PRINCEPS' FURY

Also by Jim Butcher

The Codex Alera

The Dresden Files

PRINCEPS'
FURY

BOOK FIVE OF THE CODEX ALERA

JIM BUTCHER

ACE BOOKS, NEW YORK

THE BERKLEY PUBLISHING GROUP
Published by the Penguin Group
Penguin Group (USA) Inc.
375 Hudson Street, New York, New York 10014, USA
Penguin Group (Canada), 90 Eglinton Avenue East, Suite 700, Toronto, Ontario M4P 2Y3, Canada
(a division of Pearson Penguin Canada Inc.)
Penguin Books Ltd., 80 Strand, London WC2R 0RL, England
Penguin Group Ireland, 25 St. Stephen's Green, Dublin 2, Ireland (a division of Penguin Books Ltd.)
Penguin Group (Australia), 250 Camberwell Road, Camberwell, Victoria 3124, Australia
(a division of Pearson Australia Group Pty. Ltd.)
Penguin Books India Pvt. Ltd., 11 Community Centre, Panchsheel Park, New Delhi—110 017, India
Penguin Group (NZ), 67 Apollo Drive, Rosedale, North Shore 0632, New Zealand
(a division of Pearson New Zealand Ltd.)
Penguin Books (South Africa) (Pty.) Ltd., 24 Sturdee Avenue, Rosebank, Johannesburg 2196,
South Africa

Penguin Books Ltd., Registered Offices: 80 Strand, London WC2R 0RL, England

This is an original publication of The Berkley Publishing Group.

First edition: December 2008

Library of Congress Cataloging-in-Publication Data

Butcher, Jim, 1971–
    Princeps' fury / Jim Butcher. — 1st ed.
        p.   cm.—(Codex Alera ; 5)
    ISBN 978-0-441-01638-9
    I. Title.
    PS3602.U85P75 2008
    813'.6—dc22

                                                                                            2008037151

PRINTED IN THE UNITED STATES OF AMERICA

10 9 8 7 6 5 4 3 2 1

*For Shannon and JJ,
who make life worth all the fuss and bother*

ACKNOWLEDGMENTS

Many thanks to the Beta Foo Asylum inmates, who had to work fast on this one. Their help, as always, made this a much better book than it would have been if I'd been the only one looking at it.

Many thanks also to my editor, Anne, who bravely smiled and told me "no pressure" as the clock was ticking down to zero, and who also had to do a whole lot of work in very little time, thanks to me.

And, as always, many thanks to Shannon, JJ, and my gaming gang: Robert, Julie, Shaun, Miranda, Sarah, Lisa, Joe, Alex, and, God help him, the new guy, Jeremiah. They all had to put up with me under pressure, and did so with grace and aplomb. Or at least without murdering me, which is close.

Farewell, mother Roma.
The shining columns,
The endless roads,
The mighty legions,
The peaceful fields.
Born in fire,
The light in darkness.
Farewell, mother Roma.
Never again will your sons return.

—A POEM, INSCRIBED IN STONE IN THE RUINS OF APPIA

Good riddance, gluttonous whore! Victory Germania!

—AN ADDENDUM TO THE POEM, SCRATCHED IN FAR CRUDER LETTERS

PROLOGUE

"This way, my lord!" screamed the young Knight Aeris, beckoning as he altered the direction of his windstream and dived through the twilight sky. He was bleeding from a wound in the neck, where one of the razor-sharp shards of ice the creatures hurled like javelins had slipped beneath the rim of his helmet. The young fool was fortunate to be alive, and neck wounds were notoriously treacherous. If he didn't stop flailing about and have it attended to, it might tear wider and cost the Legion an irreplaceable asset.

High Lord Antillus Raucus adjusted his own windstream to match the young Knight's dive and followed him down toward the embattled Third Antillan Legion upon the Shieldwall. "You!" he snarled, passing the young Knight without particular effort by his own, far-stronger furies. What was the idiot's name? Marius? Karius? Carlus, that was it. "Sir Carlus, get to the healers. Now."

Carlus's eyes went wide with shock as Raucus shot ahead, leaving the younger man behind as if he had been hovering in place instead of power diving for the earth at his most reckless speed. Raucus heard him say, "Yes, my l—" But the rest of the word vanished into the gale roar of the High Lord's windcrafted wake.

Raucus bid his furies to enhance his sight, and the scene below him sprang into magnified vision. He assessed the Legion's situation as he swept down upon it. Raucus spat out an oath. His captain had been right to send for aid.

The Third Antillan's situation was desperate.

Raucus had cut his teeth in battle at fourteen years of age. In the forty years since, scarcely a month had passed in which he had not seen action of one scale or another, defending the Shieldwall against the constant menace of the primitive Icemen of the north.

In all that time, he had never, not once, seen so many of them.

A sea of the savages spread out from the Shieldwall, tens of thousands strong, and as Raucus dived closer, he was suddenly enveloped by a chill far deeper than the mere bite of winter. Within seconds, crystalline laceworks of frost had formed across the surface of his armor, and he had to begin the familiar effort of low-grade firecrafting to ward away the cold.

The enemy had built mounds of snow and corpses against the Shieldwall, piling them into ramps. It was a tactic he had seen before, in the most determined assaults. The Legion had responded with their usual doctrine—burning oil and blasts of fire from their Knights Ignus.

The wall itself was very nearly a feature of the land, a massive edifice of granite furycrafted from the bones of the earth, fifty feet tall and twice as thick. It must have cost the Icemen thousands of lives to mount those ramps, to see them melted down, and to mount them again, and again, and again—but they had done it. The cold had lasted long enough to sap the *legionares* of their strength, and the battle had raged long enough to wear the Third's Knights down, until they could no longer sustain the effort needed to keep the foe at bay.

The Icemen had gained the wall itself.

Raucus felt his teeth clench in frustration and rage as the apelike creatures swarmed over the breach in the defenses. The largest of the brutes was as tall as an Aleran *legionare*, but far broader across the shoulders, far thicker through the chest. Their arms were long, with enormous hands, and their leathery hides were layered with a sparse coating of wiry, yellow-white fur that could make them all but invisible in the frozen wastes of the north. Yellow-white eyes glared from beneath shaggy brows, and a pair of heavy tusks jutted up from massively muscled jaws. Each Iceman bore a club of bone or stone in his hands, some of them edged with chips of sharp, unnaturally hard ice that, like the cold of the winter itself, seemed to bend itself to the will of the savages.

The *legionares* rallied behind the crested helmet of a centurion, struggling to push forward and seal the breach—but the furycraftings that were supposed to keep the top of the wall clear of ice were failing, and their footing had become treacherous. Their foe, more at home on the slippery surface, began to drive the Legion back into a pair of separate, vulnerable elements, as more and more of their kind surged onto the wall.

The yellow-eyed sons of crows were killing his men.

The Third Antillan had minutes of life left in it, and after that, the Icemen would be through them, and that horde would be free to ravage the lands beyond. There were a dozen steadholts and three small towns within a few hours' march for the horde, and though the militia of every town along the Shieldwall was well maintained and diligent in its continued training—Raucus would permit nothing less—against such an enormous number of the foe, they would be able to do nothing but die in a futile effort to allow their women and children time to flee.

He wouldn't allow it to happen. Not to his people. Not to his lands.

Antillus Raucus, High Lord of Antillus, let the rage boil up inside him in a white-hot fire as he swept his sword from its sheath at his side. He opened his mouth in a wordless roar of pure wrath, bellowing to his furies, calling out to the land around him, to *his* land, which for a lifetime he had fought to defend, as had his father, and his father, and his father before him.

The Aleran High Lord screamed his outrage to the land and the sky.

And the land and the sky gave answer.

The clear twilight air boiled and blackened with storm clouds, and dark streamers of mist followed him in a spiral as he dived. Thunder magnified the High Lord's battle cry tens of thousands of times over. Raucus felt his rage flow into the sword in his hand, and the blade burst into scarlet flame, burning through the cold air in a sizzling hiss, lighting the sky around him as if the sun had suddenly risen back above the horizon.

Light fell onto the desperate *legionares*, and faces began to turn skyward. A sudden roar of hope and wild excitement rose from the Legion, and lines that had begun to buckle abruptly locked into place again, shields binding together, firming, holding.

It took a few seconds more before the first of the Icemen began to look up, and only then, as Raucus readied himself to enter the fray, did the High Lord unleash the furies of his skies against the foe.

Lightning came down from the sky in threads so tiny and numerous that more than anything, they resembled burning rain. Blue-white bolts raked the Icemen on the ground below the wall, killing and burning, sending Icemen into screaming confusion—and suddenly choking the pressure of their advance onto the wall.

Raucus flung his sword's point down as he closed on the exact center of the Icemen's position atop the wall, and called fire from the burning blade, sending out a white-hot column of flame that charred flesh to ash and blackened bone in a circle fifteen feet across. At the last second, he called upon his wind furies to slow him, landed hard upon the unyielding stone of the wall—now cleared of the treacherous ice.

Raucus called strength up from the earth, shattered two hurled clubs with

sweeps of his burning blade, swept a wave of fire over a hundred of the foe between himself and the southern side of the wall, then began grimly hacking his
way northward. The Icemen were no fools. They knew that even the mightiest
furycrafter could be felled if enough spears and arrows and clubs were thrown
at him—and Raucus knew it, too.

But before the shocked Icemen could coordinate their attacks, the High Lord
of Antillus was among them with his deadly sword, giving them no chance to overwhelm his defenses with a storm of missiles—and no Iceman alive, no dozen of
the savages, was the match for the skill of Antillus Raucus with steel in his hand.

The Icemen fought with savage ferocity, each of them possessed of far
more strength than a man—but not more than an enraged High Lord, drawing
power from the stones of the land itself. Twice, Icemen managed to seize Raucus with their huge, leathery hands. He broke their necks with the use of one
hand and flung the corpses through several ranks of the enemy around him,
knocking down dozens at a time.

"Third Antillan!" Raucus bellowed, all the while. "To me! Antillus, to me!
Antillus, for Alera!"

"Antillus for Alera!" came the thunder of his *legionares'* reply, and his soldiers began to reverse the tide and drive the foe from the walls. The veteran *legionares*, bellowing their war cry, fought their way to the side of their lord,
hammering through the enemy who had been close to overwhelming them
moments before.

The enemy resistance melted abruptly, vanishing like sand washed away by
a tide, and Raucus sensed the change in pressure. The Third Aleran's Knights
Ferrous cut their way to his side and fell in on his flanks, and after that, it was
only a matter of dispatching the animals who remained on the wall.

"Shields!" Raucus barked, mounting up on a crenel, where he could overlook the Icemen's snow ramp below. A pair of *legionares* immediately came to
his side, covering all three of them with their broad shields. Spears, arrows, and
thrown clubs hammered against the Aleran steel.

Raucus focused his attention on the snow ramp. Fire would melt it, right
enough, but it would be an enormous effort. Easier to shake it apart from beneath. He nodded sharply to himself, laid a bare hand on the stone of the Shieldwall, and sent his attention down through the stones. With an effort of will, he
bade the local furies to move, and the ground outside the Shieldwall suddenly
rippled and heaved.

The great structure of ice cracked and groaned—and then collapsed, taking
a thousand screaming savages with it.

Raucus rose, nudging the shields aside, as a great cloud of ice crystals leapt
into the air. He gripped the burning sword in hand, and stared out intently,

waiting for his view of the enemy. For a moment, no one on the wall moved, as they waited to see through the cloud of snow.

There was a cry from farther down the line, one of triumph, and a moment later the air cleared enough to show Raucus the enemy, routed and in full retreat.

Then, and only then, did Raucus let the fire fade from his sword.

His men crowded against the edge of the wall, screaming their defiance and triumph at the retreating enemy. They were chanting his name.

Raucus smiled and saluted them, fist to heart. It was what one did. If it gave his men joy to cheer him, he'd be even more of a heartless bastard than he was not to let them have their moment. They didn't need to know that the smile was a false one.

There were too many still, silent forms in Antillan armor for it to be genuine.

The efforts of the day's furycrafting had exhausted him, and he wanted nothing so much as a quiet patch of dry, flat space to go to sleep on. Instead, he conferred with his captain and the Third's staff, then went to the healer's tents to visit the wounded.

Like accepting cheers one didn't deserve, it was also what one did.

Those men lying wounded had become so in service to him. They had suffered their pains for him. He could lose an hour of sleep, or two, or ten, if it meant easing that pain for a few moments for the cost of nothing more than a few kind words.

Sir Carlus was the last of those Raucus visited. The young man was still fairly groggy. His injuries had been more extensive than he had known, and the watercrafting that had healed them had left him exhausted and disoriented. Neck injuries could be that way. Something to do with the brain, Raucus had been told.

"Thank you, my lord," Carlus said, when Raucus sat down on one edge of his bunk. "We couldn't have held without you."

"We all fight together, lad," Raucus replied roughly. "No thanks need be given. We're the best. It's how we do our work. How we do our duty. Next time, it could be the Third saving me."

"Yes, my lord," Carlus said. "Sir? Is it true what they say? That you challenged the First Lord to the *juris macto*?"

Raucus snorted out a quiet laugh. "That was a while ago, lad. Aye, true enough."

Carlus's dulled eyes glittered for a minute. "You'd have won, I wager."

"Don't be daft, boy," Raucus said, rising and giving the young Knight a squeeze on the shoulder. "Gaius Sextus is the First Lord. He would have handed me my head. And still would. Think about what happened to Kalarus Brencis, eh?"

Carlus didn't look happy to hear that answer, but he said, "Yes, my lord."

"Get some rest, soldier," Raucus said. "Well done."

At last, Raucus turned to leave the tent. There. Duty done. At last he could get a few hours of rest. The increased pressure on the Shieldwall, of late, had left him wishing that he had demanded that Crassus serve his first Legion hitch at home. Great furies knew, the boy could make himself useful now. As could Maximus. The two of them, it seemed, had at least learned to coexist without attempting to murder one another.

Raucus snorted at his own train of thought. He sounded, to himself, like an old man, tired and aching and wishing for younger shoulders to bear his burdens. Though he supposed he would rather grow old than not.

Still. It would be nice to have the help.

There were just so *many* of the crowbegotten savages. And he'd been fighting them for so bloody long.

He walked toward the stairway leading down into the fortifications within the Shieldwall itself, where a heated chamber and a cot waited for him. He'd gone perhaps ten paces when a scream of wind, the windstream of an incoming Knight Aeris, howled in the distance.

Raucus paused, and a moment later, a Knight Aeris soared in, escorted by one of the Third Aleran's Knights who had been flying patrol. Night had fallen, but the snow always made that a minor inconvenience, particularly when the moon was out. All the same, it wasn't until the man had landed that Raucus spotted the insignia of the First Antillan upon his breastplate.

The man hurried to Raucus, panting, and slammed his fist to his heart in a hasty salute. "My lord," he gasped.

Raucus returned the salute. "Report."

"Message from Captain Tyreus, my lord," the Knight panted. "His position is under heavy attack, and he urgently requests reinforcements. We've never seen so many Icemen in one place, my lord."

Raucus looked at the man for a moment and nodded. Then, without another word, he summoned his wind furies, took to the air, and headed west, toward the First Antillan's position, a hundred miles down the wall, at the best speed he could manage for the distance.

His men needed him. Rest would have to wait.

It was what one did.

"And I don't care how hungover you are, Hagan!" said Captain Demos, in a perfectly conversational voice that nonetheless carried the length of the ship and up and down the dock. "You get those lines coiled properly, or I'll have you scraping barnacles all the way across the Run!"

Gaius Octavian watched the surly, bleary-eyed sailor turn back to his work, this time performing more to the liking of the *Slive*'s captain. The ships had begun leaving the harbor at Mastings on the morning tide, just after dawn. It was near to midmorning, and the harbor and the sea beyond looked like a forest of masts and billowing sails, rolling over the waves to the horizon. Hundreds of ships, the largest fleet Alera had ever seen, were now sailing for open sea.

The only ship still in port, in fact, was the *Slive*. It looked stained, old, and worn. It wasn't. Its captain simply chose to forgo the usual painting and piping. Its sails were patched and dirty, its lines dark with smears of tar. The carved female figure on the prow, so often made to resemble benevolent female-form furies and revered ancestors on other ships, looked more like a young riverfront doxy than anything else.

If one didn't know what to look for, the sheer amount of sail she could hang and the long, lean, dangerous lines of the *Slive* might go completely overlooked. She was too small to be matched squarely against a proper warship, but she was swift and nimble on the open sea, and her captain was a dangerously competent man.

"Are you absolutely sure about this?" rumbled Antillar Maximus. The Tribune was of a height with Tavi, though more heavily muscled, and his armor and equipment were so scratched and dented by use that they would never have passed muster on a parade ground. Not that anyone in the First Aleran Legion gave a bloody crow's feather about that.

"Whether I'm sure or not," Tavi replied quietly, "his ship is the only left in port."

Maximus grimaced. "Point," he growled. "But he's a bloody pirate, Tavi. You have a title to think about now. A Princeps of Alera shouldn't have a vessel like that as his flagship. It's . . . dubious."

"So's my title," Tavi replied. "Do you know of a more competent captain? Or a faster ship?"

Max snorted out another breath and looked at the third person on the dock. "Practicality over all. This is your fault."

The young woman spoke with perfect assurance. "Yes it is," she said calmly. Kitai still wore her long white hair in the fashion of the Horse clan of the Marat people, shaved to the scalp along the sides and left long in a swath over the center of her skull, like the mane of one of the Horse clan's totem mounts. She was dressed in leather riding breeches, a loose white tunic, and duelist's belt bearing two swords. If the cool of the mid-autumn morning disturbed her in her light dress, she showed no signs of it. Her green eyes, upturned at the corners, as were all of her people's, roamed over the ship alertly, like a cat's, distant and interested at the same time. "Alerans have a great many foolish ideas in their heads. Pound on their skulls often enough, and some of them are bound to fall out eventually."

"Captain?" Tavi called, grinning. "Will your ship be fit to sail at any point today?"

Demos came over to the ship's railing and leaned his forearms on it, staring down at them. "Oh, aye, Your Highness," he replied. "Whether or not you'll be on it when it does is another matter entirely."

"What?" Max said. "Demos, you've been paid half the amount of your contract, up front. I gave it to you myself."

"Yes," Demos replied. "I'll be glad to cross the sea with the fleet. I'll be glad to take you and the pretty barbarian girl." Demos pointed a finger at Tavi. "But His Royal Highness there doesn't set foot aboard my ship until he settles up with me."

Max narrowed his eyes. "Your ship's going to look awful funny with a big hole burned straight through it."

"I'll plug it with your fat head," Demos retorted with a wintry smile.

"Max," Tavi said gently. "Captain, may I come aboard to settle accounts?"

Max growled under his breath. "The Princeps of Alera should not have to ask permission to board a pirate ship."

"On his own ship," Kitai murmured, "captain outranks Princeps."

Tavi reached the top of the gangplank and spread his hands. "Well?"

Demos, a lean man, slightly taller than average, dressed in a black tunic and breeches, turned to lean one elbow on the rail and study Tavi. His free hand, Tavi noted, just happened to fall within an inch or two of the hilt of his sword. "You destroyed some of my property."

"That's right," Tavi said. "The chains in your hold you used to imprison slaves."

"You're going to replace them."

Tavi rolled one armored shoulder in a shrug. "What are they worth to you?"

"I don't want money. It isn't about money," Demos said. "They were mine. You had no right to them."

Tavi met the man's eyes steadily. "I think a few slaves might say the same thing regarding their lives and freedom, Demos."

Demos blinked his eyes, slowly. Then he looked away. He was quiet for a moment, before murmuring, "I didn't make the sea. I just sail on it."

"Here's the problem," Tavi said. "If I give you those chains, knowing what you're going to do with them, I become a part of whatever those chains are used for. I become a slaver. And I am no slaver, Demos. And never will be."

Demos frowned. "It would seem that we are at an impasse."

"And you're sure you won't change your mind?"

Demos's eyes flicked back to Tavi and hardened. "Not if the sun fell out of the sky. Replace the chains, or get off my ship."

"I can't do that. Do you understand why?"

Demos nodded. "Understand it. Even respect it. But that doesn't change a crowbegotten thing. So where are we?"

"In need of a solution."

"There isn't one."

"I think someone's told me that once or twice before," Tavi said, grinning. "I'll replace your chains if you'll make me a promise."

Demos tilted his head, his eyes narrowing.

"Promise that you'll never use any other set, any other restraints, but the ones I give you."

"And you give me decrepit pieces of rust? No thank you, Your Highness."

Tavi lifted a placating hand. "You'll get to inspect the chains first. Your promise will be contingent upon your acceptance."

Demos pursed his lips. Then he nodded abruptly. "Done."

Tavi unslung the heavy courier's bag from its strap over one shoulder and tossed it to Demos. The captain caught it, grunted under the weight, and gave Tavi a suspicious look as he opened the bag.

Demos stared for a long, silent moment. Then, link by link, he drew a set of slaver's chains out of the bag.

Every link was made of gold.

Demos ran his fingertips over the chains for an astonished minute. It was the fortune of a mercenary's lifetime, and much, much more. Then he looked up at Tavi, his brow furrowed in a confused frown.

"You don't have to accept them," Tavi said. "My Knights Aeris will fly me out to one of the other ships. You'll join the fleet. And you can take up slaving again at the end of your contract.

"Or," he continued, "you can accept them. And never carry slaves again."

Demos just shook his head slowly for a moment. "What have you done?"

"I've just made it more profitable for you to stop slaving than to continue it," Tavi said.

Demos smiled faintly down. "You give me chains fashioned to my own size, Your Highness. And ask me to wear them freely."

"I'll need skilled captains, Demos. I'll need men whose word I can trust." Tavi grinned and put a hand on the man's shoulder. "And men who have the fortitude to bear up under extreme prosperity. What say you?"

Demos dropped the chains back into the bag and slung it over one shoulder, then inclined his head more deeply than Tavi had seen him make the gesture before. "Welcome aboard the *Slive*, my lord."

Demos immediately turned and began bawling orders to the crew, and Max and Kitai came up the ramp to stand next to Tavi.

"That was well done, Aleran," Kitai murmured.

Max shook his head. "There's something broken inside your skull, Calderon. You do all your thinking sideways."

"It was Ehren's idea, actually," Tavi said.

"Wish he was coming with us," Max rumbled.

"That's the glamorous life of a Cursor," Tavi replied. "But with any luck, we won't be gone long. We sail Varg and his people back home, make some polite noises to keep diplomatic channels open, then come right back. Two months or so."

Max grunted. "Gives Gaius time to gather support in the Senate, declare you his heir all legal and official."

"And puts me somewhere that is both beyond the reach of potential assassins and of unquestionable importance to the Realm," Tavi said. "I am particularly fond of the former."

The sailors began casting off mooring lines, and Kitai took Tavi's hand firmly. "Come," she said. "Before you splatter your breakfast all over your armor."

As the ship pushed away from the dock and began to rock with the motion of the sea, Tavi felt his stomach slowly begin to roil, and he hurried to his cabin to relieve himself of his armor and make sure that he had plenty of water and an empty bucket or two available. He was a terrible sailor, and life on a ship was pure torment.

Tavi felt another twinge in his belly and thought longingly of nice, solid ground, be it ever so littered with assassins.

Two months at sea.

He could scarcely imagine a greater nightmare.

"This stinks," complained Tonnar, from five yards behind Kestus's mount. "This is like some kind of bad dream."

Kestus glanced down at the field hatchet strapped to his horse's saddlebag. It would be hard to get much strength behind a throw while riding a horse, but Tonnar's head was so soft, it probably wouldn't matter. Of course, then there would be the matter of the moron's corpse and potential murder charges.

True, Kestus had the entire deserted run of the wilderness southwest of the Waste to hide the body in, but there was the issue of the new man to complicate things. He glanced back at the third member of the patrol, the slender, wiry pip-squeak who called himself Ivarus and had enough sense to keep his mouth shut most of the time.

Kestus was a strong believer in avoiding complications. So he did what he usually did when Tonnar flapped his lips. He ignored him.

"Do you know what it's like closer to the Waste?" Tonnar continued. "Wild furies everywhere. Outlaws. Pestilence. Starvation." He shook his head mournfully. "And when old Gaius blew Kalare off the face of the earth, he sent about half the able-bodied men in the whole area away with it. Women are throwing themselves at men for a couple of copper rams or the heel of a loaf of bread. Or just to have someone around who they think will protect their brats."

Kestus thought wistfully of murder.

"I talked to this one guy from the northern march," Tonnar went on. "He plowed four women in one day." The loudmouth slashed the extra length of his reins savagely at the branches of a nearby tree, scattering autumn leaves and striking his mount's neck sharply by mistake. The horse twitched and jolted, and Tonnar barely kept from being thrown.

The man cursed the horse savagely, kicking harder than necessary with his heels and jerking hard on the reins to bring it back under control.

Kestus idly added theoretical torture to the theoretical murder, because done right, it might be funny.

"And here we are," Tonnar snarled, waving his arm in a broad circle at the silent expanse of trees all around them. "Men are making fortunes and living like lords, and Julius leads us out into the middle of nowhere. Nothing to see. Nothing to loot. No women to bed."

Ivarus, his face mostly hidden beneath the hood of his cloak, broke a branch about as thick as a man's thumb from a tree beside the trail. Then he nudged his horse up into a trot and drew up alongside Tonnar.

"We could have them lining up to spread their legs for us for the price of a piece of bread," Tonnar was saying. "But no—"

Ivarus quite calmly lifted the branch and broke it over Tonnar's head. Then, without a word, he turned and nudged his horse back into his original position.

"Bloody crows!" Tonnar bellowed, reaching one hand up to clutch at his skull. "Crows and bloody furies, what is wrong with you, man?"

Kestus didn't bother trying to hide his smile. "He thinks you're a bloody idiot. So do I."

"What?" Tonnar protested. "Because I want to tumble a girl or two?"

"Because you want to take advantage of people who are desperate and dying," Kestus said. "And because you haven't thought things through. People are starving. Disease is rampant. And soldiers get paid. How many *legionares* do you think have been murdered in their sleep for the clothes on their back, the coins in their purse? How many do you think have fallen sick and died, just like all those holders? And in case it slipped your notice, Tonnar, all those outlaws would have every reason to kill you. You'd probably be too busy trying to stay alive to spend any time humiliating women."

Tonnar scowled.

"Look," Kestus said. "Julius got us all the way through Kalare's rebellion in one piece. None of our company died. And out here, we're out of the worst of it. It might not pay as well, or have the . . . opportunities, as the patrols nearer the Waste. But we aren't dying of plague or getting our throats cut while we sleep, either."

Tonnar sneered. "You're just afraid to take chances."

"Yep," Kestus agreed. "So's Julius. Which is why we're all in one piece." So far.

The loudmouth shook his head and turned to glare at Ivarus. "You touch me again, and I'm going to gut you like a fish."

"Good," Ivarus said. "Once we hide the body, Kestus and I can switch out our mounts with yours and pick up the pace." The hooded man glanced up at Kestus. "How much longer until we get back to camp?"

"Couple of hours," Kestus replied laconically. He gave Tonnar a very direct glance. "Give or take."

Tonnar muttered something under his breath and subsided. The rest of the trip passed in blessed, professional silence.

Kestus liked the new man.

As twilight settled over the land, they rode into the glade that Julius had chosen as their camp. It was a good site. A steep hillside had provided them a place to earthcraft something that almost resembled shelter from the weather. A small stream trickled nearby, and the horses whickered, their steps quickening as they recognized the place where they would receive some grain and rest.

But just before he rode out of the shelter of the belt of heavy evergreens that surrounded the glade, Kestus stopped his horse.

Something was wrong.

His heartbeat sped up a little, as a tension with no obvious explanation seized him. He remained still for a moment, trying to trace the source of his unease.

"Bloody crows," sighed Tonnar. "What is it now—"

"Quiet," Ivarus whispered, his voice tense.

Kestus glanced back at the wiry little man. Ivarus was on edge as well.

The camp was completely silent and still.

The company of rangers patrolling this area of what had once been the lands of the High Lord Kalarus Brencis numbered a dozen strong, but three- and four-man patrols moved in and out of the camp on a regular basis. It was not inconceivable that all but a pair of the rangers were out on their rounds. It was not unthinkable that whoever was minding the camp might have gone on a quick local sweep, hoping to turn up some game.

But it didn't seem very likely.

Ivarus brought his horse up beside Kestus's, and murmured, "The fire's out."

And that pinpointed it. In an active camp, a fire was kept alight almost as a matter of course. It was too much of a headache to let it go out and continually rebuild it. Even if the fire had burned down to hot coals and ashes, there would still be the scent of woodsmoke. But Kestus couldn't smell the camp's fire.

The wind shifted slightly, and Kestus's horse tensed and quivered with sudden apprehension, its wide nostrils flaring. Something moved, perhaps thirty yards away. Kestus remained still, fully aware that any motion would draw attention toward him. Footsteps sounded, crunching on fallen autumn leaves.

Julius appeared. The grizzled ranger wore his usual forest leathers, all deep browns, greys, and greens. He stopped at the fire pit, staring down at it and otherwise not moving. His mouth hung slightly open. He looked pale and weary, and his eyes were dull and flat.

He just *stood* there.

Julius never did that. There was always work to be done, and he detested wasted time. If nothing else, the man would spend any idle time he had fletching more arrows for the company.

Kestus traded a glance with Ivarus. Though the younger man did not know Julius the way Kestus did, Ivarus's expression said that he had reached the same conclusion Kestus had as to the proper course of action—a cautious, silent withdrawal.

"Well, there's old Julius," Tonnar muttered. "Happy now?" He growled, kicking his heels into his horse's flanks and nudging the beast into motion. "Can't believe he let the fire die. Now we'll have to rebuild it before we can eat."

"No, fool!" hissed Kestus.

Tonnar looked back over his shoulder at them with an exasperated expression. "I'm *hungry*," he said plaintively. "Come *on*."

The thing that ripped its way from the earth beneath the feet of Tonnar's mount was like nothing Kestus had ever seen.

It was huge, the size of a wagon, and covered in a gleaming, slick-looking green-black shell or armor of some kind. It had legs, a lot of them, almost like a crab's, and great, grasping pincers like the claws of a lobster, and glittering eyes recessed into deep divots in that strange shell.

And it was strong.

It ripped a leg from Tonnar's horse before Kestus could so much as cry out a warning.

The animal went down, screaming, blood flowing everywhere. Kestus heard Tonnar's bones breaking as the horse landed on him. Tonnar began to scream in agony—and kept screaming as, with the other claw, the monster, whatever it was, ripped his belly open, right through his mail, and spilled his entrails into the cool air.

A half-hysterical thought flashed through Kestus's stunned mind: The man couldn't even *die* quietly.

The creature began to methodically rip the horse apart, its motions as swift and sure as a butcher hard at work.

Kestus felt his eyes drawn to Julius. His commander turned his head slowly to face them and opened his mouth in a slow, wide gape.

Julius screamed. But the deafening sound that came out was nothing even remotely human. There was something metallic to it, something dissonant, an odd, warbling tone that set Kestus's teeth on edge and set the horses to dancing and tossing their heads, their eyes rolling whitely in sudden fear.

The sound died away

And an instant later, the forest came alive with rustling.

Ivarus lifted his hands and drew back his hood, the better to hear the sound. It came from all around them, cracklings of crushed fallen leaves, rasping of pine needles against something brushing through them, snapping of twigs, pinecones, fallen branches. No one sound was more than a bare murmur. But there were *thousands* of them.

The forest sounded as if it had become one enormous bonfire.

"Oh, great furies," breathed Ivarus. "Oh bloody crows." He shot a wide-eyed glance at Kestus as he whirled his horse, his face pale with terror. "No questions!" he snarled. "Just run! Run!"

Ivarus suited action to his words, kicking his mount into a run.

Kestus tore his eyes away from the empty-eyed *thing* that had been his commander, and sent his horse leaping after Ivarus's.

As he did, he became aware of . . .

Things.

Things, in the forest. Things moving, keeping pace with them, shadows that remained only half-seen in the deepening darkness. None of them looked human. None of them looked like anything Kestus had ever seen. His heart pounded with raw, instinctive terror, and he called to his mount, demanding more speed.

It was madness to ride like this—through the forest, in the deepening dark. A tree trunk, a low branch, a protruding root, or any of a thousand other common things could kill a man or his horse if they collided with them in the night.

But the things were drawing closer, behind and on either side of them, and Kestus realized what it meant: They were being hunted, like fleeing deer, with the pack in full pursuit, working together to bring down the game. Terror of those hunters overrode his judgment. He only wished his horse could run faster.

Ivarus splashed across a creek and abruptly altered his course, sending his mount plowing through a thorny thicket, and Kestus was hot on his heels. As they tore through the thicket, ripping their hides and the hides of their mounts, Ivarus reached into his belt pouch and drew forth a small globe made of what looked like black glass. He said something to it, then spun in his saddle, shouted, "Down!" and threw it at Kestus's face.

Kestus ducked. The globe zipped over his hunched shoulders, and into the dark behind them.

There was a sudden flash of light and a roar of flame. Kestus shot a glance over his shoulder, to see fire spreading over the thicket with such manic intensity that it could only have been the result of some kind of furycraft. It washed out like a wave, spreading in all directions, burning the dried material of the thickets in eager conflagration—and it was moving fast. Faster than their horses were running.

They burst free of the thicket barely a panicked heartbeat ahead of the roaring flame—but not before two creatures the size of large cats came flying out of the blaze, burning like a flock of comets. Kestus got a glimpse of a too-large, spiderlike creature—and then one of them landed on the back of Ivarus's horse, still blazing.

The horse screamed, and its hoof struck a fallen log or a depression in the forest floor. It went down in a bone-breaking tumble, taking Ivarus with it.

Kestus was sure that the man was as good as dead, just as Tonnar had been. But Ivarus leapt clear of the falling horse, tucked into a roll, and controlled his fall, coming back to his feet several yards later. Without missing a beat, he drew the short *gladius* from his belt, impaled the creature still clinging to his mount's haunches, then hacked the second burning spider-thing from the air before it could reach him.

Before the corpse had hit the ground, Ivarus hurled two more of the black globes into the night behind them, one to the left and the other to the right. Blazing curtains of fire sprang to life in seconds, joining with the inferno of the burning thicket.

Kestus fought his panicked horse to a halt, savagely forced it to turn, and rode back for Ivarus, while the wounded horse continued to scream in agony. He extended his hand. "Come on!"

Ivarus turned and, with a single, clean stroke, ended the horse's suffering. "We won't get away from them riding double," he said.

"You don't know that!"

"Crows, man, there's no time! They'll circle that screen and be on top of us in seconds. Get *out* of here, Kestus! You've got to report this."

"Report *what*?" Kestus all but screamed. "Bloody crows and—"

The night went white, and red-hot pain became Kestus's entire world. He dimly felt himself fall from his horse. He couldn't breathe. Couldn't scream. All he could do was *hurt*.

He managed to look down.

There was a blackened hole in his chest. It went through the mail, just at his solar plexus, dead center of his body. The links surrounded it had melted together. A firecrafting. He'd been hit with a firecrafting.

He couldn't breathe.

He couldn't feel his legs.

Ivarus crouched over him and examined the wound.

His sober face became even grimmer. "Kestus," he said quietly. "I'm sorry. There's nothing I can do."

Kestus had to work for it, but he focused his eyes on Ivarus. "Take the horse," he rasped. "Go."

Ivarus put a hand on Kestus's shoulder. "I'm sorry," he said again.

Kestus nodded. The image of the creature dismembering Tonnar and his mount flashed to mind. He shuddered, licked his lips, and said, "I don't want those things to kill me."

Ivarus closed his eyes for a second. Then he pressed his lips together and nodded, once.

"Thank you," Kestus said, and closed his eyes.

Sir Ehren ex Cursori rode Kestus's horse until the beast was all but broken, using every trick he'd ever learned, seen, heard, or read about to shake off pursuit and obscure his trail.

By the time the sun rose, he felt as weak and shaky as his mount—but there was no further sign of pursuit. He stopped beside a small river and leaned against a tree, closing his eyes for a moment.

The Cursor wasn't sure if his coin would be able to reach Alera Imperia from such a minor tributary—but he had little choice but to try. The First Lord had to be warned. He drew out the chain from around his neck, and with it the silver coin that hung from it. He tossed the coin into the water, and said, "Hear me, little river, and hasten word to thy master."

For several moments, nothing happened. Ehren was about to give up and start moving again, when the water stirred, and the surface of the water stirred, rose, and formed itself into the image of Gaius Sextus, the First Lord of Alera.

Gaius was a tall, handsome man, who appeared to be in his late forties if one discounted the silver hair. In truth, the First Lord was in his eighties, but like all powerful watercrafters', his body did not tend to show the effects of age that a normal Aleran's would. Though his eyes were sunken and weary-looking, they glittered with intelligence and sheer, indomitable will. The water sculpture focused on Ehren, frowned, and spoke.

"Sir Ehren?" Gaius said. "Is that you?" His voice sounded strange, like someone speaking from inside a tunnel.

"Yes, sire," Ehren replied, bowing his head. "I have urgent news."

The First Lord gestured with one hand. "Report."

Ehren took a deep breath. "Sire. The Vord are here, in the wilds to the southwest of the Waste of Kalare."

Gaius's expression suddenly stiffened, tension gathering in his shoulders. He leaned forward slightly, eyes intent. "Are you certain of this?"

"Completely. And there's more."

Ehren took a deep breath.

"Sire," he said quietly. "They've learned furycrafting."

⬦⬦⬦⬦CHAPTER 1

On his previous voyages, it had taken Tavi several days to recover from his seasickness—but those voyages had never taken him out into the ocean deeps. There was, he learned, a vast difference between staying within a long day's sail of land and daring the deep blue sea. He could not believe how high the waves could roll, out in the empty ocean. It often seemed that the *Slive* was sailing up the side of a great blue mountain, only to sled down its far side once it had reached the summit. The wind and the expertise of Demos's crew of scoundrels kept the sails constantly taut, and the *Slive* rapidly took the lead position in the fleet.

By Tavi's order, Demos kept his ship even with the *Trueblood*, the flagship of the Canim leader, Varg. Demos's crew chafed under the order, Tavi knew. Though the *Trueblood* was almost unbelievably graceful for a vessel her size, compared to the nimble *Slive* she moved like a river barge. Demos's men longed to show the Canim what their ship could do, and give the vast, black ship a view of their stern.

Tavi was tempted to allow it. Anything to end the voyage a little sooner.

The greatly increased activity of the waves had increased his motion sickness proportionately, and though it had, mercifully, abated somewhat since those first few horrible days, it hadn't ever gone away completely, and eating food remained a dubious proposition, at best. He could keep down a little bread, and weak broth, but not much more. He had a constant headache, now, which grew more irritating by the day.

"Little brother," growled the grizzled old Cane. "You Alerans are a short-lived race. Have you grown old and feeble enough to need naps in midlesson?"

From her position in the hammock slung from the rafters of the little cabin, Kitai let out a little silver peal of laughter.

Tavi shook himself out of his reverie and glanced at Gradash. The Cane was something almost unheard of amongst the warrior caste—elderly. Tavi knew that Gradash was over nine centuries old, as Alerans counted them, and age had shrunken the Cane to the paltry size of barely seven and a half feet. His strength was a frail shadow of what it had been when he was a warrior in his prime. Tavi judged that he probably was no more than three or four times as strong as a human being. His fur was almost completely silver, with only bits of the solid, night-dark fur that marked him as a member of Varg's extended bloodline as surely as the distinctive pattern of notches cut into his ears or the decorations upon the hilt of his sword.

"Your pardon, elder brother," Tavi replied, speaking as Gradash had, in Canish. "My mind wandered. I have no excuse."

"He is so sick he can barely get out of his bunk," Kitai said, her Canish accent better than Tavi's, "but he has no excuse."

"Survival makes no allowances for illness," Gradash growled, his voice stern. Then he added, in thickly accented Aleran, "I admit, however, that he should no longer embarrass himself while attempting to speak our tongue. The idea of a language exchange was a sound one."

For Gradash, the comment was high praise. "It made sense," Tavi replied. "At least for my people. *Legionares* with nothing to do for two months can become distressingly bored. And should your people and mine find ourselves at odds again, I would have it be for the proper reasons and not because we did not speak one another's tongues."

Gradash showed his teeth for a moment. Several were chipped, but they were still white and sharp. "All knowledge of a foe is useful."

Tavi responded to the gesture in kind. "That, too. Have the lessons gone well on the other ships?"

"Aye," Gradash said. "And without serious incident."

Tavi frowned faintly. Aleran standards on that subject differed rather sharply from Canim ones. To the Canim, *without serious incident* merely meant that no one had been killed. It was not, however, a point worth pursuing. "Good."

The Cane nodded and rose. "Then with your consent, I will return to my pack leader's ship."

Tavi arched an eyebrow. That was unusual. "Will you not take dinner with us before you go?"

Gradash flicked his ears in the negative—then a second later remembered to follow the gesture with the Aleran equivalent, a negative shake of the head. "I would return before the storm arrives, little brother."

Tavi glanced at Kitai. "What storm?"

Kitai shook her head. "Demos has said nothing."

Gradash let out a rumbling snarl, the Canim equivalent of a chuckle. "Know when one's coming. Feel it in my tail."

"Until our next lesson, then," Tavi said. He tilted his head slightly to one side, in the Canim fashion, and Gradash returned the gesture. Then the old Cane padded out, ducking to squeeze out of the relatively tiny cabin.

Tavi glanced at Kitai, but the Marat woman was already swinging down from the hammock. She trailed her fingertips through his hair as she passed his bunk, gave him a quick smile, and left the cabin as well. She returned a moment later, trailing the Legion's senior valet, Magnus.

Magnus was spry for a man of his years, though Tavi always thought that the close-cropped Legion haircut looked odd on him. He had grown used to Magnus's shock of fine white hair while the two of them had explored the ancient Romanic ruins of Appia. The old man had wiry, strong hands, a comfortable potbelly, and watery eyes that had gone nearsighted after years of straining to read faded inscriptions in poorly lit chambers and caves. A scholar of no mean learning, Magnus was also a Cursor Callidus, one of the most senior of the elite agents of the Crown, and had become Tavi's de facto master of intelligence.

"Kitai has alerted Demos to what Gradash said," Magnus began, without preamble. "And the good captain will keep a weather eye out."

Tavi shook his head. "Not good enough," he said. "Kitai, ask Demos if he would indulge me. Prepare for a blow, and signal the rest of our ships to do the same. As I understand it, we've had unusually gentle weather so far, sailing this late in the year. Gradash didn't survive to old age by being a fool. If nothing else, it will be a good exercise."

"He'll do it," Kitai said with perfect confidence.

"Just be polite, please," Tavi said.

Kitai rolled her eyes as she left and sighed. "Yes, Aleran."

Magnus waited until Kitai had left before he nodded to Tavi, and said, "Thank you."

"You really can say whatever you like in front of her, Magnus."

Tavi's old mentor gave him a strained look. "Your Highness, please. The Ambassador *is*, after all, a representative of a foreign power. My professionalism feels strained enough."

Tavi's weariness kept the laugh from gaining too much momentum, but it felt good in any case. "Crows, Magnus. You can't keep beating yourself up for not re-alizing I was Gaius Octavian. No one realized I was Gaius Octavian. *I* didn't real-ize *I* was Gaius Octavian." Tavi shrugged. "Which was the point, I suppose."

Magnus sighed. "Yes, well. Just between the two of us, I'm afraid that I have to tell you, it's a waste. You'd have been a real terror as a historian. Dealt those pigheaded snobs at the Academy fits for generations, with what you'd have turned up at Appia."

"I'll just have to try to make amends in whatever small way I can," Tavi said, smiling faintly. The smile faded. Magnus was right about one thing—Tavi was never going to go back to the simple life he'd had, working under Magnus at his dig site, exploring the ancient ruin. A little pang of loss went through him. "Ap-pia was very nice, wasn't it?"

"Mmm," Magnus agreed. "Peaceful. Always interesting. I still have a trunk-ful of rubbings to transcribe and translate, too."

"I'd ask you to send some of them over, but . . ."

"Duty," Magnus said, nodding. "Speaking of which."

Tavi nodded and sat up with a grunt of effort as Magnus passed over several sheets of paper. Tavi frowned down at them and found himself studying several unfamiliar maps. "What am I looking at?"

"Canea," Magnus replied. "There, at the far right . . ." The old Cursor indi-cated a few speckles at the middle of the right edge of the map. "The Sunset Isles, and Westmiston."

Tavi blinked at the map for a moment, looking between the isles and the mainland. "But . . . I thought it was about three weeks' sailing from those is-lands."

"It is," Magnus said.

"But that would make this coastline . . ." Tavi traced a fingertip down its length. "Crows. If it's to scale, it would be three or four times as long as the western coast of Alera." He looked up sharply at Magnus. "Where did you come by this map?"

Magnus coughed delicately. "Some of our language teachers managed to make copies of charts on the Canim ships."

"Crows, Magnus!" Tavi snarled, rising. "Crows and bloody furies, I *told* you that we were *not* going to play any games like that on this trip!"

Magnus blinked at him several times. "And . . . Your Highness expected me to *listen*?"

"Of *course* I did!"

Magnus lifted both eyebrows. "Your Highness, perhaps I should explain. My duty is to the Crown. And my orders, from the Crown, are to take every ac-tion within my power to support you, protect you, and secure every possible advantage to ensure your safety and success." He added, without a trace of apology, "Including, if in my best judgment I deem it necessary, ignoring orders containing more idealism than practicality."

Tavi stared at him for a moment. Then he said, quietly, "Magnus, I'm not feeling well. But I'm sure that if I ask nicely, when Kitai gets back, she will be happy to throw you off this ship for me."

Magnus inclined his head, unruffled. "That is, of course, up to you, Your Highness. But I would ask you to look over the map first."

Tavi growled under his breath and turned his attention back to the map. The deed was done. There was no sense in pretending it hadn't been. "How accurate is this copy?"

Magnus passed over several other pieces of paper, which were virtually identical to the first.

"Mmmm," Tavi asked. "And these are to scale?"

"That remains unclear," Magnus replied. "There could be differences in the way that the Canim understand and read their maps."

"Not *that* much difference," Tavi replied. "I've seen the charts they drew of the Vale." Tavi traced a finger down one of the maps that had various-sized triangles marking the locations of a number of cities. Names had been sketched next to half of them. "These cities . . . I'm sure that . . ." He gave Magnus a sharp glance. "The population of each of these cities is enormous. As large as any of the High Lords' cities in Alera."

"Yes, Your Highness," Magnus said calmly.

"And there are *dozens* of them," Tavi said. "In this section of coastline alone."

"Just so, Your Highness."

"But that would mean . . ." Tavi shook his head slowly. "Magnus. That would mean that the Canim civilization is dozens of times larger than our own—*hundreds* of times larger."

"Yes, Your Highness," Magnus said.

Tavi stared down at the map, shaking his head slowly. "And we never *knew?*"

"The Canim have guarded their coastline quite jealously over the centuries," Magnus said. "Fewer than a dozen Aleran ships have ever visited their shores—and those have only been allowed to dock at a single port, a place by the name of Marshag. No Aleran has ever been permitted off the docks—and returned to tell about it, at any rate."

Tavi shook his head. "What about furycrafting? Have we never sent Knights Aeris to overfly it?"

"The range of any flyer is limited. A Knight Aeris could fly perhaps two or three hundred miles and back, but he could hardly expect to do so unobserved—and as we saw subsequent to the Night of the Red Stars, the Canim do possess the ability to counter our flyers." Magnus shrugged, and smiled faintly. "Then, too, it has been speculated that our furycrafting abilities would be significantly reduced, so far from Alera, and our furies' points of origin. It is possible that a Knight Aeris would not be able to fly at all."

"But no one's ever thought to test it?" Tavi asked.

"The ships that have sailed there have all been couriers and merchantmen." Magnus flashed Tavi a swift smile. "Besides, can you imagine the Citizen who would *want* to rush off to the domain of the Canim amidst a crowd of rude sailors, only to find out that he is just as powerless as they?"

Tavi shook his head slowly. "I suppose not." He tapped a finger on the maps. "Could this be a lie? Deliberately planted for us to find?"

"Possible," Magnus said, approval in his tone, "though I would consider it a very low order of probability."

Tavi grunted. "Well," he said. "This is rather valuable information."

"I thought it so," Magnus said.

Tavi sighed. "I suppose I won't have you thrown off the ship just yet."

"I appreciate that, Your Highness," Magnus said gravely.

Tavi traced his finger over several heavy lines, many of which ran ruler-straight. "These lines. Canals of some sort?"

"No, Your Highness," Magnus said. "Those are boundary lines between territories."

Tavi looked up blankly at Magnus. "I don't understand."

"Apparently," Magnus said, "the Canim do not exist as a single governmental body. They are divided into several separate, distinct organizations."

Tavi frowned. "Like the Marat tribes?"

"Not exactly. Each territory is entirely independent. There is no overriding unity, no centralized leadership. Each is governed completely separately from all the others."

Tavi blinked. "That's . . ." He frowned. "I was going to say that it was insane."

"Mmmm," Magnus said. "Because Carna is a savage world, packed with far too many different peoples, most of them in constant conflict with one another. For us Alerans, only a united stand against our foes has allowed us to survive and prosper."

Tavi gestured at the map. "Whereas the Canim have numbers enough that they can afford to be divided."

Magnus nodded. "All things considered, it makes me rather glad that our new Princeps found an honorable, peaceful, and respectful solution to the situation in the Vale."

"Can't hurt to make a good first impression," Tavi agreed. He shook his head slowly. "Can you imagine, Magnus, what would have happened if those hotheaded idiots in the Senate had gotten their way and funded a full-scale retaliation upon the Canim homeland?"

Magnus shook his head in silence.

"With numbers like this," Tavi continued, "they could have wiped us out. Furycrafting or no, they could have destroyed us at will."

Magnus's face turned grim. "So it would seem."

Tavi looked up at him. "So why didn't they?"

The old Cursor shook his head again. "I don't know."

Tavi studied the map for a time, examining the various territories. "Then Varg, I take it, is a member of only one of these territories?"

"Yes," Magnus said. "Narash. It's the only territory that has actually made contact with Alera."

The territory of Narash, Tavi noted, was also home to the port of Marshag. "Then I suppose the next question we need to ask ourselves is—"

Outside the cabin, the ship's bell began to ring frantically. Demos began bellowing orders. A few moments later, the captain himself knocked, then opened the cabin door.

"Magnus," he said, nodding to the old Cursor. "My lord," he said, nodding to Tavi. "The old sea dog was right. There's a storm coming up on us from the south."

Tavi winced, but nodded. "How can we help you, Captain?"

"Tie down anything that isn't bolted to the floor," Demos said, "including yourselves. It's going to be a bad one."

CHAPTER 2

Valiar Marcus debated the proper way to inform the proud young Canim officer that there was, in fact, a considerable distinction between telling an Aleran that he had a poor sense of smell and informing him that he smelled bad.

The young Cane, Marcus knew, was anxious to make a good showing in his language lessons in front of no less personages than both Varg, the undisputed commander of the Canim fleet, and his son and second-in-command, Nasaug. If Marcus made the young officer look foolish, it would be an insult that the Cane would carry stubbornly to his grave—and given the enormous life span of the wolf-folk, it meant that Marcus's actions could cause repercussions, good or ill, for generations yet unborn.

"While your statement is doubtless accurate," Marcus replied, in careful, slow, clearly pronounced Aleran, "you may find that many of my countrymen will respond awkwardly to such remarks. Our own sense of smell is, as you note, a great deal less developed than your own, and as such the use of language that bears upon it will carry a different degree of significance than it might amongst your own folk."

Varg growled under his breath, and muttered, "Few, Aleran or Canim, care to be informed that their odor is unwelcome."

Marcus turned his head to the grizzled old leader of the Canim and inclined his head, in the Aleran fashion. "As you say, sir."

He had only a split second's warning as the embarrassed young officer let out a snarl and lunged at Marcus, his jaws snapping.

Marcus had recognized the signs of brittle pride, which, it seemed, were as common and easily noted amongst ambitious young Canim as they were amongst their Aleran counterparts. Marcus was nearing sixty years of age, and would never have been fast enough to have met the Cane, had he been relying upon his senses alone to warn him—but foresight had always proven a far-more-effective defense than speed alone. Marcus had been anticipating the flash of temper and instant violence.

The Cane was eight feet of coiled steely muscle, fangs and hard bone, and weighed two or three of Marcus—but as his jaws darted forward, he was unable to twist away when Marcus seized his ear in one callused fist and hauled to one side.

The Cane twisted and rolled with the motion, letting out a snarl that rose to a high-pitched yelp of agony as he instinctively moved toward the source of the pull against his sensitive ear, to reduce the pressure on it. Marcus took advantage of the motion, breaking the Cane's balance, building momentum, and dropped his entire weight as well as the young Cane's full onto his furry chin, slamming him to the deck with a skull-jarring crack of impact.

The young Cane lay there stunned for a moment, his eyes glazed, his tongue hanging out of his mouth, bleeding from a small cut.

Marcus rose and straightened his tunic. "An inferior sense of smell," Marcus said, as if absolutely nothing of significance had happened, "is distinct from being told that one smells unpleasant. It's possible that someone sensitive might think you intended an insult. I personally am only an old centurion, too slow to be dangerous in a fight anymore, and find nothing insulting in either statement. I am not at all angry, and could do nothing about it even if I *were* upset. But I would hate for someone less tolerant and more capable to do you harm when, clearly, you are only trying to be friendly. Do you understand me?"

The young officer stared at Marcus with glazed eyes. He blinked a few times. Then his ears twitched in a vague little motion of acknowledgment and assent.

"Good," Marcus said, in his rough but functional Canish, smiling with only the slightest baring of his teeth. "I am glad that you make adequate progress in your efforts to understand Alerans."

"A good lesson," Varg growled in agreement. "Dismissed."

The young Cane picked himself up, bared his throat respectfully to Varg and Nasaug, then walked rather unsteadily from the ship's cabin.

Marcus turned to face Varg. The Cane was a giant of his race, nearly nine feet tall when standing, and the *Trueblood* had been built to fit him. The cabin, which, to the Cane, was as cramped as any shipboard space, was cavernous to Marcus. The Cane, a great black-furred creature, his coat marred with the white streaks of many scars, crouched on his haunches, the at-rest posture of his kind, negligently holding a thick, heavy scroll in his pawlike hands, open to the middle, where he had been reading during the language lesson.

"Marcus," murmured Varg, his basso growl as threatening and familiar as it always was. "I expect you want an explanation for the attack."

"You have a young officer who would be promising if he wasn't an insufferably arrogant fool, convinced of the invincibility of your kind and, by extension, his own."

Varg's ears flicked back and forth in amusement. His eyes went to Nasaug— a Cane who was a shorter, brawnier version of his sire. Nasaug's mouth dropped open, white fangs bared and tongue lolling in the Canim version of a smile.

"Told you," Varg said, in Canish. "Huntmasters are huntmasters."

"Sir?" Marcus asked. He understood the separate meanings of the words, but not their combined context.

"Senior warriors," Nasaug clarified, to Marcus. "They are given command of groups of novices. Long ago, they would form hunting packs, and teach the young to hunt. The teacher was called the huntmaster."

"These days," Varg growled, "the word means one who trains groups of young soldiers and prepares them for their place in the order of battle. Your Legions have something like them as well."

"Centurions," Marcus said, nodding. "I see."

"The pup would not have killed you," Nasaug said.

Marcus faced the younger Cane squarely and calmly. "No, sir," he replied, his voice steady. "He would not have. And out of respect for the Princeps' desire for a peaceful journey, I did not kill him."

"Why would you have done so, huntmaster?" growled Varg, his voice quietly dangerous.

Marcus turned back to face him without flinching. "Because I would far rather leave a dead fool behind me than a live enemy who has gained a measure of wisdom. In the future, I would take it as a courtesy if I was not used as an object lesson beyond those I have already been commanded to give."

Varg bared his fangs in another Canim smile. "It is good to see that we understand one another. My boat is prepared to take you back to your ship, if you are ready, Valiar Marcus."

"I am."

Varg bowed his head and neck, Aleran-style. "Then go your way, and find good hunting."

"And you, sir."

Marcus had just turned to the door when it opened, and a lean Cane, reddish-furred and small for his kind, entered the cabin. Without preamble he bared his throat slightly to Varg and said, "A severe storm approaches, my lord. We have half of an hour or less."

Varg took that in with a growl and dismissed the sailor with a jerk of his head. He glanced at Marcus. "No time to send you back and recover our boat," he said. "It looks as though you're staying for a time."

"Sire," growled Nasaug. There was a note of warning in his tone, Marcus thought. It was not difficult to guess at its source. Marcus had come to the immediate conclusion that he did not relish the notion of being effectively trapped within the hectic conditions of a ship under a storm with the angry young officer still smarting from his learning experience.

"The foremost cabin," Varg said.

Nasaug's tail lashed in a gesture that Marcus had come to recognize as one of surprise. The younger Cane quickly controlled himself and rose. "Centurion," he rumbled, "if you would come with me. It would be best to have you out of the way so that the sailors may do their work. We will do our best to keep you comfortable."

Marcus thought, with a dry amusement, that in this case *comfortable* was synonymous with *breathing*. But one learned rather quickly that the Canim had a viewpoint distinct from that of Alerans.

He followed Nasaug onto the *Trueblood*'s deck. Its timbers had all been painted black—something that would never have happened to an Aleran vessel. Quite the opposite, in fact. Ships were generally whitewashed. That made it easier for the crew to see what they were doing at night, particularly during bad weather, when few reliable light sources were to be had. All the black wood around them gave the ship a grim, funereal appearance, which was certainly imposing, particularly when combined with the black sails. A Cane's night vision, though, was far superior to an Aleran's. They likely had no trouble operating at night, whatever color the ship was tinted.

Nasaug led him to the foremost cabin on the ship—the one generally considered to be the least desirable, Marcus knew. On a sailing vessel, the wind generally blew in from the stern, and whoever was farthest downwind received the benefit of every unpleasant odor on board—and there were generally plenty to be had. The door to the cabin was low, barely Marcus's own height, but rather than simply entering, Nasaug paused and knocked first—then waited for the door to be opened.

When it did, the cabin beyond was completely unlit, windowless and dark. A quiet voice asked, "May we serve, son of Varg?"

"This Aleran huntmaster is under Varg's protection," Nasaug said. "My sire bids you to safeguard him until he can be returned to his people after the storm."

"It will be done," the voice said. "He may enter, son of Varg."

Marcus arched an eyebrow at that and glanced at Nasaug.

The Cane gestured toward the doorway with his snout. "Your quarters, centurion."

Marcus glanced at the dark doorway, then at Nasaug. "I'll be comfortable here, will I?"

Nasaug's ears flicked in amusement. "More so than anywhere else on the ship."

One of the critical things the Alerans had learned about dealing with the Canim, largely thanks to the Princeps himself, was that they placed a far higher priority on body language than humanity did. Words could be empty, and statements of motion and posture were considered to be a great deal more reliable and genuine indicators of intention. As a result, one did *not* display physical signs of fear before the predatory wolf-warriors, if one wanted to avoid being, for example, eaten.

So Marcus firmly clubbed down the instinctive apprehension the unseen speaker had awakened in him, nodded calmly to Nasaug, and stepped into the cabin, shutting the door behind him. In the darkened cabin, he became acutely aware of how thin his tunic and trousers were, and for the first time since the ships had left port, more than a month ago, he missed the constant burden of his armor. He did not put his hand to his sword—the gesture was too obvious. The knives he had concealed on his person would doubtless be of more use in any fight in such blackness, in any case. It would all happen in terrible proximity.

"You are no huntmaster," said the unseen Cane after a moment. It let out a chuckling snarl. "No, no warrior."

"I am a centurion of the First Aleran Legion," he responded. "My name is Valiar Marcus."

"Unlikely," replied the voice. "It is more likely that you are *called* Valiar Marcus, I should judge."

Marcus felt the tension sliding into his shoulders.

"We have been watching your spies, you know. They are largely untrained. But we had no idea that you were one of them until only yesterday—and even that was the result of an accident. The wind parted a curtain, and you were seen reading one of Varg's scrolls when he was out of the cabin."

A second voice, this one to the right and higher up, spoke. "Only chance revealed you."

A third voice, low and to his left, added, "The mark of an adept of the craft."

Marcus narrowed his eyes in thought. "Varg didn't bring in that pigheaded brat to use me to teach him a lesson," he said. "He did it to delay my departure until the storm stranded me here."

"At our request," confirmed the first speaker.

Marcus grunted. But Varg had played the entire situation out as if it had been his usual planning intersecting with chance, all the way through. It meant that for whatever reason, Varg wanted to keep this conversation concealed, even from his own people. It implied dissension in the ranks—always useful information.

It also meant that his current hosts could only be one thing. "You're Hunters," he said quietly. "Like the ones who tried to assassinate the Princeps."

There was the sound of soft motion in the dark, and then one of the Canim drew a heavy cloth away from a bowl filled with a liquid that cast off a glowing red light. Marcus could see the three Canim, lean, grey-furred members of the breed, with somewhat larger, more foxlike ears than most of the warriors he had seen. They were dressed in the loose robes patterned in grey and black that they had been described as wearing whenever they had been seen back in the Amaranth Vale.

The cabin was small, containing two bunk beds. One Cane crouched on the floor over the bowl. Another sprawled across the top bunk at one side of the room, while a third sat in an odd-looking crouch on the bottom bunk opposite. The three Canim were all but identical, down to the shade and patterning of their fur, marking them as family, probably brothers.

"Hunters," said the first Cane. "So your folk have named us. I am called Sha."

"Nef," growled the second.

"Koh," said the third.

The wind had begun to rise, deepening the roll of the ship. Thunder grumbled across the vast, open sea.

"Why have you brought me here?" Marcus said.

"To give you warning," Sha replied. "You need not fear attack at the hands of the Narash. But the other territories have given you no pledge of safety. They regard your kind as vermin, to be exterminated on sight. Varg can only protect you to a certain point. If you continue to Canea, you will do so at your own peril. Varg suggests that your Princeps may wish to consider turning back now rather than continuing on."

"The Princeps," Marcus said, "is remarkably unlikely to be swayed by the possibility of danger."

"Be that as it may," Sha said.

"Why tell me here?" Marcus asked. "Why not send a messenger to the ship?"

All three Hunters stared at Marcus with unreadable expressions. "Because you are the enemy, Valiar Marcus. Varg is of the warrior caste. His honor will no more permit him to give aid and warning to the enemy than to grow fresh fangs."

Marcus frowned. "Ah, I think I see. Varg cannot do it, but you can."

Sha flicked his ears in affirmation. "Our honor lies in obedience and success, regardless of methods and means. We serve. We obey."

"We serve," murmured Nef and Koh. "We obey."

Thunder roared again, this time from terribly nearby, and the wind rose to a howl. Far beneath the scream of the storm, another sound rolled—deeper than thunder, longer, rising in a ponderous, gargantuan ululation Marcus had heard only once before, and that many, many years ago.

It was the territorial bellow of a leviathan, one of the titans of the seas who could smash ships—even ships the size of the *Trueblood*—to kindling. Storms generally roused them, and the turbulent waters made it a great deal more difficult for each ship's water witches to conceal their vessel from the monsters.

Men and Canim were going to die in the storm.

Marcus swallowed his fear and sat down with his back to the wall, closing his eyes. If the Hunters meant him harm, they would have caused it already. So all he had to worry about was the very real possibility of an angry leviathan smashing the *Trueblood* into a cloud of driftwood and leaving everyone aboard her to the mercy of the stormy sea.

Marcus found that idea to be only moderately troublesome. He supposed it was all relative. Such a death, while horrific, would at least be impersonal. There were far worse ways to die.

For example, the Princeps could discover what the Hunters had realized— that Valiar Marcus was *not* a simple, if veteran, centurion in an Aleran legion. That he was, in fact, exactly what they had assessed him to be, namely a spy operating incognito. That he had been placed there by the Princeps' mortal enemies back in Alera was not something that the Hunters could be expected to realize, but should one of the Princeps' personnel or, great furies forbid, Octavian *himself* realize that Valiar Marcus was only a cover identity for Fidelias ex Cursori, servant to the Aquitaines and traitor to the Crown, there would be the crows to pay.

Fidelias had left the employ of the Aquitaines. Indeed, he regarded his letter of resignation as one of the more decisively eloquent messages he had ever sent—flawed only in the fact that it had not deprived the High Lady Aquitainus Invidia of her cold-blooded life. Yet that would not matter. Once he was discovered, his life was forfeit. Fidelias knew that. He accepted it. Nothing he did would ever change the fact that he had betrayed his oath to the Crown and cast his lot with the traitors who would have usurped Gaius's rule.

One day, he would be crucified for his crimes.

But until that day, he knew who he was and what he would do.

Valiar Marcus closed his eyes and, with the skill of most seasoned soldiers, dropped almost immediately to sleep.

CHAPTER 3

Amara, Countess Calderon, wiped the sweat from her brow and regarded the thinning cloud cover with a certain amount of satisfaction. Once again, the local wind furies had attempted to marshal their strength for an assault upon the folk of the Calderon Valley, one of the dangerous furystorms that so often sent its holders running for the shelter of its stone buildings. And once again, she had been able to intervene before the storm could properly take shape.

It wasn't a monumental effort, really, to unravel such an affair, provided she could reach it early enough. A great many things had to happen before a storm could build enough power to be a danger to the people under her husband's care, and if she could break it up at its earliest stages, it was a fairly simple matter to ensure that the storm never took place. It had surprised her, really.

Perhaps it shouldn't have. It was always easier to demolish something than to create it. Look at her sense of dedication to the First Lord, for example. Or her trust and love for her mentor, Fidelias.

The bitter thoughts brought quiet pain and sadness that were at direct odds with the cheery sunbeams that began to break through the disrupted storm clouds, bathing Amara with the wan, feeble warmth of early-winter sunlight. She closed her eyes for a moment, taking in whatever warmth she could get. It was always cold, once one flew more than a mile or so above the ground, as she was—particularly if one wore a dress instead of flying leathers, as she was now. She hadn't felt that she would need the heavier gear, given that she would only be up for half an hour or so—a brief errand, up to moderate heights, then back to her duties at Garrison, where the Countess Calderon had a great many very minor, undeniably useful, and extremely satisfying tasks that required her attention.

Amara shook her head, dismissing the thoughts as much as she could, and called out to Cirrus, her wind fury. At one time, she would have sped as recklessly as she possibly could have toward Garrison—but the thunder and racket of such speeds could prove an annoyance to the holders, and it seemed unthinkably impolite to her now. And it would leave the hem of her dress in tatters and her hair in a hideous mess, besides. At one time, that wouldn't have bothered her in the least—but appearances mattered to many of the people she currently had to deal with on a daily basis, and it made things easier if she *looked* like the Countess they expected.

And besides, while he'd never actually said as much—he never would—her husband's eyes had spoken volumes about his approval of her more . . . polished, she supposed, appearance of late.

Amara smirked. As had his hands. Et cetera.

She glided back to Garrison at a swift but practical pace, passing over the much-expanded town to land in the original fortress that straddled the narrow mountain pass at the eastern end of the Calderon Valley, now itself serving as a citadel in a township nearly the size of a lord's holding, rather than a simple county. What had begun as an open-air market run by a score of ambitious peddlers hawking their wares to a few hundred of the nomadic Marat passing through the area had become a regional trading post involving dozens of merchant interests and attracting thousands of visitors interested in trade, including both the pale-skinned barbarians and ambitious Aleran businessmen.

The growing town had demanded increasingly large supplies of food, and the farmers of the Valley's steadholts had expanded their households and their fields, growing more prosperous with each passing season. Alerans from other parts of the Realm, attracted to the opportunity in the Calderon Valley, had begun to arrive and settle in, and Bernard had already approved the founding of four new steadholts.

Amara frowned as she cruised in for a landing. Technically, she supposed, only two of them were actually new. The others had been rebuilt atop the ruins of the steadholts destroyed by the Vord infestation some years before.

Amara shuddered at that memory.

The Vord.

With the help of the Marat, they had been destroyed—for the moment. But they were still out there. She and Bernard had done everything they could to warn their fellow Alerans of the threat they represented, but few had been willing to listen with open minds. They didn't understand exactly how dangerous the creatures could be. If and when the Vord returned, the fools might not have time to realize their mistake, much less to correct it.

Amara had despaired of ever making enough people understand. But her husband, in his usual fashion, had simply turned his hand to another course of action. If Bernard had done all that he could to strengthen the Realm as a whole, then he had done all that he could. Instead, he returned to Calderon and began to fortify the valley, doing everything within his power to prepare to defend his home and his people against the Vord or any other threat that might come against them. And, given the revenue from the taxation of the booming business in his holding, those preparations were formidable indeed.

She exchanged greetings with the sentries on the walls and descended to the courtyard before crossing to the commander's quarters. She nodded to the *legionare* on duty outside, and went in, to find Bernard poring over a set of plans with his secretary and a pair of Legion engineers. He stood a head taller than the rest of them, and was broader across the shoulders and chest. If his dark hair was frosted with more silver at the temples than it had been in the past, it did not detract from his appearance—far from it. He still wore the short beard he always favored though it was rather more heavily salted with grey. Dressed in a forester's green tunic and leather breeches, he wouldn't have looked like a Citizen at all, but for the excellent quality of material and manufacture of his clothing. His eyes were serious and intelligent, though the faint lines of a scowl had appeared between his brows.

"I don't care if it's never been done before," Bernard told the older of the two engineers. "Once you do it, no one will be able to say that again, now will they?"

The engineer ground his teeth. "Your Excellency, you must understand—"

Bernard's eyes narrowed. "I understand that if you speak one more word to me in that condescending tone of voice, I'm going to roll up these plans and shove them so far up your—"

"Assuming that you aren't too busy," Amara interjected smoothly, "I wonder if I might have a quiet moment with you, my lord husband."

Bernard glared at the engineer, then took a deep breath, composed himself, and faced Amara. "Of course. Gentlemen, shall we continue this after lunch?"

The three men murmured agreement. The senior engineer seized his stack of plans from the table without ever taking his eyes off Bernard, quickly put both hands behind him, and began rolling the papers up in an almost-frantic hurry as he backed from the room. Amara was put in mind of a chipmunk stumbling upon a sleeping grass lion and fleeing for its life.

She found herself smiling as she shut the door behind the chipmunk.

"Rivan Legions," Bernard spat, pacing the functional, plainly appointed office. "They haven't stood to battle in so long they might as well be called Rivan construction crews. Always finding reasons why something can't be done. Most often, *because it isn't done that way.*"

"The useless parasites," Amara said, nodding in compassion. "Aren't your own men members of the Rivan Legions, my lord?"

"They don't count," Bernard growled.

"I see," Amara said gravely. "Did not you, yourself, serve in the Rivan Legions, my lord?"

Bernard stopped pacing and looked at her helplessly.

Amara couldn't stop herself. She burst out laughing.

Bernard's face twitched through half a dozen separate emotions. Then a smile broke the surface of his features, and he shook his head wryly. "Breaking up storms before they have time to properly gather themselves again, are we?"

"It is my duty as Countess Calderon," Amara said. She crossed the room to him, stood on her toes, and kissed him lovingly on the mouth. He slipped an arm around the small of her back and drew her close against him, drawing the kiss out over a slow, delicious minute. Amara let out a pleased little sound as their mouths parted, and smiled up at him. "Long day?"

"Better now," he said. "You must be hungry."

"Starving. Shall we?"

They had just stepped outside when the sentry sounded a ram's horn—a challenge to incoming Knights Aeris. A moment later, the distant sound of another horn came to them in answer, and a few seconds later, a flight of Knights Aeris swept down from overhead at maximum speed, twenty strong, bearing a wind coach amongst them.

"Odd," Bernard said. "Twenty for a single coach? The harness only needs six."

"An escort, perhaps," Amara said.

"Nearly a Legion's allotment of Knights Aeris as escorts? Who would be that important who would *need* them?"

The Knights waited until the last possible moment to slow down, and landed in the courtyard in front of Garrison's command building amidst a hurricane roar of furycrafted wind.

"Extra hands," Amara said, understanding, as the roar died down. "They're flying at top speed, taking turns as bearers."

Bernard grunted. "What's the rush?"

One of the Knights Aeris came running over to Bernard and slammed a fist to his breastplate in a Legion salute. Bernard returned the gesture automatically.

"Your Excellency," the Knight said. He offered a sealed envelope. "I must ask you and the Countess to come with me at once."

Amara lifted her eyebrows and traded a glance with her husband. "Are we under arrest?" she asked, carefully keeping her tone neutral.

"The details are in the letter," the Knight replied.

Bernard had already opened the letter, and was reading it. "It's from the First Lord," he said quietly. "We are commanded to come to Alera Imperia at once."

Amara felt a hot flash of anger. "I don't work for Gaius anymore," she stated, her tone precise.

"Are you refusing to comply, Countess?" asked the Knight, politely.

"Amara—" Bernard began.

Amara should have remained silent, but the fires of her anger sparked memories of other fires, far more horrible, and her pain got the better of her. "Give me one reason why I should."

"Because if you do not," said the Knight politely, "then I have been ordered to arrest you and bring you to the council in chains, if necessary."

Amara felt her knuckles pop in protest as her hand clenched into a fist.

Bernard put a large, strong hand on her shoulder, and rumbled, "We'll come, Captain."

"Thank you," the Knight said, his expression serious. "This way, please."

"Let me fetch a few things for the trip, please."

"Two minutes," the Knight said. "I can delay no more than that, Your Excellency."

Amara blinked at him. "Why not?" she asked him quietly. "What is happening?"

"War," he said shortly. For a moment, his eyes looked haunted. "We're losing."

CHAPTER 4

Gaius Isana, First Lady of Alera, was woken in the middle of the night by a stir in the courtyard below her chambers. The seat of the High House of Placida was shockingly staid, by the standards of the High Lords of Alera. While it was an exquisite home of white marble, it was a manor house of a mere four stories, formed in an open square around a central courtyard and garden like a common country estate. Isana had seen seasonal homes in the capital owned by other High Lords that were far larger and more elaborate than the ancestral halls of Placida itself.

Yet the home, while not gargantuan, had its own quiet integrity. Every block of stone was polished and perfectly fit. Every bit of woodwork, every door, every shutter was made of the finest woods and crafted to simple perfection. The furniture, likewise, was exactingly made and lovingly maintained.

But more than that, Isana thought it was the household staff that made her like the place the most. The capital, and many of the other large cities of the Realm she had visited, had been filled with a wide variety of the various strata of Aleran society. Citizens had swept by in their finery, while common freemen had tended to their tasks and stayed out of the way, and poorer freemen and slaves had scurried about their own duties in impoverished misery. In Lady Placida's household, there were no slaves, and Isana was hard-pressed to discern the difference, at a glance, between Citizens and freemen. More to the point, the Citizens themselves seemed to place less emphasis on their station and more upon their duties, whatever they might be—an attitude that embraced their aides and employees without the same overwhelming regard for social status that permeated most of the Realm.

The gulf between Citizen and freeman hadn't simply vanished there—far from it. But much of the sense of latent hostility and fear that went along with it certainly had. It was a reflection, Isana felt certain, of how High Lord and Lady Placida conducted themselves amongst their own people, in the halls of their own home, and Isana thought that it spoke very well of them.

Since her return from the war-ravaged region around the Amaranth Vale, Isana had been a guest of the High Lady Placidus Aria. While the abrupt end of Kalarus's rebellion and the truce with the invading Canim had ended the war, it had not halted the ongoing loss of life. The war had devastated harvests, displaced entire steadholts, ravaged the economy, and disrupted government on every scale. Throughout the territory once governed from the late city of Kalare, slaves had arisen in bloody revolt. Wild furies, their Aleran bondmates slain by war, famine, or disease, roamed the countryside, far more dangerous than any rabid animal.

The subsequent scramble to find work, food, and shelter against the elements had resulted in widespread chaos. Banditry had arisen and begun to spread almost as fast as the diseases that began to torment the countryside.

The vast monies the Crown had poured into the rush construction of enough shipping to allow Aleran forces to escort the Canim back to their homeland had been a stabilizing force—as had, ironically, the presence of the Canim themselves, who had dealt with Aleran bandits every bit as ruthlessly and efficiently as the *legionares* deployed to hunt them down. Isana suspected that it was, in fact, why their departure had been delayed for several months. She could not have proven anything, of course, but she suspected that Gaius had slowed construction of the final ships in order to make use of the Canim's presence, helping to establish a beachhead of social order amidst the chaos of the war-torn territory.

The Senatorial Guard and the Crown Legion had been slowly reasserting control, but it was an agonizingly methodical process, rife with the political maneuvering of Citizens struggling to seize new titles and power in the reclaimed territory—all while the holders who lived there coughed their lives out in the winter cold or starved to death after eating their shoes. With the financial and public support of the Dianic League, Isana had been doing all that she could to organize relief efforts into the region—until the night two men with drawn swords had reached the doors of her bedroom before her bodyguard had stopped them.

The news of the emergence of an heir to the Crown had spread like wildfire, of course, from one side of the Realm to another within days. It had brought with it a storm of fresh political infighting, as the plans of every ambitious Citizen in the Realm were abruptly sent crashing into ruin. A great many people did not like the notion at all, and many were already decrying Tavi as a fraud and demanding that the Senate declare him an illegitimate heir.

The Senate had no grounds to do so. Septimus had seen to that, ensuring that there were witnesses and evidence enough to validate his son's identity. Evidently, though, someone had decided that if some of the witnesses conveniently vanished, the Senate might be able to oppose Octavian's installation. As the foremost of said witnesses, Isana was the natural target for such schemes.

At the First Lord's suggestion, she had accepted Aria's invitation to visit Placida, ostensibly to speak at several important gatherings of the Dianic League. In truth, she knew perfectly well why she had come: It was the only place in the Realm where she could be reasonably certain of her safety. Gaius's suggestion was a tacit admission that even the First Lord could no longer protect her in Alera Imperia.

Of course, "reasonably certain" was not the same thing as "certain."

There was no certainty anymore.

Isana had no idea of the cause of the raised voices and running feet in the courtyard below her window, but she took no chances. She rose from her bed, dressed only in her nightgown, and immediately seized the long, armored coat from the stand by the bed. She slid into the heavy garment, the motion swift and automatic after the endless practice sessions Araris had forced her to endure. Though the coat seemed to be made of heavy leather, sections of the finest steel plate had been sewn into place between two layers of the lighter material. While not as effective as true lorica, the coat offered far more protection than her skin alone, and could be donned swiftly at need.

Once the coat was in place, she slid her feet into light leather shoes and, with a moue of distaste, slung a leather baldric over one shoulder, so that her sword, a standard Legion *gladius*, hung at her side. She regarded the weapon without enthusiasm. She had managed to acquire some rudimentary knowledge of self-defense using a blade, again at Araris's insistence. She'd felt that she had little choice in the matter. After all, it was Araris who had risked his own life to stop the assassins who had nearly reached her, and it seemed the least she could do to follow his advice and help him perform his duty as a *singulare* to the First Lady. She had diligently applied herself to learning the basics of swordplay—but she did not think that she would ever feel truly comfortable wearing one.

Although what made her most uncomfortable, she reflected, was the fact that the weight of the sword and armor, once settled upon her, made her feel more reassured than ridiculous.

She felt the presence of someone tense with anxiety a full second before a soft footfall sounded outside her door, and by the time it opened she had her sword in hand and held in a defensive guard. Light from the furylamp in the hallway made a black outline of the intruder, but Isana's watercrafter's senses identified him more surely than her eyes could have within another heartbeat.

"Araris," she said quietly, lowering the sword. She waited until he had shut the door behind him to say, "Light."

The little furylamp beside her bed responded to her voice, flickering to life, casting a warm yellow glow over the spacious chambers, revealing Araris. He was a man of medium height and average build. He wore his hair shorn close to his head, in the Legion style, and one side of his face was hideously marred with a mass of scar tissue in the shape of the brand the Legions used to mark men convicted of cowardice in the face of the enemy. He wore simple, well-made clothing, including a coat not unlike Isana's own, and bore a *gladius* upon one hip and a duelist's long blade on the other.

His anxiety faded a little when his eyes met hers, and Isana felt the sudden warm rush of his affection and love—among other, rather less poetic expressions of masculine approval. "Good," he said quietly, nodding at her sword. "But next time, come away from the window before you turn on the light."

She stepped away from the window with a sigh, shaking her head, and extended her hand to him. "I'm sorry. I just woke."

He stepped closer to her and took her hand, just barely touching the tips of his fingers and thumb to her skin. "It's all right. You never expected to be forced to live with this sort of thing."

She gave him a small smile. "No. I suppose not." She shook her head. "What's happening outside?"

"A courier has arrived from the capital," Araris replied quietly, lowering his hand. "Her Grace requests that you join her in her study with all possible haste. Beyond that, I have no idea."

Isana looked down at herself and sighed. Then she carefully put the sword away. She'd given herself several minor cuts before learning the sufficient degree of respect for the weapon's edge. "I look ridiculous."

"You look like someone serious about survival," Araris corrected her. He glanced back as more feet hurried down the hall outside. All around them there was a rising amount of activity in the household, evidenced by the opening and closing of doors, and the sound of rising numbers of voices. "To be frank, my lady, this kind of disruption is an ideal situation for another attack. I'm just as happy to have you in the armor if you're going to be moving around the hallways."

"Very well," Isana said. "Then let's waste no more time."

One advantage of such a modest-sized household, Isana reflected, was that one never had to plan an expedition complete with guides and pack animals to reach the other side of it, the way it had often seemed necessary in the capital, or in Aquitaine. Isana traded greetings with a young Knight, a chambermaid, and a senior scribe, all of whom she'd broken bread with on several occasions, circled the courtyard, and walked up a single flight of steps to reach the High Lady's private study. Araris followed her silently, a constant presence, two paces back and slightly to one side, his eyes wary, calm, and everywhere.

Guards were posted outside of Lady Placida's study.

Isana paused and traded a glance with Araris. This was a first. Aria was one of the more . . . confident women Isana had ever known where matters of potential violence were concerned. If the reports Isana had heard were to be believed, it was with good reason. In Alera, most female Citizens gained their status through marriage. Aria hadn't. As a young academ, she'd fought a duel with the newly installed High Lord of Rhodes—a situation arising from a rather forceful rejection of his attention during evenings at the Academy, if rumor was to be believed. She'd beaten the young man handily, too, and in front of far too many witnesses for anyone to question her claim.

Isana scarcely wished to consider what situation might have arisen that would cause Placidus Aria to post guards at her door. Her wishes, however, were quite immaterial to the matter. She strode forward, nodding to the guards, both of whom saluted her sharply. One of them opened the door for her without bothering to inquire of those within whether or not he should.

Isana felt herself begin to wince and forced the expression away. She felt quite rude, not to mention presumptuous, simply striding into the High Lady's personal study—but as odd as she might find it, Isana was, at least nominally, Aria's peer and marginal superior. In an emergency situation, the First Lady of Alera did not *need* to ask permission to enter the room. Whatever Isana might have felt personally, she had an obligation to maintain the status of her office, as well as fulfill its duties.

Aria's study could easily have been mistaken for a garden. Several fountains chuckled quietly within, and growing plants were everywhere but upon the several bookshelves spaced around the walls. The fountains drained into a pool in the center of the room, and furylights of every color twinkled at the pool's bottom like tiny, jeweled stars.

Lady Placida herself arrived less than a minute later, striding into the room with confidence, energy, and purpose. She was a very tall woman, with lovely red hair and, like Isana herself, appeared to be a young woman in her early twenties. Also like Isana, she was in fact a good deal older than that. She wore the green-on-green of the House of Placidus in her gown and long tunic, and in the trim of her white traveling cloak and gloves.

"Isana," she said, coming toward them, holding out her hands.

Isana took her hands and received a kiss on the cheek. At the touch, Isana felt the wrenching anxiety beneath the High Lady's practiced, serene expression. "Aria. What's happened?"

Lady Placida nodded politely to Araris before turning back to Isana. "I'm not yet certain, but sealed orders from the First Lord arrived, and my lord husband has already left to mobilize Placida's legions. We are commanded to leave for the capital at once."

Isana felt her eyebrows lifting. "Only us?"

The High Lady shook her head. "Half a dozen of my husband's most powerful lords have been summoned as well—and from what the messenger said, similar summons have gone out to the entire Realm."

Isana frowned. "But . . . why? Why do such a thing?"

Aria's expression remained calm, but it could not hide the woman's worry from Isana's senses. "Nothing good. Our coach is waiting."

CHAPTER 5

Isana had been to the great hall of the Senatorium only once before, during the presentation ceremony when she and several others had been brought forth in front of the Realm as a whole and introduced as new Citizens of Alera. At the time, dressed in the scarlet and sable of the House of Aquitaine, she had mostly been too self-conscious—and, she could admit to herself now, ashamed—to notice how *large* the place was.

The Senatorium was built from sober, somber grey marble, and was ostensibly large enough to hold not only the Senate, which included the Senators and their retinues, but every Citizen of the Realm of Alera as well. Isana had been told, at some point, that it could seat more than two hundred thousand souls, each and every one of them able to see and hear what transpired thanks to the cleverly arranged furycraft in the construction.

It resembled an enormous theater more than anything else. Upon the bottom and center of the Senatorium was the actual half circle of seating for the Senate, presided over by the Proconsul, the Senator with the most votes within the body of the Senate itself. Then, rising in rank upon rank upon rank, bench seating stretched up and out for hundreds of yards. Looking down upon the Senate floor, one had only to lift one's eyes up a little to see the First Lord's Citadel, the heart of Alera Imperia, rising above the Senatorium.

"What's so funny?" murmured Lady Placida.

"I was thinking how one couldn't help but notice how large and threatening is the First Lord's Citadel up above us upon entering," Isana said. "It's hardly subtle."

"That's nothing," Lady Placida replied. "When leaving, the view is of the Grey Tower. An even more poignant vista."

Isana smiled, and glanced over her shoulder to see that Aria was correct. The Grey Tower, that unassuming little fortress, was a prison built to hold powerless even the strongest furycrafters in the Realm—and was a silent statement that no one in Alera was beyond the reach of the law.

"One cannot help but wonder," Isana said, "if whichever First Lord presided over the construction meant the view to reassure the Senators or to threaten them."

"Both, naturally," Lady Placida replied. "Senators loyal to the Realm first can rest easy knowing that personally powerful, ambitious men will always be held accountable—and the ambitious receive the exact same message. I believe it was the original Gaius Secundus who constructed the Senatorium, and he— oh my."

Isana could not blame Lady Placida for breaking off in the midst of a sentence. For though the vastness of the Senatorium was generally more or less empty, hosting only the various retinues of the Senators and a few curious parties, allowed by law to watch the proceedings, that night was different.

The Senatorium was filled to the top rows of its seats.

The noise of the crowd was enormous—a sea of talk, a thunderstorm of murmurs. More than that, though, was the overwhelming emotion of those present. None of it was particularly sharp, but there were so *many* people there that the accumulated weight of all their low-intensity anxiety, curiosity, impatience, irritation, amusement, and too many others to name hit her like a sack of grain.

Isana felt it when Lady Placida called upon her metalcrafting to shield her mind against the storm of emotions, and briefly wished that she could have done something similar—but she couldn't. She simply ground her teeth for a moment, fighting back the surge of outside emotion, and found Araris's hand beneath her arm, holding her steady, his calm concern a bedrock and a shelter against the tide that threatened her. She gave him a swift, grateful smile and, working from that solid point, methodically pushed away the other emotions to let them back in gradually, bit by bit, to give herself a chance to acclimate to them. Araris and Lady Placida stood on either side of her, patiently waiting for her to adjust to the environment.

"All right," she said, a moment later, as other Citizens continued to file in. "I'm better, Araris."

"Best we take our seats," Lady Placida murmured. "The Crown Guard is beginning to arrive. The First Lord will be here any moment."

They descended to the rows of box seats just above the Senate floor. While not specifically, legally granted to the High Lords, it was well understood who would be occupying those seats, and tradition had long since established which High Lord would occupy which box in the Senatorium at the infrequent assemblies of both the Senate and lords.

The seats for Lord and Lady Placida were situated above the places of the Senators from the areas governed by Citizens beholden to them. Lady Placida took a few moments to descend to the Senate floor, exchanging greetings with several people, while Isana and Araris sat down in the box.

"Lady Veradis?" Isana asked, recognizing the young woman in the box beside theirs.

The serious, pale-haired young healer, daughter of the High Lord of Ceres, turned to them at once, and offered Isana a grave nod. She was notably alone in her father's section, and seemed all the more slender and frail for the open space around her. "Good evening, Your Highness."

"Please, call me Isana. We know one another better than that."

The young woman gave her a fleeting smile. "Of course," she said. "Isana. I am glad to see you well. Good evening, Sir Araris."

"Lady," Araris said quietly, bowing his head. He glanced around the empty box, and said, with perfectly bland understatement, "You seem less well attended than I would expect you to be."

"With excellent reason, sir," Veradis said, returning her attention to the Senate floor. "As I trust will be made clear shortly."

Isana settled back, frowning, and studied the seating behind the High Lord's boxes in general, where the visiting Lords and Counts as a rule settled in behind their own patrons. Behind Lord Aquitaine's box, for example, was a sizeable contingent of finely dressed Citizenry, mostly sporting the scarlet and black of the House of Aquitaine, while the gold and black of Rhodes made for an only slightly smaller contingent in the seats behind that High Lord's box.

By contrast, the sections behind Lord Cereus's box, and for that matter, behind the box of Lord and Lady Placidus, were rather sparsely populated. And the section behind the empty box where the High Lord of Kalarus would have been seated was entirely empty of any citizen bearing the green and grey of the House of Kalare. That wasn't a surprise, given that the House was hardly in favor after Kalarus Brencis's open rebellion against the Crown had failed so miserably and spectacularly.

Even so, the Citizens seated in that section were at its fringes, and wearing the colors of one of the other greater Houses. Surely *someone* should have been wearing Kalarus's colors, if for no other reason than out of tradition and force of habit. Some of those families had been wearing those colors for centuries.

Regardless of the actions of the most recent Lord Kalarus, they would not have abandoned their own traditional garb—indeed, many of the poorer Citizens of that region simply could not have afforded a new court wardrobe, given the devastation the rebellion had wreaked upon their economy.

Where were the Citizens from Kalare, from Ceres, and from Placida? *What has Lady Placida not told us?*

She felt a similar sense of concerned curiosity from Araris, and turned to him, expecting him to have noticed the same absences she had—only to find him staring intently across the Senate floor.

"Araris?" she murmured.

"Look at Aquitaine's box," he murmured quietly. "Where is Lady Aquitaine?"

Isana blinked and looked more closely. Sure enough, High Lord Aquitainus Attis sat in his box without the familiar, stately figure of his wife Invidia at his side.

"Where could she be?" Isana murmured. "She would never miss something like this."

"Perhaps now that an heir has appeared, they finally decided to kill one another," murmured a wry, familiar voice. "Though if so, I lost money in the pool the Cursors had going as to the victor."

Isana turned to find a short, slight man with sandy hair smiling at them from the row above the Placidan box, his elbows casually resting on the railing.

"Ehren," Isana said, smiling. "What are you doing here? I thought you were going to Canea with my son."

The young man's expression grew sober, and Isana felt him close down, concealing his emotions—but not before she felt his flash of weary frustration, anger, and fear. "Duty called," he replied, mustering up the effort for another smile as Aria returned to the box. "Ah, Lady Placida. I wonder if I could impose upon you for a seat during the First Lord's address?"

Lady Placida glanced at Isana, lifting an eyebrow. "By all means, Sir Ehren. Please join us."

Ehren inclined his head in thanks and swung his legs calmly over the railing, slipping down into the box with a rather cavalier disregard for the solemnity of the Senatorium. Isana had to make an effort to keep from smiling.

Ehren had barely been seated when a single trumpeter blew the fanfare of a Legion captain—and *not* the notes of the First Lord's Processional. Murmurs rose through the Senatorium at once as those seated all rose to their feet together— the First Lord only employed that protocol in time of war.

Gaius Sextus, First Lord of Alera, entered as the last notes of the fanfare rang out, flanked by half a dozen Knights Ferrous in the crimson cloaks of the Crown Guard. A tall, powerfully built man, Gaius looked more like a man in his late prime than an octogenarian—except for his silver-white hair, which was, if Isana was not imagining it, even thinner and wispier than it had been the last time she had seen him, several months before.

The First Lord moved like a much younger man, descending the steps from the Senatorium's entrance to the Senate floor in rapid strides. He passed between the boxes of Lords Phrygius and Antillus—both of which were empty of a High Lord. Lady Phrygia was present, though an elderly, one-eyed lord was evidently standing in for High Lord Antillus and bore the signet dagger of the House of Antillus on a sash across his sunken chest. The murmuring rose to a low tide of sound as Gaius descended to the floor.

"Citizens!" the First Lord said, raising his hands, as he took the Senate floor. His voice, enhanced by the furycraft of the building, rolled richly through the evening. "Citizens, please."

The Speaker of the Senate—Isana wasn't sure who it was this year, someone from Parcia, she thought—quickly took the podium. "Order! Order in the Senatorium!" His voice thundered through the enormous theater like a titan's, quelling the voices of the assembled Citizenry. Isana had the brief, uncharitable thought that the man probably found it quite satisfying. Though upon reflection, how often did the opportunity to have both the justification and the means to shout down half the Citizenry of the Realm present itself? She could think of several days that she would have found it more than mildly satisfying, herself.

Once the noise had dwindled to a low murmur, the Speaker nodded, and said, "We welcome you to this emergency convocation of the Senate, convened at the request of the First Lord. I will now yield the floor to Gaius Sextus, First Lord of Alera, so that he may present information of key importance to the Realm before the august members of this assembly."

Almost before he was finished speaking, Gaius had stepped up to the podium, confidently assuming the space the Speaker had been occupying a moment before. There was no sense of bluster or swagger in the movement, nor did the Speaker react with anything like chagrin—yet Gaius somehow managed simply to displace the man, the way a large dog will a far smaller one at the food dish, and did so as smoothly and naturally as if the entire world had been expressly ordered that way—and as a consequence, it was. Isana shook her head, simultaneously exasperated with the man's sheer arrogance and admiring of his restraint. Gaius never used more of his considerable force of personality, will, or furycraft than he absolutely required.

Of course, he never let anything stand between him and what he deemed "required," either. No matter how many innocent people it might kill.

Isana pressed her lips together and restrained her thoughts on the matter of the ending of Lord Kalarus and his rebellion—and his city and its inhabitants, and all the lands around it and everyone who lived in them. It was not the time to review once again Gaius Sextus's actions, or to judge them as acts of war, or necessity or murder—or, most likely, all three.

"Citizens," he began, his sonorous voice serious, sober. "I come to you to-night as no First Lord has for hundreds of years. I come to you to warn you. I come to you to call you to duty. And I come to you to ask you to go beyond all that duty requires." He paused, to let the echoes of his voice roll through the darkening evening. "Alerans," he murmured. "We are at war."

CHAPTER 6

"Well of course we're at war," Amara murmured crossly to Bernard. "We're practically always at war. There's constant low-level conflict with the Canim, an ongoing conflict on the Shieldwall that's been in progress for generations, the occasional argument with a horde of screaming Marat and their beasts . . ."

"Shhhhh, love," Bernard said, patting her hand with his. They were fairly far up in the seating above the box of the High Lord of Riva, but Bernard hadn't bothered establishing his own colors to reflect those of Riva's. The green and brown of the Count of Calderon tended to fade into the landscape around his home—but among the scarlet-and-gold-clad Citizens of Riva, it had the opposite effect. That did not, Amara reflected, appear to disturb her husband.

"I just don't see the point in playing up the drama of this," Amara said, folding her arms. "He's let the dramatic pause go on long enough."

"It's a large room," Bernard said, glancing around. "Give him a moment. Can you see where Ehren's gotten off to?"

"He's sitting with your sister in Lady Placida's box," Amara said idly.

"Isana?" Bernard scowled. "Of course it was too much to ask for Gaius to leave her in peace."

"Hush, pause over," Amara said, squeezing Bernard's hand.

"An enemy which has previously only been a theory, a vague concern, has become a very real, very present threat to the Realm," Gaius continued. "The Vord have come to Alera."

Amara felt Bernard's body grow tense beside her.

"At the moment, it would appear that they landed and established themselves sometime late last summer, after the end of the Kalare Rebellion, in the wilderness region to the southwest of the city."

"Good place for it," Bernard rumbled.

Amara murmured her agreement. The area was an ideal place for the Vord to establish themselves and begin to spread. It was richly forested and thick with game, while simultaneously being almost empty of human inhabitants. It was, in fact, for that very reason that they had approached the city of Kalare through that region with the First Lord, when he had made his now-famous furyless trek to Kalare to unleash Kalus, the great fire fury beneath the mountains near the former city of Kalare, before the mad High Lord Kalarus could use it to take down as many people as possible with him when the Legions finally brought him to bay.

"We discovered their presence just under one month ago," the First Lord continued. "When they began attacking the southernmost patrols from the area around the Waste. A number of teams of Cursors and combat patrols of Knights were dispatched to determine enemy numbers and whereabouts." He paused and swept his gaze around the Senatorium. "Casualties were heavy."

"Bloody crows," Bernard snarled. His right hand closed into a fist, his knuckles popping. "If they'd been careful enough, they should have . . . No one *listened*."

"You tried," Amara murmured. "You tried, love."

"The nearest Legion, one of the re-formed interim Kalaran Legions, was dispatched to secure the region," Gaius continued. "They engaged the Vord under near-ideal circumstances thirty miles south of the Waste and were overwhelmed within an hour. With the exception of two Knights Aeris, who escaped to bring word of the Legion's fate, there were no survivors."

The murmurs died.

Gaius continued speaking in a dispassionate tone. "The entirety of the other forces in the region, including the Senatorial Guard and both interim Kalaran Legions, marched at once, linked up, and gave battle to the enemy at the northern edge of the Waste. We cannot be certain what happened at that point—there were apparently no survivors from the second engagement."

Shocked silence ruled the Senatorium.

Gaius turned to the broad, shallow pool in the center of the floor and waved his hand at it. The water's smooth surface rippled at once, then resolved itself into the familiar mountains, valleys, and rivers of a map of Alera itself, in full color, the cities of each High Lord marked by a disproportionately large model of their respective citadels—including the sullen, fiery mountaintop of Mount Kalus, where the city of Kalare once stood. Thanks to the furycrafting of the

Senatorium's builders, Amara could clearly see the model in the pool, even from the high seats, and she regarded it intently, along with every other soul present.

As she watched, the entire coastline southwest of Mount Kalus began to turn a dirty brown-green, as if being coated with some sort of moldy sludge that began to spread steadily over the ground to the north and east, sliding inexorably forward, over the Waste that was all that remained of the city of Kalare, and continuing toward the Amaranth Vale beyond it. Amara recognized it after a moment—the *croach*, the strange, waxy substance that grew all around the Vord wherever they began to spread, choking out all other life.

The *croach* continued to spread, sweeping into the Vale and halfway through it.

"The enemy has come this far—a distance of nearly two hundred miles from the first point of contact—in less than a month. The substance you see represented on the map is known as the *croach*. It is some kind of mold or fungus that grows in the Vord's wake, killing all other plant and animal life."

A befuddled-looking, portly old country Count, his gold-and-scarlet tunic patched and faded, sat on the bench beside Amara, shaking his head. "No," he murmured beneath his breath. "No, no, no. This is some kind of mistake."

"Our aerial scouts have confirmed that the entire area represented here has been covered entirely," Gaius continued. "Nothing lives there now that is not Vord."

"Oh come now," sputtered Lord Riva, rising, his jowls flushed and sweating. "You cannot expect us to believe that some kind of fungus is a threat to our Realm?"

The First Lord glanced at the High Lord of Riva and narrowed his eyes. "My lord, you have not been recognized by the Speaker of the Senate. You are out of order. The floor will open for questions and debate as soon as it is practical, but for the moment, it is essential that—"

"That you force these histrionics upon us?" Riva demanded, gathering momentum. "Come now, Gaius. Winter is all but upon us. The first freeze will destroy this . . . infestation, at which point *competent* military leadership should suffice to contain and destroy the invaders. I see no reason why these theatrics—"

Gaius Sextus turned toward the High Lord of Riva.

"Grantus," Gaius said in an even tone. "I do not have time for this. Every moment of delay puts more lives at risk." His expression hardened. "Perhaps even your own."

Riva stared at Gaius for a startled moment, his eyes wide, then flushed dark red with anger. His hands opened and closed several times as he realized that the First Lord had all but openly threatened him with the *juris macto*.

Lord Aquitaine's gaze snapped to Gaius like a falcon's and locked upon him.

Amara tensed suddenly.

The First Lord was taking a terrible risk. In his prime, Amara would have thought Gaius the match of any crafter in Alera—but she knew, better than almost anyone, how much of the First Lord's apparent strength was an act of bravado, a display of sheer will. Beneath the outer show of energy and drive, Gaius was a weary old man, and Riva, despite his less-than-legendary intellect, was, after all, a High Lord of Alera, and wielded tremendous power.

The status of Octavian's legitimacy was far from set in stone. Should the First Lord die today, especially given the need for strong leadership, Aquitainus Attis might well attain the throne he'd been seeking for so long.

Gaius had to know that. But if the thought troubled him, it did not show in his expression or bearing. He faced Riva with perfect aplomb, waiting.

In the end, Riva's uncertainty proved a better defense than any furycraft. The portly High Lord harrumphed, and growled, "My apologies for speaking out of turn, Speaker, Senators, my fellow Citizens." He glowered at Gaius. "I will refrain from pointing out the obvious until the proper time."

Aquitaine's mouth spread into a lazy grin. Amara couldn't be certain, but she thought she saw him incline his head, very slightly, to Gaius, a fencer's gesture of acknowledgment.

Gaius went back to speaking as though nothing had happened. "The Vord have not limited their attacks to military forces. Civilian populations have been attacked and massacred without mercy. Given the nature of our defeats on the battlefield, a great many people never received word about their presence, or did not hear about them until it was too late for them to escape. The loss of life has been staggering."

Gaius paused to sweep his gaze around the Senatorium. Again, when he spoke, he did so with detached precision. "More than one hundred thousand Aleran holders, freemen, and Citizens alike have been slain."

Cries rang out amidst an ocean-surf swell of gasps that ran through the Senatorium.

"Four days ago," Gaius said, "the Vord reached the southernmost holdings of High Lord Cereus. Lord Speaker, honored Senators, his daughter and heir, Veradis, is here to give testimony to the Senate and to speak on behalf of His Grace, her father."

Gaius stepped back as the Speaker rose and leaned into the podium again for a moment. "Will the Lady Veradis please come before the Senate?"

Amara watched as a slender, serious-faced young woman rose, her pale, wispy hair drifting like cobwebs as she moved. Bernard leaned close to her, and murmured, "Cereus has a son, does he not? I thought he was the heir to Ceres."

"He was," Amara said. "Apparently."

"Thank you," Veradis said, the building's furies projecting her words throughout the Senatorium. She had a voice to match her face—low, for a woman, and quite somber. "My father sends his regrets that he cannot be here himself, but he is in the field with our Legions, slowing the Vord in an effort to give our people a chance to flee. It is at his command that I have come here to beg the aid of the First Lord and of his brother High Lords in Ceres' most desperate hour." She paused for a moment, frozen, then cleared her throat. The first several words of her next sentence were tight, constricted. "Already, my brother Vereus has fallen to the invaders, along with half of the Legion under his command. Thousands of our holders have been slaughtered. Nearly half of the lands in my lord father's care have been consumed by the Vord. Please, my lords. After what Kalarus's rebellion did to our lands . . ." She lifted her chin, and though her expression was perfectly composed, Amara could see the tears glistening on her cheeks. "We need your help."

With perfect poise, Veradis descended from the podium and returned to her seat in her House's box, and Amara abruptly felt certain that the young woman was unaware of her own tears, or she would have contained them, using her watercrafting if necessary.

Pausing to elicit a nod from the Speaker, Gaius resumed the podium. "Our current estimates place the enemy numbers at somewhere between one hundred and two hundred thousand—but frankly, this tells us relatively little. We have limited knowledge of their capabilities as individuals, but know almost nothing of their potential working in mass coordination."

"You know one thing," interjected a quiet voice, enhanced despite the fact that the speaker was not standing at the podium. Lord Aquitaine regarded Gaius steadily. "You know that they are extremely dangerous. In all probability, more so, pound for pound, than an Aleran Legion."

The uproar raised by *that* statement was instant and vociferous. Everyone knew that the Legions were invincible. For a thousand years, they had been the wall of steel and muscle and discipline that had held against every attacker—and while a *legionare* might not leave a battle with victory in his grasp, it would only be because it had been pried tooth and nail from his fingers.

And yet . . .

It had been a very long time since the Legions as a whole had faced any real threat. The Icemen had been largely neutralized by the Shieldwall, centuries before. Conflicts with the Canim had rarely involved more than a few hundred of the wolf-warriors—at least until Kalare had conspired with one of their traitors to bring a literal horde to Aleran shores three years ago. The Marat had won battles against the Legions here and there, but they had never been lasting victories and had only served to make Aleran counterattacks all the more intense and punitive.

The Children of the Sun were long since dead, their Realm rotted back into the Feverthorn Jungle. The Malorandim had been driven to extinction eight centuries ago. The Avar, the Yrani, the Dekh—all gone, nothing left of them but names that Amara dimly remembered from her history lessons. Once they had all been rivals and tyrants to a younger, smaller, weaker Alera.

But the Legions had changed all of that. In conflict after conflict, battle after battle, season after season, century after century, the Legions had laid the foundations for the present-day Realm.

It was boldly done—but boldness had rarely been at a premium in the Legions since Alera had become more settled. High Lords had placed more value upon stable, conservative captains, who would have a care for the pocketbook as well as their *legionares*.

Could it be that the legendary might of the Legions had passed into legend? Suppose they were not the invincible bulwark against Alera and her foes? Amara folded her arms. She found the idea uncomfortable. To others it would simply be unacceptable—as the occupants of the Senatorium had proven by their reaction to Aquitaine's statement.

Amara called upon Cirrus with a murmur, bringing Gaius's expression into clearer view, and saw the steady gaze he exchanged with Aquitaine. Though she was no watercrafter, she could clearly sense the understanding the two men exchanged in that gaze and felt a leaden sense of fear sink into her bones.

Gaius had no trouble accepting the statement.

The First Lord already believed it.

"Order!" called the First Lord, his voice thundering over the roar of the assembled crowd. "Citizens! We *will* have order in the Senatorium!"

It took a moment more for the crowd to settle down again, but they did. The air of the Senatorium seethed with anger and tension and, though Amara doubted most of the folk there would have admitted it, with raw fear.

"Over the past several years, representatives from every Legion have been briefed on what we know of the Vord," the First Lord said. "They represent a unique threat—one that can expand very rapidly. We must respond rapidly and with overwhelming force if we are to repel them. To that end, I am ordering every High Lord, saving Phrygia and Antillus, to dispatch two Legions immediately for detached operations against the Vord."

"Outrageous!" bellowed Riva, his round face flushing scarlet as he rose from his chair. "You go too far, Sextus! No First Lord in five hundred years has acted with such arrogance!"

Once again, Gaius turned to face High Lord Riva—but this time, he remained silent.

"Yes, the founding laws of the original Primus give you that authority," Riva seethed, "but it is well understood that we have grown beyond such ancient measures! This fearmongering is nothing but a pathetic and transparent attempt to continue grasping at power—exactly like the announcement of the sudden appearance of your so-called legitimate grandson.

"You are not a tyrant, Gaius Sextus! You are a first among equals! Among equals, the crows take your egotistical eyes, and I will go to the crows before I will submit to your—"

Calmly, in no apparent rush, High Lord Aquitainus Attis rose from his seat in his box, turned to the railing dividing it from Lord Riva's, and drew his sword in a blur of silver. There was a hissing sound, a chime of steel, and the heavy wooden railing fell into two pieces, their ends smoking and glowing orange.

Lord Aquitaine pointed his sword at Riva, and fire abruptly licked its way down the length of the weapon, fluttering up out of the steel, which began to glow with a sullen orange heat. "Grantus," Aquitaine said, loud enough for everyone to hear. "Close your cowardly lips over that void in your head where your brains went missing and keep them there. Then put your lazy, shapeless ass back into your chair and do it swiftly. Or face me in the *juris macto.*"

Riva's eyes grew so round that Amara could clearly see the whites all the way up where they sat, even without Cirrus's help. His mouth opened and closed several times, then he abruptly sat down.

Aquitaine nodded sharply and turned a slow circle, burning sword's point sweeping around the boxed seats of the High Lords. He spoke in a quiet, hard tone, carried all the way through the Senatorium by his own furies, Amara had no doubt. "Does anyone else have an objection to obeying the lawful commands of the First Lord?"

Evidently, no one did.

Aquitaine lowered his blade, the flames upon it dying down. He turned toward Gaius, descended from his seating, and crossed the Senate floor to the podium. There he bowed to the First Lord and offered him the hilt of his sword over one arm. "My Legions are yours to command, sire. I will dispatch them at once. Further, I offer you my personal services in the field."

Gaius nodded gravely and took the sword, then offered it hilt first back to Aquitaine. "Thank you, Your Grace. Your support is most welcome. It was my hope that you would be willing to serve as captain for this campaign."

Aquitaine sheathed his sword, struck his fist to his heart in a *legionare's* salute, and moved to stand at Gaius's right hand. "Who will stand with us?" he demanded, eyes sweeping sternly around the room.

Lady Placida rose. "My lord husband is already on the march to support our friend and neighbor Lord Cereus," she said. "Veradis, dear, he should be arriving at Ceres within a day."

"Atticus?" Aquitaine said. "Parcia?"

Both lords rose and began to pledge their support, and estimate how long it would take for their troops to arrive.

"Huh," Bernard grunted, folding his arms. "There's something I didn't expect."

"What's that?" Amara said.

"Aquitaine turning into a supporter for Gaius."

Amara arched an eyebrow. "Is that what you think he's doing?"

"It *does* look something like that, love."

Amara shook her head. "Look at what he's done. He's uniting the Realm. Serving as its protector. Leading everyone against the deadliest threat Alera has ever known—all while the Princeps is entirely absent." She smiled grimly. "Some might even say, conspicuously absent."

Bernard blinked. "That's absurd."

"Of course. But not everyone will know that. Tavi is an unknown quantity. A great many people would prefer a known, proven veteran of Aleran politics to be the next First Lord. Should Aquitaine lead this war and win, he will be a hero as well. At that point . . ." Amara shrugged. "Gaius will not live forever."

Bernard stared down at the Senate floor, a sickened expression on his face. "And Gaius just . . . just let him do it?"

"Wanted him to do it, I should think," Amara said.

"Great furies, *why?*"

"Because whatever else Aquitaine is, he is *very* capable in the field," Amara said quietly. "Because if we are to survive, we will need him." She rose. "They won't be much longer here. Let's go before we get caught in the crowd."

"Where to?"

"The Citadel," Amara said. "Unless I miss my guess, Gaius is going to have a favor to ask of us." She glanced down at the far side of the Senatorium. "And of your sister."

CHAPTER 7

Amara and Bernard were standing outside the First Lord's study when a pair of Crown Guardsmen arrived. The two men nodded to them, confirming Amara's suspicion that Gaius wished to speak to them privately, and one of them went into the study and emerged again. A moment later, the First Lord himself appeared, flanked by four more Guardsmen.

"Gentlemen," Gaius said, nodding to the Guardsmen. "Your Excellencies, if you would join me, please."

One of the guards opened the door, and Gaius went inside. Amara stared after him for a moment, her lips compressed into a hard line. A quietly violent tide of emotion surged through her at the sight of the First Lord, there before her, at the sound of his voice, at his blithely competent, peremptory manner. He had unleashed the great fury Kalus upon the people of Kalare with the same kind of immediate, decisive calm, killing tens of thousands of innocent Alerans, civilians, along with the forces of the rebellious High Lord Kalarus.

And she had stood upon a mountaintop overlooking the city with him and watched those people die.

Amara hated him for making her see that.

Bernard put his large, warm hand on her shoulder. "Love," he said quietly. "Shall we?"

Amara gave her husband as much of a smile as she could manage, then straightened her back and followed Gaius into his study.

Like all the rest of the Citadel, the chamber was lavishly, exquisitely appointed without being overdone. There was a broad writing desk made of green-
black hardwood from a Rhodesian tree found near the Feverthorn Jungle,
surrounded by matching shelves that groaned with books of every description.
Amara had seen many such studies in which the books had been nothing more
than decoration. She had no doubt that in that room, every book had been both
read and considered.

Gaius crossed to a sideboard with brisk strides, opened it, and drew out a
bottle of wine and a cup, every motion precise and focused—until Bernard shut
the door behind him.

Then the First Lord bowed his head for a moment, shoulders sagging. He
took a couple of slow breaths, and Amara could hear them rasp in his lungs.
Then he opened a bottle of what smelled like particularly pungent spicewine,
fighting down a cough as he did, and drank a glass in several quick gulps.

Amara traded frowns with her husband.

The First Lord, it seemed, was not nearly as strong and fit as he would have
the Citizenry believe. Granted, Amara had no doubt that he had permitted
them to see his true condition deliberately, and for reasons of his own. Or perhaps he hadn't. After all, Amara and Bernard had seen Gaius in far worse condition, during their trek through the swamps of Kalare. There would be no harm
in letting his mask slip in front of them now.

Gaius half filled his cup again and walked quietly over to his desk, settling
carefully down behind it, wincing a bit as several joints creaked and popped.
"First, Amara, allow me to apologize to you for the . . . rather uncompromising
nature of the orders given to the Knights sent to bring you here. Given the situation, sensitivity had to be sacrificed to haste."

"Of course, sire," she said stiffly. "I have never known you to employ a
means which you did not feel justified by its ends."

He sipped from his cup, eyes studying her, and when he lowered it a faint,
bitter smile was on his lips. "No. I suppose not." He looked from her to Bernard,
and said, "Count Calderon, I was impressed with your crafting, your skills, and
most importantly, your judgment during our enterprise last year. I have need of
your services again—and of yours, Countess, if you are willing."

Bernard inclined his head, his expression guarded and neutral. "How may I
serve the Realm?"

How may I serve the Realm? Not, Amara noted, *How may I serve the Crown?*

If Gaius took note of the phrasing, no gesture or expression revealed it. He
reached into a drawer of his desk and unrolled a heavy parchment—a wide map
of the Realm. Upon it, detailed much as the map shown in the Senatorium, was
an illustration of the spread of the Vord invasion.

"What I did not tell our Citizens," Gaius said quietly, "is that the Vord have somehow developed the ability to use furycraft."

"That's not new," Bernard rumbled. "They did so in Calderon."

Gaius shook his head. "They were able to use the taken bodies of the local holders to respond to furies a living Aleran had caused to manifest. It is a subtle but important distinction. At that time the Vord could only make any use of furycraft if Alerans engaged in its use first." Gaius sighed. "It seems that this is no longer the case."

Bernard drew in a short, sharp breath. "The Vord are manifesting furies independently?"

Gaius nodded, swirling his cup in a slow circle. "Multiple reports confirm it. Sir Ehren saw it with his own eyes."

"Why?" Amara demanded, surprising herself with how harsh and rough her voice sounded. "Why aren't you telling them?"

Gaius's eyes narrowed. He was silent for several long seconds before answering. "Because news of such a thing would frighten the Citizens of Alera into a unity of purpose they could otherwise never achieve."

Bernard cleared his throat. "I know I'm not a politician or a Tribune or a captain, sire. But . . . I don't quite see how that's a bad thing."

"Two reasons," Gaius replied. "First is that when the High Lords are well and truly frightened, their initial instincts will be to protect their homes. It would almost certainly cause them to reduce the quality and quantity of troops they would be willing to commit to the campaign—which could prove fatally disastrous for the entire Realm. If the Vord are not stopped in the next few weeks, they could become so widespread and numerous that we might never overcome them.

"Second," he continued, "because of this, Count. The Vord can't be sure that we know about their newfound abilities—and if I do *not* disseminate such an obviously critical fact, it is my hope that they will assume that we remain ignorant as to what they can do."

Amara nodded, following the line of thought. "They'll want to save their secret weapon for use at a critical moment, when shock and surprise will decide the course of a battle. They'll have the crafting at hand, but they won't dare use it, at least at first, for fear that they'll be squandering their element of surprise."

Gaius nodded. "Precisely."

"But what does that accomplish, sire?" Bernard asked.

"It buys time."

Bernard nodded. "To do what?"

"Find the answer to an important question."

"What question?"

"The one I should have been asking from the start," Amara said quietly. "Why? Why are the Vord now able to utilize furycraft when they could not before?"

Gaius nodded again. "Your Excellencies, your skill in the field and your dedication to the Realm are beyond question. But I cannot make an order of this. Instead, I make this request." He paused for another sip of spicewine. "I wish you to pass into Vord-occupied Alera, discover the source of their furycraft, and, if possible, determine a way to end it."

Amara stared incredulously at the First Lord for a heartbeat. Then she shook her head, and said, "Unbelievable."

Bernard slashed his hand in a horizontal motion, and said, "Absolutely not. I will not take my wife with me into something that dangerous."

Amara jerked her head around to stare at her husband.

He folded his arms, set his jaw, and met her glare with his own.

Gaius never looked up from the contents of his cup, but a small smile graced his mouth. "Bernard. Amara. The fact of the matter is that I am asking you to take on a mission which will in all probability result in your deaths—if you are fortunate. Just as I have asked several other small teams to attempt the same. But it is my belief that if anyone is to succeed, it will be the two of you." He looked up at Amara. "Regardless of what may have passed between us before today, the fact of the matter is this: Our Realm stands on the brink of ruin, and most of the people in it do not even realize that this is so. Alera needs you."

Amara bowed her head for a moment and sighed. "Crows take you, Gaius Sextus. Even when you make a request, you leave me no choices."

"They do seem to have grown a bit sparse, these past few years," he agreed quietly.

Bernard frowned quietly, and stepped up to study the map. "Sire," he said, after a moment, "that's a lot ground to cover. You could send a full cohort of scouts into that area and not find what we're looking for."

"You won't have to cover all of it," Gaius said. "As the Legions arrive, we will be massing them at Ceres."

Bernard grunted. "Ceres is all open land. Bad place to fight a force that outnumbers you so badly."

"It's an extremely bad place, in fact. We would have very little chance of holding it if the Vord outnumber us as thoroughly as I fear that they do. It's a guaranteed victory for the enemy—who won't be able to resist it. The Vord will concentrate their heaviest numbers there—including their crafters. It is my hope that there will be enough confusion to allow you to infiltrate their territory and slip away again when your mission is completed."

"When in fact," Amara said, "you have no intention of holding the city."

Gaius finished off the rest of his wine and set the glass down with a weary gesture. "I will draw them and hold them in place for as long as I can. Perhaps three days. That should be time enough to impress upon the High Lords exactly how much danger the Vord represent. You may draw upon my personal treasury for any expenses or equipment you feel you may need. If you wish any additional mounts, et cetera—they are yours for the asking. Speak with Sir Ehren, and he will arrange them for you."

It was clearly a dismissal, but Amara paused at the doorway.

"You're keeping a lot of people in ignorance, Gaius. A lot of them are going to die because of it."

The First Lord moved his head in a gesture that might have been a nod of acquiescence, or just a weary sag of the muscles in his neck. "Amara, a lot of people are going to die. Regardless of what I do. Nothing can change that. All I can say for certain is that if we cannot find a way to prevent the Vord from using furycraft against us, we are already lost."

CHAPTER 8

As Ehren led them to the First Lord's study, Isana crossed the path of her brother in the hall outside.

"Bernard!" she said.

"'Sana," he rumbled in his deep, gentle voice. They embraced, and she felt him actually lift her a few inches from the floor—utterly improper treatment, for a First Lady, but she hardly cared. After the first rush of happiness and affection, she began to sense his deep worry, and when she drew away from him, her own face was drawn with concern.

"What are you doing here?" she asked him, as he exchanged grips with Araris. Then she looked past him, toward Gaius's study. Amara, her own features strained, waited a few steps back from her husband. She gave Isana a deep nod but did not even attempt to smile.

"Gaius," Isana said, understanding. "Gaius has some insane errand for you."

"We got here late, and the sane ones were already taken," Bernard said, forcing a smile to his mouth. It faded after a moment, and he said, "It must be done, 'Sana."

Isana closed her eyes for a moment, her stomach twisting with fear for her brother's safety. "Oh, bloody crows."

Bernard burst out in a laugh. "Now we know how serious the situation is, if even you are driven to such coarse speech."

"It's the company she's been keeping," Aria said smoothly, stepping forward and extending her hand. "Count Calderon."

Bernard took her hand and bowed politely over it. "High Lady Placida." He glanced over his shoulder at Amara, then smiled at the High Lady. "I hear good things about you."

She smiled at him. "I can say as much about you. Which shows how much we know." She inclined her head to Amara. "Countess. That's a lovely dress."

Spots of color appeared on Amara's cheeks, but she inclined her head a shade more deeply in respect. "Thank you, Your Grace."

"Dress!" Bernard blurted, looking at Amara.

She tilted her head slightly, then said, "Oh. Those things cost a bloody fortune."

"But not *our* bloody fortune," Bernard said in a reasonable tone of voice.

"Oh," Amara said. "Yes, then, I like that."

Aria looked back and forth between the two of them, and said, to Isana, "Have you any idea what they're talking about?"

"They're saying that they chose well when they married," Isana said, smiling faintly at Bernard. "I take it you need to keep the details to yourself?"

"I'm afraid so," Bernard said. "And—"

Isana held up a hand. "I can guess. Time is an issue."

Ehren, who had been standing aside respectfully, silently, cleared his throat. "Well said, milady."

Isana leaned up and kissed her brother on the cheek, then held his face in her hands. "Be careful."

Bernard traced his thumb gently over her chin. "I've got too much work waiting for me back home to let anything happen now."

"Good," she said, and hugged him. He hugged her back, and they parted, without looking at one another again. She had felt him start to tear up as he'd held her, and she knew he wouldn't want her to see the tears in his eyes. He'd know that she knew, of course—but after a lifetime near one another, certain fictions were simply understood. She smiled at Amara as they passed one another, and clasped both hands briefly. Isana didn't think the two of them would ever really be close—but the former Cursor had made her brother happy. That was no small thing.

She heard Araris and Bernard trade a few quiet words, then Ehren was leading her into Gaius's study, the one that was supposed to impress everyone with how restrained, erudite, and learned he was.

Oh, certainly, Gaius Sextus *was* likely one of the more erudite and learned Citizens in the Realm, but all the same. Isana had never understood men who made it a point to put trophies of their hunts on the walls, either. Gaius's study, its walls lined with the carcasses of books he had torn open and devoured, reminded her of nothing so much as old Aldo's hunting lodge, back in the Calderon Valley, and she thought it only marginally less boastful.

Isana considered all the books thoughtfully, as Araris and Lady Placida entered behind her, along with Sir Ehren. She'd read a tiny fraction of the books there—even in winter, there had generally been more work than quiet, free time on the steadholt. Books were expensive, as well. But she'd read enough of them to know that they were only as valuable as the contents of their writers' minds—and to her it seemed that a great many writers, had they been merchants, would have precious little inventory.

Still, she supposed it said something in the First Lord's favor that he considered intellectual achievement something to be boasted over at all. Not all men thought as he did upon the subject.

"Isana," Gaius said, rising from his seat and smiling.

"Sextus," she responded, nodding to him. So. They were not standing on formality it seemed.

"Your Grace," Gaius continued. He put his hand to his chest and bowed slightly toward Lady Placida.

"Sire," Aria replied, managing an elegant curtsey.

"Ladies, please." He gestured toward a pair of seats before his desk, and Isana and Aria settled into them. He poured himself half a cup of what smelled like spicewine from a bottle on a sideboard and sat down behind the desk.

"How much trouble are we in, Gaius?" Aria asked bluntly.

He lifted an eyebrow at her, and took a sip of wine. "A very great deal," he said quietly. "The Vord have already overwhelmed multiple legions in the field, so thoroughly as to leave no survivors."

"But . . . surely now, with the rest of the Legions taking the field . . ." Isana said.

Gaius shrugged a shoulder. "Perhaps. The reputation of the Legions is thousands of years old, Isana, with the strength of centuries of tradition—and with the shortcomings of centuries of rigid thought. We are used to thinking of our Legions as invincible bulwarks. Yet they were bloodied and beaten by the Canim during Kalare's rebellion last year, just as they were overwhelmed by the Marat a generation ago."

The First Lord's face flickered with some harsh, bitter emotion, and Isana felt the faintest flicker of it through her link with Rill, more than she usually ever felt from Gaius. She could hardly blame him. It was one of the few points upon which they shared similar emotions. The Marat incursion, more than twenty years gone, had wiped out the Crown Legion and killed the Princeps, Septimus, her husband and Tavi's father.

"Earlier in Alera's history," Gaius continued, gesturing at the walls of books, "our Legions fought practically every year against a veritable host of enemies—enemies who are no more." He shook his head. "For several centuries, Alera has been the entire continent. We have held the Marat at the Calderon Valley, the Canim at the shore. Our Legions have fought comparatively rarely and only in certain places."

Aria lifted her chin. "You're saying that they aren't up to the task."

"I'm saying that most of our *legionares* have never lifted a blade in anger," Gaius replied. "Particularly in the southern cities, which are those now threatened by the Vord. The only Legions who had any recent experience at combat were Kalarus's forces and the Senatorial Guard—both of which were destroyed. The Crown Legion and the First Ceresian are the only other two veteran Legions in the area. The rest are . . . frankly, to all purposes, well trained but untested."

"The First Placidan should probably be considered very nearly a veteran Legion as well, sire," Aria said, her spine stiff. "My lord husband recruits heavily from veterans of the Antillan Legions, and you know that our officers all rotate through terms of service on the Shieldwall."

"Quite," the First Lord agreed. "Antillus and Phrygia represent the only two cities to maintain anything like true traditional Aleran Legions. Every *legionare* there has seen action. Every man of those cities has served his term in the Legions, seen real combat, so that even their militias are arguably better prepared for actual battle than the first-rank Legions of Attica, Forcia, Parcia, and Ceres—and, frankly Your Grace, your own Second and Third."

Isana lifted a hand. "Gaius, please. I am not a Tribune or a *legionare*. What does this have to do with me?"

"If I am to defend Alera, I need the Legions of the Shieldwall," Gaius said, gazing steadily at Isana. "Legions, militia, every Knight, every sword and spear of the north."

"Antillus Raucus will never leave his people to the Icemen," Lady Placida said. "Neither will Phrygius Guntus. And both of them have seen heavier fighting than ever, the past two years."

Isana met the First Lord's gaze and abruptly understood. "But if the war with the Icemen can be ended, those Legions will be freed to fight."

Lady Placida's coppery brows rose nearly to her hairline. "Ended? Peace talks with the Icemen have never been successful."

"Neither have they ever had a moderator," Gaius said. "A neutral third party with respect among the Icemen, willing to mediate a negotiation."

Isana drew in a sharp breath. "Doroga." She glanced at Aria, and said, "The foremost chieftain of the Marat. A friend."

Gaius inclined his head. "I've been in regular correspondence with him ever since his daughter took up residence here. The Marat learned to write in less than six months. He's surprisingly astute, really. He is already on the way to the site of the meeting."

"And you're sending me?" Isana said. "Why?"

"Because I need to be here," Gaius replied. "Because by sending you, the most highly positioned woman of the House of Gaius, I am making a statement of trust. Because Doroga trusts you, and he most definitely does not trust me."

"You did say he was astute," Isana said wryly.

Lady Placida's eyes widened slightly, and she glanced at Isana, but Gaius only lifted one corner of his mouth in a small smile and took a sip of his spicewine. "Aria," he said, "I want someone with her who can protect her and Doroga in the event that things go awry—but who doesn't appear to be overtly threatening."

"Sire," Lady Placida protested, "if the Vord take Ceres, Placida is next. My place is at home, protecting my people."

The First Lord nodded calmly. "It's up to you, of course, Aria, to decide if your people will be better protected by yourself or by Antillus Raucus, all of his Citizenry, and sixty thousand Antillan veterans." He took another sip of wine. "To say nothing of the Phrygians."

Lady Placida frowned and folded her hands in her lap, staring down at them.

"Isana," Gaius said quietly. "Alera needs those Legions. I am issuing you full authority to make a binding treaty with the Icemen."

Isana drew in a sharp breath. "Great furies."

Gaius waved a hand in a deprecating gesture. "You'll get used to it. It isn't as enormous as it seems."

Isana felt a small, hard smile stretch her lips. "And if Octavian's mother arrives unlooked for from the north with a critical force at her back, loyal to the Crown, in an hour of dire need, it just might steal quite a bit of the glory Lord Aquitaine is going to gain for himself in the field—winning support for Octavian by proxy, even if the Princeps himself can't be here."

"I confess," Gaius murmured, "that had occurred to me in passing."

Isana shook her head. "I can't stand these games."

"I know," Gaius said.

"But you ask me to save lives by helping to end a war that has gone on for centuries. I can't refuse, either."

"I know that, too."

Isana stared at Gaius for a moment. Then she said, "How can you live with yourself?"

The First Lord stared at her for a moment, his eyes cold. Then he spoke in a very quiet, precise, measured voice. "I look out my window each day. I look out my window at people who live and breathe. At people who have not been devoured by civil war. At people who have not been ravaged by disease. At people who have not starved to death, who have not been hacked apart by enemies of humanity, at people who are free to lie and steal and plot and complain and accuse and behave in all manner of repugnant ways because the Realm stands. Because law and order stands. Because something other than simple violence shapes the course of their lives. And I look, wife of my son, mother of my heir, at a very few decent people who have had the luxury of living their lives without being called upon to make hideous decisions I would not wish upon my worst enemies, and who consequently find such matters morally appalling when they consider them—because they have not had to be the ones who dealt with them." He took a short, hard swallow of wine. "Feh. Aquitaine thinks me his enemy. The fool. If I truly hated him, I'd *give* him the Crown."

A shocked silence followed the First Lord's words—because though Gaius's speech had been quiet and calm, the sheer rage and raw . . . *passion* . . . behind the words had shone through like a fire through glass. Isana realized that in his anger he had allowed her to see a portion of his true self—some part of him that was dedicated far beyond himself, very nearly beyond reason, to the preservation of the Realm, to its ongoing survival, and beyond that, to the welfare of its people, freeman and Citizen alike.

Behind the bitterness, the cynicism, the weary suspicion, she had felt that passion before—in Septimus. And in Tavi.

There had been something else, too. Isana glanced at Aria, but though Lady Placida seemed a little startled by the slip in Gaius's usual mask, there was nothing of the shock that she should have been feeling if she'd sensed what Isana had.

Lady Placida met her eyes and misinterpreted what she saw there. She nodded at Isana, then turned to Gaius. "I will go, sire."

"Thank you, Aria," Isana said quietly, and rose. "Everyone. If we could have a moment alone, please, I would appreciate it."

"Of course," Lady Placida said, rising. She curtseyed to the First Lord again and withdrew. Sir Ehren, silent the whole while, also retreated, as did Araris, after frowning at Isana in concern. He shut the door behind him.

Isana sat facing the First Lord, alone in the room.

Gaius arched an eyebrow and, for a fleeting second, she sensed uncertainty in him. "Yes?" he asked her.

"We're private here?" she asked.

He nodded.

"You're dying."

He stared at her for a long moment.

"There's . . . an awareness. When the mind and body know the time is near. I don't think many would know it. Or see you at such an . . . unguarded moment."

He set the cup of wine down and bowed his head.

Isana rose. She walked calmly around the desk and laid her hand on his shoulder. She felt the First Lord's frame tremble once. Then his hand rose and covered hers briefly. He squeezed once before withdrawing it again.

"It's rather important," he said, after a moment, "that you not speak of it."

"I understand," she said quietly. "How long?"

"Months, perhaps," he said. He coughed again, and she saw him fighting to suppress it, his hands clenching into fists. She reached for the cup of spicewine and passed it to him.

He swallowed a sparing measure and nodded his thanks to her.

"Lungs," he said after a moment, recovering. "Went swimming in the late autumn when I was young. Took a fever. They always were weak. Then that business in Kalare . . ."

"Sire," she said, "would you like me to take a look at them. Perhaps . . ."

He shook his head. "Furycrafting can only go so far, Isana. I'm old. The damage is long done." He took a careful, steadying breath, and nodded. "I'll hang on until Octavian returns. I can do that much."

"Do you know when he'll return?"

Gaius shook his head. "He's beyond my sight," he replied. "Crows, but I wish I hadn't let him go. The First Aleran is probably the most seasoned Legion in Alera. I could use them in Ceres right now. To say nothing of him. Hate to say it, but growing up the way he did, no furies at all—it's given him a crow-begotten tricky mind. He sees things I wouldn't."

"Yes," Isana agreed in a neutral tone.

"How'd you do it?" Gaius asked. "Stifle his furycraft, I mean."

"His bathwater. It was an accident, really. I was trying to slow his growth. So no one would think him old enough to be Septimus's son."

Gaius shook his head. "He should be back by spring." He closed his eyes. "One more winter."

Isana could think of nothing further to do or say. She moved quietly to the door.

"Isana," Gaius said quietly.

She paused.

He looked up at her with weary, sunken eyes. "Get me those Legions. Or by the time he comes home, there might not be much of Alera left."

CHAPTER 9

After the first six days of the storm, Tavi more or less gave up trying to keep track of time. In the brief periods when he was not too sick to think coherently, he practiced his Canim—mostly the curse words. He'd learned to manage himself well enough to keep from constantly retching, at least, but it was still a miserable way to live, and Tavi did not bother hiding his jealousy at those around him who did not seem subject to the brutal pitching of the *Slive* under storm.

The winter gale was violent and relentless. The *Slive* did not simply rock. It positively wallowed, rolling wildly as it pitched back and forth. At times, only the lines fastened across his bunk kept Tavi from being tumbled completely out of it. Between the clouds and the long winter nights, it was dark the vast majority of the time, and lights were only permitted where absolutely necessary and where they could be constantly monitored. A fire on the ship, during such a storm, while unlikely to destroy the vessel on its own, would almost certainly cripple it and leave it easy prey for wind and wave.

Meanwhile, out on the deck, in the howling wind and driving rain and sleet, the sailors of the *Slive* shouted and labored continuously, constantly lashed by the bellowing voices of Demos and the ship's officers. Tavi would have joined them if he could, but Demos had flatly refused, on the grounds that serpents and worms had better sea legs, and that he wasn't going to explain to Gaius Sextus how the heir to the Realm had managed to trip over something while trying to tie a knot he didn't know very well and fallen to his death in the sea.

So Tavi was left to sit there in the dark, most of the time, feeling vaguely guilty that he stayed in his bunk while others labored to bring the ship through the storm, and bored out of his skull—in addition to being sicker than anyone really ought to be.

The entire business was enough to make him somewhat surly.

Kitai was there with him the whole while, her presence steady, calming, reassuring, always passing him bland food that he could keep down, or urging him to drink water or gentle broth—at least until the seventh day, at which point she said, "Aleran, even I have limits," and left the cabin with her fists clenched, muttering under her breath in Canim.

That part, at least, he spoke better than she did. But then, he'd been practicing.

An interminable time later, Tavi awoke to an odd sensation. It took him several moments to realize that the ship was riding smoothly and that he did *not* feel horribly ill. He unfastened the line across his chest and sat up at once, hardly daring to believe it, but it was true—the *Slive* rode steady in the waves, no longer tossed and shaken by the storm. The insides of his nostrils were painfully dry, and when he sat up out of his bunk, he felt the cold at once. Grey sunlight trickled drearily through cabin windows rimed with frost.

He got up and dressed in his warmest clothes, and found Kitai sleeping hard in the bunk beside his. Maximus was in the bunk across the room, the first time Tavi had seen him in days, in a similar state of exhaustion. Tavi added his blanket atop Kitai's. She murmured sleepily and curled a bit more closely beneath the additional warmth. Tavi kissed her hair, and went out onto the deck of the ship.

The seas were strange.

The waters, for one, were odd. Even at their smoothest, they had always rolled gently. These seas were as flat as a sheet of glass, hardly rippled by a mild, cold breeze from the north.

Ice was everywhere.

It coated the ship in a thin layer, glistening over the spars and masts. The deck, too, was covered in a thicker film of ice, though it had been pitted and scarred by some means, making it less treacherous than it might have been. Nonetheless, Tavi walked cautiously. Lines had been strung up in several places on the ship, obviously there to provide the crew with handholds where they could not reach a railing or other portion of the ship's superstructure to support themselves.

He went to the railing and looked out over the sea.

The fleet was spread out around them, raggedly, out into the distance. The nearest ship was too far away to make out any details, but even so, Tavi could see that its profile was wrong. It took him a moment of staring to realize that its mainmast was simply missing, snapped off in the storm. At least two more ships were close enough for him to identify similar damage, including one of the over-sized Canim warships. Tavi could see no one moving on any of the ships, in-cluding his own, and it gave him the odd, uncomfortable sensation that he was the only person alive.

A gull let out a lonely-sounding cry. Ice crackled, and an icicle fell from a line to shatter on the deck.

"It's always like this after a long blow," came Demos's quiet voice from be-hind him.

Tavi turned to find the ship's captain emerging from belowdecks, moving calmly over the icy planks to stand beside Tavi. He looked the same as he always did—neat, calm, and dressed in black. His eyes were undershadowed with weariness, and he had several days' growth of beard. But otherwise he showed no signs of his days-long battle with the elements.

"The men have been working as hard as a man can, without proper food or sleep for days, sometimes," Demos continued. "Once the danger is passed, they just drop down and sleep. I practically had to beat them to get them to go to their racks first, this time. Some of them would have slept right on the ice."

"Why aren't you sleeping, too?" Tavi asked.

"I'm not as tired. I spent the time watching them work," Demos drawled. Tavi didn't believe him for a moment. "Someone has to keep his eyes open. I'll sleep when the bosun wakes up."

"Is everyone all right?"

"I lost three," Demos said, his voice never wavering. Tavi didn't mistake it for a lack of feeling. The man was simply too tired to become energetic about anything at all, be it joy or agony. "Sea took them."

"I'm sorry," Tavi said.

Demos nodded. "She's a cruel mistress. But we keep coming back to her. They knew what could happen."

"The ship?"

"My ship is fine," Demos said. Tavi didn't miss the very quiet note of pride in his voice. "Rest of them, I don't know."

"Those two look damaged," Tavi said, nodding out to the sea.

"Aye. Storms can take masts like a waterbuck cropping reeds." Demos shook his head. "The larger ships had it bad in this one. The fleet's witchmen were able to keep us from getting completely separated. Seas are calm enough, we might be able to send some flyers around, gather everyone in—once folks start waking up. Give it a couple of hours."

Tavi ground his teeth. "There must be something I can do. If you like, get some rest, and I'll keep an eye on—"

Demos shook his head. "Not on your life, my lord. Maybe you're a mad genius at war, but you sail like cows fly. You aren't commanding my ship. Not even in this pond."

Tavi grimaced at Demos but knew better than to argue with the man. Demos had certain views about the order of the universe—simply put, that upon the deck of his ship *he* should be the foremost policy-making entity. Given that the *Slive* had survived the storm in fine condition when many of the other ships seemed to have been horribly mauled, Tavi supposed Demos's opinion was not entirely without foundation.

"I've been lying around like a lazy dog for days," Tavi said.

"Like a sick dog," Demos said. He gave Tavi a direct look. "You don't look good, my lord. The Marat woman was worried about you. Worked herself harder than any of us, trying not to."

"She just got sick of my bellyaching," Tavi said.

Demos smiled faintly. "I'll wager your work will begin shortly, my lord. Then none of us will want to be you."

"That's shortly. I want to do something *now*," Tavi said. He squinted around the ship. "The men are going to wake up hungry."

"Like baby leviathans, aye."

Tavi nodded. "Then I'll be in the galley."

Demos arched an eyebrow. "Set fire to my ship, and I'll see you roasted alive before she sinks. My lord."

Tavi started for the galley and snorted. "I grew up in a steadholt, Captain. I've worked in a kitchen before."

Demos folded his arms on the ship's railing. "If you don't mind me saying, Octavian—you really don't have any idea at all how to be a Princeps, do you?"

Men began stirring sooner than Tavi would have thought. Partly, that was due to the day's growing swiftly colder, making sleep in still-damp shipboard clothing difficult. Partly, it was due to the minor injuries and strains associated with hard, dangerous labor. But it was due in large measure to their raw hunger, driving them from rest to fill their growling bellies.

The ship's galley included a frost cabinet large enough to require a pair of coldstones, and he was surprised to see how much meat it stored. By the time the men began to rouse themselves, he'd managed to prepare a large amount of mash and sliced and fried four entire hams, in addition to the stacks of ship's biscuit and gallons of hot, bitter tea. The mash wasn't much clumpier than the ship's cook normally made it, and the ham, while perhaps not of gourmet quality, was certainly in no danger of being undercooked. As Demos predicted, the crew dug in with abandon, while Tavi, just as the cook normally did, slapped food onto waiting plates as the men lined up.

He spent the time talking with each of the sailors, asking them about the storm, and thanking them for a job well done. The sailors, all of whom had become familiar with Tavi on their journey the previous year, spoke with him in familiar, friendly terms that never quite edged all the way into open disrespect.

The last people in line for food were Maximus, Kitai, and Magnus. The latter had a decidedly disapproving glare on his face.

"Not a word," Tavi said quietly as Magnus approached. "Not a crowbegotten word, Magnus. I had to lay there like a bloody infant for more than a week. I'm in no mood to be scolded."

"Your Highness," Magnus said, rather stiffly and just as quietly. "I would not dream of doing so in public. For fear that it would lessen the respect due your office."

Max stepped in front of Magnus without hesitation, seized a plate, and plunked it down on the counter next to Tavi. "Hey, cooky," he said, yawning. "Give me a piece of ham that isn't burned black. If you made such a thing."

"The rats knocked these three onto the floor before they were finished cooking," Tavi replied, loading Max's plate. "But then the crowbegotten little things refused to eat them for some reason."

"Rats are wise and clever," Kitai said, putting her own plate down as Max collected his. "Which makes the meat suitable for you, Maximus." She collected the plate and smiled at Tavi. "Thank you, Aleran."

Tavi winked at her and returned her smile, then turned to Magnus.

The old Cursor lifted his eyes skyward, sighed, and picked up a plate. "Extra mash, please, Your Highness."

"All right," Max sighed, shutting the cabin door behind him. The big Antillan held up a small sheaf of paper and tossed it onto the small writing table in front of Magnus. "The Knights Aeris found another two dozen that had wandered astray, and they've changed course to rendezvous with us. Crassus says he thinks we've found every ship that came through the storm."

Tavi exhaled slowly. "How many did we lose?"

"Eleven," Magnus said quietly. "Eight of the Free Aleran, three belonging to the Legion."

Eleven ships. With crews and passengers, more than two thousand souls, in all, lost to the fury of the storm.

"The Canim?" Tavi asked quietly.

"At current count, eighty-four," Magnus said quietly. "Most of them transports carrying noncombatants."

No one said anything for a moment. Outside, the mourning songs of the Canim, wild and lonely howls, drifted over the icy, placid sea from the dark ships.

"What condition are we in?" Tavi asked.

"The Legion transport ships have sustained considerable damage," Max replied. "Shattered masts, splintered hulls, you name it."

"Most of those tubs are still in danger of going under," Demos said. "We'll be lucky to make half our normal sailing speed. If the next storm catches us in the open sea, our losses will be a great deal worse."

"According to Varg's letter," Tavi said, gesturing with another piece of paper, "the Canim ships aren't much better off than we are. Also according to Varg, the storm has taken us several hundred miles out of our way, north along the Canean coast—hence the calm seas, the cold, and all the ice that we've seen in the water. He says that there is a port we might be able to reach nearby. He did not, however, specify our exact location."

"Give the overcast a few days to clear, and we can read the stars," Demos said quietly.

"I don't think fortune-telling is the answer here," Max said. "No offense, Captain."

Demos gave Max a level look, then glanced at Tavi.

"He isn't talking about fortune-telling, Tribune," Tavi said. "Sailors over deep water can guide their course by taking a measurement of the positions of the stars."

"Oh," Maximus said, chagrined. "Well. One of our Knights Aeris could take someone up above the cloud cover. It lifts a couple of thousand feet up."

"There isn't a windcrafter alive that could hold steady enough for an accurate measurement, Tribune," Demos said, without rancor. "Besides, we use points of reference on the ship to accomplish it. So unless they can take the *Slive* with them . . ."

"Oh," Max said. "Probably not."

"In any case, we can't afford to wait, my lord," Demos said. "This time of year, another storm is only a matter of time. We might have a few days. We might have hours."

Magnus cleared his throat. "If I may, Your Highness. While we are not sure of our precise position, our general location is much more easily determined." He offered a folded piece of paper to Tavi.

Tavi took it and unfolded it to reveal a map of what was labeled as the coastline of Canea. A cursory scan of the drawing showed him what Magnus was driving at. "We know we were bound for Narash, Varg's home," Tavi said. He traced his finger north along the coast. "And the only Canim realm along the coast to the north of Narash is this one. Shuar."

"Pronounced with a single syllable," Magnus corrected him absently. "It's another of those words one has to growl from between clenched teeth to speak properly."

"Does it really make a difference?" Max asked.

"Since it seems we will be making landfall there," Kitai said tartly, "perhaps we should make it a point to pronounce the name of our hosts' home properly, as opposed to offering them an insult every time we speak it."

Max's spine stiffened, and the muscles along his jawline tightened.

"*Chala*," Tavi said quietly.

Kitai's nostrils flared as she gazed steadily at Max. But she glanced aside at Tavi, nodded to the Antillan in a vaguely conciliatory gesture, and settled farther back into the shadows beneath the lower bunk.

Another worry. The storm and the length of the trip, plus the condition of the ships, the distance from home, and the pure uncertainty of the situation would be putting tremendous pressure upon his people—and if it was showing that overtly between Kitai and Maximus, who had been friends for years and who lived in the comparatively roomy conditions of the *Slive*, it would be a far-more-intense problem on the more crowded ships of the fleet. He wasn't sure it would be a problem he could do anything about, either. It was only natural, after all, for men to worry when they were far from home, in strange circumstances, and uncertain if they would return.

After all—some of them wouldn't.

Eleven ships.

"The point is," Tavi said, "that if we're to land within a clear-weather window of hours or days, with a fleet that can barely make half its usual pace, then we'll be landing somewhere in Shuar." He made the effort to speak the word properly. "Do we know anything about this . . . realm? Is it a realm, Magnus?"

"The word the Canim use for their states translates more accurately to 'range,'" Magnus replied. "The range of Shuar. The range of Narash."

"Realm, range," Tavi said. "What do we know about it?"

"That it occupies an enormous and highly defensible mountain highland," Magnus said. "It is one of the three largest ranges in terms of pure area, along with Narash and Maraul—and it has only a single port city, which is called Molvar."

"Then it would appear that we're bound for Molvar," Tavi said. He smiled. "I wonder if we're going to have to take the city to be able to land."

"Ugh," Max said. "Do you think it will come to that?"

"I don't think it's impossible," Tavi said. "If the ranges really are hostile to one another, Varg might have to take the port to be able to land there. Even if they aren't openly hostile, I can't imagine that they'll be overjoyed to see a force of this size come over the horizon."

"If that's the case, maybe we should land elsewhere. It isn't as though we need a shipyard to make repairs," Max said. "Once the ship is together, we should be able to craft hulls back together again—we just need some time and quiet for our crafters to work in. Right, Demos?"

Demos frowned pensively for a moment and nodded. "Yes, for the most part. Masts are more difficult, but they can be remounted even without a yard."

Magnus frowned. "Marcus sent me a very interesting report. He was approached by a group of Hunters, who evidently delivered a covert message on behalf of Varg."

Tavi pursed his lips. "Go on."

"The Hunters indicated to Marcus that while you had Varg's respect, he might not be able to protect you from other Canim once we reached Canea. He suggested that you might consider turning back rather than continuing the rest of the way."

"A warning," Kitai murmured. "But one he could not deliver personally."

"Possibly," Tavi said.

"Then let's take him up on it," Max said. "No offense, Tavi, but there's a big difference in fighting an expedition of Canim on our home ground and taking them *all* on in their house. Especially if there are as many of them as it looks like there are."

Tavi scratched absently at his chin. "Exactly. Exactly." He shook his head. "I don't think it's a warning."

Kitai tilted her head. "What else would it be?"

"A test," Tavi said. "To see if I was serious about dealing with them in good faith."

"What?" Magnus spluttered. "You have amply demonstrated that already. We built them a fleet of ships, for goodness' sake."

"If you'll remember, they were well on the way to building the fleet all on their own," Tavi said. "And while the Legions most likely would have destroyed them before they could have completed the task, you and I would have not have been alive to see it, Magnus. Nasaug had the First Aleran and the Guard at his mercy, and we all know it."

"Regardless, you settled with them peaceably and abided by your word," Magnus said.

"Which means nothing," Kitai said. "It was simply the swiftest, most certain, and least costly way to be rid of the enemy."

"If I turn back now," Tavi said, "then the trust that the Canim extended to us goes unanswered. It sends them the message that while we may be good to our word, we are uninterested in building faith."

"Or," Max said, "you could avoid being eaten. And all of us being eaten with you."

Tavi took a deep breath. "Yes. There is that." He pointed a finger at Max. "But as you pointed out, Max, there would appear to be a lot more Canim than we ever imagined. Perhaps more than we could fight, should they ever decide that we need to be destroyed. What do the rest of you think?"

"What *else* do we not know about them?" Kitai asked.

"We don't know what the insides of their bellies look like," Max said. "We could go home, and we'd never know, and I think I'd never lose a moment's sleep over it."

Tavi grinned at him. "Magnus?"

"I think this would be an excellent opportunity for someone else to pursue, Your Highness," Magnus said. "If you proceed, I urge you to do so with extreme caution."

"Demos?"

The captain shook his head. "Don't ask me about politics, my lord. I can tell you this much—our ships won't make it back across the open sea, and even if we found all the materials needed to repair them, it would be dangerous to cross before spring. I also think we don't have time to sit around chatting about it. The weather won't wait."

Tavi nodded once. "Get word to our captains. We make for Molvar with Varg. Any port in a storm."

CHAPTER 10

Gradash stood beside Tavi at the *Slive*'s prow and watched with him. The lookout in the crow's nest had spotted land several moments before, so they waited for it to come into sight from their position on the deck. Tavi finally spotted the dark, solid shadow on the horizon.

Gradash squinted forward, but it was another minute or more before the greying old Cane grunted and flicked his ears in satisfaction. "Ah."

"Glad to be home?" Tavi asked him. "Or at least, back in the general area."

Gradash grunted. "We are not there yet. You will see."

Tavi arched a brow at the old Cane, but Gradash did not elaborate. It was almost an hour later before Tavi understood. The *Slive* drew even with the "land" the lookout had spotted—and it proved to be an unthinkably large slab of what looked like muddy ice. The fleet had to change formation to maneuver around it. The thing was the size of a mountain, fully as big as the city of Alera Imperia.

"Glacier spawn," Gradash said, nodding toward the ice mountain. "Come winter, more ice starts forming, and there are a couple of spots that push those mountains of ice into the sea."

"That must be a sight," Tavi murmured.

The Cane gave him a brief, speculative glance. "Oh, aye. Not one to be seen from up close, though." He waved a paw at the ice. "They're dangerous.

Sometimes they spread out, beneath the surface. Sail too close, and it will rip out the belly of your ship like it was made from lambskin."

"Are they common, then?"

"In these waters," Gradash said, flicking an ear in agreement. "Leviathans don't care for them, so any Cane who has sailed in the northern regions for any time at all has spent some time sailing close to one to get away from a rogue or to cross a beast's range."

"I've always wondered," Tavi said, "how your folk deal with the leviathans. I mean, crossing the first time, I'm given to understand that the storm that pushed you moved you very quickly, kept them from gathering on you, and that there were so many of you that you only lost a few ships. But you could hardly provide all those conditions on a regular basis in your home waters."

Gradash's battle-scarred, stumped tail swished once in mild amusement. "No great secret to it, Aleran. We chart their ranges throughout the waters near our homes. And then we respect them."

Tavi lifted his eyebrows. "And that's all?"

"Range is important," Gradash said seriously. "The territory one claims and defends is important. We understand that. The leviathans understand it. So we respect their claim."

"It must make for some complex sailing routes."

Gradash shrugged. "Respect is elder to convenience."

"And besides," Tavi said drily, "if you didn't respect them, they'd eat you."

"Survival is also elder to convenience," Gradash agreed.

The lookout shouted from high above again, a second cry of, "Land!"

The Cane grunted, and the pair of them returned to gazing ahead.

"There," Gradash growled. "*That* is Canea."

It was a bleak, black land—or so it seemed from Tavi's viewpoint aboard the ship. The shoreline was an unbroken wall of dark stone that rose from the sea like the ramparts of some vast fortress. Above the bluffs of dark granite rose the shadowy forms of cloud-veiled mountains, covered to the hips in snow, and higher than any Tavi had ever seen. He let out a low whistle.

"Shuar," growled Gradash. "Their whole bloody crowbegotten range is one frozen rock." The grizzled Cane had learned his Aleran curses from Maximus, and used them fluently. "Makes them all bloody insane, you know. They spend both days of summer getting ready for winter, and then all bloody winter chasing things around frozen mountains so that their hunters can fall to pointless deaths in some crevasse. When they get the meat home, their females prepare it in spices that would set these ships on fire, and tell the surly bastards it's for their own good."

Tavi found himself grinning, though he kept himself from inadvertently showing his teeth. The gesture carried different connotations with the Canim than it did with Alerans. "You don't care for them, then?"

Gradash scratched under his chin with the dark claws of one paw-hand. "Well. I will say this much for the snow-addled, crow-eating slives in Shuar—at least they aren't the Maraul."

"You don't care for the Maraul, then?" Tavi asked.

"Mud-loving, swamp-crawling, tree-hopping fungus-eaters," Gradash said. "Not one of them has been born that doesn't deserve to go screaming to his death in the jaws of a mad leviathan. But I will say this for the Maraul—at least they are not Alerans."

Tavi barked out a sharp laugh, and this time he *did* show Gradash his teeth. The Cane had, he thought, just made an obscure joke. Or perhaps he had paid the Alerans a backhanded compliment, by comparing them to enemies whom Gradash obviously respected, to spend such time and attention on his insults.

Likely, he had been doing both at the same time. Among the Canim, a respected enemy was as valued as a friend—perhaps more so. To the Canim way of thinking, while a friend might one day disappoint you, an enemy could be relied upon to behave as an enemy without fail. To be insulted in company with already-respected foes was no insult at all, from the Canim perspective.

Tavi scanned the tops of the bluffs as the fleet turned to follow them southward, perhaps half of a mile off the coast. "We're being watched," he noted.

"Always," Gradash agreed. "The borders between ranges are always watched, as are coastlines and rivers."

Tavi frowned, peering at the cliff tops, and wished yet again that his limited mastery of furycraft had included the ability to craft wind furies into a farseeing. "Those are . . . riders. I didn't realize your people employed cavalry."

"Taurga," Gradash supplied. "They are unsuited to sea voyages and have not come to Alera."

A shadow stirred on the deck, and Tavi glanced up to see Kitai lounging in the rigging on the nearest spar, apparently balanced like a cat and asleep. But a flash of green through her silver-white eyelashes told him that she was awake, and the faintest curve of her mouth betrayed her satisfaction. Already, they had learned something else of interest by continuing on.

Tavi mouthed the words, "I know. You told us so," toward her.

Her mouth opened in a silent laugh, and her eyes closed again, perhaps into genuine sleep.

"How far is it to the port from here, elder brother?"

"At our pace? Two hours, perhaps."

"How long will it take Varg to get an answer from the Shuarans, do you think?"

"As long as it takes," Gradash said. He glanced back down at his tail. "It would be better if it was soon, though. We have less than a day before the next storm is upon us."

"If they have dry ground to land upon, some of my people can probably do something about the storm," Tavi said.

Gradash gave Tavi an oblique look. "Truly? Why did they not do so during the previous storm?"

"A windcrafter needs to be up there within the storm to affect it. The wind they use to fly would kick up a lot of spray from the ocean whenever they were near the ship," Tavi replied. "Seawater carries a great deal of salt, which damages and inhibits their wind furies. In rough weather, it makes takeoffs dangerous and landings all but suicidal."

Gradash let out a coughing grunt. "That is why your fliers will bear messages in calm seas, then, but you use boats when there is any swell."

Tavi nodded. "They can land safely on the deck, or if there is a chance bit of spray, they can fall into the sea and be taken up by the crews of the ships with minimal risk. I won't take chances with them, otherwise."

"Your people can stop the storm?"

Tavi shrugged. "Until they've seen it and can judge its size and strength, I have no way of knowing. They should, at the least, be able to slow and weaken it."

Gradash's ears flipped back and forward in acknowledgment. "Then I would suggest that they begin their work. It may be of use to your people as well as mine."

Tavi mused over that statement for a moment, and came to the conclusion that Gradash was speaking of negotiations. The Shuar would hold a much stronger bargaining position for making demands of the Narashan Canim and the Alerans if the storm was breathing down their necks.

"That might not be a bad idea," Tavi agreed.

"This is a terrible idea," Antillar Maximus growled. "I'd even go so far as to call it insane—even by *your* standards, Calderon."

Tavi finished lacing up his armor, squinting a little in the dimness. The sun had not yet set, but for the first time in several weeks, the mass of the land to the west meant an actual twilight rather than the sudden darkness of a nautical sunset, and the shadows were thick inside his cabin.

He leaned down to peer out one of the small, round windows. The enormous, dark granite walls of the fjord rose above the ships on either side, and what looked a great deal like the old Romanic stone-throwing engines he and Magnus had experimented with back in the ruins of Appia lined the top cliffs on either side at regular intervals. The approach to the port of Molvar was a deadly gauntlet should their hosts decide to take umbrage with any visitors.

Only the *Slive* and the *Trueblood* had been permitted to enter the fjord itself. The rest of the fleet still waited in the open sea beyond the fjord—vulnerable to the weather threatened by the darkening skies.

"The Shuarans haven't left us with many options, Max. They won't even discuss landing rights until they've spoken to the leaders of both contingents of the fleet, alone. We've got too many ships out there that aren't going to make it if we don't find a safe harbor."

Max muttered the cabin's sole furylamp to life and folded his arms, frowning. "You're walking into a city full of Canim *by yourself*. Just because it's necessary doesn't make it any less insane. Tavi . . ."

Tavi buckled his belt and began fastening the heavy steel bracers to his forearms. He gave his friend a lopsided smile. "Max. I'll be all right."

"You don't know that."

"The Canim are good about one thing—they don't make any bones about it when they want to kill you. They're quite direct. If they wanted me dead, they'd have started dropping rocks on the ship by now."

Max grimaced. "You shouldn't have sent the Knights Aeris out. We'll wish we had them if those stone throwers start up on us."

"Speaking of which," Tavi said. "Has your brother reported back yet?"

"No. And the wind is rising. We're going to lose men to the sea when they come back if they don't have solid ground to land on."

"All the more reason for me to go now," Tavi said quietly. "At least we know that they're slowing the storm. Crassus wouldn't keep them up there if they weren't doing any good."

"No," Max admitted. "He wouldn't."

"How long can they stay aloft?"

"Been there since noon," Max said. "Another three or four hours at most."

"Then I'd better hurry."

"Tavi," Max said, slowly. "What happens if they come back and we haven't worked something out with the Shuarans?"

Tavi took a deep breath. "Tell them to land onshore within sight of the fleet. Take some earthcrafters, create a way to the top, and get them back aboard."

"You want them to land on a hostile shore, while we craft a dock and an assault stairway in what is obviously intended to be an impregnable defense." Max shook his head. "The Shuaran Canim might call that an act of war."

"We'll be as polite about it as we can, but if they do, they do. I'm not letting our people drown over protocol." He finished buckling on both bracers and rose to slip the baldric to his *gladius* over one shoulder. Then, after a moment's consideration, he picked up the strap to Kitai's *gladius* and hung its baldric the opposite way, so that the additional weapon lay against his other hip.

Max looked pointedly at the second weapon and arched an eyebrow.

"One for the Shuarans," Tavi said. "And one for Varg."

Tavi and Max were the only ones to climb into the longboat.

"Are you sure about this, Aleran?" asked Kitai, her eyes worried.

Tavi looked across the short distance to the *Trueblood*, where a larger longboat was being lowered to the water. He could recognize Varg's enormous figure in the prow. "As sure as I can be," he said. "Making a good first impression might do more to head off trouble than anything else we could do." He met Kitai's gaze. "Besides, *chala*, the ships are going to be back at sea. If it comes to a fight, having more men with the longboat wouldn't change anything."

"It's simpler if I'm working alone, Kitai," Max assured her. "That way if there's trouble, I don't have to play gentle. If the Shuarans start treating us the way Sarl did, I can just level everything that isn't His Royal Highness."

"His Royal Highness appreciates that," Tavi said. "Where's Magnus?"

"Still furious that you would not allow Maximus to take your place," Kitai said.

Tavi shook his head. "Even if he crafted himself into my twin, Varg would have known the second he got close enough to smell him."

"I know. Magnus knows. He is angry because it is true." Kitai leaned over the side of the longboat and kissed Tavi hard on the mouth, her fingers tight in his hair for a moment. Then she broke it off abruptly, met his eyes, and said, "Survive."

He winked at her. "I'll be fine."

"Of course he will," Maximus said. "If there's a lick of trouble, Tavi will set something on fire—it's easy to set something on fire, believe me—and I'll see the smoke, knock down all the buildings between him and the dock, come get him, and we'll leave. Nothing simpler."

Kitai gave Maximus a steady look. Then she shook her head, and said, "And the truly incredible part is . . . you actually believe it."

"Ambassador," Max said, "in the course of my life, I have more than once been too ignorant to know that something was impossible before I did it anyway. I see no reason to jeopardize that success."

"It certainly explains your study habits at the Academy," Tavi noted. "We're ready, Captain."

Demos, who had been directing the affairs of the ship from nearby, called out an order to the crew, and the sailors of the *Slive* lowered the boat to the chill waters of the fjord.

Tavi flung his scarlet cloak about his shoulders and hooked it to the clasps on his armor, while Max sat down at the rear of the boat. The big Antillan thrust one hand into the water for a moment, murmured something, and a second later the longboat surged silently forward, propelled by a burbling current that pressed against its stern.

Tavi rose to stand in the prow, and the wind threw his cloak back as the longboat glided silently for the shore.

"First impressions, eh?" Max muttered.

"Right," Tavi said. "When they get close enough to get a look at you, try to look like someone who isn't impressed."

"Got it," said Max.

The longboat altered course to run parallel to the boat coming from Varg's vessel. Varg's boat was crewed by seven warrior-caste Canim, six of them pulling oars while a seventh held the longboat's tiller. Varg, like Tavi, stood in the prow of his boat. He wore no cloak, but the fading light of day managed, somehow, to glitter upon the bloodred gem hanging from a gold ring in one ear, here and there upon his black-and-crimson armor, and upon the hilt of the curved sword hanging at his side.

"Carrying a lot of bloodstone on him," Max noted.

"I get the impression that Varg hasn't made a lot of friends among the ritualists," Tavi said. "If I were he, I'd carry a lot of bloodstone, too."

"Beats being annihilated by red lightning or melted into sludge by a cloud of acid, all right. You brought your stone, right?"

"Got it in my pocket. You?"

"Crassus loaned me his," Max confirmed. "Do you really think that showing up with only two of us will impress the Shuarans?"

"It might," Tavi said. "Mostly, I feel better knowing that I'm not leaving anyone helpless to Canim sorcery standing around on the dock behind me to be taken prisoner or wounded and used to slow me down."

Max snorted. "You didn't say anything about that aboard the ship."

"Well. No."

"Just did it to impress the girl, eh, Your Highness?"

Tavi threw a sly glance over his shoulder. "It *was* a pretty good kiss."

Max snorted, then they fell silent until they reached the sea-gate of Molvar.

Huge bars of black iron rose from the cold sea, supported on either side by walls made from hand-hewn granite blocks. Even without the use of furycraft, the Canim had been able, somehow, to raise the seabed into something solid enough to support massive walls, built out from the sides of the fjord. Tavi could not imagine how much sheer, brute effort, how much raw sweat and muscle power had gone into their construction, or what techniques must have been used, even with the incredible strength of the Canim laborers, to maneuver the enormous blocks of stone. They made the ruins in Appia look like children's projects by comparison.

As the two boats approached, the sea-gates groaned and began to move, slowly parting. Phosphorescence flickered up and down the metal bars, and eerie, fluttering waves of light danced over the surface of the water. Metal rattled on metal, an eerie, regular thump-thump-thump as the gates opened, swirling water in their wake.

The boats passed through, and Tavi spotted several Canim on the walls above them, in dark armor and strange, long, slippery-looking cloaks, all but hidden within their garments. Each of them bore one of the steel bolt throwers in his hands, the deadly balests that had claimed the lives of so many Knights and *legionares* in the wars in the Amaranth Vale, and Tavi's shoulder blades developed a distinct itch as the boat passed them. A bolt hurled by one of the deadly weapons could slam through his armor's backplates, his body, and his breastplate in an instant, and still carry enough momentum to kill a second armored man on the other side of him.

Tavi did not allow himself to turn his head or alter his straight-backed, confident stance. Posture and gesture were of enormous significance among the Canim. Someone who looked as if he expected to be attacked quite possibly *would* be, simply as an outgrowth of unspoken, unintended, but very real statements being made by his body.

A cold trickle of sweat slid along Tavi's spine. It was no time for bungled communications to spoil an otherwise reasonably fine day. After all—he was about to get off the bloody water for the first time in weeks.

He let out a little breath of laughter at the thought and calmed himself as his boat, along with Varg's, crossed the harbor of Molvar.

It was huge—half a mile across at the least, large enough to house the whole of his fleet and the Canim's, too. Indeed, in the failing light he counted at least thirty Canim ships of war, whose designs differed subtly from those designed and built by Varg's shipwrights. Granite bluffs framed the harbor, except for a long stretch of stone piers, as large as any Tavi had seen in Alera, where warships and other vessels, built more along the lines of merchants, were docked.

One pier was set apart from the others. Torches had been lit at its end and burned scarlet with more intensity than any normal fire. It was crowded with Canim, also in their odd, wet-looking cloaks, but Tavi caught glimpses of midnight blue steel armor beneath their cloaks and similarly tinted weaponry in their hands.

Varg's longboat headed for that pier, and without being told, Max altered his heading slightly to do the same. The two longboats pulled up on opposite sides of the pier in almost-total silence. The only sound was the rattle of wood and metal fittings as the rowers in Varg's craft shipped their oars.

From there, Tavi thought, looking up at the pier, it certainly looked like a great many more Canim were present than had been there a moment before. They also looked quite a bit taller. And their weapons looked a great deal sharper. Doubtless, he thought, it was all just a trick of the light.

"No fear," he muttered to himself. Then he took a long step up to the pier and stepped out of the longboat and onto the Shuaran stone.

Opposite him, Varg was doing the same, albeit having less difficulty with the scale of the construction. He tilted his head slightly toward Tavi, who returned the gesture at precisely the same depth and timing. They turned simultaneously to face the warriors gathered on the pier.

Silence ruled.

Tension mounted.

No one stirred.

Tavi debated saying something to break the ice. His time in the Academy, both in academic studies and in training as a Cursor, had included considerable exposure to diplomacy and protocol. Both fields of knowledge offered several potential courses of fruitful action he might pursue. He mused over it for a moment, then discarded them entirely in favor of a lesson his uncle Bernard had taught him on the steadholt: that hardly a man ever made a fool of himself by keeping his bloody mouth shut.

Tavi held his tongue and waited.

A moment later, footsteps sounded, and a runner approached. He was a young adult Cane, lean and swift, running very nearly as fast as a horse might, his odd cloak flying behind him. His fur was a strange color that Tavi had never seen in the wolf-warriors, a kind of pale golden brown fading to white at the tips of his ears and tail. He loped up to the end of the pier, bared his throat deeply to one of the warriors, and growled, "It is done as agreed," in Canish.

The warrior in question flicked his ears in acknowledgment and stepped forward. He faced Varg, stopping a few inches outside the range of what Tavi judged would be the reach of Varg's sword, should he draw it.

"Varg," growled the strange Cane. "You are not welcome here. Go."

Varg's eyes narrowed, and his nostrils flared for a few seconds. "Tarsh," he snarled, pure contempt in his voice. "Did Lararl lose his wits in the snow, that *you* are pack leader here?"

Tarsh reached up a paw-hand to rip back the hood of his cloak, revealing another golden-furred Cane. This one's muzzle was heavily scarred, including an odd-looking ridge of scar tissue across the black skin of his nose. He was missing one ear halfway up, and Tavi noted that instead of a sword, he bore at his hip an axe with a long, vicious spike protruding from the back.

"Have a care, Varg," he spat, harshly. "A word from me will spill your blood into the sea."

"Only if someone listens," Varg replied. "I do not bargain with scavenging muzzle-lickers like you, Tarsh. You will order your men to prepare to receive my people. I will give you my pledge of peace. We will debark here and camp outside the walls of your city, so that you will feel safe. You will provide me with a priority courier, that I may send word to Lararl of our presence and our need for the presence of someone with the stature to treat with me."

Tarsh bared every fang in his head. "This is not Narash, tree-runner. You have no authority here."

"I am *garada* to Lararl, Tarsh," Varg rumbled. "And every warrior in your range knows it. Lararl will have the throat of anyone who denies him the pleasure of spilling my life's blood."

Tarsh snarled. "I will send a courier to Lararl, of course. But that is all. You may abide here to await an answer. Your ships will stay where they are."

"Unacceptable!"

Tarsh coughed out a growling laugh. "You *will* accept it, Varg. I am pack leader here."

"A storm approaches," Varg said. "Many of my vessels are damaged. Lives will be needlessly lost if they are not given the shelter of the harbor."

"What are they to Shuar, Narashan ape? My warriors have their orders. If your ships attempt to sail up the fjord, we will destroy them."

Varg's lips peeled back from his fangs. "Is this Shuaran hospitality, then? Shuaran honor?"

"If you do not care for it," Tarsh suggested, his voice openly mocking, "seek elsewhere."

Varg's eyes narrowed further. "Were I not honor-bound to take up quarrels with Lararl instead of with his pack leaders, I would have your throat."

Tarsh's leering snarl seemed to grow more self-satisfied. "Many decrepit old creatures have used such an excuse to hide their weakness."

Varg, instead of answering, glanced aside, just for an instant, at Tavi.

Tavi blinked.

Insults like those Tarsh was offering Varg were more than a mere invitation to a challenge to a fight—they were practically demanding it. Under any normal circumstance, any Cane who spoke to another that way could expect an instant and violent response. Varg, in particular, was not one to gladly suffer either insults or fools, and from what Tavi had seen, he didn't know *how* to back down from a fight. Which meant that for whatever reason, something to do with the Canim concept of honor, Varg *couldn't* act against this windbag.

But perhaps Tavi could.

It seemed that this was the moment for diplomacy.

"Varg is correct," Tavi said calmly, stepping forward. "There is no time for this foolishness. His people and mine seek safety from the winter and give you our word that our intentions are peaceful. We need to work out the best way to get them all into the harbor before the storm arrives."

Every set of eyes on the pier swiveled to Tavi and hit him like a physical weight.

"Oh bloody crows," Maximus whispered, somewhere behind him.

"This creature," Tarsh said after a moment. "It is the Aleran leader?"

"I am," Tavi said.

Tarsh growled and turned to the warriors behind him. "Kill it."

Oh, bloody crows, Tavi thought.

Uncle Bernard had been right after all.

CHAPTER 11

The nearest Cane, a particularly muscled brute, drew and threw his axe in the same underhanded motion, a smooth and professional cast that sent the weapon through a single tumble before its razor edge sliced at Tavi's face.

Tavi had both of his short blades free of their sheaths before the axe had begun to fly. Rather than dodging aside, he deflected the heavily tumbling weapon back upward and over his head. Tavi had time for the brief thought that most sensible men would, at that point, dive for the boat and run like mad for the *Slive*.

Instead, Tavi borrowed speed from the cold wind circling the cauldron of Molvar's harbor, and as time seemed to slow, he launched himself toward Tarsh.

The warriors on the dock tried to stop him. Two more axes tumbled toward him, spinning gracefully. Tavi rolled his shoulder from the path of one weapon, though its blade cut a perfectly straight slice from the hem of his cloak. The other he deflected with a sweep of his armored forearm. The shock of impact shook him hard enough to rattle his teeth, but he simply tightened his jaw and moved on.

The heavily muscled warrior who had first thrown his axe managed to step in front of Tarsh, but Tavi was on him before he could get his secondary weapon into a proper guard position. As he closed, Tavi could sense the strange midnight blue metal of the warrior's sword, and instinctively sensed a flaw in its manufacture, a weak point a few inches above the tang. He thrust high, forcing the Cane to lift the weapon to protect his throat and face. Tavi then swung with his other weapon, striking the weak spot of the sword, shattering it.

The Cane reeled as flying shards of steel cut into his face. Tavi laid a whipping slash across one of the warrior's thighs—painful, but not deadly, forcing him to put his weight upon his other leg. Then, with a single, powerful motion, he called upon the earth for strength enough to sweep that foot from beneath the Cane with his own leg, toppling the wolf-warrior to the ground.

The sweep likely saved the Cane's life. Tarsh's wavy-bladed sword thrust straight for Tavi's throat, and would have transfixed the Canim warrior's left lung had he still been standing.

Tavi never lost his forward momentum, dropping under the thrust, reversing his grip on one blade as he went. He fended off the Cane's sword with the blade in his left hand, while with fury-assisted strength, he drove the sword in his right hand down like a spike through Tarsh's paw-foot and into the stone of the pier.

Tarsh howled in agony and hacked down at Tavi with his blade. The blow was swift and as powerful as any earthcrafter's—but it was not nearly as skilled as Tavi would have expected. It lacked the instantaneous reflex response that would have made it a deadly counterattack, and Tavi was able to strike it aside with his *gladius*, then surge to his feet and shove the point of his weapon up and into the soft underside of Tarsh's throat.

"Do not move!" Varg thundered in a voice whose raw authority rang from the stones and echoed around the harbor. And as swiftly as that, the dock was motionless, the other warriors, one in the very act of drawing his arm back to throw his weapon, holding their positions as if frozen in a sudden arctic gale.

Tavi had already stopped his motion, even before Varg had spoken. The very tip of his sword, no more than a quarter of an inch of steel, lay buried in Tarsh's throat. A tiny rivulet of blood trickled from it and down the shining steel of Tavi's weapon. Tarsh stood frozen, hardly daring to breathe. His sword clattered from his hand and to the pier.

Without taking his eyes from Tarsh, Tavi gave Varg an acknowledging nod. "I appreciate the courtesy."

"Of course, *gadara*," Varg rumbled.

Tarsh's ears quivered in shock and his eyes widened.

"Hear me, pack leader," Tavi said quietly—too quietly for the nearby Canim warriors to hear, he hoped. "Varg has named me *gadara*, and I have responded in kind. I will not permit you to take advantage of his sense of honor in order to abuse it and thus cheapen his reputation." He narrowed his eyes. "I wish it to be intact when I kill him. Do you understand me?"

Tarsh continued to look shocked for a few seconds. Then his lips quivered on one side of his muzzle, briefly baring his fangs.

Tavi promptly stomped on the foot that his *gladius* held pinned to the stones.

It took Tarsh several moments to regain his breath.

"I asked you a question," Tavi said.

Tarsh bared his fangs in earnest. "I understand."

"Good," Tavi said. He reached down and jerked his *gladius* clear of the stone and the luckless Tarsh's foot. Then he withdrew his blade from the golden-furred Cane's throat and stepped two quick paces back from Tarsh. He raised his voice, and said, "Now. Pick up your sword."

Tarsh just stared at Tavi for a blank second.

"Did you lose your hearing with your ear, Tarsh?" Tavi asked tartly. "Pick up your sword."

The Cane let out a snarl and snatched up his weapon—careful, Tavi noted, to keep his weight off his injured foot.

"Out of respect for Lararl, who holds the respect of Varg, I have not killed you out of hand," Tavi said. "Instead, I give you this choice. Behave honorably toward Varg, as you know Lararl would have you act—or face me, here and now, in front of everyone, to the death. And after I've killed you, I will give your second the same choice."

Tarsh's eyes glittered. "What makes you think that you are worthy of my attention, Aleran scum?"

Tavi spread his swords in mocking invitation. "I'm the size of a half-grown puppy, Tarsh. You've got twice my reach, three times my weight, several times my strength, you're fighting on your home ground and with your own men all around you. Except for that little hole in your foot, you hold absolutely every advantage. Surely only a coward of legendary proportion would be afraid to fight *me*."

From the ranks of Canim warriors came a number of coughing growls—the Canim approximation of Aleran chuckles, or so Tavi judged them. The loudest such sound came from the wounded Cane on the ground—the one Tavi had put there.

Tarsh's eyes swept back and forth across the ranks of his men, and his ears flattened slightly toward his skull.

Tavi could follow his line of thought easily enough. A moment ago, Tarsh might have been able to order his men to dispatch Tavi as he would tell them to kill any other animal. Now, however, the situation had changed. Varg had recognized Tavi as *gadara*, a respected foe, a word more highly regarded than "friend" among the wolf-warriors. More to the point, Tavi had issued a direct and personal challenge, changing the situation from a group assault to an issue of dominance and personal strength. And, most importantly, Tavi had demonstrated the virtues most unquestionably held valuable by Canim warriors—courage, confidence, and most importantly, *competence* in the arts of violence.

"Think carefully Tarsh," Varg growled, unmistakable amusement in his voice. "I would, before I dueled this Aleran." He turned to the assembled warriors. "Who is the second to this pack leader?"

The wounded, heavily muscled Cane on the ground tilted his head slightly to one side. "I serve in that capacity, Warmaster Varg."

Varg's nostrils twitched. "You are of the bloodline of the Red Rocks."

"Anag," the Cane said, flicking his ears in the affirmative. "You slew my grandsire, Torang, at Blackwater Fen."

"Torang Two-Swords, that tricky old bastard," Varg said, jaws dropping open in a grin. He gestured with a paw-hand at one line of white hairs among the black fur along his jaw, just above his throat. "He gave me this scar." He gestured at his chest and belly. "And two more, here and here. I was under the healers for an entire moon after I fought him, and his pack stopped our advance cold."

Anag lifted his head slightly in pride. "When I was young, he spoke well of you, Warmaster. He died in good company."

Varg turned to Tarsh. "Fight the Aleran, Tarsh. I would rather deal with a true Cane than you."

Tarsh's huge chest bubbled with a growl, but he did not meet Varg's gaze or show any teeth. "Warmaster," he said after a moment, keeping most of the snarl out of his words. "I will make arrangements for your people."

"And the Alerans," Varg said. "I will speak to Lararl about them. Until then, I expect the same treatment of Tavar and his people that you give to me."

Tarsh gave Tavi a look of flat hatred, but said, "It will be done." He turned and stalked away, pausing only to stand over the wounded Anag and say, "See to it." Then he walked off the dock and into the darkness of the city.

Tavi stepped over to Varg, and asked, quietly, "Tavar?"

"If you are to be here, you need a proper name," the Cane said with a shrug—a gesture shared by both races. "It is close to your own, and has an appropriate meaning."

Tavi tilted his head, waiting for him to continue, but Varg only parted his jaws in a small smile, then nodded to Anag. "Perhaps this is an opportunity."

Tavi glanced at the wounded Cane, then nodded at Varg and turned to walk back toward the longboat. Maximus, his face somewhat flushed, said, "Bloody crows, Calderon. That was a near thing." He tossed Tavi a cloth.

Tavi caught it and immediately began wiping the blood from his swords. "We were lucky Varg was on our side."

"On our *side*?" Max demanded, barely keeping his voice down. "He just forced you into a position where you had to fight twenty Canim and take their leader prisoner to keep from being cut to ribbons."

"It worked out," Tavi said calmly, sheathing each weapon as he finished wiping it clean. "Now come on. I want you to heal Anag."

"You want me to heal one of the Canim who tried to kill you," Max said.

"The one who came closest, really," Tavi replied. "Shouldn't be too much work. I was careful not to hit anything delicate. Just stop the bleeding and get him back on his feet so he can make arrangements for the fleet."

Max sighed and began climbing out of the boat. "I'm glad Magnus isn't here." Max gained the dock, and said, "You know, Tavi, it occurs to me that this might not work."

"What might not?"

"Watercrafting," Max said.

"You just crafted the boat all the way in," Tavi replied.

"Through the sea," Max said. "The same sea that touches the shores of Alera. But if we put this Cane into a tub of the local freshwater, I have no idea if it will work. There might not even *be* any furies in it."

"I had no problem with metalcrafting, and a little windcraft, just now."

"Metal from an Aleran sword," Max said. "Wind from the same air that touches Alera."

"I just used a bit of earthcrafting, too," Tavi said. "Don't tell me these stones are Aleran rock."

Max frowned. "That doesn't . . . everyone I've ever talked to, every paper I've ever *read* on the subject said that . . . Tavi, it just shouldn't work like that."

"Why not?"

"Because," Max said. "No one thinks it *should.* And I read up on it before we left, too, believe me."

"What happened to accomplishing the impossible through ignorance?"

Max grimaced. "I suspended my usual policy on this subject. I wanted to . . . you know. Be sure that if you needed . . . that I'd be able to . . ."

"Protect me?"

"I didn't say that," Max said quickly.

"Max, my father had full command of his furycraft. By all reports, he was nearly as strong as the First Lord himself—even without inheriting Gaius's furies. And someone murdered him." Tavi shook his head. "I'm not going to get picky about my friends doing what they can to make sure it doesn't happen to me."

Max nodded, though his expression was undoubtedly relieved. "Glad you're not being a fool about it."

"Fortunately, I *was* fool enough not to know that furycrafting shouldn't be possible here, when it clearly is," Tavi said. "Now, as your Princeps and captain, I hereby order you to forget that nonsense you read and heal Anag so that he can get our people safely to shore."

"Already forgotten, Your Royal Highness," Max drawled, banging a fist to his armored chest in salute.

Tavi nodded, and the two of them walked forward, to rejoin Varg, who was crouched on his haunches, speaking quietly to the wounded Anag.

"What a bloody mess," Max said, in Canish. The big Antillan leaned down to squint at Anag's wounds. Max had learned his swearing from Gradash, and was fluent. "Did you have to carve his bloody thigh all the way to his cursed bone? Look, you slashed right through his fire-gnawed armor, and the bloody edges were hot enough to sear the wound partly shut, or he'd have been worm fodder by now."

One of the other warrior Canim had stepped forward protectively behind Anag and had one paw-hand on the handle of his axe. He growled throatily at Max.

"Don't draw that bloody axe, you puppy-mating furball," Max growled back, without even looking up. "Unless you've decided you want to eat it." He looked up at Anag. "I'm a healer. I've got to stop the bleeding before we move you to a tub and repair the muscle. So I need to touch your leg. All right?"

Anag looked steadily at Max, his eyes wary.

"Their sorcery is not like ours," Varg rumbled. "It has saved my life once before. They made no claim on my blood thereafter."

Anag glanced at Varg, then Tavi, and nodded once at Max.

Max laid his hand on the Cane's blood-smeared leg and closed his eyes. There was a rippling sound, something like knuckles popping in rapid succession. Anag let out a short, surprised, growling sound. Then Max exhaled and drew his hand away. The gaping wound was closed, no more muscle visible beneath it, and no fresh blood leaked out onto the stones of the pier.

That drew a round of surprised mutters from the Canim, along with a great deal of interest. Twenty of the enormous wolf-warriors crowded around, noses quivering and sniffing as they eyed the wound, then Max. There wasn't any overt hostility in them, but simply being amidst a crowd of eight-foot-tall armored, warrior Canim, muttering to one another in their growling, snarling tongue, was more than unsettling enough, even without a naked weapon in sight.

"It's closed," Max said, breathing a little heavily from the exertion of the crafting, "but it will tear open again if you try to use it. If we get the wound into a tub of clean water, so that the entire wounded limb is under the surface, I can repair the muscle, and it should be good as new by the time you wake up in the morning."

That statement drew another round of interesting growl-mutters, and within a moment, two of the warriors had found a barrel, filled it with freshwater, and unceremoniously deposited their commanding officer in it.

Tavi had been correct in his assessment of the wound. It had incapacitated the Cane with pain and debilitating damage to major muscles, without destroying tendons or slicing open major blood vessels. The crafting used to repair such damages was not precisely easy, but it was fairly simple and straightforward, and Antillar Maximus excelled at such tasks. Within moments, he withdrew his hand from the water and chanted what every Legion healer did after he wrapped up work with a *legionare* on a comparatively minor injury, "Done. You'll be hungry and tired tonight. That's normal. Eat plenty of meat, drink plenty of liquid, sleep as much as you are able."

The Canim began to help Anag out of the barrel, but he waved them out and climbed out on his own. He sprang down to the pier and landed on the leg that had been wounded, taking most of his weight on it. He let out a small growl of discomfort—Tavi knew from experience that the leg would ache like the devil for an hour or so yet—but he was able to use it.

The Canim warriors watched with ears forward and eyes bright as Anag practiced a pair of sword-practice footwork sequences including a long lunge, performing them smoothly. They flicked their ears in acknowledgment afterward. It was something along the same lines of cheers or applause from Aleran troops.

Anag approached Tavi and bared his throat. Tavi matched the gesture, but a little less deeply.

"The use of your healer's skills is appreciated," Anag growled.

"He is a warrior, and no true healer," Tavi replied. "My healers would be mildly insulted at the comparison."

"I meant no offense," Anag said, perhaps a shade more quickly than he might have.

"None is perceived," Tavi replied. "As I was responsible for your injuries, it seemed fitting to me to restore you."

Anag tilted his head, his eyes searching. "You were responsible for sparing my life when you might have killed me. You owed me nothing."

"You were doing your duty, protecting your pack leader—even one such as he," Tavi replied. "I would not offer an insult to Lararl by depriving him of a valuable warrior's service, even temporarily, when I had the means to make it otherwise."

Anag nodded, then bared his throat again, a shade more deeply. "I will see to accommodating your people as well, Tavar of Alera. You have my word."

"It is appreciated," Tavi said gravely. "And I give you mine that my people will abide peaceably here and will not lift a weapon save to defend themselves from attack."

"It is appreciated," Anag replied. "Your weapons, please."

Tavi arched an eyebrow.

Varg looked at him, then smoothly drew his sword and passed it over, hilt first, to Anag. "Aleran," he prompted.

Tavi understood that the surrendering of weapons carried multiple levels of significance to the Canim, but he was unsure exactly what was contained within this particular gesture. Still, it wasn't something worth jeopardizing their hosts' willingness to grant them shelter over, not with the ships still at sea and bad weather on the way, so he slipped both baldrics from his shoulders and passed over the swords hilt first. "Why?"

"We have sought shelter and refuge from Lararl, a Warmaster of the Shuar," Varg said. "The local pack leader has granted it, provisionally. Now we must go and speak to Lararl, and he will decide our fate."

That sounded fairly ominous. "Meaning what?" Tavi asked.

Varg blinked at Tavi as if he had asked a rather foolish question. "Meaning that we have surrendered to the enemy, Aleran. You are a prisoner of war."

CHAPTER 12

The air coach lurched wildly to one side and suddenly plummeted. If Ehren hadn't been wearing the safety strap secured around his waist, he'd have slammed his head against the roof of the coach. As it was, his stomach lurched up into his throat, and his arms flew upward, seemingly of their own accord. The book he'd been holding flew up and smacked into the ceiling of the coach, bounced, then simply floated there, as the coach continued to fall, faster and faster.

The wind roared, but Ehren could hear the sounds of men screaming to one another over it.

"What's happening?" Ehren shouted.

The First Lord, his expression calm, leaned over to look out the coach's window. "It would seem that we're under attack," he called back, as the coach continued to dive.

"But we're still miles from the Vord's territory!" Ehren protested.

"Yes," Gaius said. "Rather inconsiderate of them."

Ehren snatched at his book. "What do we do?"

"The spin has stopped, which means we're in a controlled dive," Gaius replied, and settled back into his seat as if they were having an idle discussion while waiting for tea. "We let our Knights Aeris do their jobs."

Ehren swallowed and clutched his book to his chest. A few seconds later, the floor of the coach suddenly pressed up hard against him, and he found himself almost doubled over by the abruptly enormous weight of his own body. The coach pitched to the left abruptly, then to the right. There was a scream of agony from one of the men outside.

Something slammed against the side of the coach, and blood-smeared fingers smashed through the window beside Ehren, clutching desperately to the window frame despite the jagged teeth of broken glass remaining. Ehren leaned over to see a young Knight Aeris, his face pale, one arm dangling uselessly, hanging on for his life.

Ehren tore off his straps and shoved open the wind coach's door. The sudden drag made the cart slew toward the door side, creating a windbreak by the door. Ehren wrapped one safety strap around his wrist and leaned out the door of the coach, reaching for the wounded Knight.

He seized the man by the collar of his mail. The Knight let out a shriek at the sudden touch, then focused bleary, terrified eyes upon Ehren.

The Cursor gritted his teeth, let out a scream, and hauled with all of his strength, using his legs and back as well as his arm. It occurred to him that if the strap broke, he and the young Knight would doubtlessly fall to their deaths together—but there wasn't time to spare for worrying about such things.

Fortunately, the young Knight wasn't on the brawny or heavy side, and Ehren was able to drag him into the coach, all but throwing him to the floor.

"The door!" the First Lord called, helping to pull the wounded man the rest of the way in. "Close it! It's slowing us down!"

Ehren staggered in the wildly swaying coach, trying not to step all over the wounded Knight, and leaned out to grasp at the door.

He had a short look at the outside. The coach was racing along at a dangerous pace, skimming thirty feet above the six-foot-long grass stalks of the central plains of the Amaranth Vale. The sun had all but set, and the sky was scarlet and midnight blue.

It was also full of Vord.

Ehren wasn't sure exactly what he was looking at. He recognized the shapes of the Knights Aeris readily enough, the familiar armored forms streaking by, supported by their furies' windstreams. But there were more—many more—of the strange, black, glistening shapes with wings like dragonflies, greenly translucent.

An instinct made him look up in time to see one of the enemy plunging down toward him. He had a second, perhaps two, to get a look at it.

It almost looked human.

It had two arms, two legs, a head, with a face that was human in shape—but eerily featureless except for its segmented eyes. Dragonfly wings buzzed behind its shoulders, and its arms terminated not in hands, but in a single, gleaming, scythe-shaped talon a little less than two feet long—almost precisely the same length, Ehren realized, as a *legionare's gladius*. Its armor, too, resembled a *legionare's* lorica, though it melded seamlessly with its skin, all of it made from the same gleaming, dark chitin.

It looked, in fact, a great deal like a Knight Aeris.

And it was coming straight for him.

Ehren scrambled back, pulling the door shut, and flung his back against the rear wall of the coach. One of the vordknight's vicious scythes slammed through the wood of the door where he'd been crouching an instant before. The eerie, featureless face appeared at the side window, not six inches from Ehren's own, staring in at him through the glass.

Ehren was never sure precisely when he had drawn the knife, but in the same instant he saw that face, his right arm snapped forward, to shatter the window and bury his knife to the hilt in the vordknight's glittering eye.

It screamed, a wailing shriek that sounded like tearing metal and the snarls of a wounded dog. Green-brown blood sputtered from the wound in a miniature fountain.

Ehren let go of the knife, braced his back, screamed for strength again, and lashed out with the heel of his boot, kicking at the scythe still transfixing the door. It snapped and broke cleanly, like the edge of a horse's hoof, and the vordknight vanished from sight, falling away from the racing coach.

Gaius looked up from where he knelt over the wounded Knight and gave Ehren a sharp nod of approval.

And then he heard a piercing trumpet, a clarion call that carried even over the roar of wind and the shouts and cries of battle.

"Ah," Gaius said, glancing up briefly. "Excellent."

From outside the coach came a flash of light and a deafening racket of thunder—and another, and another. Interspaced within the head-rattling thunderclaps were smaller flashes of light, accompanied by hollow, heavy booms, and Ehren turned to see a vordknight, its wings burned completely away, its body twisted and cracked by fire, plummet past the coach's window. The coach banked smoothly to the right and began to gain altitude again—smoothly, this time, instead of with the sharp panic of combat.

A moment later, there was a knock on the coach's door. Ehren didn't remember actually deciding to draw another knife, but he was just as glad that his fingers had preempted him.

"Stay your hand," Gaius said calmly. "Let him in please, Sir Ehren."

Ehren swallowed and opened the coach door, to find an elderly man dressed in very fine but rather outdated armor, riding a windstream parallel to the coach. He had shorn his head, but the stubble of his beard was mostly silver, and his eyes were sunken with fatigue—but shone with bitter rage.

"Your Grace," Ehren stammered. He stepped back from the door, nodding to the High Lord Cereus to enter.

"Sire," Cereus said with a nod, closing the door behind him.

"Your Grace," Gaius replied. "A moment." He closed his eyes briefly, then lifted his hand from the wounded Knight. The man lay there pale and still, but his chest was still moving, and he was no longer bleeding. "Thank you."

"No thanks are necessary, sire. Whatever those other jackals want to pretend, Sextus, you are the First Lord of Alera and my lord. I only did my duty."

"Thank you all the same," Gaius replied quietly. "I'm sorry about Vereus. He was a fine young man."

The High Lord glanced out the coach's window at the coming darkness. "Veradis?"

"Safe," Gaius said. "And will be so while I have breath in my body."

Cereus bowed his head. He took a deep breath, and said, "Thank you."

"No thanks are necessary," Gaius said, smiling faintly. "Whatever those jackals want to pretend, I am your lord. Duty flows uphill and down." He frowned again and looked out the window. "I'll have our Legions in position to support Ceres in another week. What can you tell me about the Vord advance?"

Cereus looked up wearily. "That it is accelerating, despite everything we can do."

"Accelerating?" Ehren blurted. "What do you mean?"

The old High Lord shook his head and spoke without any inflection. "I mean, Sir Ehren, my lord, that my city does not have a week.

"The Vord will be upon us in two days."

CHAPTER 13

Amara held the arrow nocked firmly against the bowstring, and kept enough steady pressure against it to ensure a swift and certain draw, but not too much to tire her arm. It had been a surprisingly difficult skill to learn, at least until she'd developed enough of the proper musculature to use the bow her husband had made for her. She took a slow step forward and put her foot down silently, her eyes focused into the middle distance, at nothing, the way she'd been trained. The forest was almost silent in the stillness just before dawn, but Cirrus, her wind fury, carried every tiny sound to her ears as clearly as if it'd been a voice speaking from directly beside her.

Trees creaked in tiny breaths of wind. Sleeping birds stirred, their feathers rustling. Something scuttled among the higher branches of a tree, probably a squirrel getting an early start on the day, or a night rodent of some kind crawling back to its nest. Something rustled, perhaps a deer making its way through the brush—

—and perhaps not.

Amara focused Cirrus on the sound and located a second rustling, that of cloth on cloth. Not a deer, then, but her target.

She pivoted toward the sound, in perfect silence, moving slowly to keep it, focusing on maintaining her own invisibility. Learning to master the use of the furycrafted cloth had been simpler than she had expected—certainly easier than employing a windcrafted veil. All she had to do was maintain a low level of concentration, focusing on the colors of her surroundings, drawing them in from what she saw, and the cloth would absorb and mimic them, rendering her into little more than a blur of background color. Granted, the original designer of the cloth, an expensive clothier in Aquitaine, had nearly shrieked the skies down when she'd heard how her invention, designed as the absolute pinnacle of wealthy fashion, was to be used.

The thought made Amara smile. Just a little.

She couldn't see anything where her ears told her something should be, but that didn't matter. She drew the bow in a slow, practiced motion, and loosed the arrow.

The arrow flew, swift and straight, and from the empty air appeared a form of blurred color that eventually resolved itself into the shape of her husband. The blunted wooden arrow hadn't been a deadly threat, but as he cast back his own color-shifting cloak and rubbed at his ribs, wincing, Amara found her own side twinging in sympathy.

"Ouch," she murmured, parting her cloak and revealing herself. "Sorry."

He looked around for a moment until he spotted her and shook his head. "Don't be. Well done. What did you think?"

"I had to use Cirrus to track the sound of your movement. I never saw you, not even when I knew where you where."

"Nor I, you, even tracking you with earthcraft. I'd say the cloaks work then," Bernard said, his wince of pain broadening into a grin. "Aquitainus Invidia may not have given a crow's feather about the Realm, but it seems that her fashion sense is going to be of service."

Amara laughed and shook her head. "When that seamstress heard we wanted her to break those gowns down and refashion them into traveling cloaks, I thought she was going to start foaming at the mouth—the more so when one was to be made for you."

Bernard made his way quietly through the brush, as always seeming to pass through it with hardly a branch or leaf disturbed by his presence, despite his size. "I'm sure a liberal dosing of silver and gold eased the symptoms."

"That will be up to Gaius's accountants," Amara said smugly. "I had a letter of credit with the Crown's seal upon it. All she could do was pray that I wasn't some sort of confidence artist watercrafted into the semblance of Calderonus Amara."

Bernard paused for a moment, blinking. "My."

She tilted her head. "What is it?"

"That's . . . the name of my House."

Amara wrinkled up her nose at him and laughed. "Well, yes, my lord. So it would seem. Your letters are all signed His Excellency, Count Calderonus Bernard, remember?"

He didn't smile in reply. His expression was, instead, very thoughtful. He fell into a pensive silence as they walked back to their camp, after the final tests of their new equipment. Amara walked beside him without saying anything. It never helped Bernard to prod at him while he was forming thoughts. It sometimes took her husband time to properly forge the things in his head into words, but it was—at least usually—worth the wait.

"It's always been a job," Bernard said at last. "My rank. The way being a Steadholder was. Something I did for my livelihood."

"Yes," Amara said, nodding.

He gestured vaguely toward the northeast, toward Riva, and their home in Calderon. "And it's been a place. Garrison. The town, the fortress, the people who lived there. The problems to be solved and so on. Do you follow?"

"I think so."

"Calderonus Bernard was just that fellow who was supposed to make sure everyone had somewhere to go during furystorms," Bernard rumbled. "And who made sure that men with more time on their hands than sense didn't bother people trying to work for a living, and who was trying to build up a lasting peace with his neighbors to the east rather than occasionally being eaten by them."

Amara laughed at that and slipped her fingers between his.

"But Calderonus Amara . . ." He shook his head. "I've . . . never heard it said aloud. Did you realize that?"

Amara frowned and thought about it. "No. I suppose it's because for so long we were . . ." Her cheeks flushed. "Improper."

"Illicit lovers," Bernard said, not without a certain amount of satisfaction. "*Frequent* illicit lovers."

Amara's cheeks grew warmer. "Yes. Well. Your people, whom we spent most of our time together among, hardly wished to throw that in your face. So they just called me your lady."

"Exactly. So now there's this new person, you see. Calderonus Amara."

She looked obliquely up at him. "Who is she?" she asked quietly.

"A temptress who seduces married men in their bedrolls in the depths of the night where all the stars can see, apparently."

She laughed again. "I was *cold*. As I recall, the rest was your idea."

"I don't recall it that way at all," he said gravely, his eyes shining. His fingers tightened gently in hers. "She is also the wife of that Calderonus fellow. The founder of House Calderonus. Something that . . . something that could last a good long while. Something that could stand, and grow. That could do a lot of people a lot of good."

Amara felt herself quail a little inside, but steeled herself against it. "For that to happen, a House needs children, Bernard," she said quietly. "And I'm not . . . We haven't . . ." She shrugged. "At this point, I'm not sure it's going to happen."

"Or it might," Bernard said. "Some things can't be hurried along."

"But what if I can't?" she asked, without malice or grief in the tone. After a second, she felt startled to realize that she didn't *feel* any, either. Or at least, not nearly so much as she had in the past. "I'm not trying to gather sympathy, love. It's a rational question. If I can't provide you with an heir, what will you do?"

"We adopt," Bernard said promptly.

She arched an eyebrow. "Bernard, the laws regarding Citizenship—"

"Oh, to the crows with those codes," Bernard spat, grinning. "I've read them. They're mostly an excuse for Citizens *not* to give up their money and status to anyone but their own children. Great furies know, if it was all based upon blood, all those bastard children, like Antillar Maximus, should certainly be inheriting Citizenship."

"Adopt the bastard of a Citizen," Amara mused.

"They'd have every bit as much potential for strong furycraft as a child born of us would," Bernard said. "And crows, there are enough of them, the way some Citizens carry on. Why not provide some kind of positive direction for a few of them? I'd bet every sword in my armory that nearly every one of those mercenary Knights of the Aquitaines is a bastard child of a Citizen."

"Suppose we manage to get away with it?" she asked him. "Then what?"

He arched an eyebrow at her. "We raise them."

"Raise them."

"Yes. You'll be a good mother."

"Ah. It's that simple, is it?"

He laughed, a warm, booming laugh that rolled through the trees. "Raising a child isn't complicated, love. It isn't easy, but it isn't complicated, either."

She tilted her head, looking up at him. "How's it done, then?"

He shrugged. "You just love them more than air and water and light. From there, everything else comes naturally."

He stopped and tugged gently on her hand, turning her to face him. He touched her cheek, very lightly, with the blunt fingertips of one hand.

"Understand me," he said quietly, his eyes earnest. "I haven't given up on the idea of your bearing my children, and I never will."

She smiled quietly. "Depending on what nature has to say," she replied, "we may have to agree to disagree on that issue."

"Then let me tell you exactly where I'm drawing the line, Calderonus Amara," he rumbled. "I'm building a future. You're going to be in it. And we're going to be happy. I'm not willing to compromise on that."

She blinked up at him several times. "Love," she said in a near whisper, "in the next few days, we're going to begin a mission for the Crown that, in all probability, will kill us both."

Bernard snorted. "Heard that before. And so have you." He leaned down and kissed her mouth, and she was suddenly overwhelmed with the enormous, warm, gentle power behind that kiss, and the touch of his hand. She felt herself melt against him, returning the kiss measure for measure, slow and intent as the light began to change from wan grey to morning gold.

It ended a time later, and she felt a little dizzy.

"I love you," she said quietly.

"I love you," he said. "No compromises."

The last ridgeline between them and their eventual area of operation was at the top of a long slope, and Amara's horse reached it several moments before Bernard's. The poor beast labored mightily under Bernard's sheer size, and over the course of many miles, it had added up to a steep toll in fatigue.

Amara crested the rise and stared down at the broad valley, several miles south of the city of Ceres. The wind was from the north, chill without being unpleasant—even the depths of winter were seldom harsh, there in the sheltered southern reaches of the Realm. She turned her face into the wind and closed her eyes for a moment, enjoying it. Ceres lay several leagues north of their current position, at the end of the furycrafted causeway that ran through the valley below. From there, she and Bernard would be able to wait for the Vord to pass by, then slip among them.

The wind suddenly felt a little colder. She shivered and turned her head to survey the valley below her.

The sky to the south was smudged with a dark haze.

Amara drew in a sharp breath, lifted her hands, and called to Cirrus. Her fury shimmered into the space between her hands, bending light, letting her see into the far distance much more clearly than she could have on her own.

Dozens and dozens of plumes of smoke rose into the sky, far to the south—and crows, so many of them that from where she stood they almost seemed like clouds of black smoke themselves, wheeled and swirled over the valley.

Amara turned her gaze to the causeway, and with Cirrus's help, she could now see, as she had not before, that the furycrafted road was crowded with people, traveling with as much haste as they could manage—holders, mostly, men, women, and children, many of them half-dressed, barefoot, some of them carrying unlikely bits of household paraphernalia, though most carried nothing. Some of the holders were doing their best to herd livestock. Some drove carts—many loaded with what looked like wounded *legionares*.

"It's too soon," Amara breathed. "Days too soon."

She was hardly aware of Bernard's presence until he rumbled, "Amara. What is it?"

She shook her head and wordlessly leaned over, reaching out to let him see through the sightcrafting Cirrus had provided.

"Crows," Bernard breathed.

"How could this have happened?" Amara asked.

Bernard was silent for a second, then let out a sharp, bitter bark of laughter. "Of course."

She arched an eyebrow at him.

"We were told that they're furycrafting now, correct?"

"Yes."

He gestured at the road below. "They're using the causeways."

A chill went through Amara's belly. Of course. The explanation was utterly simple, and yet she had never even considered it. The furycrafted roads of Alera, whose construction allowed Alerans to travel swiftly and almost tirelessly across the countryside, were a staple of life, practically a feature of the land-scape. They were also the single most reliable advantage Alera had in defending the Realm against the foes that so often outnumbered her. The causeways allowed the Legions to march a hundred leagues in a single day—more, if the need was dire. They meant that the Legions would always be able to field a maximum amount of force to ideal positions.

Of course, none of those enemies had used furycraft.

If Bernard was right, and the Vord could make use of the causeways, Amara wondered, then what else could they do? Could they intercept messages sent by water fury through the rivers of the Realm? Could they tamper with the weather? Could they, bloody crows, rouse the sleeping wrath of one or more of the Great Furies, as Gaius had done with Kalus, the previous year?

Amara stared at the fleeing holders and the rising smoke and the circling crows, and in her heart became abruptly certain of a simple, undeniable fact.

Alera could never survive what was coming.

Perhaps if they had acted sooner, in accord, instead of bickering and in-fighting, something could have been done. Perhaps if more people had heeded their warnings, and had been willing to back their belief with resources enough to create some kind of sentinel organization, it might have been nipped in the bud.

But instead . . . Amara knew—not feared, not suspected, but *knew*—that they were too late.

The Vord had come, and Alera was going to fall.

"What are we going to do?" Amara whispered.

"The mission," Bernard replied. "If they're using the causeway, they've got their crafters with them. In fact, it should make them easier to find. We just follow the road."

Amara began to reply, when her horse suddenly threw back its ears and danced sideways for several steps with several harsh breaths of apprehension. Amara steadied the animal only with difficulty, keeping the reins tight and speaking quietly. Bernard's mount reacted in much the same way, though he had far more skill at calming the beast. A touch of his hand, a brush of earthcraft, and a murmur of his rumbling voice calmed his mount almost immediately.

Amara swept her gaze left and right, to see what had startled the horses so.

She smelled it before she saw it—putrescence and rotting meat. Then a breath later, she saw the grass lion emerge from the shadows beneath a stand of scraggly pine trees.

The beast was eight or nine feet long, its golden hide dappled with greenish stripes that would blend perfectly with the tall grasses of the Amaranth Vale. A powerful creature, far more heavily muscled than anything resembling a common house cat, the grass lion's upper fangs curved down like daggers from its upper jaws, thrusting past its lower lip, even when its mouth was closed.

Or, more accurately put, a *living* grass lion's fangs would do so. This grass lion no longer *had* a lower lip. It had been ripped or gnawed away. Flies buzzed around it. Patches of fur had fallen away to reveal swelling, rotted flesh beneath, pulsing with the movements of infestations of maggots or other insects. One of its eyes was filmy and white. The other was missing from its socket. Dark fluid had run from its nostrils and both its ears, staining the fine fur surrounding them.

And yet it moved.

"Taken," Amara breathed.

One of the more hideous tactics employed by the Vord was their ability to send small, scuttling creatures among their enemies. The takers would burrow into their targets, killing them and taking control of their corpses, directing them as a man might a puppet. Amara and Bernard had been forced to fight and destroy the remains of scores of taken holders, years before in the Calderon Valley, during the first Vord outbreak—the one that had been stopped before it could become too large to contain. The taken holders had been oblivious to pain, swift, strong beyond reason—but not overly bright.

The grass lion stopped and stared at them for the space of a breath. Then two.

Then, moving with a speed that a living beast could not have bested, it turned and bounded into the trees.

"A scout!" Bernard hissed, kicking his horse into motion after it. "We have to stop it."

Amara blinked for a second, but then slapped her mount's neck with the reins, left and right, and sent it after Bernard's mount. "Why?" she called.

"We've killed one Vord queen," Bernard shouted back. "I'd rather whichever one was commanding this force didn't learn that we were in the area, and set out to actively hunt us down."

Amara lifted a hand to shield her face as branches slapped against her. "Useless," she spat. "I'm going high!"

"Go!"

Amara seized her bow and quiver. She slipped her feet from the stirrups, lifted them to the saddle, then smoothly rose, and all as part of the same motion, leapt into the air. At her silent bidding, Cirrus rushed into the space beneath her, catching her up and sweeping her skyward. Her wind fury brushed aside tree branches from her path until she shot up into the open air over the ridge and wheeled south, to follow the path of the fleeing Vord scout. She spotted Bernard at once, and focused ahead of him until she caught a flash of racing motion perhaps thirty or forty yards in front of him.

The taken grass lion was not running the way a true grass lion would. Such a beast, running through the trees and brush, would have been all but invisible, even to Amara, moving with lithe, silent grace through its natural habitat. Possessed by the Vord, though, the grass lion simply ran in a straight line. It smashed through thickets, heedless of brambles and thorns. It tore through brush, shouldered aside saplings, and altered course only to avoid the trees and boulders it could not plow aside or leap across.

For all that it lacked grace, it was *fast*, though. A true grass lion was not a cross-country runner, even if it could move very swiftly over short distances. Taken by the Vord, it ran at its best speed, tirelessly, and it was steadily leaving Bernard's horse behind.

Stopping the scout was up to Amara. Bernard was right in that—their mission was already dangerous enough. Should the Vord learn that they were in the area and dispatch even a relatively small portion of their forces to hunting Bernard and Amara down, that mission would become impossible. As Amara had demonstrated to Bernard only that morning, if the Vord knew more or less where they were located, no amount of stealth would provide protection for long.

Amara gained a little more altitude, the better to look ahead, and saw that the fleeing Vord's straight-line path crossed a clearing in the woods, up ahead. That would be the best place to strike. She was a fair hand with a bow, for someone without any appreciable skill at woodcrafting, but hitting a target racing among the trees while she herself rode a gale-force wind was out of the question.

Of course, one would have to be mad or desperate to stand in the path of a fleeing grass lion armed only with a medium-weight hunting bow—much less that of a Vord-possessed grass lion. Amara supposed she qualified as at least one of those things, though she did not care to examine too closely which one. She poured on the speed, flashing ahead to the clearing, and touched down in the open grass.

She had little time. She drew two arrows from her quiver, thrusting one into the earth at her feet and setting the other to her string. She took a deep breath to steady herself, raised her bow, and the Vord scout came crashing out of the brush.

She called upon Cirrus to borrow from the wind fury's swiftness, and time seemed to slow, giving her ages and ages to aim the arrow.

The possessed lion ran with its half-rotted tongue hanging out. Its ears, which would normally have been stiff and upright, flopped and wriggled like wilted leaves of lettuce. There was some kind of greenish mold or lichen growing on its fangs. Its shoulder struck the edge of a windfall as it came into the clearing and a small shower of woodchips exploded into the air with the sheer power of the impact, ripping the insensate flesh with no noticeable effect whatsoever.

Amara loosed the arrow. It leapt gracefully over the forty yards between her and the grass lion, struck its skull just over the brow, and glanced off the hard bone to bury itself in the powerful, hunched shoulders.

The Vord scout did not so much as twitch.

Amara snatched up another arrow.

Clods of earth flew up from beneath the lion's feet, propelled by the raw power of its legs. Amara tried not to think of what would happen if a battering ram of four hundred pounds of rotting meat and hard bone slammed into her at the rate the beast was moving. She set another arrow to string as the lion's passage startled a covey of birds from the grass, sending them up in a slow-motion panic of feathers and beating wings and glassy eyes.

She dropped to one knee, drew the arrow to full extension, and held it, waiting, timing each plunge of the taken lion's ruined body, tracking its motion, waiting for the timing to be perfect.

Twenty yards. Fifteen. Ten.

When it was ten feet away, she loosed her arrow and flung herself flat to one side.

The shaft stabbed out and vanished into the lion's open mouth, its broad point plunging into the back of its throat.

The lion's front limbs suddenly went loose, and its jaws and muzzle snapped down, smashing violently into the earth, plowing a shallow furrow as its momentum carried it forward. Its spine and hindquarters twisted and flipped up and over, then came smashing down onto the earth as well, forcing Amara to jerk her knees up to her chest, lest her legs be crushed underneath the beast's descending weight.

The impact ruptured the grass lion's innards, and an explosion of noxious fumes washed over her. Her stomach twisted in revulsion, and she scrambled away as it began to empty itself.

She looked back at the lion several unpleasant seconds later, to see it still twitching, and realized that she could hear . . . something, making a tinny, wheezing sound of pain. The Vord taker. When one of them inhabited a body, it was usually somewhere inside the skull. The arrow must have wounded the thing.

The job wasn't done. The grass lion had never been the danger—the taker was. It could not be allowed to return to the rest of the Vord.

She looked around until she spotted a stone a little smaller than her head. She took it up, steeled herself against the stench, and walked back over to the still twitching corpse of the grass lion. She lifted the stone and, with all her strength, brought it smashing down on the grass lion's skull.

The wheezing scream of pain stopped.

She looked up to see Bernard plunge from the trees and draw his horse to an abrupt halt, bow in hand. He stared at her for a moment. Then he simply slid his bow back into the holder on his saddle and nudged his horse into a walk again. Her own mount had followed his horse once she had left it, and came following along.

She walked over to meet him and get out of the stench.

He passed her a flask of water. She rinsed and spat the bad taste out of her mouth, then drank deeply.

He studied the grass lion gravely. "Nice shooting."

From him, it was no idle comment. "Thank you," she said.

He clucked to her horse, who docilely came over to his outreached hand. He collected the reins and offered them to Amara. "We'd better get moving. Where there's one scout, there will be more."

"Bernard," she said, staring at the corpse. "I don't want to end up like that. I don't want them to use me against my own people. I'd rather die." She turned her face to him. "If it comes to that, I want you to make sure of it."

"It won't," Bernard said.

"But if it does—"

His eyes hardened. "It won't," he said, with harsh finality, and all but threw the reins at her chest. "No compromises, Countess. Not for anyone. Including the Vord."

CHAPTER 14

"The art of diplomacy is the art of compromise," Lady Placida said calmly, as the wind coach began its descent to the Shieldwall. "The key here is finding the compromise that will satisfy everyone involved."

"That presumes that everyone involved is willing to compromise," Isana replied. "The Icemen have been at war with Alera for centuries. And I can't imagine that the lords of Antillus or Phrygia will be particularly inclined to be gracious, after generations of combat with the northern tribes."

Aria sighed. "I wasn't presuming. I'd hoped you hadn't realized it. I thought perhaps that a positive attitude on your behalf might put everyone sufficiently off-balance enough to allow you to get something accomplished."

Isana smiled faintly. "What can you tell me about Antillus Raucus?"

"He's a great fighter, probably the most accomplished tactician in Alera, almost unquestionably the most practiced battlecrafter in the Realm. He's won significant battles against—"

Isana shook her head, frowning as the air grew noticeably colder. She drew her cloak tighter around herself. "Not that," she said gently. "That isn't what I need to know. Tell me about *him*."

Aria closed her eyes for a moment and shook her head in self-recrimination. "Of course. I'm sorry, I've been thinking in military terms for most of the trip. How to make sure I can keep getting food and supplies to my husband and his men, that sort of thing."

"Understandable," Isana said gently. "Raucus?"

Aria folded her hands in her lap and frowned out the window for a moment. "Passionate," she said, finally. "I don't think I've ever known a man more passionate than Raucus. That's partly what makes his firecrafting so strong, I think. He believes furiously in whatever it is he's doing. Or only does whatever it is he believes in most furiously. I suppose it depends upon one's point of view."

"He's loyal to the Realm?" Isana asked.

Aria took a slow breath. "He's . . . loyal to the concept of loyalty," she said finally.

"I'm not sure I see the distinction."

"Raucus believes that every High Lord does, and should, owe fealty to the First Lord," Aria said. "He can't stand power-seekers like the Aquitaines, Rhodes, and Kalarus, and he will scrupulously adhere to what he sees as the ideal for how a High Lord should behave—but he detests Gaius. He'd rather gouge out his own eyes than show the least amount of voluntary personal respect for the man currently wearing the Crown, as opposed to the respect due the Crown itself."

"Why?" Isana asked. "Not that Gaius hasn't done a number of things to earn enemies in his time—but why Raucus?"

"He and Septimus were close when they were young," Aria said. "Inseparable, really, after a year or so of initial difficulties. After Septimus died, Raucus stopped attending Wintersend, stopped writing to the Citadel, and refused to answer any letters from the First Lord directly."

Isana felt her eyes widen. Septimus had not truly died in battle with the Marat, as the Realm at large had been led to believe. He had been killed during the battle as a result of the actions of a group of Citizens, a conspiracy of crafters powerful enough to neutralize Septimus's furies and leave him vulnerable to the barbarians. In fact, the successful attempt had not been the first but merely the last in a series of half a dozen such incidents. Isana knew that Septimus had believed that he had puzzled out who were the ones behind the conspiracy—and that he had been in the process of gathering evidence when he died.

If Raucus had been close friends with Septimus, it was possible that her late husband had shared what he knew with the then-young lord of Antillus. "Great furies," Isana breathed. "He knows something."

Aria arched a red-gold eyebrow. "Knows something? What do you mean?"

Isana shook her head quickly. "Nothing, nothing." She gave Aria a quick, apologetic smile. "Nothing I can share at the moment."

Aria opened her mouth in a silent "ah" and nodded. She frowned and gathered her own cloak closer to her body. "Always so cold up at the Wall."

Isana looked out the window, to see the Shieldwall, an enormous construction of dark stone, perhaps twenty yards below them. It was early evening, and a circle of lights marked a landing space on the wall. The countryside around, blanketed in snow, glowed with the eerie half-light of winter.

"Tell me this, Aria," Isana said. "In your judgment—is he a good man?"

Aria blinked at Isana. She hesitated for several seconds, as if wrestling with a concept she had never encountered. "I . . ." She spread her hands helplessly. "I'm not sure how to answer. There have been days when I haven't been proud of the things I've needed to do for the sake of duty."

Isana smiled faintly. "I've had days like that as well," she said quietly. "And it doesn't change anything or make the question invalid. Ask your heart. Is he a good man?"

Lady Placida regarded Isana slowly for a moment, before a rather worn half smile appeared on her mouth, along with a sardonic little chuckle. "For a High Lord. Yes. He's bullheaded and arrogant, his ego is bloated to the size of a mountain, he's headstrong, often inconsiderate, more than occasionally rude, intolerant to anyone he doesn't respect, and short-tempered with anyone who challenges him. And underneath all that—there's more of the same, only better cured." She shook her head. "But beneath that, yes. I sent my own sons to Antillus to train under him when they came of age. That is how much I trust Antillus Raucus."

Isana smiled at her, and said, "Thank you, Aria. That's encouraging. Perhaps we have a chance to make something work out after all."

"Perhaps you didn't listen to most of what I just said," Aria replied, her tone dry.

The coach settled down with a gentle bump, and the winds died down. A second later, a Legion band began playing the Crown Anthem.

Isana grimaced.

"It is traditional," Aria murmured.

"Yes, yes." Isana sighed. "But the tune is ghastly. It sounds like a sick gargant dying. What precisely qualifies it to be the Crown Anthem?"

"Tradition," Aria replied promptly.

"And tradition alone, apparently," Isana said. "Though perhaps my taste in music is simply . . . uneducated."

"Oh, no, not at all," Aria said. "I am well versed in several musical traditions, and assure you that the Crown Anthem is perfectly hideous."

Araris, who had sat silent and motionless through most of the trip—asleep, actually, though he'd dozed with that catlike lightness that could have come instantly to waking, had the need arose, opened his eyes as the Knights who had borne the air coach came to the door and opened it. "Ladies," he murmured. "If you will excuse me." He exited the coach first—as he insisted upon doing every time, these days—and a moment later leaned his head back inside and extended his hand to Isana. "Very well, ladies."

Isana took Araris's hand and left the coach, emerging into, not the light of furylamps, but instead raw torchlight atop the wall. It was far dimmer and, somehow, more primal than the tiny, clean, blue-white furylamps inside the wind coach. Red light and shadow lay heavily over everything, and she found herself instinctively becoming more wary of her surroundings.

Standing atop the Shieldwall was, Isana realized, more like standing upon a road or bridge than any building—or more accurately, like standing in the square of a small town. The wall was fifty feet wide, and a number of structures existed atop the Wall, within sight of where the cart had landed, framed by four towers that rose up from the Wall, standard Aleran ramparts rising another twenty feet above the surface of the already-towering Wall. Several knee-high stone walls rose up here and there around them, and Isana realized that they must be guard-walls around stairwells that sank down into the structure of the Wall itself. A moment's estimate showed Isana that the area of the Wall they stood upon could have contained enough structures to comprise a town.

That might, she supposed, do something to explain the number of *legionares* assembled to meet the coach, despite the late hour. There was the better part of two full cohorts—or, she supposed the Legion's Prime Cohort—turned out in ranks in front of the coach, while at least five times as many *legionares* were obviously on duty within sight of her position, on guard upon the battlements at the edges of the Wall, at each level of the ramparts, and at lighted positions up and down the length of the Wall, to either horizon, as far as she could see.

Every *legionare's* breastplate bore the three scarlet diagonal bars of the Legions of Antillus—though upon several helmets and shields, Isana saw a more graphic representation of the heraldic design, evidently painted on by individual *legionares*: three ragged, bloody wounds, as if torn by the claws of one of the massive northern bears.

A man in the finer breastplate and elaborate helmet of a Tribune stepped forward and saluted. He was tall, clean-cut, and looked every inch the professional soldier. "Your Highness, Your Grace. On behalf of my lord, His Grace, Antillus Raucus, welcome to the Wall. My name is Tribune Garius."

Isana inclined her head to him. The chill in the air made her shiver despite the warmer clothes and heavier cloak she had worn. "Thank you, Tribune."

"May I ask, Tribune," Aria said, "why Lord Antillus is not here to greet us personally?"

"He regrets that his duties prevented him from being here," the man said smoothly.

"Duties?" Aria asked.

Garius stared at her levelly, his gaze unwavering, and gestured toward the southern side of the wall. "See for yourself, Your Grace."

Aria glanced at Isana, who nodded, and the pair of them, accompanied by Garius and the silent Araris, walked to the southern side of the Wall. The first thing Isana noticed was that the temperature rose noticeably—by several degrees, at least—in the few short feet she traveled. The second, was that the ground on the far side of the Wall was brightly lit.

About a hundred men were spread out on the ground below, working by torchlight. They had, apparently, just finished building some kind of low wooden framework to support several score crates—and then, with a chill that had nothing to do with the cold of the season, Isana realized that the boxes weren't crates.

They were coffins.

The men—Legion engineers, she could see now, formed up into ranks, facing the coffins, which she could see had been arranged upon a wooden byre.

"Ah," Aria said quietly. "Now I see."

"They burn the dead here?" Isana asked.

Aria nodded calmly. "The *legionares*, at any rate. Those who fall against the Icemen are almost always covered in frost. It has become a custom among the Legions to promise one's fellows that no matter what happens, they will never lie cold upon the earth."

A tall, silent form with broad shoulders and a crimson cloak appeared from among the engineers. He put a hand on the shoulder of a grizzled veteran, evidently the leader of the engineering cohort, then stepped forward, and gestured with a hand.

The torches exploded into white-hot, eerily silent fire that opened and spread with an almost tender deliberation from the sources, at each torch, blooming out into spheres until it had enveloped the framework and the coffins below. The tall lord below—Antillus, Isana had no doubt—cupped both his hands and lifted them abruptly to the sky, and in time with the gesture, the white fire gathered and rose in a sudden fountain that dispersed into the air and diffused into the night sky, as if scattering to join the stars themselves.

A moment later, the usual colors and brightness of winter night returned. The ground below the wall was empty of coffins, byre, bodies, and ash. Nor was there snow, or grass, or anything but naked earth. The fire had swept the ground clean.

"Actually," Garius commented idly, "those weren't *legionares*, Your Grace. We lost nearly two hundred *legionares* in our last action against the Icemen, and we burned them three days since. Those men were veterans. The Icemen slipped over the Wall in several places two nights ago. Those men fell defending their steadholts and families, before our cavalry and Knights could arrive to help." He spoke in a quiet, matter-of-fact tone. "But they fought and fell as *legionares*. They deserved to be sent off as *legionares*."

On the ground below, High Lord Antillus bowed his head, and covered his face with both his hands. He just stood that way for a moment, not moving. Even from there, Isana could feel the echoes of his grief and guilt, and the sympathetic pains that rippled through the men around her who could see him—men who obviously cared about him.

Aria let out a low sigh. "Oh," she whispered. "Oh, Raucus."

The grizzled centurion growled an order, and the engineers below marched out in good order. A moment later, Antillus, too, departed, walking back toward the base of the Wall and out of sight.

"I'll remind him that you've come," Garius murmured.

"Thank you, Garius," Aria murmured.

"Of course, Mother." The young Tribune walked briskly away.

Within a few moments, Antillus Raucus came up one of the staircases Isana had noted before, Garius walking just behind his left shoulder, the grizzled engineering centurion behind his right. The High Lord walked straight over to Isana and bowed politely, first to her, then to Aria.

"Your Highness. Your Grace."

Isana returned the gesture as gracefully as she could. "Your Grace."

Raucus was a large, rawboned man, brawny as a house built from raw timber. His craggy face reminded Isana startlingly of Tavi's young friend Maximus—though it was worn with more years of care and discipline, and sharpened with more bitterness and anger. His hair was dark, shot through with flickers of iron—and his eyes were hollow with weariness and grief. "I regret that I could not be on hand to greet you myself," he said, his voice empty. "I had duties that required my personal attention."

"Of course, Your Grace," Isana said. "I . . . Please accept my condolences for the suffering of your people."

He nodded, the gesture empty of any real meaning. "Hello, Aria."

"Hello, Raucus."

He gestured at the bare patch of earth and something hot and unpleasant shone in his eyes. "You saw what I just did?"

"Yes," Aria said.

"If my men didn't make it a point to steal their swords and take them home at the end of their service, while I make it a point to look the other way, it would have been the women and children of those steadholts in the fire," he snarled.

Aria pressed her lips together and looked down, saying nothing.

Antillus turned his hard gaze back to Isana, and said, "There's only one kind of peace you can make with the Icemen."

Isana lifted her chin slightly and took a slow breath. "What do you mean?"

"They're animals," Antillus spat. "You don't bargain with animals. You kill them, or you leave them alone. You can talk all you want, First Lady. But the sooner you realize the truth of that, the sooner you can help me and Phrygia do what is necessary to get some real help down to the south."

"Your Grace," Isana said cautiously. "That isn't what the First Lord—"

"The First Lord," Antillus said, scorn seething from every syllable. "He has no idea what life is like up here. He has no idea how many *legionares* I've buried—most of them sixteen- and seventeen-year-old children. He has no idea what the Icemen are, or what they are capable of. He's never seen it. Never had to wash the blood off him. I have. Every day."

"But—"

"Don't you *dare* think you can walk in here for half of one hour and tell me about my own domain, Your *Highness*," Antillus snarled. "I will *not* be bullied around by Gaius's pet—"

"*Raucus*," Aria snapped. Her voice was barely more than a whisper, but it shook the air between the three of them with its intensity.

The High Lord closed his mouth and glared at Lady Placida. Then he looked away from her and shook his head.

"Perhaps you could use some rest," Aria suggested.

Raucus grunted. A moment later, he said, to Isana, "Your savage is here. Camped out with my savages. You're to meet in the morning. Garius will show you to your chambers."

He spun, his scarlet cloak flaring out, and stalked away, out of the torch-light.

Isana shivered again and rubbed her arms with her hands.

"Ladies," Garius said, "if you'll follow me, please, I will show you to your rooms."

The art of compromise?

How in the world was she supposed to find a compromise when one side of the conflict, at least, simply did not *want* to find a peaceful resolution?

CHAPTER 15

Marcus paused outside the Princeps' cabin at the sound of raised voices within.

"What is it you think we're supposed to do, Magnus?" Maximus demanded in a blunt tone. "The Princeps—and every Cane in the range of Shuar, apparently—believes that it is necessary."

"It is an unacceptable risk," answered the Legion's valet, his voice crackling with precisely restrained anger. "The Princeps of Alera simply does *not* wander the land of a foreign power alone, vulnerable and unsecured."

"It's not as though he's a helpless babe," pointed out Antillus Crassus's calmer, more measured voice. "Perhaps my brother has a point, Magnus."

Marcus smiled faintly. He knew Crassus well enough by then to know that the young man had a better head on his shoulders than to agree with Maximus about sending the Princeps into the heart of a Canim nation alone. But siding with his brother would neatly undermine Maximus's objection when Crassus capitulated.

"Octavian's life is irreplaceable," Magnus stated. "If every single life in this expedition had to be sacrificed to see him safely back to Alera again, it would be our duty to do everything in our power to make sure that it happened as rapidly and efficiently as possible. We are expendable, gentlemen. He is not."

"I am neither a gentleman nor expendable," the young Marat woman interjected. "Nor do I see how the deaths of all of your people could possibly get my

Aleran safely home again. You've seen him on the open water. Do you honestly think he could manage a ship on his own?"

There was a beat of startled silence, then Magnus said, his tone sour, "I was speaking in hypothetical terms, Ambassador."

"Ah," Kitai said, her tone wry. "Explain again to me the difference between hypothesis and make-believe."

"All right," said Octavian in his resonant baritone. Already, Marcus thought he could hear the gravity of greater authority settling into the young man's voice. "I think we've beaten this particular gargant to death."

"Your Highness—" Magnus began.

"Magnus," Octavian said, "I am, for all practical purposes, a prisoner—as is our fleet. The Shuarans control the harbor. If I do not go to see Warmaster Lararl after claiming the protection of his respect, there's nothing to stop them from turning those stone throwers on us and sending us all to the bottom of their harbor—including me. That isn't the way to get me safely back to Alera."

"We could win free," Magnus said stiffly.

"Perhaps. If we broke the truce and our word, betrayed the trust they've extended, and attacked them first." Octavian's voice hardened slightly. "That isn't going to happen, Magnus. It could prove every bit as dangerous in the long term."

"Your Highness—"

Octavian didn't raise his voice with his anger. In fact, it grew quieter, if sharper and more clearly pronounced. "Enough."

Marcus lifted his hand, knocked once on the door, and opened it without waiting for a response, as he usually did. His entrance surprised everyone within. They all turned to blink at him.

Marcus saluted. "Your Highness. I overheard your discussion as I approached. If it isn't too forward of me, sir, may I offer a suggestion?"

Octavian's eyebrows climbed nearly to his hairline. "Please."

"Sir, when Varg was at the capital, didn't he have a bunch of his own honor guards with him? Tokens of his station or some such?"

"Certainly."

"Seems to me you could claim the same."

Maximus scowled and shook his head. "The Canim told him that he had to travel alone."

"An honor guard is appropriate to a man of his station," Marcus replied. "What are they going to do? Back down because they're afraid of a few men he takes with him?"

Octavian smiled faintly and pointed a finger at Marcus. "Point. If it was phrased that way, they'd have little choice but to accept it or look like cowards. A few men couldn't be a threat to the Shuarans."

Magnus shook his head. "That's precisely the problem. I'd much rather the Princeps' bodyguard could annihilate a thousand attackers at least."

Octavian sat forward in his seat. "I don't need to annihilate thousands, Magnus. But a few men *could* fly me out of trouble and back to the ships if they happened to be Knights Aeris. Or hide us and let us travel back hidden behind a veil if they were woodcrafters. I'd say I would need to take as much guile as power. Would you agree, Marcus?"

"In essence," Marcus said. "Yes, sir. Even if the entire force was with you, sir, we couldn't fight a country full of Canim and win—but we do have strength enough to take and hold this port for a time, if we must. What you need is a group small enough to avoid alarming the Canim—but with enough muscle to get out of a tight spot and enough finesse and skill to get back here through a hostile countryside if need be."

Octavian nodded sharply. "That sounds quite reasonable."

"By what madman's standard? Reasonable relative to *what*?" asked Magnus. His voice was dry, but the bitter undertones had gone out of it.

"Suggestions?" Octavian asked, giving Magnus an amused and tolerant glance.

"Me," Maximus said at once.

"Concur," Marcus agreed. The big Antillan was an engine of destruction in a fight of any scale.

"Me," Crassus said a second later.

"Yes," Magnus said. "You said you'd need finesse as well."

"I am going," Kitai stated.

"Lady Ambassador," Magnus began, "it might be better if—"

"I am going," Kitai repeated, in exactly the same tone of voice, as she rose and walked over to the cabin's door. "The Aleran will explain it to you."

Marcus stepped aside as the Marat woman left the cabin and shut the door behind her.

Octavian shook his head and sighed. "That's three. Who else, do you think? Radeus? A fast flier might be handy."

"Durias, sir," Marcus said, without hesitation.

Octavian arched an eyebrow at the suggestion.

Crassus frowned. "He's . . . Isn't he the First Spear of the Free Aleran Legion?"

Marcus nodded.

"Ridiculous," Magnus said. "We know almost nothing about the man. He owes nothing to the Realm and has no interest in keeping the Princeps safe. In point of fact, he's a traitor."

"Let's not wave that brush around too wildly, Magnus," Octavian said. "You never know whom it will stain."

Marcus found himself smiling faintly, and Octavian answered the expression with one of his own. The young man would think Marcus was smiling about the young Princeps' actions of the year before, when he had infiltrated the Grey Tower in Alera Imperia and kidnapped Ambassador Varg out from under the noses of the Grey Guard. Let him. Octavian had enough on his mind without burdening him with another bit of unpleasant knowledge.

"Why Durias, First Spear?" Octavian asked.

"He knows the Canim, sir," Marcus replied. "He worked closely with them, marched beside them, trained with one. He'll know them better than any of us—even better than you, sir. Know their capabilities in comparison to ours, know their methods, know the way they think. He'll be better able than almost anyone in the expedition to tell you what the Canim do and do not know about Aleran capabilities, and unless I miss my guess, he's no slouch with his own earthcrafting or knowledge of fieldcraft."

The old Cursor stared quietly at Marcus for a long moment before he finally spoke. "The question is," Magnus said, "whether or not he'll be *willing* to share that knowledge with you, my lord. Durias has no love for Alera or her Citizens."

"Nor would I, had I lived as he did," Octavian replied. "Alerans enslaved him. Varg's people freed him from bondage and taught him to fight so that he could protect that freedom. I'd be more than half-willing to let Alera hang, if I'd grown up in the same circumstances."

"Then I advise you to choose someone else," Magnus said.

Octavian shook his head. "The First Spear is right, Magnus. Max and Crassus, between them, have all the furycraft anyone could need. Kitai is one of the better scouts and trackers in the Legion. I'd trust her to be able to find her way back to the ship if the Canim blindfolded her and tossed her in a sack for the journey to visit their Warmaster." He thumped a finger against the side of his head. "What's more valuable to us now than any number of swords or furies is knowledge—all we can get. Durias has it. We need it. So we need him."

"And what makes you think he'll cooperate?" Magnus said.

Octavian smiled. "I did him a good turn once."

Maximus snorted. "Aye. His nose never did heal up straight from your good turn, either."

"Leave Durias to me," the Princeps said, his tone confident. "Magnus, would you see to it that he gets a message. Invite him to come see me at his earliest convenience, please."

"Of course, my lord."

"Good. Gentlemen, if you would excuse me, I would speak with the First Spear for a moment."

The others took their leave and departed the cabin, leaving Marcus alone with the Princeps.

"Sir?" Marcus said, once they were alone.

"Sit down, please," Octavian said, gesturing at the other chair in the cabin.

Marcus pulled up the chair and did so, frowning. "You about to demote me or something, sir?"

Octavian's mouth turned up into a quick grin. "Something like that. Magnus tells me that you did some excellent work gathering intelligence during the voyage. That you managed to get a look at several of their charts—and that you were the one the Hunters contacted when they wanted to pass information along to us."

Marcus shrugged. "The *Trueblood* is their largest vessel, and their flagship. It's got the most people coming and going, the most traffic, the most activity. I imagine anyone could have done what I did."

"Nevertheless, you were the one who did it," Octavian said. "You went beyond anything you could reasonably have been expected to do, Marcus." He folded his hands and frowned. "And I'm about to ask you to go even further."

Marcus frowned and waited.

"I'm leaving you in command of the Legions," Octavian said.

Marcus lifted his eyebrows. "Sir? You can't do that."

"The crows I can't. I'm the Princeps of bloody Alera and the commander of this expedition. I can establish whatever chain of command I think appropriate."

Marcus shook his head. "Sir, there are a number of Tribunes in the First who outrank me—and I'm not at all sure that the Captain of the Free Aleran is going to like the idea of a centurion in the First Aleran giving him orders."

"You've got more field experience than any two Tribunes in either Legion," the Princeps replied. "And there aren't many men alive who are members of the Crown's House of the Valiant. Even in the Free Aleran, the name of Valiar Marcus carries respect."

Marcus frowned and looked down at the scarred knuckles of his hands.

"It's more or less an open secret by now," Octavian continued. "Magnus isn't really a mere valet."

"Cursor?" Marcus asked, purely for form. Valiar Marcus would need to confirm a suspicion, after all. He wouldn't be one hundred percent certain.

The Princeps nodded. "My grandfather appointed him my advisor in political matters. I intend his decisions to guide the expedition in diplomatic matters while I am gone. You have authority over security or military decisions. In the end, though, Marcus, I expect you to keep everything together until I get back."

Marcus exhaled slowly. "Understood, sir."

"I'll be meeting with the Tribunes shortly, to let them know how I expect things to run in my absence—and with the officers of the Free Aleran, after that. All things considered, I think they'll be nervous enough at being surrounded by hostile Canim to be willing to be cooperative, provided they're treated with respect."

"I'll break enough heads to get that point across, sir," Marcus promised.

"Good," Octavian said, rising, and Marcus mirrored the gesture.

"Sir?" Marcus asked. "May I ask you a question?"

"Of course."

"Do you really expect to come back from this meeting with the Shuaran Warmaster alive?"

The young Princeps' face became an expressionless mask. "You don't think he's going to meet with me in good faith?"

"Your Highness," Marcus said, "from what I've heard, there is a bloody idiot in charge of the warrior caste here."

"Yes," the Princeps said. "That's true."

Marcus grimaced. "Then they're hiding something, sir."

"Why do you say that, First Spear?"

"Think about it. If you had one bloody fortified port on your entire shoreline, would you leave an incompetent in charge of it? Or would you put the best commander you could find in that position."

Octavian frowned, his brow furrowing.

"Doesn't make any sense," Marcus said. "There's got to be some kind of pressure forcing that kind of appointment. Which says to me that this Warmaster doesn't have the kind of control he would like to have. If I were you, sir, I'd want to know why not. Might be important."

"You're right," Octavian said quietly. "I hadn't thought of it in quite those terms, but you're right. Thank you."

Marcus nodded. "Sir."

"I'll be departing within two hours," Octavian said. "In that time, I want you to make me a list of anything you think you'll need my approval to get done. Draw them up as separate items, and I'll sign off on them before I go."

"Yes, sir," Marcus said. "Best of luck on your journey, sir."

"To both of us, Marcus. Though I'd rather neither of us needed it."

CHAPTER 16

The journey from Molvar to Shuar took four days, all of them along a stretch of hilly, windy country that supported little but yellowed grass, peeking up through early snows, and rounded black stone. By the end of the third day, the taurg Tavi was riding had only tried to kill him twice—since lunchtime. By the standards of Canim cavalry, the beast was behaving admirably.

The taurg most closely resembled a bull, Tavi had decided. It was a bit bigger, and considerably humpier about the shoulders. Its rear quarters were much more heavily muscled, as well, and its legs were longer, springier, more in proportion to a hare's than to anything so large as it was. The beast was covered with thick, curly fur that ranged from deep grey on its blunt muzzle to blueblack on its shoulders and haunches. Its neck was thick, its head was rather tiny, and its brow was half-encircled by a massive, bony ridge that was capable, so the Canim claimed, of smashing through stone walls. Its eyes were tiny and pink and hostile, its wide nostrils drooled a constant stream of slobbery mucus, and its cloven hooves struck at a speed that rivaled that of any warhorse in Alera—and hit with several times the power.

Anag raised a hand and signaled for the group to halt near a circle of standing stones beside the road—the campsite for the night. Forty taurga drew off the road at their long-legged, swaybacked walk, in a maneuver as familiar to them as making camp was to any *legionare*, and began filing into a circle within the standing stones, three beasts to each. Three blued-steel rings had been set into each stone, each to tether a single taurg.

Tavi slid down from the saddle, keeping a hand on it to control his descent to the ground. He winced at the shock to sore muscles as he landed. The first couple of days in the strange saddles, made for large Canim riders, had been nightmarish, but his body had finally begun to adjust.

The taurg promptly whipped its head at Tavi in an effort to crush his windpipe with the heavy ridge of bone on its skull.

Tavi ducked the attempt without really thinking about it and slashed at the taurg's vulnerable nose with the ends of his reins, still gripped in his hand. The taurg jerked its head away and tried to kick him with one of its rear legs, lashing a cloven hoof forward in an effort to disembowel him, but Tavi had already slipped forward, alongside the taurg's head, slipped the reins through the ring in its slimy, sensitive nose, and tied them securely through the ring on the standing stone.

Thus secured, the taurg settled down placidly onto its belly, as most of the rest of the riding beasts were doing.

"Crows take you, Steaks," Maximus snarled from the far side of the taurg beside Tavi. The beast was dancing in place, shuffling its mass left and right, evidently trying to kick at Max with the rear leg on the far side of its body. "One more kick out of you and I'm walking the rest of the way with a full stomach."

Tavi stepped forward, slapped the other taurg's ear to startle it, then seized its nose ring with his hand and jerked firmly. The taurg let out a startled little bawl of basso discomfort, and Maximus appeared, stuffing the reins through the ring and securing the beast as Tavi had, muttering a dark string of curses beneath his breath as he did. "Roasted. Spit on a nice long lance and roasted over a roaring fire. Then boiled. Boiled in a pot big enough to fit your entire lazy, ornery, smelly ass."

"You're taking it awfully personally," Tavi murmured. "I think Steaks and New Boots is probably treating you the same way he does everyone else."

"It isn't that's he treating me badly," Max growled. "It's that he's too stupid to understand something everything with brains enough to see the sky should know."

Tavi found himself grinning. "What's that?"

"*Legionares* are not afraid of dinner," Max growled, giving the taurg a dire glare. "Dinner is afraid of *legionares*."

Steaks and New Boots returned Max's glare with a placid stare, and began chewing cud where it lay in place.

"Bastard," Max muttered, and began unfastening the straps of the high-cantled saddle. "Spends all day trying to murder me, and still gets to sack *and* chow before I do." The pace and volume of his complaints began to increase steadily. "If I didn't need his legs, I'd carve them into steaks and serve them up with a nice red wine. Though I'll bet he doesn't taste any good, when you get right down to it. Why, I'll bet you could . . ."

As Max's complaints grew steadily louder and more outrageous while he tended to the taurga, Tavi gathered the saddles from his beast, Max's, and Durias's, next to Max's, and began brushing them down from the day's use.

"Well?" he asked Durias quietly, under cover of Max's noise.

The Free Aleran centurion was a rather short man, with shoulders so wide that he almost looked deformed. His neck was thicker than a lot of women's waists, his blocky face plain and scarred here and there with the irregular, fine, jagged cuts of a life spent under slavery, where the lash had wrapped around. He had dark, very intelligent eyes, and thick-knuckled, capable hands that immediately set to the task of cleaning and coiling the saddle straps.

"I counted four more supply trains today," Durias said. "All of them military, all of them escorted, all of them headed the same direction we are. None of them were ones we've passed before."

"That makes eighteen, total," Tavi said. "How sure are you about the estimates on what a Canim soldier needs for rations?"

"How sure are you about estimating what your *legionares* need for rations, Captain?" Durias replied, grinning.

"Point taken," Tavi said. "We passed two maker settlements today closely enough to get a good look at them, and I didn't see a single male Cane among them."

"Nor I," Durias said. "I think your theory is sound, Captain. From all the signs, the Shuaran Canim are at war."

Tavi liked Durias. The young Free Aleran had met Tavi—rather forcefully—in Tavi's capacity as the Captain of the First Aleran Legion. The public revelation of his heritage, made since then, was something Durias found too uncomfortable to confront directly, and, as a result, the young man was one of the few people who still referred to Tavi in the same terms he had *before* Tavi had revealed himself as a scion of the House of Gaius.

"We were expecting something like it," Tavi said quietly, looking around as he finished the last saddle.

Kitai and Crassus arrived a moment later. Crassus took up conversation with Max, whose complaints only gathered in volume and capacity—and sincerity. Max *really* couldn't stand the taurga.

"Anag was polite and revealed very little," Kitai reported quietly. "But some of the other warriors nearby were less disciplined. They are excited that we are drawing near to the front. They are glad that they might be able to see action and prove themselves in battle."

"Remind me, Durias," Tavi said. "Isn't it Canim practice to place hotheaded young idiots in rear-area positions precisely to avoid having attitudes like that near the actual fighting?"

"Aye, it's common enough," Durias said. "The theory is that they'll grow out of it. Someday."

"Then how do you explain Anag?" Kitai asked. "He seems sensible."

Durias shrugged. "Maybe it took."

Tavi shook his head. "More likely, someone assigned a young but competent subordinate to mitigate the sins of an incompetent senior officer." He squinted into the glowering winter sky, where occasional snowflakes were already starting to come down. "I'm getting a better picture now. Tarsh had somehow attained too much rank for his level of competence. In an actual war, he was going to get a lot of otherwise-decent soldiers killed—so Warmaster Lararl stuck him in a position where his incompetence wasn't going to get in the way of the war effort, in charge of a bunch of hotheads who needed time to season. He probably regretted losing a decent junior officer to ride herd on the lot of them, but he couldn't leave them entirely unattended."

"That would make sense if the post was in the middle of nowhere," Durias countered. "But it's still their only significant port, Captain."

"True," Tavi admitted. "Unless . . . unless Molvar has *become* the middle of nowhere."

Durias frowned. "What do you mean?"

Tavi held up his hand for silence as he followed that line of thought to several chilling conclusions.

Kitai's head snapped around to him, her eyes narrowed and intently focused. *"Chala?"*

Tavi shook his head.

Durias frowned and looked at the two of them. "What's wrong?"

"I hope I'm not right," Tavi said. "But if I am . . . we're in trouble." He looked up at Kitai. "I need to talk to Varg."

She rose and padded away without a word.

". . . and not even *she* would do that with *you*, no matter *how* much money or how many burlap bags were involved!" Max bawled at the peacefully reclining Steaks and New Boots, and kicked the taurg in the side. He might have slammed his foot into a stone for all the reaction the animal showed.

Crassus put a hand on his seething brother's shoulder, and said, "Honestly, Maximus. You're really taking this way too personally. You need to look on the bright side."

"I've got blisters and muscle cramps in places not meant for the touch of anything but a beautiful woman," Max spat back sullenly. "I've bitten my tongue so many times in the past three days that I whistle in musical chords when I exhale. And the smell isn't ever going to come out of my armor, I just know it." He narrowed his eyes and glared at Steaks and New Boots. "Where, precisely, is the bright side?"

Crassus considered that gravely. Then he offered, "If nothing else, the crowbegotten beast has given you something legitimate to complain about."

Max's eyebrows lifted, and his expression became that of a man who is mulling over a new thought.

Kitai returned with Varg a moment after that.

"Aleran," Varg rumbled. "How do you like Shuar?"

"Cold and flat. And my men don't care for taurga," Tavi replied.

"Sane beings do not," Varg agreed, settling down on his haunches, the posture a casual one among the Canim. He tossed a waterskin to Durias, who caught it casually, opened it, and drank it Canim-fashion, squirting the water into his mouth without touching it to his lips. Durias tossed it back to the Cane with a nod of thanks.

"Varg," Tavi said, "from what I have seen of the maps of Shuar, the place is essentially a single enormous plateau. A natural fortress."

Varg drank from the waterskin and nodded. "Yes. Close enough to it. There are three passes into the plateau, all of them heavily fortified. The Shuar's range has always been all but impregnable." He yawned, and flicked his ears dismissively. "Not that anyone wants it."

"That's what has made them strong," Tavi said.

"That and the mines in these mountains," Varg said. "They make arms, armor, and goods of acceptable quality here. Their warriors often make alliances with other battlepacks, lend aid and support in battle."

"I noticed that Molvar was built with impressive defenses."

Varg showed his teeth. "Shuarans are lords of the mountains. Narash rules the seas. Shuarans know that they cannot challenge us there. But if there is one thing their warriors know better than any other pack, it is fortifications."

There was an outcry from the other side of the ring of stones, as four of the young warriors evidently erupted into some kind of personal brawl. Weapons were drawn, and blood followed a moment later. It might have gotten more serious if Anag had not stepped in with a taurg-goad—essentially a long-handled, heavily weighted club with a sharp spur sticking out of one side. Anag knocked half of the brawling foursome unconscious with two efficient swings, dragged another to the ground by one ear, and bludgeoned the last into docility by sheer force of will.

Once order was restored, Tavi stared at Varg for a long moment. Then he said, "Tarsh. Defending Molvar. With this band of crack troops."

Varg fell silent and returned the stare for a moment. Then he said, his voice deep and barely audible, "You see well, Aleran."

The Cane rose and stalked silently away.

Durias stared after him, an expression very like shock on his face.

Max and Crassus watched Varg go. Max came back over to Tavi, and said, "What was that all about?"

"He doesn't know," Durias said. He glanced at Tavi. "Varg isn't sure what's happening, is he?"

Tavi shook his head and said, "I don't think he's certain."

"But you are," Kitai said quietly.

Tavi grimaced. "I'm certain we'll see for ourselves tomorrow."

They slept on the cold ground, bedrolls laid out close together for simple warmth. Though there were no wood-burning fires, as there would have been in a Legion camp, the Canim instead built fires in trenches that burned low, hot, and slow on some kind of thick bricks of springy moss. The fire trenches made the nights survivable, but just barely. Max and Crassus were both familiar with firecrafting techniques used along the Shieldwall for keeping oneself warm in the bitter cold, but they couldn't be done when sleeping, and their nights were as miserable as everyone else's.

The next day began with the bawling of hungry taurga waking everyone from their sleep. Max, who had begun bringing a stone to his bedroll with him specifically to hurl at the first taurg to begin bellowing near him, threw nothing more than a muttered oath, and the day got under way almost immediately. Canim camp procedure was elementary in the morning: feed the taurga and shovel their leavings out of the ring of stones and into the mound where they would be allowed to dry and used to supplement the fuel for the fire trenches. Then saddle the beasts and mount up. The warriors ate dried jerky from their own packs as they worked or as the morning's ride began.

As on the other days they'd spent on the road, they rode at the swaying, swift pace of the taurga's loping walk, following the road southwest, continuing farther inland, as they had for the previous three days, and stopping only once at midday, to feed and water the beasts. By the time evening approached, the wind had begun to rise, swift and cold, and pellets of stinging ice fell in irregular intervals with spats of chilling rain.

Kitai drew her beast up beside Tavi's. The taurga slammed their heads together, bawling and huffing at one another until they had settled which of them had herd precedence over the other—though Tavi had no idea which of them was the superior once it was done. They behaved exactly as they had before the ruckus.

"Aleran," Kitai said quietly, "do you smell it?"

Tavi looked at her sharply and shook his head. "Not yet."

The Marat woman grimaced at him and tugged at the guide straps, to haul her taurg back into line. "Keep your nose to the wind."

It took perhaps another half an hour for Tavi's less acute senses to pick up on the scent. But once he did, the hairs on the back of his neck rose, and flashes of hideous memories flickered through his mind.

From the line of taurga ahead of him came a sudden bellowing, then one of the beasts broke out of the line. Tavi looked up to see Varg employing his goad, jabbing his taurg from the routine comfort of the company of its herdmates, driving it into a pace that was less a run than it was a continual series of bounding leaps that covered ground at an astounding rate.

One of the young warriors in the column ripped a balest from the holster on his taurg's saddle, slapped a bolt home, and raised the weapon to his shoulder, but Anag flung his goad, sending it whirling end over end, and the club slammed into the warrior and sent him tumbling from the saddle before he could send a deadly missile into Varg's back.

"Stand down!" Anag roared, his voice carrying down the entire column. "Stand down, you fool, or I'll have your throat!" The young Cane glowered at Varg, then up and down the line. "Column halt! Dismount! Ready yourselves for inspection before we arrive at the fortifications!"

The command began to echo down the length of the column as it was relayed, but Anag did not dismount. Instead, he pulled his taurg out of line and rode back down the column until he drew even with Tavi. "Aleran," he growled. "I think you should bring your people."

Tavi frowned at Anag but nodded to him. He signaled to Kitai and the others with a hand, and they turned their mounts out of the column, to follow Anag. They rode in pursuit of Varg, though at a far more sedate pace.

The dark-furred Warmaster had ridden to the top of a low rise half a mile away and halted his mount. As they approached, Varg was nothing but a black shadow against a grey sky, an outline of silent menace atop the still-puffing form of the massive taurg.

The wind grew stronger, and less chilly as they neared the crest. The rain, less frozen, grew into a steady, stinging shower that would shortly make outdoor travel all but unbearable.

And the scent grew stronger.

They crested the little rise and looked down over the edge of the Shuaran plateau, onto the lands below.

Tavi had tried to prepare himself for what he knew was coming.

Even so, his heart went sick with raw terror.

The rise upon which they stood thrust slightly out from the plateau, like the prow of some unimaginably large ship, offering a vista of the lands below that would have been spectacular if not for the dim veil of rain. Varg had not exaggerated when he said that their land was a fortress, and that the Shuarans knew how to defend it. Below them, the land dropped away into sheer cliffs and bluffs that fell hundreds, if not thousands, of feet to the plains below.

A few miles ahead of them, along the wall of the plateau, Tavi could dimly make out the dark slash of an opening in the rock, doubtless one of the passes Varg had named. Even from there, Tavi could see the shapes of stone fortifications built into it, over it, around it, through it—a citadel the size of a city in its own right, every bit as complex and grand, in its fashion, as Alera's Shieldwall. More fortifications ran along the top of the plateau.

And they were filled with warrior Canim.

Tavi could see the banners, the blue-and-black steel of their armor, rank upon rank of them, manning the battlements, the parapets, the towers, the gates. Tavi remembered all too vividly the shock and terror of facing the assault of ten thousand warrior-caste Canim, during the desperate battle for the Elinarch. He remembered the terrifying precision of their onslaught, the speed, the aggression, the discipline that had carried them through one successful engagement after another.

Oh, certainly, Tavi had managed to contain the Canim invasion—but he had no illusions about how he had done so. When he had beaten Nasaug's troops in the field, he had pitted his *legionares* against the Canim raiders, the equivalent of their militia. He had used his cavalry and the furycraft of his Knights to disrupt their communications and their supply lines. He had harried and danced with them, struck at them where they were weakest, and never left his forces standing still long enough to be hammered down by the foe.

Had he done so, they would have been crushed in short order—by the warrior caste. Despite their successes, the First Aleran had never been able to claim anything more than a marginal victory in any conflict with Nasaug's ten thousand elite.

If Tavi was not mistaken in his estimate, Warmaster Lararl of the Range of Shuar had something like a quarter of a million of them.

And *they* weren't what had frightened him.

The plains at the base of the plateau, all of them, *all* of them, for as far as the eye could see . . . glowed softly green.

They were covered in the *croach*.

And the *croach* was covered in Vord.

There was no way for him to count them. Simply no way. There were too many. It was like staring down at an uprooted anthill. Black forms moved everywhere, seething over the landscape below, rushing and flowing in organized channels that reminded Tavi uncomfortably of a network of veins pulsing with dark blood. They spread from horizon to horizon, all moving forward, an inexorable pressure being exerted upon the massive Shuaran fortifications.

The Canim fought. They had already piled chitinous black corpses into miniature mountains, but still the Vord came on.

And the world behind them was nothing but dark, alien shadows and eerie green light.

Varg stared down on the land below with an expression and posture Tavi had never seen on any Cane. His ears had simply slumped, falling limply in slightly different directions. The dark fur not covered by his armor almost seemed to go flat against his skin. He stared for long, silent moments before he finally said, in a whisper, "Tarsh in command of Molvar. Molvar, the mighty fortress. Built to defend Shuar against my people."

Max made a hissing sound of sympathetic pain.

Tavi bowed his head.

Varg turned flat, dull eyes to Anag. "When?"

"Almost two years ago," Anag said. He looked from the battle back to the rest of them. "Narash was only the first to fall, Warmaster. The other ranges are gone. They're all gone."

"Gone?" Varg said.

Anag looked back down to the battle, his manner weary. "Only Shuar remains."

CHAPTER 17

"Suddenly," Max said, "I feel very small. And as though I have been somewhat arrogant."

"Um," Crassus said. He swallowed and cleared his throat. "Yes."

Durias stared out at the sight below them, his craggy face bleak.

"Now we know why Sarl decided to abandon Canea and invade Alera," Tavi murmured, thinking aloud. "He must have seen it beginning and guessed where it would lead."

Kitai turned her green eyes toward Tavi and stared at him intently.

So did everyone else.

Bloody crows, Tavi thought. *They're all looking at me.*

Tavi surveyed the massive struggle raging below once more, careful to keep his face calm and relaxed, nodded once as if it had told him something, though he had no idea at all—yet—what that might be, and turned to Anag. "I'd say that we have matters to discuss with your Warmaster. Let's waste no time."

Anag inclined his head slightly to one side and immediately turned his taurg and began riding back to rejoin his column.

Tavi and the others set out after him, but when Tavi noticed that Varg had not moved, Tavi drew his mount up short. He gestured for the others to keep going, and rode back to Varg's side.

The Cane stared down at the battle below with dull, unfocused eyes.

"Varg," Tavi said.

The Cane did not respond.

"Varg," he said, louder.

There was no response.

Tavi glanced after the others. The freezing rain had come on thicker, and combined with the dark they were out of sight, as was the battle below. He and the Cane were alone.

For the first time since mounting the beast, Tavi took his taurg prod from where it hung on its saddle hook. It weighed as much as a smith's hammer, at the end of a three-foot handle to boot. He debated reaching down through the taurg to the earth below for strength but decided against it. He had enough raw muscle, barely, to control the heavy tool.

Tavi whirled it once and slammed it as hard as he could into Varg's chest.

The ball of the prod thudded against the Cane's armored chest, and sent Varg sprawling back, nearly knocking him out of the taurg's saddle entirely. The taurga immediately bellowed at one another, butting heads and ramming shoulders for half a minute before they backed away, settling down again.

Varg stared at Tavi in shock, then bared his fangs and reached for his sword.

Tavi smiled at him, showing teeth, and put the prod back on its hook. "I have work to do. I have a duty to my people back at Molvar." He turned his mount back toward the column, adding, over his shoulder, "So do you."

Tavi wasn't sure how Varg was going to react to what he had just done. Physical violence among the Canim was . . . not what it was among Alerans. And while it was commonly employed as a disciplinary measure, it was also seen as something of an insult; it was how one dealt with an unruly puppy, not how one treated a respected subordinate. Certainly, that kind of action was not how one treated an equal. Then again, their concept of *gadara*, respected enemy, put an entirely different light on that kind of interaction. Enemies were *supposed* to hit you.

All the same. It was entirely possible that he had just effectively offered Varg a challenge. Such things, among the Canim of Varg's status, were not confined to first blood.

Varg's mount came hurrying out of the chilling rain behind Tavi, and fell into pace beside his own beast. After the mounts settled, Tavi glanced aside, to find Varg watching him.

The big Cane's eyes were still dull. His fur was being plastered flat to his skull by the rain, making him seem, to Tavi, somehow smaller, more vulnerable, and more dangerous.

Varg inclined his head slightly to one side.

Tavi returned the gesture.

The Cane turned away, and they rejoined the troop. As the group of taurga took to the trail again, Varg rode slightly apart from everyone else.

"Shuar," Anag said, gesturing.

The road had led to the fortifications they had seen from the top of the bluffs. As a military camp, it would have to be enormous. With all the supporting folk needed to keep so many warriors in condition to fight, it had to be almost unimaginably large to hold them all—a city that easily outshone Alera Imperia in sheer scale and in grim splendor, all made of dark, bleak stone, with oddly shaped, too-narrow doors and windows. The Canim did not, it seemed, put much stock in building high towers. No building in sight was more elongated than a cube, though several of them were several stories tall. All told, it must have made for some truly cavernous architecture, with buildings capable of holding many more occupants than was customary in Alera.

Even this city, though, had been strained to its limits, Tavi could see. Dome-shaped tents stood in precise groups around the city's walls, stretching for thousands of yards over the open ground of the plateau, surrounded by simple earthworks patrolled lightly by warrior Canim in blue-and-black armor. Beyond them, cruder tents had been erected in a far-more-chaotic fashion. As they passed through them, Tavi could see evidence of tanners, smiths, and all manner of other tradesmen necessary to support such a gathering of troops. Members of the maker caste, the tradesmen had evidently overflowed whatever quarters had been intended for their use in the city proper. The cold and the rain kept most of the occupants of the tents inside them, but a few laborers— notably smiths—were still hard at work under flimsy canopies, and wide-eyed Canim children came rushing to the flaps of the tents to watch as the taurga came huffing and swaying through the tent city.

"They're cute," Max commented idly. "The little ones."

Durias snorted.

Tavi glanced over his shoulder at the former slave and arched an eyebrow. "Not cute?"

"They're adorable," Durias said. "But I once saw a slave owner who was being taken to his trial try to escape by taking one of them hostage. Little female, maybe five years old. He grabbed her by the scruff of the neck, picked her up, and put his arm around her throat. Held her like you might a child you had half a mind to strangle. Had a knife in his other hand."

Kitai, riding in front of Tavi, turned all the way around in her saddle, comfortably balanced in the rhythm of the walking taurg, her expression intently interested. "What happened?"

"That little female puppy opened up her jaws and just about tore that bad man's hand off at the wrist," Durias said. "She *did* dislocate his shoulder in the process."

Tavi lifted his eyebrows. "Strong little things."

"They don't develop the same way our children do," Durias said, nodding. "By the time they can run, their muscles are functioning almost at an adult level."

"What happened to the slave owner?" Kitai asked. "Was he found guilty at the trial?"

"No," Durias said shortly. "The puppy's mother was there. So was her uncle. Once the child was out of reach of the knife . . ."

Tavi winced. Not that he mourned the loss of any man who would take a child prisoner—even the child of an avowed enemy invader—but he couldn't imagine that a slave owner, no matter how benevolent or law-abiding, could have expected to survive a trial in the hands of a government composed of ex-slaves. Such pressure could drive any man to desperate acts.

"Don't trouble yourself, Captain," Durias said, a few seconds later, as though he had read the thoughts behind Tavi's expression. "The man was a rapist and worse. We did all that we could to spare the lives of those who hadn't actually abused women or taken a slave's life themselves."

Tavi shook his head and chuckled wryly. "There's going to be a lot of things to be worked out once we get home, you know."

"Slavery must end, sir," Durias said. His tone was quiet and respectful, but the words were made of granite and steel. "From there, we are willing to abide as any other freeman. But not until all Alerans are free."

"That isn't going to be simple or easy," Tavi said.

"Worthy things often aren't, sir."

They drew near the gates of the fortifications themselves—massive things that rose forty feet above the level of the plateau. The falling rain had begun to coat them in ice. Low-burning torches blazed at wide intervals on the walls, providing barely enough light for the Alerans to see. That could become a problem. The Canim had excellent night vision. The light they preferred to use, when they used any at all, was a dim, red form of illumination that was hardly enough for Aleran eyes to separate solid shapes from shadows. There was no reason to suppose that the interior of their fortress would be lit well enough to prevent the Alerans from looking extremely foolish—which was to say, helpless and weak.

And that, Tavi thought, would be a very bad message to send to the Shuaran nation.

A horn blew atop the gates, and Anag bellowed for the column to halt. He began exchanging what sounded like formal greetings with the guard atop the gate, introducing their company.

"Max," Tavi said. "Crassus. Once we get into the dark, we'll need to see our way. I think your swords should strike the proper tone."

Crassus nodded and Max grunted in the affirmative. A moment later, the huge gates swung open, wide enough to allow the column of taurga to enter three abreast.

Max and Crassus fell in on either side of Tavi, with Durias and Kitai bringing up the rear. As they passed into the blackness beneath the gates, into the tunnel that ran beneath walls a hundred feet thick, the two brothers drew their long blades and held them upright, at rest beside them. As they did so, bright tongues of flame suddenly rushed out from the hilts of the blades to their tips, golden white light that wreathed the steel and drove back the cavernous night beneath the Shuaran gates.

As the company rode out of the tunnel and into the city beyond it, they entered what looked like a large square or marketplace, where hundreds of Canim, makers and warriors alike, were hurrying past through the rain, purpose in their strides. As the light of the blazing swords began to cast harsh, long shadows against the buildings on the far side of the square, several dozen passersby stopped to stare at the troop and the Alerans as they entered the city.

Then an Aleran Legion trumpet abruptly rang out behind Tavi, sharp and silvery, crying out against the dark stones of Shuar. The opening bars of the Anthem of Eagles, the clarion call of the Princeps of Alera, shivered through the rain and the night, proud and cold and defiant. Tavi shot a quick, surprised glance over his shoulder, to see Durias lowering the trumpet, returning it to hang from its baldric at his side. The young centurion inclined his head to Tavi with a very small smile and winked.

If the glare of light had slowed foot traffic around them, the cry of the trumpet stopped it completely.

The square went deathly still and silent. Hundreds of dark Canim eyes stared intently at the visiting strangers.

Varg nudged his mount forward, glancing once at Tavi.

Without knowing precisely why, Tavi felt that the Cane wanted him to do the same. He guided his own taurg to stand beside Varg's.

"I am Varg of Narash," the grizzled Cane called out, his voice carrying throughout the city around them. "This is my *gadara*, Tavar of Alera. We ride to seek audience with Warmaster Lararl. Let any who would bar our way stand forward now."

Within seconds, a path leading to one of the exits on the far side of the square was entirely unoccupied.

"Huh," Max muttered. "Guess they know him here."

Varg let out a satisfied sound somewhere between a grunt and a growl, and made a polite, beckoning gesture to Tavi. The two of them started their mounts forward, followed closely by Max and Crassus, with their burning blades, then Durias and Kitai, and finally followed by Anag's troops, formed into a hasty honor guard.

Word apparently rushed ahead of them as they rode. Though the cavern-dark city was filled to overflowing with Canim, the street before Tavi and Varg was, without exception, perfectly empty.

It was an eerie ride. What would have been familiar crowd murmur in Alera Imperia was instead the continuous chorus of rumbling growls and snarls that comprised the Canim tongue. Though the light cast by the brothers' swords was bright, outside of that circle there were only dark shapes and thousands and thousands of gleaming red eyes—and the occasional glimpse of white fangs.

The atmosphere was not helped by the fact that Max and Crassus, at Tavi's suggestion, had slowly decreased the intensity of the flames surrounding their swords, until the Alerans' eyes had adjusted more adequately to the dim red luminescence the Canim favored for light. They still could not see *well*, but neither had they been entirely blinded as they entered the city, and avoiding moments of apparent weakness was critically important in any dealings with their predatory hosts.

Short of a miracle, there would be no chance whatsoever of escaping the fortress at night, Tavi realized. The simple lack of light would make it impossible, even if the sheer numbers of Canim hadn't made the entire idea laughable in the first place. To have enough light to see by, they'd have to light themselves up like a beacon, announcing to any Cane with eyes exactly where they were. And in daylight, of course, sneaking about was almost as unlikely. Which meant that they'd have to rely entirely upon furycraft, if it came to that—and surrounded by so much bleak stone, a woodcrafted veil would be out of the question, a windcrafted one frail and difficult to hold.

Best to avoid the need to escape, then.

If he could.

Anag took them down several steeply sloping streets that wound down the side of the plateau, all of them built with strong gates and battlements at regular intervals—the road through the pass that led up to the range of Shuar proper, until, near the base of the plateau, they stopped before the largest building they had seen so far, an enormous cube of black stone at least two hundred feet high.

After dismounting, they passed through several guard stations and past several higher-ranking officers. It took them the better part of two hours to work through the chain of command, but eventually they were shown to a chamber somewhere toward the center of the building. It was a large room, stretching out beneath a high dome overhead. Tavi was impressed by the sheer skill involved in engineering such a thing. The weight from above must have been enormous, yet the chamber's smooth dome arched gracefully, apparently unsupported by any pillar or buttress.

A red-coal fire burned in a pit in the center of the room. Beside it, a circular table no more than two feet high but nearly ten feet across sat, supporting the weight of a scale model of the fortress's defenses, complete with markers of blue stone for Canim troops, black stones for Vord, and colored green sand that, Tavi realized, represented the presence of the *croach*.

Several Shuarans, with their distinctive golden fur, were crouching on their haunches around the table, rumbling and growling at one another—except for one. That one, a rather small but burly specimen of his breed, his fur showing streaks of silver to mix with tawny gold, sat in silence, staring down at the pieces on the table, following the conversation around him with attentive twitches of his narrow ears.

Anag approached the table and inclined his head deeply to one side. "Warmaster."

The burly Cane lifted his eyes—odd, for a Cane's, since they were bright blue against the bloodred background—to the young officer and inclined his head slightly in response. The other Canim at the table immediately fell silent. "Pack second," rumbled the Warmaster. His voice was extremely deep, even for a Cane. "Where is your pack leader?"

"At Molvar, my lord," Anag replied, his tone neutral and polite. "Wounded."

"Unto death, one supposes?"

"I am uncertain, my lord," Anag responded. "Though if I may volunteer: I am no healer, my lord, but I have yet to hear of a warrior expiring from a clean, properly attended injury to the foot."

"For that to happen," the Warmaster replied, "he would need to be a warrior. Not the spawn of a forced mating of some jackal of a ritualist to a female barely more than a pup."

"As you say, my lord."

"Bring me better news next time, Anag."

"I will do my best, my lord."

The Cane rose to his feet and prowled over to them. He moved with a slight limp, though Tavi judged that only a fool would think him crippled, slow, or incapable. His armor, like Varg's, was ornate, battered, and heavily decorated with bloodred gemstones. Also like Varg's, most of the dark steel had been enameled in color, though in his case it was deep blue instead of Varg's crimson.

He inclined his head slightly—very slightly—to Varg, who matched the gesture with precise timing.

"Varg," the Warmaster rumbled.

"Lararl," Varg replied.

Lararl turned his attention to the others, eyes probing, his nose quivering. "We thought you long dead."

"Not before I kill you."

Lararl's eyes went back to Varg, and he bared his fangs in a slow, almost-leering smile. "I am pleased to see that the demons across the sea have not deprived me of the pleasure of showing your guts to the sky."

"Not yet," Tavi said. "But who knows? The night is young."

Lararl's ears quivered back and forth in a gesture of brief surprise, and his gaze shifted to Tavi. "You speak our tongue, little demon?"

"I speak it adequately. I understand it fairly well."

Lararl narrowed his eyes. "Interesting."

"Lararl, of Shuar," Varg growled. "Tavar of Alera. He is *gadara* to me, Lararl."

"As Varg is to me," Tavi added, guessing that it was the proper thing to say.

Lararl's ears quivered again, and he shook his head. "Tavar, is it? A demon *gadara*." He glanced back at the table and the model there. "Sometimes I think that the world is changing. That I am too old to change with it." He shook his head. "Varg, your word of peace for this night?"

"You have it."

Lararl nodded. "And you mine. Will you vouch for Tavar and his pack?"

Varg looked at Tavi. "Will you give your word that you and your people will abide peacefully here tonight, so long as no harm is offered to you?"

"Of course," Tavi said. "Provided we receive the same word in return."

"He will," Varg told Lararl.

The golden-furred Warmaster nodded. "And will you vouch for my word to him?"

Varg looked at Tavi. "I will. Lararl keeps his word."

Tavi nodded. "Done, then."

Lararl nodded to the other Canim in the room. "Leave us."

His officers filed out rapidly and quietly. Anag was the last out the door, and he shut it behind him.

Lararl crossed to the coal fire and crouched beside it, holding out his hands. "Sit, sit."

They did so. Tavi was grateful for the fire's warmth. The interior of Lararl's command tower was quite literally as cold as a cavern.

"There is much work for me to do," Lararl said. "What would you have of me?"

"First, your protection," Varg said. "I am here with nearly one hundred thousand of my people."

Lararl froze for a second, blue eyes locked on Varg. "Where?"

"Molvar," Varg replied. "We arrived five days ago."

Lararl sat in silence for several seconds. "And what protection do you ask of me?"

"My intention when I came here was to ask only for room enough to debark until our ships could be repaired to a condition suitable to return to Narash. Now . . ."

Lararl nodded. "No longer. Narash is no more. None of them are anymore, Varg. It's all . . ." His hand lashed out behind him and struck at the table, cracking its surface and scattering green sand. "All that hideous offal. And those things. Those Vord."

"You're sure?" Varg asked.

"Yes."

"How did it happen?" Tavi asked quietly.

"It started in Narash," Lararl replied. "The ritualists and their sects among the makers rose up against the Warmasters, with these Vord as their allies. But soon it became clear that ritualists from the other ranges were eagerly smuggling more Vord into their lands to help with their own uprisings. Soon, Warmasters in every range were putting down one rebellion after another."

Tavi could see where this was leading. "And once the Vord had a solid foothold everywhere, they turned on the ritualists."

Lararl nodded. "The stupid taurga. Now, they are all but extinct. Within days, every range was in flames. Battlepacks roamed over every portion of the countryside. There was no communication, no order. Some fought longer than others, held on longer than others—your own line, Varg, longer than any, even though the poison began in their own range. But in the end, it didn't matter. They fell. One by one, they all fell."

Tavi shivered and held his hands closer to the coals.

After a silent minute, Varg said, "Then I must ask you for sanctuary for the makers under my charge. And pledge my warriors to aid in your defense."

Lararl grunted. His eyes flicked to Tavi. "And you, Tavar?"

"I would like to ask your permission to spend a few days here, resupplying my ships and repairing damage. Then I intend to sail back to my home and, with any luck, never bother you again."

Lararl grunted, stood, and walked to the door. They all watched him.

He paused at the door.

"Varg. There is not enough food in my range to feed my own people, much less yours."

Varg's lips peeled away from his fangs.

"There may not be many ritualists left," Lararl continued. "But they are mine, now. Your people are going to die, Varg. At least I can make their deaths have meaning. At least I can give their blood to the ritualists to use to defend Shuar."

"Lararl," Varg snarled, rising. "Do *not* do this."

"My people are dying," Lararl spat. "My duty is to them. Not to you. Were our positions reversed, you would do the same, and you know it."

Tavi rose. "And what of us? What of my people?"

Lararl turned and gave Tavi a look that was pure, cold, bloodthirsty hate.

"Demon," he snarled. "Do you think we are so foolish that we do not *know* that the Vord came to Canea upon one of *your* ships? Do you think us so stupid that we have not puzzled out that it is *you* who unleashed this terror upon us, to destroy our people?"

"That is *not* true!" Tavi snarled.

"Aleran demon," Lararl spat, "you have no honor. Every word from your lips is a lie. I have a range to defend, and no time to waste on your deceit. But your people's blood will serve as well as Varg's people's." He slammed open the doors. "Guards!"

A great many warrior Canim appeared in the doorway.

Lararl turned to face them. "You will go with these guards, or you will die, here and now. Choose."

CHAPTER 18

The Shuaran guards offered them no violence or disrespect. They simply escorted Varg and the Alerans to the roof of Lararl's dark granite tower, closed the heavy metal door, and locked it, sliding home large bolts that would make it impossible to open.

Then they left them there, on the flat, open expanse of the cubic building's roof. It was nearly the size of a cohort's training field, and overlooked every other structure in the fortified city. Tavi did not need to look to know that there would be no way to climb down, no other building close enough to leap onto. There was no need for bars, locks, or guards. One would need to be able to fly to escape this prison cell.

Max stared at the closed door for a moment, then said, "They can't possibly be serious."

Crassus nodded. "It does seem a tad ingenuous. A trap?"

"They're trapping us into taking advantage of an opening that will give us a chance to warn our people and possibly escape?" Tavi asked. "That's clever of them." He shook his head and looked at Varg. "They don't know what Alerans are capable of doing, do they?"

Varg twitched one shoulder in a shrug. "Shuarans are stubborn, proud, narrow-minded. As they must be to survive this range. They have never been to your shores. They regard our reports of Aleran demons as tall tales. They do not believe you are capable of anything beyond what our ritualists can do. Our ritualists cannot fly. Therefore, you cannot either."

"I think it is nice that Alerans are not the only arrogant fools on Carna," Kitai said.

Tavi gave her an arch look. "It's a small piece of fortune that isn't going to last," he said. "Anag and some of the other Shuarans saw our Knights Aeris come back in from holding off that storm. He'll tell Lararl sooner or later. They'll realize that this is a mistake and take steps." Tavi turned to Crassus. "How long will it take you to get there and back?"

Crassus squinted up through the chilling rain at the overcast sky, evidently thinking out loud. "Depends on the weather. I can't see in this soup. I'll have to follow the road to find my way back. That means flying low. That's hard work, and slower. Also means I'll have to veil or risk getting a balest bolt shot through me." He nodded. "I can be back to Molvar by midmorning, and have our Knights Aeris back here by sundown tomorrow. Faster, if the weather clears."

"If one of our people is missing, Lararl might take it badly," Kitai pointed out.

"I took being imprisoned and sentenced to death badly," Tavi said. "It's going around."

Kitai flashed a swift, fierce grin at him.

Tavi winked at her, and turned to Crassus. "Whatever happens, we've got to open up some options. Tamper with the weather if you need to—but do *not* begin action against the Shuarans unless you absolutely must. Tell Magnus and the First Spear that as well."

"Understood, Your Highness."

Tavi turned to Varg. "Warmaster," he said formally, in Canish, "is there any word you wish passed on to your people?"

Varg showed a flash of teeth for a bare instant, then looked away, saying nothing.

"You anticipated this contingency," Tavi concluded aloud. He looked at Crassus. "Go now."

Crassus nodded, saluted sharply, clapped a hand against his brother's shoulder, and frowned in concentration. He vanished from sight behind a wind-crafted veil, and a moment later a miniature gale rose, whipping droplets of falling rain into a painful, stinging mist. Then the winds faded as the young heir of Antillus took to the skies.

Max stood silently looking up into the rain for a long moment after his brother had departed, his expression blank. Perhaps it was the rain. Tavi's ability to sense others' emotions was nowhere near as reliable as he would like it to be, but he could clearly feel the conflicting welter of worry and affection and sadness and pride and seething jealousy that poured off his friend.

Max looked down to find Tavi watching him. He averted his eyes, and Tavi felt Max close down on his emotions, walling them away from observation.

"Wish I could do that," Max said.

Tavi nodded. "Me too." He put a hand on Max's shoulder. "Max, I need your help here. The rain's getting heavier and the night's getting colder. If we don't get some shelter, we could freeze to death."

Max closed his eyes, took a deep breath, and nodded. "Right. I'm on it."

"Durias," Tavi said. "Would you assist him, please?"

The burly centurion nodded. "Yes sir, Captain."

Kitai walked over to Tavi. "You. Armor. Off."

Tavi had been wearing the Legion lorica for so long that he had virtually forgotten it was there, but Kitai was right. The temperature was dropping fast. Once it was cold enough, any flesh that touched the armor would freeze to it— and besides, wearing it under those weather conditions was rather like putting on a coat made of icicles.

Tavi felt distinctly vulnerable as he shed the steel casing, and he doubted that Max and Durias liked it any better. The two men knelt at the center of the tower, bare hands flat to the dark stone, their eyes closed. Within a moment, there was a trembling vibration in the soles of Tavi's boots, then a smooth, round half dome of stone, like a partial bubble made of solid granite, rose out of the top of the tower.

Max and Durias sat back on their heels once it was done. Then Durias rose, considered the eight-foot dome for a moment, and with casual precision drove his fist through an inch of solid rock. He ran his fingertips horizontally over the surface and did it again. Then he moved down the dome and went through the same process, until he had broken out a rough doorway leading to the dome's interior.

Max bowed and rolled his hand in an elegant flourish. "Your summer palace awaits."

They gathered their things and hurried out of the rain. It was not nearly the improvement Tavi had hoped for. They were out of the wet, but the inside of what was in essence a small cave was not precisely warm. At least, not until Max frowned ferociously in concentration, the tip of his tongue between his lips, and laid his fingertips on one wall of the dome. His hands shimmered with heat—not the savage white flame of a battlecrafted fire, but something infinitely more gentle, hardly visible, and within a moment or two the dome was as warm as a baker's kitchen.

Kitai let out a purring sound and stretched out full length upon the floor. "I like you."

Max smiled wearily at her and slumped down. "Should keep us for a while. If we can hang a cloak over the doorway, longer."

"I'll see to it," Durias said, taking off his own plain green cloak. "We should get some sleep."

"Kitai," Tavi said.

"No," she said. "I'll do it."

Max looked back and forth between them. "Do what?"

"Stand first watch," Kitai said.

Durias glanced back at them. "Do you think we need to do that? I know we're prisoners, but Lararl did give us his word that he wouldn't harm us tonight. When the Canim give their word, they mean it."

"It seems to me that Varg has Hunters that he sometimes employs when he needs to get around portions of his codes of behavior and honor that somehow conflict with his interests," Tavi said. "So far, Varg seems to have used them in order to protect the spirit of those codes, if not their letter. But it occurs to me that it would be a very small step for a Warmaster to employ his Hunters to get around the spirit while preserving the letter, if you see what I mean."

Durias frowned. "You don't think it's possible that you're judging Lararl wrongly?"

"Of course it's possible," Tavi said. "But it isn't probable. He gave us his oath of peace tonight, then stuck us on a roof in these conditions and left us here without shelter, food, or water. He's keeping the letter of his word. But not the spirit of it. So we're standing watch."

"I am standing watch," Kitai said. "Your lips are still blue."

Tavi frowned and glanced at Max's dim form. "Are they?"

"Can't tell," Max said. "Too dark in here."

"There, you see?" Kitai said. "I am the only one qualified to judge."

She pushed Durias's cloak aside and slipped out of the shelter.

The rest of them had been Legion long enough to know what to do next.

They were asleep in seconds.

Tavi woke later. The rock of the tower was hard and uncomfortable under his back, but not painfully so—he hadn't been sleeping longer than two or three hours. The stone was cool, but true to Max's word, the air inside the little shelter was still toasty warm. Tavi had passed worse nights in the field with the Legion.

The cloak over the dome's doorway moved aside, and Kitai appeared in the door. She padded silently to Tavi's side, knelt, and kissed him. Then she gave him a sleepy-eyed smile and stretched out on the floor. "Your turn."

Tavi gathered up his cloak, dry after several hours in the warmth inside the shelter, and threw it on over his shoulders before heading out into the cold and the mild sleet atop the tower. He drew the hood over his head and looked around the top of the blocky building, identifying Varg's silent form, crouched at the westernmost edge of the building. Tavi padded quietly across the wet, cold stone to stop several feet away from Varg, where he could still see the enormous Cane in his peripheral vision, and stared out over the sight below them.

Lararl's command building overlooked the fortifications below, where the battle against the Vord was raging. As far as Tavi could tell, it was going at precisely the same furious pitch as it had hours before. Still the Shuarans, in their blue-and-black armor, fought to hold the battlements, and still the Vord came on in a gleaming black tide.

From above, though, it was possible to make out far more detail.

The Vord had changed from those Tavi had seen and heard described before. Previously, he had encountered only the many-legged Keepers, bizarre, spiderlike creatures who haunted the green-glowing *croach*, the strange growth that covered the land wherever the Vord went. They were about as big as medium-sized dogs, weighing perhaps thirty or forty pounds each, had a venomous bite, and were frighteningly swift and nimble.

But he had also read his uncle's reports concerning the Vord warrior-creatures, enormous things each the size of a bull, hunched and crablike in their thick shells, with huge pincer-claws and buzzing wings that could launch them skyward.

These were different.

All of the Vord attacking the fortifications were covered in the same slippery-looking black chitin, with the same eerie angularity to it, the same oddly shaped limbs—but the similarities went no further than that.

Some of the Vord went upon two legs, monstrosities more than ten feet tall, and impossibly wide. They moved with slow, ponderous steps, lifting stones that must have weighed well over a hundred pounds, and hurled them at the fortifications like an idle boy flinging rocks into a pond. Some of them went mostly on all fours, their lower limbs freakishly oversized and overdeveloped. They were able to make tremendous leaps of forty and fifty and sixty feet at a time, like huge, hideous frogs, or fiendishly oversized crickets, attacking by slamming their spine-covered bodies violently into their foes.

The majority of the Vord in the assault had powerful shoulders and heavy arms, ending not in grasping hands but in vicious, scythelike hooks. The head was elongated, apparently eyeless, though it sported a nightmarishly oversized mouthful of curving black fangs—a bizarre fusion of wolf and mantis.

Tavi realized with a start that the Vord had somehow taken inspiration from the foe that they faced.

They had made themselves more like the Canim.

Tavi's gaze went to the fortress's defenders. The Shuaran warriors favored axes over the curving swords commonly carried by Varg's Narashans, and they used the weapons against the armored chitin of the Vord with crushing effect. The Shuarans worked methodically, in teams of two and three warriors, as the Vord tried to breach the walls. One or two warriors would pin a single Vord with spears fitted with heavy crosspieces, while a third, wielding an axe, would close in for a killing stroke.

Here and there among the defenders, Tavi spotted the figure of a black-robed ritualist, wearing the usual hooded mantle. These ritualists, however, did not sport the usual garment of pale leather Tavi had become accustomed to. Instead, theirs were made of gleaming black scales of chitin. The ritualists, Tavi realized, wore mantles made from the flesh of their foes.

Which meant that the pale leather of the mantles Sarl and the Narashan ritualists had been wearing was made of . . .

Tavi shuddered.

As he watched, one of the ritualists thrust a clawed paw-hand into a leather basket-pouch at his side, and withdrew it soaked in dark crimson blood. He flung the blood out over the edge of the battlements he defended just as a number of Vord scaled the top simultaneously, threatening to create a breach in the defenses. Tavi couldn't hear the Cane from his position, but he saw the ritualist lift his muzzle to the night sky, jaws parted in a primal howl.

There was a flicker in the air as the droplets of blood flew, green-gold sparkles, and suddenly a cloud of sickly green gas billowed forth from the empty air. The gas rolled out in an instant, engulfing the threatening Vord—who simply dissolved, convulsing in agony, their bodies liquefying with terrifying abruptness as the green cloud touched them. The ritualist lifted the bloodstained paw-hand and slammed it down, as if smashing a book down upon an insect, and the green cloud descended over the edge of the battlements just as abruptly.

Tavi had seen some of his own men slain by an identical ritual-working during his two-year battle with the Narashans. He had no qualms with watching the Vord be slain, but he was just as glad that he did not see the carnage that the ritualist had just visited upon whatever creatures were unfortunate enough to be below that section of the wall.

The Shuarans were professionals. Their tactics were calculating, brutal, and efficient. They were not battling the Vord, so much as simply butchering them as they attained the walls. From what Tavi could see, forty, perhaps even fifty Vord fell for every single casualty suffered by the Shuaran warriors.

Even so, he thought, the Vord stretched to the horizon.

They could afford to pay that price.

Tavi did not think that the Shuarans could.

"Tell me what you see, Aleran," Varg rumbled quietly.

Tavi glanced over at the grizzled Warmaster. Varg had unrolled the heavy cloak carried by all Narashan warriors. He crouched on his haunches, the cloak completely covering him, the sleet and rain sheeting down it to the surface of the tower. His hood covered all but the last inch or two of his muzzle.

"The Vord aren't using any taken," Tavi said quietly.

Varg grunted and nodded to Tavi's left. "Down there."

Tavi looked that way, to the first street above the active battlements. He spotted a number of young Canim there, adolescents and children mostly, spread out every ten or twenty feet. All of them bore short clubs and crouched beneath their cloaks against the rain, just as Varg was doing.

"Sentries," Tavi surmised. "To keep the takers from getting into the city."

"Takers smell bad," Varg said. "Make odd noise when they move. Young ones have the sharpest senses. And the takers are only a threat if one is not aware of them. Lararl has the young ones positioned all over the city." The Cane turned to look at Tavi, eyes gleaming within the depths of his hood. "But you know that is not what I mean."

"No." Tavi returned his eyes to the battle. "The Vord aren't using aerial troops. They could have created half a dozen breaches by now if they were, and forced Lararl to fall back to his next line. Instead, they're just throwing away tens of thousands of their soldiers. They're up to something."

Varg turned his gaze back to the fight. "When we were both young, I tried to teach Lararl to play *ludus*. He refused. He said that to learn war, one studies war. That games and books are a waste of time."

Tavi shook his head. "Will he truly attack your people?"

Varg nodded.

"With a foe like this out to destroy us all, he would truly put others of his own kind to death. It seems foolish to me," Tavi said.

Varg shrugged. "Shuar could barely produce enough food to sustain itself in the best of years. They imported food from other ranges. From Lararl's perspective, my people are doomed to death by slow starvation in any case. It is a dishonorable way to die. Far preferable for their lives to be spent in a useful purpose."

"Were I Lararl, I would reach for every possible weapon I could find against a threat like that."

"Were you Lararl, the one whose decisions defended your people's children, you would use the weapons you knew you could trust to destroy the enemy. You would be forced to choose who would live and who would die, Aleran. And given a choice between sacrificing the lives of your own people and the lives of neighboring enemies who were also in danger, you would protect your people, just as I would protect mine—and Lararl protects his." Varg shook his head. "He fears that he will fail his people's trust in him. It makes him almost blind. He cannot see even that much."

Tavi sighed. "Even though he's just told you he intends to murder all of your people, including your own son, and even though he's broken the spirit of his word of peace to us by putting us up here in this weather, you defend him."

Varg's chest rumbled in a warning growl. "No," the Cane said. "I understand him. There is a difference."

Tavi nodded, and was silent for a time, watching the battle below. Then he said, "What will he do next?"

Varg's ears twitched slightly, this way and that, as he pondered. "Lararl knows that when Sarl fled, he took ten thousand warriors with him. He will think Nasaug has no more than ten thousand under his command at Molvar. And so he will send thirty thousand to assault them in order to force a surrender."

"Will they?" Tavi asked.

"Ten thousand warriors against thirty thousand, in hostile territory? Only a fool would throw away his warriors' lives in such a hopeless battle." Varg showed his teeth. "But Lararl does not know that Nasaug has trained our makers into something very like warriors themselves. His thirty thousand will meet something more like sixty thousand. And Nasaug will hand them their tails."

"And then what?" Tavi asked.

Varg tilted his head slightly, staring at Tavi.

"After that, what will your people do?" Tavi asked. "Fortify Molvar? Hold it? Wait for the Vord to break through Lararl's defenses and besiege them? Then fight until they are pushed into the sea?"

Varg turned back to the fight. "What would you have me do?"

"Return to Alera with me," Tavi said.

Varg snorted, eyes glittering. "You just spent years convincing us to leave."

Tavi gestured at the land below and said, quietly, "That was before I saw this."

"And the sight made you wish to help us, Aleran?"

"If it helps, let's just say that I consider you and your people to be dead already. And you know as well as I do that it will only be a matter of time before the Vord arrive in Alera. I simply wish to spend your deaths more profitably for my own people."

Varg's ears twitched in amusement, and his mouth dropped open for a bare second.

"My people at Molvar are in danger as well," Tavi said. "It makes sense for us to assist one another until we are out of the current crisis."

"You propose an alliance," Varg mused.

"I do."

The Cane was silent for long moments more. Then he nodded once, and said, "Done."

CHAPTER 19

Amara and Bernard watched from a position of perfect concealment as the Vord annihilated the remnants of the Ceresian rear guard. The doomed *legionares* took their stand in the ruins of a nameless village beside the causeway. They locked shields, faced the foe, and fought with desperate determination to slow the oncoming enemy, to give the holders still trying to flee for the safety of the city's walls a chance to escape.

Four-legged creatures that looked something like the deadly predator-lizards of the southwestern swamps near Kalare dominated the enemy numbers. Long, low to the ground, swift, and powerful, their bodies were covered with the same dark chitin as the other Vord Amara had seen—with the addition of raised, serrated ridges down the lengths of their spines and flanks. As Amara watched, one of them snapped its jaws closed on the thigh of a *legionare*. In a flash, it had wrapped its body around the man, the motion bonelessly swift—and then it simply *writhed*, its body gliding in constant motion like a serpent circling its way up a tree branch.

The ridges ripped through steel and flesh alike, and the *legionare* screamed as he died.

The Ceresian cohort, more than three hundred men, were overrun by the Vord. Their lines held for ten seconds, then fifteen, then twenty. Then they seemed to sag and collapse inward, and the black tide of Vord swarmed over the men, rending and ripping, barely slowing down before they continued in pursuit of the band of refugees the *legionares* had given their lives to protect.

They had died for nothing.

The Vord caught the holders within two minutes.

Amara couldn't watch the holders, most of them very old or very young, die. She closed her eyes.

But she could still hear them screaming.

With so much chaos, so much confusion, so much destruction in the lands of Ceres, it had been inevitable, she told herself, desperate to distract herself with a flow of simple fact and calm deduction. Some of the steadholts had received word in time to avoid the oncoming terror. Many had not. Of those that hadn't, the majority had reacted by taking to the causeways to flee for the shelter of their High Lord's Legions—and rushed directly into the waiting talons and mandibles of the Vord.

Lord Cereus had spent his *legionares'* lives in an effort to shield the refugees for as long as possible, sending out his small cavalry forces in an effort to guide fleeing holders off the causeways and around the worst areas of danger, but there simply had not been enough time or enough men. The slow, the foolish, or the merely unlucky perished by the hundreds upon the roads of Ceres over those few desperate days.

There was nothing she and Bernard could have done. The Vord were simply too many. Any action on their part would have accomplished nothing but to reveal their presence and seal their own fates along with those of the slain refugees. Their mission was more important than that. It could save hundreds of thousands of lives. She could not afford to let compassion for those who were directly in front of her blind her to the fact that she had a greater responsibility to the whole of the Realm. Doing her job was the proper thing to do, the logical thing to do.

Still, she wept for the brave *legionares* and the poor holders, and logic was no comfort whatsoever.

She wept, but she did so in silence. In the hours that followed, the Vord overran their position in greater and greater numbers, some of them passing within yards of where she and her husband lay hidden by veil and stealth and furycrafted cloth. The enemy was gathering for the attack that would certainly fall soon upon the single Aleran strongpoint that remained to challenge them.

Ceres itself.

She had not spoken to her husband for four days.

That was, Amara thought, the worst part of the entire arrangement. Speech was a luxury that could not be afforded, not when the enemy could literally lurk beneath virtually any fallen leaf. They could move in nearly perfect silence, and complete invisibility—but the sound of voices, even in whispers, would betray the presence of Alerans more surely than nearly anything else they could do.

Legion scouts had long since developed a fairly complex series of hand gestures, capable of signaling critical information in the field, but it was by no means a substitute for speech. There was no signal language gesture for "I can't bear to look at this anymore," or, "someone is going to pay."

In the four days since they had entered occupied territory, they had discovered the scenes of multiple massacres of holders and *legionares* alike—and instances where the Vord had met less success, as well. Twice, wide swaths of woodland had been burned black, down to the very soil, and the charred remains of Vord armor and bits of tree trunk were all that remained, evidence of the fury of the Knights and lords of Ceres. In other instances, the destruction had been more limited and prosaic, but no less brutal—groups of desperate holders, some of them gifted strongly enough to make a fight of it, had unleashed all the crafting at their command, and left Vord crushed and broken on the earth, among the bodies of Aleran dead. In still other places, a lone Vord would be found dead, destroyed by what was doubtless a rogue fury, running wild and uncontrolled after the death of the Aleran who had previously guided it. And in still other places, the slaughter would be, not of Alerans, but of deer, or wild boar, or other animals of the forest, destroyed as remorselessly and ruthlessly as if they had been thinking foes of the Vord, not harmless beasts of the wild. In some places, even some of the plants had been systematically destroyed.

They had also found several pockets of the glowing green *croach*, growing and spreading, tended by no more than a handful of the spiderlike Keepers. Whatever the substance was, it seemed to feed upon the very stuff of Alera itself. The Keepers seemed to pack the living and the dead, plant and animal alike, beneath the surface of the *croach* with equal amounts of indifference. Standing several yards from the edge of one such growth, Amara fancied she could actually hear the stuff spreading, rustling leaves, here and there, as it oozed slowly outward.

They did not dare linger long near the *croach*. It quickly became clear that the area served as some kind of deposit of food or supplies for the enemy. Individiual Vord, or fast-moving groups would stream rapidly into a pocket of *croach* and thrust their heads and jaws into the stuff, wallowing like pigs at a trough, gulping down the foul-smelling sludge beneath the waxy surface in seconds before turning to race off about their business again.

At first, Amara dared to hope that their haste indicated desperation—but after the incident had repeated itself several times with precisely regular intervals, it became clear that the Vord as a whole were moving at the direction of an unseen choreographer on a scale more massive than she could have imagined. Though they rarely made sounds, and though they never spoke, the Vord *knew* where to move, when to strike, where to go to find food, to reinforce weak points. They made the communications and discipline of the Legions look crude and childish by comparison.

It was madness, all of it, sheer insanity, there in Ceres, within the Amaranth Vale itself, the longest-settled, gentlest, most-tamed heart of the Realm. Yet it was her duty to see it, to take it all in—and so she did. She looked, and she took notes, writing down everything that she saw, and comparing her notes with Bernard's, to make sure that she had not missed anything her husband had observed, and vice versa.

Sleep was difficult. They had to rest in turns, for only a few hours at a time, when they thought they could afford to stop for a bit and catch what rest they could. What Amara had seen tended to replay itself before her eyes if she lay still too long, and a single outcry during a dream could have had dire consequences. She didn't dare allow herself to sleep too deeply—and yet the constant tension, the wearing strain of unrelenting caution and stress and worry had taken a toll.

She knew it had, because even if she felt that she had somehow gone numb, herself, she could see the pressure wearing on Bernard, on his face and on the set of his shoulders. His own eyes, which had grown steadily more careworn over the past few years, were positively haunted, even if they maintained their constant, cool green vigil around them—when she saw him at all, at any rate. Most of the time, he was as invisible to her as she was to him, and they kept track of one another only by the shared knowledge of where they had intended to move and by the faint sounds of their passage.

But not speaking to Bernard, especially after watching the Vord catch that last group of refugees, was the worst of it.

The worst by far.

She intertwined her fingers with his and clutched his hand tightly. He squeezed back, a little less gently than she would have expected, and she knew that he was every bit as disturbed and furious and outraged as she was.

But they only had to last a little longer. If the First Lord was right, the battle for Ceres would draw the Vord's furycrafters into the open and allow Bernard and Amara to get a look at them. Once that was done, they could leave this nightmare and report upon what they had learned.

They leaned against one another in the darkness, while the Vord gathered to assault Ceres.

It took the foe less than a day to concentrate their forces and launch the assault upon the city.

Amara and Bernard were less than a mile and a half away from Ceres' walls, looking out over the broad valley from an abandoned steadholt running along the top of a low ridge. They crouched in the ruins of an old brick storage building that had collapsed when a particularly large old tree had toppled onto it. In normal circumstances, the Steadholder probably would have taken the opportunity to replace the old storehouse with a newer building—it had been old enough that time had been taking bites out of it in any case. Instead, the old building had just been left to lie in pieces, with the ancient tree still sprawling in the wreckage, and it provided a perfect hiding place. Bernard was able to use the branches and leaves of the tree, along with the grass still growing around the storehouse, to surround them with a woodcrafted veil, and Amara had layered it with her own subtle windcrafting, to hide the heat of their bodies from the Vord, as well as their scents. Bernard was also able to settle his earth fury into the foundation of the building beneath them, hiding them from any possible observation by means of earthcrafting. With the added security of their color-shifting cloaks, they were as well hidden as it was possible to be.

Half an hour after night fell, the Vord surged forward in silence and perfect unison.

For several moments, nothing happened—and then, without warning, Ceres blazed into light.

Amara found herself holding her breath. Had this been a normal engagement, the Legions would have engaged with arrows and flame, their archers and their Knights striking with their heaviest ranged salvos from the walls as the enemy closed in. The idea would have been to break enemy morale in the opening charge, to force him to pay heavily in the first moments of the attack on the city, to stamp heavily into the minds of the opposing soldiers and commanders that if they wanted Ceres, they would have to buy it dearly.

But against the Vord, such warfare of the mind was pointless, as were many of the rote techniques and tactics of the Legion—as too many of Ceres' *legionares* had already learned.

No arrows flew from Ceres' walls. No fire leapt out from the battlements. The city, still pitted and battle-scarred from the siege against the Legions of High Lord Kalarus, stood brilliantly lit, silent, and apparently vulnerable as the black tide washed forward.

Amara found her fingers searching for Bernard's. She grasped her husband's hand and squeezed tight as the wave of Vord crashed against the walls of Ceres.

Not a sound or motion came from the brilliantly lit city. Not a sword was lifted in resistance, not a *legionare* stood against the enemy.

The Vord swarmed against the walls, their claws sinking into the stone, climbing up it like enormous black insects. They disdained the tactics of armies, attacking gates and towers, simply scaling the walls wherever they reached them instead. The Vord blackened the land to the south, covering the fields of the broad valley around Ceres like one enormous shadow. For a moment, it looked as though the city would fall without any resistance whatsoever.

Amara knew better. Gaius Sextus commanded her defenses, and the First Lord had planned to make a fight of it.

The first Vord to climb began to crest the walls and mount the battlements.

From deeper and higher within the city, trumpets sounded, sudden and sharp and clear. Amara felt the instantaneous, massive stirring of windcrafting in the air, felt the hairs on her neck and at the base of her scalp begin to stir and rise of their own accord. The air itself seemed to dance and glitter with a hundred thousand flickering pinpoints of silver-white light, a host of miniature stars erupting into brilliant, brief life in the air and upon the trees across the whole of the Ceresian valley.

And then, with a roar that shook the city to the stones of its foundation, lightning leapt up from the city's walls to the Aleran skies, great, savage spears of scarlet and azure flame, twisting into the shapes of eagles leaping into flight, the colors and symbols of the House of Gaius. That sheet of thunder and power shattered the leading wave of Vord, tearing them from the walls by the hundreds, charring them to black powder in the air, and scattering them back over the stunned forms of their fellows following in their wake.

Once the echoes of that titanic stroke of thunder had rolled once over the land, they were followed by a chorus of smaller flashes that rained down from the skies above—by the hundreds. Strokes of lightning crashed down among the Vord, shattering and smashing dozens at a time. There, fiery gold hornet shapes of Rhodes fell to earth, and there, blazing green lightning shaped like the twin bulls of Placida sent Vord sailing fifty feet into the air. Crimson falcons of Aquitaine fell like fiery rain, each stroke tiny by comparison to the others, but striking with deadly precision and in terrible waves.

Amara stared in raw terror at the power being unleashed before her, and wished that she and her husband had found a rather safer distance from which to observe the battle. This was not the admittedly deadly power of a century of Knights attached to a Legion, or even that of multiple Legions' Knights working in concert—it was the concentrated furycraft of the lords of Alera, and it literally tore the earth asunder beneath the feet of the Vord as they advanced. The light was blinding, and she had to lift her hand to shield her eyes against it. Debris—and not all of it earth and stone, either—began to rain down all around them, cast out to the abandoned steadholt by the power of the furycraft unleashed upon the Vord. The sound was deafening, even where they crouched, and Amara desperately shifted some of Cirrus's effort into shielding their ears from the terrible din. Amara had never seen or imagined such sheer, awe-inspiring power unleashed—save once—and she suddenly wanted nothing in the world so much as to be in a very deep hole, hiding quietly until the entire business was concluded.

She did not know for how long that horrible storm of power and death raged. She knew it could not have been as long as it felt. It seemed that she crouched there for hours while lightning fell from a crystal-clear sky, raking the valley in a curtain of raw destruction.

When the silence came, Amara thought at first that her ears had simply burst under the sound. It took her a moment to realize that the flashes of light had died away, that the ground had ceased its shaking. Her eyes, dazzled by the flashes of light, could see nothing but the furylamps upon the walls of Ceres as night reclaimed the land. For a long minute, there was no sound at all—and then, once more, trumpets cried out from within the city, sharp and clear, and the gates of Ceres swung open wide—as did a dozen more openings in the wall, portals furycrafted open, the stone itself simply flowing aside like water, creating neat, new arches.

Cavalry thundered forth from the city—thousands of horses in columns, their hooves a vast pounding upon the lightning-scoured earth. The united alae of every Legion the First Lord had been able to gather took the field together, flying the colors of every city south of the Shieldwall. Fully half of their number, Amara saw, bore colors of Placidan green. The rumors they had heard about Lord Placida mounting an entire Legion had not, it seemed, been exaggerated.

As the cavalry took the field, flights of Knights Aeris winged up from the city behind them—Knights flying in formations around groups of Citizens who had taken the field against the Vord threat. As the cavalry surged forward, the aerial troops raced ahead of them, striking and disrupting the already-stunned Vord in the field. Amara saw more bolts of lightning and spheres of flame begin to blossom, illuminating the black armor segments of the Vord in stark, violent flashes. Then the cavalry reached them. Amara could only distantly hear the sound of their unit trumpets and drums, and could see little of them in the darkness, but she could not imagine that the battle could be going well for the heavily stricken Vord, caught in the open farmlands of the valley around Ceres, where they would find no refuge against the rage of the Aleran cavalry, nowhere to hide from the Knights Aeris and the furycraft of the Citizens they escorted.

After days of seeing the terror the Vord had visited upon the holders of Ceres, Amara felt only a surge of vicious satisfaction at the sight. Even if the Vord's furycrafters went into action—assuming they had survived that titanic assault at all—it might well be too late to turn the tide of this battle. The First Lord, it seemed, had broken the back of the enemy's advance.

And then, Amara watched the stars on the southern horizon began to go black, one by one.

It took her husband a moment longer to notice it, but she felt him suddenly go tense as he, too, saw it.

The darkness, whatever it was, kept swallowing the stars, more and more quickly—and a low, heavy thrumming sound filled the air.

Oh great furies, Amara thought. *Aerial troops. There must be thousands of them. Tens of thousands. Bloody crows, they blot out the stars.*

The creatures that had assaulted the city, their ground troops—the Vord had sacrificed them willingly, thrown them into the jaws of the Aleran's trap in order to draw out their Citizens and furycrafters, to goad the Alerans into revealing the positions of their most potent weapons.

The counterstroke fell with inhuman ferocity.

Amara could see very little from where she sat. But flashes of light erupted in the night sky, each revealing dark figures. All of them looked human, though she could hardly bring herself to believe that was possible. Surely the Vord could not have taken so many Knights Aeris. And certainly, it was not solely the Vord who were using firecrafting in the night skies.

The dull thud and pop of firecraftings echoed across the valley, and the calls of the cavalry's horns became more harried, disorganized, and desperate. Once, the roar of multiple windstreams deafened them and kicked up clouds of dust as several Knights Aeris went streaking over their position in a long, arching curve, perhaps seeking to flank some enemy element back in the main area of the fray.

And then from the walls of the city, a small group of heavily armored Knights Aeris leapt skyward, and, as they did, the sword of a single man at the center of the group kindled into brilliant golden light. That sword blazed brighter and brighter as the group of Knights streaked toward the battle, trailing streaks of fire behind it, like a living comet.

Not a single eye in the entire Ceresian valley could help but see that light, soaring toward the combat, and no one who saw it mistook it for anything other than precisely what it was—a naked challenge, a statement of raw defiance. She drew in a sharp breath, identifying the flickering golden flame as the banner colors of the High Lord of Rhodes.

The old man was a schemer, a man of dangerous ambition, and only the fact that his city neighbored that of the Aquitaines had prevented him from being a more serious threat to the Realm than Kalarus had been. As it was, Aquitaine had made it his first order of business to gain and maintain a solid margin of advantage and control over his predatory neighbor—but even so, Rhodes was widely known as a crafter of particular skill among the Citizenry.

Amara wondered if the man's arrogance had blinded him to the fact that Gaius was sacrificing him like a piece in a *ludus* game, hoping to draw out one of the Vord's major weapons in turn.

From somewhere to the south, on the ground or in the skies, Amara could not tell, came a piercing sound—a shriek that blended the sound of tearing metal and agonized lions, a sound that tore at her ears and ripped at her frayed nerves, that filled her with an insane desire to leap to her feet, screaming in mindless, instinctive response.

Amara had heard that sound before, and the memory filled her with icy terror.

It was the war cry of a Vord queen.

High Lord Rhodes and his personal bodyguards—Counts and Lords themselves, they had to be—streaked into the air to the south, a golden globe of light, that was suddenly surrounded by flickering, swift-moving black forms, like mosquitoes and moths gathering by the thousands around the flame of a candle in a forest at night.

A globe of sickly green-white light suddenly surged up from the earth to meet him.

Light flashed, sparks exploding in a cloud so thick that for a moment it obscured every single form in the southern sky, so bright that every broken stone, every dead branch and fallen leaf of the ruin around them cast a crisp-edged black shadow. A detonation rolled across the valley, so loud that it slapped against Amara's chest like a physical blow.

For a second, she could see nothing.

She blinked her dazzled eyes several times—and when she could see again, her stomach wrenched sharply, turning a slow circle within her belly.

A dying golden star was falling in slow, fading majesty toward the ground far below.

Amara watched, unable to move, unable to look away.

A High Lord had fallen.

Rhodes, a High Lord of Alera, surrounded by Citizens, prepared, on his guard, determined, and doing battle with all the might of the Realm around him, had fallen to the Vord queen, fallen in the instant of their meeting.

The golden light died away before the body reached the earth.

The Vord queen shrieked again, and that time Amara *did* let out a cry, the sound torn from her chest by a surge of involuntary terror. Green lightning suddenly filled the southern sky, spreading in a webwork that was *miles* across, centered upon the sphere of green-white light, upon the Vord queen, at last revealing the frantic battle being fought to the south.

The sky was filled with winged, humanoid Vord, the green lightning gleaming off the shining black plates of their chitin.

Not thousands of them.

Not tens of thousands.

Hundreds of thousands.

The Aleran forces who faced them were outnumbered, so laughably outnumbered that the very thought of giving battle was as ridiculous as that of a man with a shovel attempting to stem the ocean's tide.

The lightning faded to darkness.

The roar of approaching windstreams began to rise. Cavalry trumpets sounded the retreat, and panicked horn calls within the city began to echo them.

Amara watched numbly as the rout began—then she shook herself, focusing her mind to the task at hand. Gaius had sent one of his strongest assets out to die for that precise reason, to reveal the source of the Vord's power and give her a chance to find it.

She did not dare delay. The Vord would be overhead soon, and it would be madness to lower their veils for long—but she could not get a clear look from that distance, even with Cirrus's help, without lowering the concealing furycraftings.

She touched Bernard's wrist, and he nodded once. An instant later, the faint blurring of shadow and shape that was his woodcrafted veil was gone. She lowered her own veil as well, then held up her hands, and willed Cirrus to bring the green sphere into closer view.

The night sky blurred, then her eyes almost seemed to rush forward as her wind fury bent the light to let her see more clearly. The green sphere leapt up into crystalline clarity, and Amara focused upon High Lord Rhodes's killer.

Her breath caught in her throat, and for an instant it seemed her heart forgot to keep beating.

At the center of the sphere was a cloaked figure, skin smooth and dark, black cloth billowing about her, green-white eyes gleaming from within the depths of a heavy hood—the Vord queen.

She was the only Vord there.

Around her was a score of heavily armored Knights Aeris—Alerans, every one of them. All of them wore armor that looked like some kind of bizarre imitation of Legion lorica, made from the black chitin of the Vord, and they bore weapons of the same material. To a man, they were young—no, Amara corrected herself. They were young-*looking*.

Citizens.

The Vord queen was attended by Citizens of her own.

As Amara stared, horrified, she saw several of the Vord shaped like Knights Aeris streak by in the background. Each of them bore the limp form of a fallen Knight Aeris or Citizen. Though some were clearly wounded, none was obviously dead, and Amara realized with a sick heart that they were being captured.

The Vord would add them to their arsenal, just as they had the Citizens surrounding the queen.

One more person rode a windstream within the Vord queen's sphere.

At first Amara thought she was naked. Then she realized that the beautiful woman was covered with the dark chitin-armor as well, as close-fitting as a second skin. Her dark hair was long, flying out wildly in a cloud as she hovered there, a slender sword of Aleran steel in her hands. Her skin was pale, her expression cold and confident. Upon her chest, between the woman's breasts, rested . . . something, a gleaming lump the size of Amara's doubled fists. Amara stared for several seconds before she realized that the object was *alive*, like some kind of burrowing insect or tick, its head thrust beneath the surface of the woman's flesh.

Invidia Aquitaine flicked her sword to one side, clearing the blood of the late High Lord of Rhodes from its blade. .

The light of the green sphere faded, leaving Amara and Bernard in darkness.

CHAPTER 20

Ehren stood atop the highest tower of the citadel of Ceres, watching as the High Lord of Rhodes fell, and the battle turned against the Aleran forces. Horns frantically sounded retreat, and Knights Aeris and Citizens came racing back toward the city upon roaring gales of wind.

"Your opinion, Cursor?" the First Lord murmured.

Ehren swallowed. "Frankly, sire, I believe I'm entirely too terrified to offer you a useful opinion for the time being."

"I see," Gaius said, mild disapproval in his tone. "When you've regained control of yourself, I should appreciate it if you would please let me know."

"Very good, sire."

The First Lord clasped his hands behind his back and paced back and forth along the battlements atop the tower, his steps measured, his expression thoughtful. Thirty feet away, only ten or twelve yards overhead, a pair of Knights Aeris flew past, carrying a wounded companion between them. The young man was screaming in sheer agony, his breastplate pocked in several places by dents around horizontal slits, puncture marks that leaked scarlet. Gaius glanced up at the passing trio, then back out to the battle—though it was less a battle than a full-fledged rout, Ehren thought—without pausing his steps.

"Cursor," Gaius said. "Give me the roof, please."

"Sire?"

Gaius stopped in his tracks and gave Ehren a steady look, one eyebrow quirked in displeasure.

"As you wish, sire," Ehren said hurriedly, and padded to the stairs from the tower's roof. He went down them and took a moment to steady his breathing, then began the familiar, comforting ritual of checking each of his knives. It helped him begin to push aside the images of the battle and sort through his thoughts.

Foremost among them was that there really were a great many vordknights coming toward the city. Ehren imagined that they would be no less deadly and terrifying while hacking their way through the halls of Ceres than they had been in the skies above it. He had no desire whatsoever to discover whether or not his estimation was an accurate one.

It was not so much that Ehren was afraid to fight, as such. Oh, the thought and act alike of genuine mortal combat terrified him. It *should* terrify anyone who wasn't an idiot or a lunatic. And though he knew he was well trained and far more capable than most would guess by looking at him, he was also well aware of his limitations and, being neither a moron nor a madman, he much preferred the idea of avoiding a fight altogether.

That being the case, it seemed wise to leave the city. The vordknights, it was thought, could not match Aleran fliers in terms of sheer speed, except in short bursts of effort. Surely, the First Lord would summon his coach, and they would fall back to the next fortified position before much more time had passed. He couldn't remember the name of the position at the moment—a large town about fifty miles to the northeast on the causeway leading toward Alera Imperia.

They all lead to Alera Imperia, genius, Ehren said to himself. He put the last of his knives away, shook his head, and suddenly realized what they needed, at the moment, more than anything else. It was obvious, and the First Lord would likely have realized it already, but at least Ehren's brain was in motion again. He turned to go back up the stairs, and paused at the sound of voices on the roof of the tower.

". . . beside the point," Gaius's mellow baritone murmured. "It must be done."

A woman's voice, one Ehren had never heard before, answered him. "There will be lasting repercussions."

"Worse than the instability already unleashed, and what is likely to be added to it if you do not do as I ask?"

"That depends upon one's point of view, child," replied the woman's voice, amused.

Ehren blinked. Child? *Child?* Who could *speak* to the First Lord like that?

Gaius replied with wry amusement in his own voice. "Behold my own."

"Mmmm," she murmured, a pensive sound. "Some of your folk are among them."

"Nonetheless."

"I have no preference," she said. "Not of my own accord. Though I admit that I have grown . . . accustomed to you and yours, child."

"I ask for no exemptions," Gaius responded. "Only prevailing conditions."

She laughed, a gently mocking sound. "You, child? Seeking to prevail? Surely not."

"Time presses," Gaius said, his tone polite, but thick with an underlying urgency.

"With you and yours, it seldom does otherwise." She paused for a moment, then said, "It is entirely possible that we may never speak again."

"I have made my wishes known."

"Your father would be . . . what is the phrase?"

"Rolling in his grave," Gaius supplied.

"Yes. Were such a thing possible."

"But you will honor them?"

Ehren blinked again, not so much at the words the First Lord had used as at the intonation.

It had been a question. Not a command.

To whom would the *First Lord* speak like that?

"It has never before been done this way. But I believe so."

The First Lord's voice dropped to a lower register, relief evident in it. "Thank you."

"Gratitude?" the woman asked, her tone quietly merry. "What is the world coming to?"

Ehren, burning with curiosity, eased up the last few stairs and opened the door as silently as he possibly could, peering around it.

Gaius stood where he had before. A woman stood beside him, facing him, his equal in height. Her skin was a deep bronze, her hair silver, threaded with rare strands of scarlet and gold, though her face was younger than Ehren's own, strong and beautiful in a way he had never seen before. She wore a simple gown and shawl of what Ehren first thought was homespun, but at a startled second glance he realized that the clothing was made purely of what looked like opaque grey mist, as thick and swirling as any storm cloud, but holding its solid shape as if it were cloth.

The woman turned her head abruptly to one side, her eyes flicking toward him. They were brilliant gold. As Ehren watched, they flickered to silver—metallic silver, not simply grey—and a heartbeat later became sky blue, then green and faceted, like a masterfully cut emerald, then dark and glossy as obsidian.

Gaius turned as well, and the woman was abruptly gone. There was no flicker of a veil coming up, no blur of motion as of a windcrafter's drawing upon a fury for additional speed, nothing. One instant she was standing, regarding Ehren calmly, and the next she was simply . . . not.

Which was clearly impossible.

"Cursor," Gaius said, nodding calmly. "Something to report?"

"Sire?" Ehren blinked and recovered himself. "Ah. Yes, sire. Pardon me, I did not mean to interrupt."

Gaius lifted both eyebrows and asked, a hard little edge on his words, "Interrupt?"

"Your conversation . . ."

Gaius narrowed his eyes. "Conversation?"

Ehren coughed. "I was thinking, sire, that the vordknights depend upon wings for flight. Like birds. Birds depend upon using the air. They won't fly in a storm."

"I'd been thinking the same thing," Gaius replied with an approving nod. "What else?"

"I would also advise cutting the causeway behind us periodically as we retreat. Every mile or so should be sufficient to ensure that the enemy can't use it."

Gaius winced, but blew out a sigh. "Yes. I suppose that would be for the best."

A cold wind suddenly washed across the tower from the north, a chill blast that felt as if it must have begun at the Shieldwall and come to Ceres without crossing the intervening space between. The First Lord turned into the wind and closed his eyes for a moment, stretching out his hand with his fingers spread. Ehren saw him murmur something under his breath, then nod once. Ehren went to the tower's edge beside the First Lord, and saw the wind as it crossed the city below, and spread out into the fields beyond. Almost at once, it seemed, fog began to rise from streams and ponds.

In the air above the fields, Ehren saw that the disastrous rout had somehow been arrested, and it did not take long to see why. A second bright star of light, the glowing blade of a High Lord, had risen into the skies, and around that brilliant core of light, the battered Aleran forces had rallied. The bright scarlet of the star identified the High Lord of Aquitaine, and he had gathered what fliers remained into a cohesive force that had moved together in close formation, the sheer power of its combined windstreams sending vordknights scattering wildly through the air—a Legion shieldwall, taken to the skies.

Scarlet lightning flashed through the night, raking Vord from the air and slowing the advance of the oncoming tide. The fleeing cavalry began to emerge from beneath the shadow of the Vord, running for their lives, and only the courage and power of the few men who remained aloft and fighting the Vord sheltered them from being destroyed en masse.

The First Lord lifted his face to the evening sky and closed his eyes. He did not speak or move, but his expression became strained.

The vordknights began to reach the walls of the city, mostly the strays who had been blown that way by the disrupting gale of the Aleran aerial rear guard. The Legions defending Ceres had moved back into position after the first massive salvo of furycraft had taken them from the walls. Knights Flora and Ignus began hammering the Vord from the air with fire and arrow.

One vordknight streaked toward the tower where Ehren and the First Lord stood, only to be struck by half a dozen arrows loosed from the bows of the Knights Flora of the Crown Guard positioned on the neighboring towers. It dropped instantly, smashing into the battlements with a brittle, crackling sound, one of its wings still buzzing uselessly as it fell toward the courtyard fifty feet below.

The cold wind from the north grew colder yet, and Ehren shivered, his cloak suddenly inadequate against it. He turned to look over his shoulder, to the north, and saw the stars change from sharp, clear pinpoints of light to murky, blurry spots of silver in the night sky.

Gaius nodded once, and said, "Let's begin, then, shall we?" He turned his palms to the sky and lifted them in a single, sharp gesture.

The low-lying fog that had formed on the ground, somehow untouched by the wind, suddenly leapt skyward. It boiled up over the walls of Ceres and swallowed the tower in a sudden rush of warmer air. The fog passed them, and Ehren saw it lifting away into the sky like some enormous blanket.

Gaius sighed and lowered his arms, his shoulders slumping wearily. "Let's see if this works."

Ehren swallowed. "Sire? You don't think it's going to work?"

"The theory is sound. But we've no way of being sure, have we?"

"Ah," the young Cursor said. "What will we do if it doesn't?"

Gaius arched an eyebrow and said, calmly, "I expect we will die, Sir Ehren. Don't you?"

Thunder rumbled through the greyness overhead.

Ehren shivered, but before he had time to respond, he felt the first ice-cold raindrops begin to fall. They came one by one at first, then began to fall more and more thickly. He walked over to stand beside Gaius, who stared out at a battlefield that had been almost entirely occluded by rain. The burning sword of High Lord Aquitaine was leaving a plume of steam behind it, even as the Aleran fliers began to turn back toward the city, losing altitude as they came.

"You knew Rhodes was going to be killed when you sent him out there," Ehren said quietly.

"Did I?" Gaius asked.

"And when this is over, Aquitaine is going to look like the man who created an orderly retreat out of a rout."

"Not to quibble," Gaius murmured, "but Lord Aquitaine *is* the man who created an orderly retreat out of a rout." He shook his head. "I'll give Attis this; he always understood that the strength of a High Lord—or a First Lord, for that matter—is in the hearts and minds of those who support him."

"The sword," Ehren said. "He's using it to hold a firecrafting together. He's giving them courage."

"Mmmm," Gaius agreed. "Rhodes was powerful, in a personal sense, but he never saw any further than the ends of his own fingertips. No different than Lord Kalarus, really, except that Rhodes was more intelligent and had more dangerous neighbors."

"Far more dangerous," Ehren said. "So much so that Rhodes's life was the price of said neighbor's allegiance."

The First Lord smiled, a wintry expression that meant nothing. "The Citizenry has been blind to the threat the Vord represent, certain they would be easily overcome. That arrogance was as dangerous to us as the Vord. After tonight, it will no longer be an issue." He glanced up at the rumbling sky, where the rain continued to fall more and more thickly, and added, his tone wryly amused, "One way or another."

Then he staggered and fell to one knee.

"Sire!" Ehren said, starting forward.

The First Lord coughed, the sound horrible and hollow, over and over, each one wracking his entire body with clenching motion.

Ehren knelt beside the old man, supporting his weight when Gaius's balance failed again.

After a moment, the fit of coughing passed. The First Lord shuddered and leaned wearily against the young Cursor, his head bowed. His lips looked blue, to Ehren, his face pallid and grey.

"Sire?" Ehren asked quietly.

Gaius shook his head and spoke in a rasp. "Help me up. They mustn't see."

Ehren blinked at the First Lord for a heartbeat, then slipped one of Gaius's arms over his shoulders and rose, helping the older man to his feet.

Gaius leaned against the battlements for a moment, his hands spread across the cold, wet stone. Then he drew in a deep breath and straightened, his features composed, as the Aleran forces returned to Ceres.

Aquitaine's sword burned more and more clearly, until he and the men he had gathered around him, some two hundred or so Citizens and Knights Aeris, sailed over the walls of the city and down into the streets beyond, heading for the rally points where the Legions had already planned to gather before withdrawing. The cavalry was not far behind them, their exhausted horses running hard as they streamed back toward the city.

Aquitaine himself, instead of accompanying his men, soared up to the tower, cutting his windstream with masterful timing, landing like a man who had decided to hop over the last step in a stairway. He nodded once to Ehren, transferred his sword to his left hand, and saluted Gaius, putting his fist to his heart.

Though the fire of Aquitaine's sword was out, the metal still glowed and hissed with every raindrop. His armor, elaborate, beautifully made lorica, was crusted with a thin sheath of ice across the shoulders and upon the bracers that covered his forearms.

"It's working," Aquitaine said shortly. "Their wings can't handle the ice."

"Naturally," the First Lord replied calmly. "We'll fall back to Uvarton, cutting the causeway every mile as we go."

Aquitaine frowned and turned to stare back out toward the south. "Their greatest advantage is their mobility, their flight. We should move forward with every *legionare*, now, and take them head-on."

"Their greatest advantage is the ability of the Vord queen to coordinate their movements," Gaius countered. "If we march our men out there into the dark and the storm, it will be a hopeless mess. The Vord will have no such disadvantage. We retreat. More of our reinforcements will meet us every day."

"As will theirs," Aquitaine said. "We should hit them now, hard, try to thin them out."

"If need be, I'll ground them again, Your Grace." Gaius's eyes hardened. "We retreat."

Aquitaine frowned steadily at Gaius for a long moment. Then he said, "This is the wrong move."

"Were I a young man," Gaius said, "I would think so as well. If you would be so kind, please notify the other High Lords. Sir Ehren, please take word to the Crown Legion and to the First and Third Imperian."

Ehren and Aquitaine both saluted the First Lord. Aquitaine simply stepped up onto the battlements and dropped off the tower. The roar of his windstream came up to them a beat later. Ehren turned toward the door, but paused, looking back at the First Lord.

"Are you going to be all right, sire?"

The First Lord, his silver hair plastered to his head by the rain, stared down at the valley to the south and shook his head slowly. "None of us are going to be all right." Then he glanced at Ehren and jerked his chin in a sharp gesture toward the door. "On your way."

"Sire," Ehren said, and turned to go back down the stairs and tell the Legion commanders which way to run.

CHAPTER 21

When the sun rose the next morning, Isana was already awake. She took a brief, simple breakfast that Araris brought from the Legion's mess hall, and then put on her warmest cloak and went up to the top of the Shieldwall again. Aria fell into step beside her along the way, as she passed the High Lady's chambers.

Isana felt Aria's tension and worry at once, thick enough to breach her self-control. She frowned at the other woman. "Aria?"

"Word from the south. The First Lord has engaged the Vord."

Isana traded a quick look with Araris. "And?"

"The Vord have taken Ceres. The Legions are falling back toward Alera Imperia, trying to slow the Vord enough for refugees to stay ahead of them."

Isana drew in a quick breath. "Your husband?"

"He's well. For now." Aria shook her head. "But they confirmed that the Vord are using furycrafting, and on a significant scale. Rhodus Martinus was slain in the battle. Several dozen Citizens and nearly a hundred Knights Aeris were also killed or are unaccounted for."

Isana shuddered at that last. Unaccounted for. In the course of a normal war, one could generally expect such soldiers, missing after a battle, to have been killed and their bodies fallen in some hidden place, to have been scattered by the tides of conflict, or to have been captured by the enemy and taken to some sort of prison. When fighting the Vord, though, capture could mean something infinitely more hideous than death. Worse, it could mean that the Vord had *gained* several of the furycrafters that Alera had *lost*.

"Then we had best get to work," Isana said, doing her best to sound calm and confident.

Placidus Garius met them at the head of the stairs as they emerged into the light of predawn. He saluted crisply. "Your Highness. If you'll come this way, our engineers have just finished crafting a stairway down the northern face of the Wall."

Isana lifted an eyebrow. "There weren't any already?"

Garius fell into pace beside Isana and shook his head. "No, milady. It would be too easy for the enemy to use it against us, were we to leave a permanent stairway." His eyes flicked uneasily to the north. "They're dangerous enough without giving them any help."

"Garius," Aria asked, "did your father contact you?"

Garius turned back to look at his mother and nodded grimly. "He did. Here we are, milady." He'd led them to a staircase that ran down the northern face of the Shieldwall and into the snow-covered country beyond. He pointed to a slight rise of ground to the north. "That hill there is where the meeting is set to take place. We'll be watching from here, and you'll have help right away when things get violent."

"'When'?" Isana asked. "Not 'if'?"

Garius shook his head. "Milady . . . you haven't been up here. You don't understand. You might talk to them for an hour, or a day. But in the end, there's only one way this is going to fall out." He touched a hand to the hilt of his sword to illustrate his point.

"You don't think it's possible to reach an agreement with the Icemen?"

"No, Your Highness," Garius said, without malice. "Realistically, I just don't think it can happen."

"When is the last time anyone tried?"

Garius sighed. "You just don't—"

"Understand?" Isana asked quietly. "No. I don't. The conflict between the Icemen and Alera has been nothing but a plague on our land. I doubt it's done anything better for theirs. And given what's coming at us, we have little choice but to secure some kind of armistice, if not a peace. We need it to survive."

He gave her a brief, strained smile and a nod. "I sincerely wish you the best of luck, Your Highness."

Isana nodded. "Thank you, Garius." She turned to Araris. "Ready?"

Araris, dressed again in his mail, a sword hanging from either hip, nodded. "I'd better go down first," he said quietly. Then he started down the stairs. Isana and Aria followed.

The Shieldwall, Isana decided, looked a great deal smaller from the air than it did from ground level. The face of the enormous Wall, pitted and pocked by time and weather and war, rose beside her into a massive cliff face as she went down the stairs. Upon reaching the bottom, they found the ground covered in several inches of snow. Araris turned and began slogging through the snow, breaking a path for Isana and Aria.

As she followed Araris, Isana glanced back at the Shieldwall with an irritated frown. How was she to forge a peace amidst such mistrust? Garius might be a good soldier and a good son, but his mind was completely closed with intolerance. Couldn't the young idiot see that a peace was not merely desirable but crucial to survival?

It was enough to make Isana want to slap him.

Though the hill wasn't far away, it took them a solid quarter of an hour to reach it through the snow—only to find no one waiting for them. A slow scan around the land beyond the hilltop showed them stands of evergreens clothing increasingly high hills, but no delegation from the Icemen.

Aria frowned, looking around them, and Isana felt a surge of impatience escape the High Lady's restraint. "Where are they?"

"If Doroga is with them, they'll be waiting for the sun to rise," Isana replied.

"Why?"

"The Marat regard the sun as a higher power. They worship it, and conduct all their most important business only under its light."

"I see," Aria replied. "I suppose barbarians have many strange customs."

Isana fought down her own surge of irritation, attempting to rein it in before Aria sensed it. "Doroga is quite urbane, in most senses of the word. Furthermore, he has put himself in harm's way for the sake of the Realm twice over, and has personally saved the lives of my brother and my son. I would appreciate it if you would refrain from insulting him."

Aria's lips compressed, but she only nodded once and turned away to watch for the Iceman negotiators. The cold wind continued to blow from the north, and Isana wrapped her cloak more tightly around herself. She looked back at the Shieldwall behind them, looming black and massive in the dim light. She could see, here and there, the dark form of a *legionare* on guard, the outlines of their spears slender and wicked against the grey sky.

What must it look like, to one of the Icemen, she wondered. Isana had seen more furycraft at work than most, including the raising of siege walls, and even to her the Shieldwall seemed almost unreal in its sheer mass. Did the Icemen still tell stories of the empty hills that were suddenly rived by the great Wall? She had been told that the engineers that built it had raised the Wall in sections about half a mile long—an effort of furycrafting so massive that Isana could hardly imagine how many artisans and Citizens had been required to complete its construction.

If it seemed that way to her, what must it seem like to one of the enemy? Something out of a nightmare, perhaps, a fortress wall that spanned the length of a continent. A wall that resisted any efforts to break it down, a wall that was always watchful, always guarded, always sure to spill forth Aleran *legionares*, no matter how stealthily or carefully the Icemen approached. Alerans saw the Shieldwall as a massive defensive construction. How might the Icemen view it? As a massive prison wall? As the first of what might be many such barriers, each encroaching upon more of their territory? Or might they view it simply as an obstacle, something that had to be overcome, the way that some Alerans regarded high mountains and remote forests?

Impossible to say, since no one had asked. Or at least, no one of whom Isana was aware.

Beside her, Araris stood resolutely still, facing to the north, but his eyes were restless, flicking from one group of evergreens to the next. "I don't like this," he muttered.

"Relax," Isana said quietly. "Don't borrow trouble."

He nodded once in reply—but he kept his hands near the hilts of his weapons.

Something stirred in one of the nearby stands of trees. Araris stepped in front of Isana and turned toward it at once, his fingers wrapping around the hilts of his swords. Aria, in response, turned in the opposite direction, watching their backs in case the first movement was some sort of distraction from the true assault, and Isana could clearly sense her wariness and tension.

The trees shook and swayed. Snow fell from their needles and branches to the ground. They shook again, and a massive creature plodded into sight from among the trees, shouldering the smaller evergreens aside without detectable effort. The gargant was huge, even for its breed, a great, dark-furred beast, with tusks as thick as Isana's forearms thrusting up from its lower jaw. The large beast would have outweighed a dozen prize bulls, easily, and Isana was familiar with the sheer, overwhelming physical power of a gargant—and with the rider who rode on the back of this one.

He was a Marat, one of the pale-skinned barbarians who lived to the east of Isanaholt in Calderon. Like the beast he rode, he was large for his kind, nearly as tall as Isana's brother and even more heavily layered in muscle. His white hair was held back from his face by a band of plaited red cloth, and a sleeveless tunic of the same color, open down the front, barely managed to stretch across his chest and shoulders without splitting. Despite the snow and cold, beyond the tunic and a pair of deer-hide trousers, he wore nothing—neither a cloak, nor shoes, nor a hood, although he did carry a long-handled cudgel in his right hand. He looked perfectly comfortable in the freezing weather and lifted a hand to the Alerans in greeting as his gargant shambled steadily through the snow and up the little hillock.

"The Marat mediator?" Aria asked.

"Doroga," Isana called.

The Marat lifted a broad hand. "Good morning," he rumbled in reply. He seized a braided leather cord hanging from the saddle blanket that covered the gargant's back, and swung down to earth as lightly as a boy coming down from an apple tree. "Isana and Scarred-Face," he said, nodding to Isana and Araris. He peered at Araris, and said, "Cut your hair. You look different."

Araris inclined his head. "Somewhat, yes. And not very."

Doroga nodded judiciously and studied Aria for a moment. "This one I do not know."

Isana sensed Aria stiffen, as she replied, voice cold, "My elder brother was killed at the First Battle of Calderon. He died defending Gaius Septimus from your kind."

Isana barely stopped herself from sucking in a surprised and outraged breath through her teeth and half turned toward Aria. "Doroga is a friend—"

Doroga grunted as he held up a hand, casually interrupting Isana. He eyed Aria without excitement. "My father, three brothers, half a dozen cousins, my mother, her two sisters, and my closest friend died there as well," he answered in a steady voice. "All of us lost the battle at the Field of Fools, lady of the cold voice."

"So all is forgotten?" Aria spat. "Is that what you mean?"

"There is no use in chewing at old wounds." He stepped in front of Aria, whose eyes were level with his, and met her gaze. His voice came out a low rumble, calm, steady, and not in the least bit yielding. "That battle ended more than twenty years ago. Today's battle is fought far to the south, where many good Alerans, your own husband among them, now fight the Vord. In case you have forgotten, our purpose here is to make peace." Doroga's eyes flashed, and though his expression never changed, behind him the enormous dark-furred gargant suddenly let out a warning rumble that shook snowflakes from the surface of the snowbound ground around them. "Let it be, Aleran."

The High Lady of Placida's eyes narrowed, and Isana could clearly sense her tension and anger. She held her breath, hardly daring to add anything to an already-overstrained situation. She could hardly imagine talks progressing smoothly were Aria to roast their mediator to the ground—or, she supposed, if the enormous Marat, his nose only inches from Lady Placida's, snapped her slender neck. Isana realized, belatedly, that in delivering his words, Doroga had closed the distance purposefully, in order to be too close to be cleanly struck by the long dueling sword Aria wore at her hip should she attempt to draw it. The Marat was no fool.

Aria's hand twitched once toward the hilt of her blade, then she slowly moved both hands down to her thighs and smoothed her dress. She nodded once, sharply, to Doroga, the gesture in itself a kind of wordless concession, and turned to walk several paces away through the snow and stand facing the Shieldwall.

Isana stared at Aria, still surprised at the woman's vehemence. Surely Doroga's presence had come as no surprise to her. Had she been overwhelmed by her emotions at the sight of one of the Marat, despite herself? The High Lords and Ladies of Alera were, generally speaking, past masters of controlling their responses—yet Aria had nearly attacked Doroga outright. Isana felt certain that had he demonstrated any aggression in response, beyond simply standing up for himself in the face of a threat, violence almost certainly would have ensued.

She decided that it was most politic to simply regard the incident as over. It would also, she thought, be a fine idea to ignore the way the snow had swiftly melted away to nothing out to an arm's length all around Aria's feet.

She turned to Doroga, to find him frowning pensively at the High Lady as well, his dark eyes thoughtful. His gaze met hers, and she clearly sensed his puzzlement and concern. He, too, had found something odd in Aria's reaction.

No, Isana thought. The barbarian chieftain was definitely no fool.

Isana smiled at him, and gestured toward the sun. "We stand before The One, Doroga. When will the Icemen arrive?"

Doroga leaned casually on his cudgel, and drawled, "The Gadrim-ha were here before either of us." He called out something in a tongue she did not understand.

Isana's eyes widened as half a dozen mounds of snow within thirty feet of them trembled, then rose into the forms of the white-furred Icemen. They simply stood, like men rising from a nap, and shook themselves, flinging fine, powdery snow from their pelts unmelted. Though none of them were as tall as Doroga, their overlong arms and overbroad shoulders carried the same suggestion of tremendous power. They bore crude weapons—axes and spears, made from wood and leather bands and stone—but Isana noted that the weapons looked far thicker and heavier than anything any but the strongest of Alerans could wield without using earthcraft.

She also noted that the Icemen rose in a circle around the Alerans. Araris was at her side in an instant, sword in hand, raised to a low guard. His eyes were focused into the middle distance, keeping track of all movement in his field of view with his peripheral vision, rather than watching any single foe. Aria, moving in the same instant, put her back to Araris's, her own sword in hand.

The Icemen finished shaking themselves and turned to face Isana in a motion curious for its unison. One of them, a bit larger than the others, growled at Doroga. The Marat rumbled something in reply. The leader of the Icemen repeated his original growl, shaking his spear for emphasis.

"Hngh," Doroga said, shaking his head. He turned to Isana, and said, "Big Shoulders says that you have drawn weapons. Your actions say that you did not come to speak of peace."

Isana stared around at the Icemen for a moment. Then she licked her lips, and said, "I might say the same by the way they have arranged themselves all around us."

Doroga snorted in dark amusement, and rumbled at the Icemen, evidently conveying her words.

Big Shoulders, apparently the leader of the group, narrowed his eyes to slits, staring at Doroga. Then he simply looked around the circle of Icemen.

Isana felt a sudden surge of emotion, a mixture of feelings so complex and tangled that she could not possibly have given it a name. There was no source to the feeling—just the sensation itself, as loud and as clear and as pure as the emotions of an infant suddenly finding itself hungry or uncomfortable. Had it been a physical sound, it would have left her ears ringing. Even so, the sensation was overwhelming. She shuddered and swayed in place.

The Icemen, meanwhile, moved as a group, careful to come no closer to the Alerans as they all gathered behind Big Shoulders, watching the Alerans from beneath heavy, shaggy brows. None of them spoke.

None of them *spoke*.

"Good," Doroga said, nodding to Big Shoulders. He turned to Isana. "Your turn, Alerans. Put away your weapons."

"Do it," Isana said quietly.

"Isana—" Aria began, her eyes narrowed.

"That wasn't a request, Your Grace," Isana said in a quietly firm tone. "Weapons away, both of you."

Isana fancied that she could hear Aria's teeth grinding—but both she and Araris sheathed their swords.

"There," Doroga said in satisfaction. "Now you are all acting like something more than honor-hungry whelps." He gestured at Isana. "Tell him what you want."

Isana lifted her eyebrows. "What do you mean?"

"Alerans like to make this kind of thing complicated," Doroga said, shaking his head. "Should see all the papers some scribe of Sextus's kept sending me to mark on. Couldn't read them, even when I learned to read. What is the *point* of your letters if you don't use them to make yourself understood?"

Isana blinked at the Marat.

Doroga gestured impatiently. "Tell him what you want, Isana. It is not a complicated task."

Isana turned to Big Shoulders. "We want peace," she told the Iceman. "We wish our peoples to stop fighting one another."

Doroga rumbled quietly. From Big Shoulders, Isana felt a surge of surprise, then confusion, then outrage. His heavy brows lowered even farther.

Doroga said something else, the thick-sounding words spilling out rapidly.

Big Shoulders pointed at the Shieldwall with his spear, speaking in a clear, anger-edged voice.

Doroga nodded and told Isana, "He wishes to know if your words will bind Fire Sword."

Isana frowned at the Marat.

"The High Lord back there," Doroga clarified.

"Yes," Isana replied. "I speak with the voice of the First Lord himself. High Lord Antillus is obliged to honor my words as Sextus's own."

Doroga relayed her words to Big Shoulders, who grounded the butt of his spear upon hearing them, frowning at Isana. The Iceman stared at her for a silent minute.

On an impulse, Isana withdrew the control she normally used to restrain her emotions entirely. She turned toward Big Shoulders. Her words wouldn't be important, she somehow knew. What was critical was the intention behind them.

"I know that much blood has been spilled. But we now face a threat that could prove deadly to both of our peoples. We wish to make peace, so that more of our folk will be able to fight this enemy. But this is also an opportunity to create a lasting peace between our peoples, the way we have begun to do with the Marat."

Big Shoulders stared for another silent minute, as Doroga relayed her words. The Iceman glanced aside at Doroga when he was finished. They exchanged words several times, while Doroga nodded, his expression calm.

Big Shoulders grunted. There was another surge of that complex emotion, too fast and dense and thick for her to sort out, then as one the Icemen turned and shambled off into the snow. They entered the nearest copse of trees and vanished from sight.

Isana let out her breath slowly and realized that her hands were shaking— and not with the cold.

"And so," Aria said. "They decline."

"I'm not sure they do," Isana replied. "Doroga?"

Doroga shrugged. "Big Shoulders believes you. But his word is not the word of all the Gadrim-ha. He is the youngest of his station, the least influential. He goes now to confer with the other war leaders."

"They couldn't be bothered to send a senior representative?" Aria asked.

"They assumed it was a trap," Doroga replied with a shrug. "And acted accordingly."

"How long?" Isana asked. "How long before he returns?"

"As long as it takes," Doroga replied calmly. "Patience is important when dealing with the Gadrim-ha."

"Time is critical," Isana replied quietly.

Doroga grunted. "Then perhaps Sextus should have sent someone sooner than today." He nodded to them, then went back to the gargant, Walker, and hauled himself swiftly up the saddle rope. He lifted his cudgel in salute, and said, "I will signal your *legionares* when they have returned."

"Thank you," Isana replied.

The Marat nodded to them and muttered something to Walker. The gargant turned and plodded calmly through the snow, following the footsteps of the Icemen.

Isana watched him go, then exhaled heavily and nodded. "Come on," she said quietly to her companions.

Aria's eyes lingered on the trees where the foreigners had disappeared. "Where are we going?"

"Back to the Wall," Isana said. "There are questions that need answers."

CHAPTER 22

Amara leaned close to her husband to whisper directly into his ear, and said, "We must talk."

Bernard nodded. Then he put his hand on the ground, and Amara felt a faint tremor in the earth beneath their feet as he called upon his earth fury, Brutus, to create a hiding place. A few seconds later, the ground under them simply began to flow away, a slithery sensation in the soles of her feet, and they sank downward.

Amara shuddered as walls of earth reached up to surround them. The view, as the night sky with its sudden, horribly cold sleet receded, must have been almost exactly like that had by a corpse as it was lowered into a grave. A moment later, all view of the sky vanished as the earth above them flowed into the form of a roof to the small chamber Bernard had created, leaving them in complete, subterranean darkness.

"We can talk here," he murmured. He spoke in little more than a whisper, but even so, after days of silence, it almost seemed like a shout to Amara.

She conveyed to him everything she had seen at the end of the battle.

Bernard exhaled heavily. "Lady Aquitaine. Taken?"

Amara shook her head, then realized that in the darkness he could not see the gesture. "I don't think so. The people we've seen taken were just walking corpses. They never had any expressions on their faces. They weren't . . ." She sighed in frustration. "They all looked like something was missing."

"I know exactly what you mean," Bernard rumbled.

"Lady Aquitaine looked . . . I'm not sure. Smug. Or excited. Or afraid. There was something underneath the surface. And she looked quite healthy. So did the Citizens I saw near her."

"Bloody crows," Bernard said. "Would even *she* side with the Vord against Alera?"

"I don't know," Amara said. "Once, I wouldn't have thought anyone would do such a thing."

"No," Bernard said. "It's got to be some other kind of control. If you saw them taking prisoners, then it would appear that the Vord intend to place them under similar constraints."

"That was my thought as well," Amara said. "But what are we to *do* about it?"

"Take our findings to the First Lord," Bernard replied.

"The Legions are already running," Amara countered. "We would have difficulty catching him—never mind the fact that we have not yet completed our mission."

"We observed their crafters during the battle, just as he wished."

"Observing and understanding are not the same thing." She fumbled for his hand and squeezed it. "Right now, I can't tell the First Lord anything but superficial details. We need to understand more before it will do any good. We've got to see what's going on before we go back."

Bernard made an unhappy growling sound, low in his chest.

"You don't agree?"

"I'm getting tired of sleeping on the ground. Must be getting old," Bernard said. "What do you have in mind?"

She squeezed his hand tight. "We have an idea which direction they took the prisoners. I think we should find out what's being done to them."

Bernard was quiet for a moment before he said, "Whatever they're doing, it seems obvious that they're going to be doing it in a very well-protected location."

"I know."

"We won't be dodging the occasional patrol or outbound raiding party. They'll have real sentries. A lot of them."

"I know that, too," she said. "But so far, none of the Vord have spotted us. If I didn't think we had a real chance of succeeding, I wouldn't even suggest it."

Bernard was silent for a long moment. Then he said, very quietly, "One condition."

"All right," she said.

"Once we get what we need, I want you to get out, immediately. Fly, fast as you can, back to the First Lord."

"Don't be ridiculous," she snapped.

"Nothing ridiculous about it," he said. "If you leave at once, odds are excellent that you'll make it back to the First Lord. If you stay with me, you'll double your risk of being found and killed before you can get the information back."

"But you—"

"Have worked alone before, love. I'll be harder to locate alone in any case. You won't be doing anything but improving my odds of getting out."

Amara frowned at the darkness. "And you're quite sure that you're not doing this simply to protect your poor little helpless wife?"

He let out a quick, amused chuckle. "Don't let her hear you refer to her like that. She'll call up a windstorm that rips the hide right off you."

"Bernard, I'm serious."

His fingers stroked over hers, the motion somehow reassuring. "So am I. If we're going to take on additional risk, I want to be crowbegotten sure that what we learn gets back to Gaius." He paused meditatively, then added, "And if it makes my poor little helpless wife a little more likely to come out of it in one piece, that's a happy coincidence."

She reached out in the dark and found his face, cupping his cheek with the fingers of her free hand. "Maddening man."

"I am what I am, Countess," he replied, and kissed her palm gently. "We'd best get moving. There's not much air in here."

Amara sighed. "Back to quiet again. I miss talking to you."

"Patience, love. We'll have plenty of time for that when the work is done."

She leaned over and kissed his mouth, lingering for a moment, mouth moving slowly and intently on his.

Bernard let out a growling exhale. "There are some things I miss, too."

"Such as?"

"We'll discuss them when we're finished," he said. "At length."

Amara found herself smiling into the dark. "Good. Anything to make you more determined to get home."

His fingers squeezed hers. Then she felt the earth begin to tremble again, and the light of the gloom-shrouded night bloomed like a darkling sunrise above them. They rose slowly and emerged into the cold, sleeting evening. Without needing to signal one another, they brought up the concealing furycraftings again, their furies winding layers of veils around them even as their cloaks changed their hues, darkening to become one with the night.

Bernard signaled that he would take the lead, then started out into the night, the sound of rattling sleet blanketing the few sounds he made as he moved. Amara wasn't sure of their direction, in the gloom, but she knew that Bernard had a nearly supernatural facility with fieldcraft. He would lead them to the south, in the direction the Vord had taken the Aleran prisoners—and away from their friends and allies, who were retreating from the Vord.

Amara shivered against the cold and the sleet, and fervently hoped that she had been right in her assessment of their abilities—and that she had not just committed herself and her husband to cold and pitiless deaths at the hands of their inhuman foes.

CHAPTER 23

"There's frozen ground back in Alera, too, soldier," Valiar Marcus barked. "Without a palisade, we'll be easy meat for the first gang of Shuarans to come along. So put your back into it and dig, or I'll have you at a whipping post until your balls freeze and drop off."

The startled *legionare*, one of the Free Aleran troopers, started up from where he sat, his face showing chagrin that quickly turned to sullen anger. The spear of *legionares* working on that section of the palisade wall turned darkening faces toward him.

Bloody crows, Marcus thought. *It was perhaps unwise to threaten a fanatical former slave with a lashing.* He had no desire to fight eight men by himself, but neither could the First Spear back down from any show of open insubordination.

Marcus turned to square his shoulders and face the men, keeping them all within his field of vision. "You know how the Legions maintain discipline, *legionare*, or ought to."

The recalcitrant *legionare*, perhaps bolstered by the support of his fellows, drawled, "And maybe it's time that changed, centurion."

Marcus took one step forward, called up strength from the earth, and struck the man with a backhanded blow. The *legionare* was flung from his feet and crashed into the stack of loose poles that the Legions had brought with them from Alera. The man and the material spilled into a disorderly sprawl. The *legionare* moaned once and lay in a senseless puddle.

Marcus regarded the man distantly for a moment, and said, "I disagree." He turned his gaze to the other *legionares*, who stood stunned and staring, and said in a quiet voice, "You'll have to work a bit harder to get your section put up in time, gentlemen."

A tall, wiry man in the helmet of a centurion from the Free Aleran came striding down the line of men erecting the camp's palisade and paused, glowering at the men in front of Marcus. His eyes swept back and forth across them, and fastened on the man on the ground. He grunted, turned to Marcus, and gave him a nod. "First Spear."

"Centurion," Marcus replied.

"Problem with these men?"

"I've been giving them a motivational talk," Marcus said.

The Free Aleran centurion glanced at the unconscious man. He didn't quite smile. "You men are lucky. I'd have had you all at the whipping post."

"But—" protested one of the ex-slaves.

"And I'd have been right to do it," the centurion snapped. "We told you when you signed on that the Free Aleran Legion was not about taking vengeance. We told you that you would be held to the standards of behavior of every other Legion, dealt with in the same way as any free soldier. Now get your lazy asses to work before I decide that the First Spear was too lenient on you, interpret your actions as refusal to obey a direct order while the Legion is in enemy territory, and have you all hanged."

The men were shocked from their stasis by the centurion's words, perhaps. In any case, they leapt back to the work with a will.

Marcus faced off with the centurion and nodded to him. "Thank you," he said in a quieter tone.

"Bugger off, you crowbitten piece of Citizen bootlicking trash, *sir*," the centurion responded in a voice just as quiet as Marcus's. "You don't know these men, or what they've seen. If you have a problem with our *legionares*—even idiots like Bartillus, there—you deal with it through our officers. Sir."

"There is no *our*, here, centurion," Marcus replied, narrowing his eyes. "We're all Alerans here. We'll all die together if it comes to a fight with the Shuarans."

The centurion glared at Marcus a moment longer. Then he grunted, a tone of vague assent, and turned to start back down the line of laboring men. He barked orders for a pair of them to carry the unconscious Bartillus to the healers.

Marcus watched him go and shook his head. Bloody crows, he must be going senile not to have realized how sharp the division between the former slaves and the First Aleran had been. In the wrong situation, they would be as eager to fight the First Aleran as they would the Canim.

And besides that, he admitted to himself, the Free Aleran centurion had a point. Had the men he'd been passing been members of the Crown Legion, or of the First Imperian, he would most likely have spoken to the centurion in charge of the men, though he was technically within his rights to brace the men directly for such an obvious breach of discipline.

Within his rights, but unwise. And it sent the wrong message to the men of both Legions—that the command of the expedition did not trust the Free Aleran's officers. He would avoid a repetition of such foolishness in the future.

"First Spear!" Marcus looked up from his thoughts to spot one of Magnus's runners charging toward him. The young man came to a panting halt and saluted him. "Sir!"

Marcus restrained a sigh, and declined to tell the valet that "sir" was used to address officers, not centurions. "What is it, son?"

"Sir, Sir Magnus's compliments, and a message from the Princeps has arrived, sir. He said you would wish to be informed immediately."

Marcus nodded once, sharply. "Take me to the messenger."

Marcus watched Foss and his best men struggle to save Antillus Crassus's life. The young Knight Tribune, wounded in a dozen places, lay almost completely still in the healing tub, his breathing barely disturbing the water. His skin showed fresh, pink patches where he must have, in desperation, closed a dozen more such wounds as the ones he still sported. Given that he had likely done it while flying—and likely while fighting as well—it was a wonder the boy was alive at all.

He had flown into the Legion's camp, barely conscious, and collapsed two of the Legion's white canvas tents as he crashed to earth. He had been taken from the wreckage directly to the healers, and had not yet woken to give any message.

"Foss?" Magnus asked again. The old Cursor Callidus stood at the healer's right hand, intently focused upon the wounded man.

Foss shook his wide shoulders in irritation and growled under his breath. The big man's black hair and beard were too long for the letter of the regulations, but the Tribune Medica was, frankly, too good at his job to be called to task for them. "I'm trying to stack up grains of sand, here, Magnus, and you keep bumping my bloody arm. Go to the bloody crows and let me work."

Marcus turned and hurried from the tent, crossing the open stretch of ground that lay between the tents of the First Aleran's healers and those of the Legion of ex-slaves. He strode into the tent and looked around.

The Tribune Medica rose from where he sat at a small table, writing in a ledger. He frowned at Marcus warily. "First Spear."

"Sir," Marcus said, saluting the man. "We have word from the Princeps, but his messenger is gravely wounded. I had hoped that you would lend us Dorotea."

"I would," the other man said. "But she's busy. It seems one of our *legionares* was rather badly injured by some overzealous centurion."

Marcus looked past the Tribune to see the hapless Bartillus lying senseless in a healing tub, his lower face bruised and swollen all along his jawline. Kneeling behind him, her fingers resting lightly on his temples, was a woman in a plain grey homespun gown. She was lean, dark-haired, and exquisitely beautiful. She wore no jewelry or adornment, save for the slender, sinister metal band of a discipline collar at her throat.

Even as Marcus watched, he saw the wounded man's jaw shift weirdly beneath his skin. Seconds later, the swelling began to subside and the bruises began to lighten.

"This is a minor and routine injury, sir," Marcus said. "And the messenger's life might depend on securing the most skilled healer in the camp. Our Tribune Medica is pressing hard at his limits."

The Free Aleran Tribune grunted. "I'll send her over presently."

"With respect, sir," Marcus said, "Antillus Crassus is dying now."

The woman's eyes opened instantly, and she met Marcus's gaze with her own. Her stare was penetrating. She removed her hands from Bartillus's head and rose to approach the Tribune Medica.

"I've knitted the bone and controlled the swelling, sir," she said in a soft voice, her eyes downcast. "I'd be happy to help Tribune Antillus."

The Tribune frowned at her, then at Marcus. Then he waved his hand in a vague gesture, and said, "Don't be gone any longer than you need to be."

"Yes, sir," Dorotea answered. She looked up at Marcus briefly. "I'm ready, First Spear."

Marcus nodded to her, and they hurried to cross the field back toward the First Aleran's healers.

"The Princeps told you who I am," the woman observed.

"Aye, Your Grace."

She shook her head wearily. "No, no, no. I am no longer that woman."

"Because of that collar," Marcus said. "There must be some way to remove it."

"I don't want to remove it," she said calmly. "To be honest, I like the person I am now a great deal more than who I once was."

"That's the collar talking," Marcus said quietly.

Dorotea, the former High Lady of Antillus, walked for several steps before she admitted, "Possibly. However, the fact is that there is no future for High

Lady Antillus, whereas Dorotea has saved lives, helped people, and done more good in the past three years than she had in her entire previous life."

"But you're trapped there," Marcus said. "Bound to obey the commands of others. Forbidden to do harm, even to defend yourself."

"And liking it that way, First Spear." She looked ahead to the healer's tent. "How severe are my son's injuries?"

"I'm no healer," Marcus replied. "But I've seen Foss handle very serious injuries. Some of them were my own. If he's struggling . . ."

Dorotea nodded once, her expression serene. "Then we shall see what we shall see." She glanced obliquely at Marcus. "Does my son know?"

Marcus shook his head.

She nodded. "I should prefer to keep it that way. It's better for everyone."

"Of course."

"I thank you." Dorotea's eyes flickered with uncertainty and fear, and her footsteps increased in speed as they drew near the tent. "Oh," she breathed. "Oh, I can . . . He's in so much *pain*."

Marcus did not follow her. A few seconds after Dorotea entered the tent, Magnus pushed the flap aside and walked up to Marcus, his eyes hard.

"What in the name of the great furies do you think you're doing?" he hissed at Marcus. "You know who she is."

"Yes," Marcus said placidly.

"And it never occurred to you that she might well hold a grudge against the Crown for the way her brother and his resources were destroyed? That she might resent her current status intensely enough to strike out at the Crown in vengeance?"

"She's bound to do no harm," Marcus pointed out.

"And she'll not *need* to do any harm to kill the Princeps, if he is in trouble. All she'll have to do is fail to save the messenger. Given her limits, how often in a *lifetime* of waiting could such an opportunity for vengeance present itself?"

"If the messenger was anyone else, I'd agree with you," Marcus said calmly. "She won't allow her child to die to satisfy her vengeance—presuming that she wants such a thing."

The Cursor stared steadily at Marcus for a long moment. Then he said, softly, "And if you're wrong?"

"I'm not."

The old Cursor's eyes narrowed. "You've given it much more thought than I would have expected from a career soldier."

Tension made an iron bar of the First Spear's neck, but he forced himself not to allow it to spread to his shoulders and back, where Magnus would have no trouble observing it. "Wasn't a hard batch of thinking," Marcus said, keeping his tone even and confident. "I was there when the two of them came down to join the First Aleran. Saw them together. She doted on that boy."

Magnus made a noise that seemed to be a grudging agreement. His worried eyes shifted from Marcus to the healer's tent. "I'd best be inside, in case Crassus wakes."

"Go ahead," Marcus said. He glanced across the open ground to the walls of the city of Molvar, barely half a mile away. "There's plenty of work to be done on the palisade, still, and we want it in place before we move the stores up from the ships."

Magnus nodded. "What of the Narashans?"

"They're making camp on the plain on the opposite side of the city," Marcus said. "I'm making arrangements to establish runners between our camps."

Magnus arched an eyebrow in silent question.

"They're the closest thing we have to an ally," Marcus said.

"The enemy of my enemy is my friend?" the Cursor asked.

"The enemy of my enemy is just that," Marcus replied. "It's foolish to assume anything more. But we share a common interest that is threatened by a larger foe. If Narashan relations with the Shuarans fall to bits, Nasaug is practical enough to take any help he can get."

"And if our relations with the Shuarans fall out, there is a bond between Nasaug and the Free Aleran," Magnus murmured. "Enough of one to convince them to assist us?"

"No knowing," the First Spear replied. "Can't hurt to keep talking to them."

"Agreed," Magnus said. "I'll send someone as soon as we know something. Meanwhile, let the Knights Aeris know that they may be needed to fly at a moment's notice."

"Aye."

The elderly Cursor nodded and turned to head back into the healer's tent.

Marcus watched him go, then raised a hand to rub at the wooden muscles on the back of his neck. *Crows take it, what is the matter with me today?* Magnus was right to be suspicious. Valiar Marcus might be a consummate soldier, a stalwart veteran, but such men did not tend to make such delicate and dangerous wagers with the safety of someone like the Princeps—or if they did make them, they put their money on the conservative side of the bet. What in the world had prompted him to fetch Lady Antillus to assist Crassus without first conceiving a convincing explanation as to why Marcus would bring her?

The First Spear turned on a heel and marched back out toward the palisades, taking a route that would let him walk past the barracks area of the Legion's Knights.

There was plenty of work to occupy his mind—which was likely the problem.

Crassus survived.

Marcus strode into the healer's tent three hours later, to find the young Tribune lying on a cot, covered by a blanket. Lady Antillus was nowhere to be seen, but Magnus was sitting on a camp stool beside the cot, a simple wooden framework with a sheet of canvas serving as the bed. Foss hovered nearby and seemed to be busy cleaning out a tub—but Marcus could all but feel the man itching to tell them to leave his patient to recover in peace.

Magnus nodded to the First Spear as he entered. "He's dozing," he said quietly. "But I wanted you here when I asked him to speak."

"Certainly." Marcus came to stand beside Magnus, frowning down at the young man. Crassus was pale, but whole. Where there had been three or four wounds on his shoulders and head, there was only the pink skin of freshly healed flesh. The wounds were all punctures—lines no more than two inches wide that had gaped like open mouths over deep wounds. Marcus would have thought them to be dagger wounds, had it happened to the boy on the streets of an Aleran city.

But what the crows had given the boy such wounds in the skies over Canea?

"Crassus," Magnus said quietly, touching the boy's shoulder. "Tribune. Report."

Crassus opened his eyes, and took a moment to focus them, first on the roof of the tent, and then upon Magnus. "The Princeps. He's imprisoned on the roof of a tower. Sent me to let you know what was going on, and to lead the Knights Aeris back to be ready to extract him if need be."

Magnus spluttered, "If *need* be? He's been imprisoned. What more need does he *need*?"

The First Spear firmly stopped himself from beginning his next sentence with the word "obviously." "Could be that he thinks there might be some advantage to be gained if he stays where he is," Marcus said.

Crassus looked up at him and nodded. In short, simple sentences, he described their journey to the fortified city of Shuar, what they had learned about the events of the past three years in Canea, and of their encounter with its master.

"He's after information," Magnus said. "Whatever the Shuarans know about the Vord. Crows take his arrogant eyes, that boy will be the death of me. He should never expose himself to such danger. This is why there *are* Cursors in the *first* place!"

"He's the Princeps," Marcus said firmly. "Crassus, what are his orders?"

"To bring the Knights Aeris back with me to Shuar," Crassus replied. "But he doesn't know everything."

"At least someone realizes it," Magnus muttered darkly.

The First Spear restrained himself from shaking the Cursor. "What did you see on the way back?"

"Survivors," Crassus said. "Narashan survivors. Twenty, maybe thirty thousand. They're being held in a camp about ten miles from Shuar. Lararl's ritualists are draining their blood to fuel their sorcery."

"Bloody crows," Marcus breathed. "If Nasaug hears that . . ."

"His entire force will march within the hour," the Cursor said grimly. "Is that where you got hurt, son?"

"No, sir," Crassus replied. "I was attacked when I was about halfway back here."

Marcus clenched his jaw and kept quiet.

"The Vord," Crassus said. "Lararl has his entire force at Shuar, defending the fortifications. But they've tunneled their way beneath them, into the center of the plateau. They're pouring up out of the ground like ants." He grimaced. "And some of them fly. They dropped on me when I was off my guard, trying to get a good look at the forces on the ground."

Dead silence filled the tent.

Magnus began to speak, then paused, swallowed, licked his lips, and rasped, "How many?"

"I can't be certain. My best guess is that there are eighty, maybe ninety thousand of them. They're marching toward Shuar. They'll be there in a day, two at most."

"Bloody crows," Foss breathed. Marcus turned to see the healer staring at Crassus, his expression stunned.

"Well," Magnus said, his voice a monotone. "Well, well, well. First Spear?"

Marcus blew out a breath. "I'd say this just turned from a diplomatic mission into a retreat. We need to get the Princeps back here and take him back to Alera before the Vord overrun Shuar and come for us. We should send the Knights Aeris to get the Princeps and his companions. We'll expedite repairs and get off this frozen rock."

Crassus pushed himself up, and swung his legs down off the cot.

"Hey," Foss snapped. "You can't do that. Lie down before you tear those wounds open again."

Crassus shook his head. "I've got to go with them."

"The crows you do," Foss replied. "Lie down. That's an order."

Magnus lifted a hand to forestall the healer. "Crassus is right, Foss. Our Knights Aeris have only a vague idea of where the city is, much less where the

Princeps is located within it. And I daresay, they cannot fly as well concealed as the boy was. They'll need to take a route that leads them around the Vord in the interior."

Crassus nodded to Foss. "If they go without me, there's no guarantee that they'll even reach the Princeps, much less find him and get him out in one piece."

Foss shook his head. "If you go haring off right now, flying and fighting like you haven't a care in the world, you're going to rip open those wounds." The big healer moved to the side of the cot, put a hand on Crassus's shoulder, and looked the young man in the eyes. "Do you hear me? If you don't rest now, you are likely going to die."

"Yes," Crassus said, his voice calm and utterly weary. "Where is my armor?"

CHAPTER 24

Tavi sat with his feet dangling over the edge of Lararl's tower and watched the on-going battle below. Farther along the tower's roof, Varg and Durias sat together, also watching, speaking quietly to one another. The next day had dawned cold but clear, and without the constant chill of the rain and sleet, the rooftop was bear-able, given short breaks inside the warmth offered by the earthcrafted shelter.

Tavi could only admire the effectiveness and efficiency of the Shuarans' de-fense against the Vord, against an enemy so vast that he literally could not read-ily number them, despite a clear day and hours of trying. A few hours ago, it had occurred to him that it was more like watching the sea surge forward than ob-serving an enemy army in action. The Shuarans stood defiantly against that tide, and wave after wave broke upon the granite of their determination.

Tavi shivered. It had not been a pleasant realization.

Though the mountain might stand for a while, the sea would eventually wear it away.

In the end, the sea always won.

Maximus approached, his bootsteps distinctive on the stone roof. Tavi glanced back and saw Max's shadow puddled against his feet. Noon.

"Two days. He should have been back by yesterday evening," Max said qui-etly. "We should have heard from him or seen something."

"There's no need to panic yet," Tavi said calmly. "There might have been a delay on the other end, something that required his help. Or he might be out there, waiting for nightfall before making the run in."

"He'd have found a spot in line of sight, and windcrafted his voice to you," Max disagreed.

Privately, Tavi had begun to think along the same lines, but there was no point in deepening Maximus's concern for his brother by agreeing with him. Besides which, it was not as though they had a great many options, short of attempting to smash their way clear of Shuar. That wouldn't go well, at least not for long. It was a simple question of numbers.

"Be patient, Max," Tavi said. "I know it's difficult for you when there's nothing around to smash or flirt with, but I'd take it as a favor."

Max grunted and set one of his boots lightly against the back of Tavi's armor and mimed a faint push. "Would you care for a flying lesson, Your Highness? Though in all fairness, I should warn you that it might give the lie to your honorific."

Tavi looked back over his shoulder and grinned at his friend. Max settled down on the edge of the roof with him and watched the fight.

"They can't win this," Max said quietly.

"I know that," Tavi said. "They know it, too. A lot of them won't admit it to themselves, but they know."

"The Vord aren't going to stop here," Max said. "Are they?"

"No," Tavi said. "Alera was fortunate and decisive enough to smash them when they were weakest. We established ourselves as the primary threat to them. So they came here to where they would have more opportunity to spread and reproduce. They won't make the same mistake twice."

"Bloody crows," Max sighed. "I thought you would say something like that." He jerked his chin at the vast force of nightmarish Vord. "We couldn't stop that. Not with all the Legions in Alera, and every crafter to boot."

"Not with standard tactics, no," Tavi said.

Max grunted. "You have something in mind?"

Tavi smiled slightly. It was a better answer than "I have no idea how we'll survive this," without actually crossing the line into speaking a falsehood to his friend.

Max eyed him for a moment, then nodded, his big frame relaxing visibly. "Fine," he said. "Be that way."

"Thank you," Tavi replied. "I will."

Max was quiet for a moment more, watching the battle. "Seems a shame. Great furies, the Canim have guts."

"That wasn't exactly unexpected. Not after what the Narashans did to us."

Max waved a hand. "Even so."

Tavi nodded. "I know what you mean."

"Is there anything that can be done for them?"

Tavi shook his head. "I don't think so. Not given their attitude toward us. Lararl is determined to hold out, and enough of his people believe it's possible to enable him to keep his position of authority."

"I suppose," Max answered. "I'm not sure our people would act any differently. Most of the High Lords would die fighting rather than be driven from their lands."

"We'll see. And before too long."

The words had a sobering effect upon Tavi's friend. He was quiet for several more moments.

"What do we do about Crassus?" Max asked.

"We wait," Tavi replied. "For now. If he hasn't made contact by this evening, we'll consider our alternatives."

"He's all right," Max said. "He's faster than a hungry crow, and bloody near impossible to see while he's flying. He's fine."

Of course, if that was true, where *was* Crassus? Again, Tavi refrained from speaking his mind. "I haven't seen anything here that could present a real threat to him."

Max nodded, then sighed. "Maybe old Magnus is up to something. Holding him back for some reason."

"Maybe."

Max growled and rose to his feet, pacing restlessly. "I just can't stomach waiting around and doing nothing."

Tavi reached into one of the leather pouches on his belt and produced a stick of charcoal and several folded pieces of parchment. "Here," he said. "Take these and draw a map of the city. Every building you can see from up here. It might come in handy if we need to walk out for some reason."

Max took the paper and charcoal. "You aren't going to last long as First Lord if you go around handing your *singulares* compulsory homework, my lord."

"I know. But if I'm forced to spend my time listening to all their complaining, I'll knife myself and save the assassins the bother."

Max snorted and ambled away, surveying the Canim city and beginning to draw on the topmost sheet of paper.

Kitai emerged from the shelter and settled down beside Tavi, watching the battle with mild disinterest. "That was kind of you."

"Hmm?"

"Giving Max something to occupy his mind."

"Oh, that," Tavi said. "He's quite a bit brighter than he lets on. He kept passing marks at the Academy for two years, despite the fact that he debauched himself practically every night. If I didn't give him something to do, he'd drive us all insane."

"A pity there is not more privacy," Kitai murmured. "I could certainly use something to occupy my . . . mind." She smiled and found Tavi's hand with hers. "Walk with me?"

Tavi gave her a bemused smile. "That won't take long."

Kitai jerked her chin toward the carnage at the fortifications. "I'm tired of looking at that. You should be, too."

Tavi gave the battle one last glance and shook his head. "Perhaps you're right, but . . ." They rose and began pacing the edge of the roof. When they were the farthest they could get from the others on the roof, Tavi asked, "What's on your mind?"

"We should have heard from Crassus by now," she said.

"Yes."

"And so you do nothing?"

"I am waiting."

Kitai absorbed that for a moment, her expression serious. "Since I have known you, I have learned the single greatest activity at which you have little skill—sitting patiently." Her green eyes searched his. "Especially not in the face of so massive a threat, *chala*."

Tavi gave her half of a smile. "You're worried that I've given in to despair."

She opened her hand, palm up, and shrugged. "It is one possibility. But I am mostly worried because you are not acting like yourself. I expected you to have formulated half a dozen overly complicated escape plans by now."

Tavi shook his head. "No."

Kitai nodded. "Why not?"

"Because we need to wait," Tavi said. He turned his gaze to the city below. "The air's full of it. Nothing we do will accomplish anything—yet. We need to wait."

"For what?"

Tavi shrugged. "Honestly? I'm not sure. It's just . . ." He searched for words and found none. He shrugged at her again.

"Instinct," Kitai said.

"Yes," he said.

"You've had them before."

"Yes."

Kitai studied his eyes, then nodded, and said, "Reason enough."

Horns suddenly brayed in the streets below the tower.

Tavi had to take several steps to be able to see their source, on the street at the tower's base. Half a dozen taurga came down the street at full speed, lungs heaving loudly, bellowing their complaints. Canim of the city scattered before them, and one of the mounted Canim sent up another warning blast on his horn. The party of blue-armored warriors thundered to a halt at the base of the tower, and the leader of the column dismounted without bothering to secure his beast, and hurried inside.

The Canim left outside to care for the mounts looked exhausted. Their armor was battered, and minor wounds were in evidence on most of them. They'd obviously seen combat recently.

Tavi frowned. All the fighting was at the western edge of the city. These riders had entered from the east. Which raised the singular question: Whom had that patrol been fighting?

The Shuarans wouldn't be fighting one another—not in the face of a threat like the Vord. Only three other parties could possibly be responsible. There was no way the taurga could have outrun Aleran Knights Aeris, and after two years of fighting Nasaug back in the Amaranth Vale, Tavi knew well how difficult it was to get the drop on the Canim commander. If Nasaug had gone on the offensive, Tavi thought it unlikely that so many riders would have escaped an attack.

Which left only one likely suspect . . .

Tavi felt his heartbeat begin to quicken and a trembling sensation low in his belly.

"There," he told Kitai. "That's it."

Anag and a contingent of guards came to take them to Lararl within the hour.

"No," Tavi told them calmly. "We're not going anywhere. Tell Lararl that we've come to see him once already. If he wants to speak to us again, he can come up here."

Anag stared at him for a moment. Then he said, "This is Lararl's tower. Here, you do what he says."

Tavi showed Anag his teeth as he folded his arms. "Apparently not."

Anag growled and put his paw-hand to his sword.

Tavi sensed it when Maximus and Kitai, standing close behind him, tensed up. He did not move himself. He simply stared steadily at Anag.

Varg stepped forward in the precise instant that Anag's anger began to waver. He stopped beside Tavi, and said, "Lararl has shamed himself enough without you adding to it, Anag."

The younger Cane hesitated, his eyes flicking from Tavi to Varg.

Varg didn't reach for his weapon. He strode forward to stand within range of Anag's as-yet-undrawn blade without a flicker of apprehension. "You will go to Lararl," Varg said. "You will tell him that we await him here." Varg moved his arm then, slowly putting his hand to his weapon in a display made quietly deadly by the utter stillness in the rest of his body. "You will tell him that I am disinclined to be moved anywhere by any will but my own."

Anag was still for a few seconds more, then leaned his head to one side in acknowledgment and vanished from the rooftop, taking the other guards with him.

Max let out an explosive breath. "Bloody crows, Tavi."

Varg turned his head slightly to stare at Tavi. He had not, Tavi noted, taken his hand from his weapon. His voice came out in a deep, threatening basso growl. "Why?"

Tavi met Varg's gaze as he answered. "Because circumstances have changed. Lararl needs us, or he would have left us to rot up here."

Varg let out a rumbling growl, and Tavi found himself centering his balance, in case he needed to avoid a sudden strike—but the sound proved to be more pensive than angered, and Varg lowered his paw-hand from his sword's hilt.

"Besides," Tavi said, "Lararl abused your people's sense of honor and obligation. I find myself unconcerned with protecting his pride."

Varg made another thoughtful rumbling sound. "Have a care, Tavar. Lararl is not swift to forgive. And he never forgets."

"I am not one of his subordinates," Tavi replied.

Varg flicked his ears in acknowledgment. "No. You have declared your intention to replace him as a leader."

"In a manner of speaking," Tavi said, showing Varg his teeth in another smile, "that is precisely what I intend to do."

Lararl came to the rooftop alone.

Anag and several other apprehensive-looking Canim stood by while Lararl shut the door in their faces and turned to Varg. "My guards may be going deaf," the golden-furred Warmaster snarled. "Because only a fool or a madman would have spoken the words they brought to me."

Varg faced Lararl without any kind of movement.

Lararl stepped forward to stand directly in front of Varg, and the two Canim put their hands to their swords in precisely the same instant.

Silence reigned on the rooftop for a full minute, the sounds of the battle below rising and falling with the breeze, like some enormous, gruesome surf pounding upon a seashore.

"Give me one reason," Lararl snarled, "not to kill you here and now."

"I will give you three," Varg answered, and inclined the tip of his nose slightly toward the stone shelter the Alerans had crafted.

There was a vague sense of movement in the darkness within, then a slender-looking Cane clad in soft grey-and-black cloth glided silently out of the darkness. Immediately after, two more similarly clad, younger Canim flowed out behind the first, taking up a silent, passive stance on either side of the first.

Behind Tavi, Max hissed in a breath of surprise, and he did not need to look to see that Max's hand had gone to the hilt of his sword. "Bloody crows. Hunters."

Tavi suppressed his own startled reaction. He recognized the gear of the three Canim. The trio that had nearly gutted him during the war against Nasaug had been dressed identically.

Beside him, Kitai narrowed her eyes in suspicion, and Tavi felt the surge of surprise and . . . annoyance, he thought, as she spoke. "When did *they* slip in there?" She paused, and something faintly impressed entered her whisper. "*How* did they get up here at all?"

"They can't have been in there more than half an hour," Tavi murmured. "That was the last time one of us went inside to warm up."

"I saw and heard nothing." Kitai's eyes glittered, and her teeth showed in a quick smile. "That was well done."

Lararl eyed the three Hunters for a moment, then turned his attention back to Varg.

"Since the battle with your enemy seems to have clouded your vision," Varg said, "I will explain matters to you. It is possible for you to kill me. But you cannot be sure of stopping my Hunters from carrying word of such an act to Nasaug. Even if you do, Nasaug is my wisest student. He will very likely assume that you have killed me and react accordingly.

"If you can count, you will see that the Alerans are missing a member of their party. Doubtless, he has already returned to their Legions to report what you have done so far. It is my belief that they remain imprisoned largely as a matter of respect—which they have given, even when it has not been given to them." Varg showed his teeth. "Finally, it is possible that I kill you, in which case your people are left without a Warmaster.

"Nothing you do with that weapon," Varg concluded, "will help your people. It will leave them without a Warmaster—or it will create more enemies. Is that what you want for them, Lararl?"

The other Cane shivered, and Tavi could all but see the rage rolling off him.

Then Lararl let out an explosive snarl and turned to stalk several paces away.

Varg released the hilt of his weapon and glanced at Tavi.

Tavi raised his voice. "Your defenses are the most impressive I have ever seen, Warmaster," he said to Lararl.

The Canim glanced back at Tavi, his eyes angry, wary.

"But impressive or not, they are still fortifications. You can't move them, adjust them—and they are all positioned to prevent an enemy from entering your range at all. The highest wall in the world is useless if the enemy can march around it." Tavi took a slow breath. If he'd guessed correctly, his next words would show it. If he hadn't . . . well. At least he was armed. "How did the Vord bypass your defenses?"

Lararl's eyes narrowed still farther. "I did not say the Vord had done so."

"Those soldiers who arrived earlier were wounded by something," Tavi said. "If they'd been fighting my people, they never would have escaped on taurga. If they'd been fighting Varg's warriors, you would have sent someone to execute him or just let him rot on this rooftop. Instead, you sent Anag, whom we have reason to trust and respect. It was not a gesture of anger or retaliation." Tavi nodded out toward the battle. "The enemy are many. Once behind your defenses, it would take only a fraction of the forces out there to devastate your range."

Lararl said nothing. Tavi's mouth felt dry.

"Warmaster," Tavi said, "it seems clear to me that if you wish to protect your people, you need our help to do it."

Lararl bared his fangs. They were impressive. Tavi forced himself to keep his expression steady and blank. Then the golden Cane looked away. His ears twitched, almost imperceptibly, in assent.

Tavi let out a slow breath. It was harder to keep the relief from his face than it had been to disguise his apprehension.

After a stilted pause, Lararl spoke, biting off the words savagely. "My forces are stationed at the entry points to the range. The Vord tunneled under them. A large force is now among the estates and markets of the makers. Killing."

Varg rumbled, a sound of unmistakable hatred.

"More of them pour in by the hour," Lararl continued. "It will not be long before we are outnumbered in the rear areas as well as at the fortifications. Then . . ." He spread his hands and closed them together, as if squeezing the juice from a fruit.

"You need our help," Tavi said quietly.

"Help?" Lararl said. An almost-hysterical edge of frustration entered his voice. "Help? What could you do?" He drew his sword and jabbed it at the horde spreading over the plains below. "What could *anyone* do against that? We will fight. But there can be no victory. This is the end."

"That depends upon your definition of victory, Warmaster," Tavi said quietly.

"Shuar cannot be held," Lararl snarled.

"Is Shuar the land?" Tavi asked. "Is it the hills and stones and trees? Is Shuar the rivers, the walls, the towers?"

Lararl had turned to stare at Tavi intently.

"Or is it the people?" Tavi said quietly. "Your people, Warmaster."

Lararl's ears shivered in reaction, a portion of Canim body language Tavi had never seen.

"What," Lararl growled, "do you mean?"

"It's possible that your people could be saved, sir. Some of them, in any case."

"How?"

Tavi spread his hands. "I'm not yet sure," he said. "I need more information."

"What information?"

"Everything you have regarding the war with the Vord, in every range. All of it."

Varg was also staring hard at Tavi. "What do you expect to learn?"

"I cannot tell you that."

"For what reason?" Varg demanded.

"Because among the enemy is at least one queen. The Vord queens are able to sense the thoughts of others if they can get close enough. Your Hunters have proven that it is possible to approach closely to Lararl's command by means of stealth. It is entirely possible, even likely, that the queens have been gathering information directly from the thoughts of the Shuaran officers—possibly even from your own thoughts, Warmaster Lararl."

Lararl growled in his throat, the sound pensive. "You know this enemy."

"I would not presume to say that," Tavi said. "But I know them better than you. And, for now, whatever secrets your intelligence on them might reveal is best kept safe by being locked in one location." He tapped his temple with one finger. "I believe that it may be possible to help you and your people, Warmaster. If you will extend me a measure of trust."

Lararl stared steadily at Tavi, but remained silent.

"It is obvious that simple force of arms is insufficient. We must outthink them, outmaneuver them." Tavi glanced at Varg and inclined his head slightly to one side. "As I did to Sarl in Alera."

Lararl's gaze moved to Varg. "Well?"

Varg nodded slowly to Tavi, the Aleran gesture peculiar on the Cane. "Lararl. You have said yourself that you have no way to defeat the foe. Were this range mine and these people my own, I would listen to him." He looked over at his Shuaran counterpart. "Tavar took a force of barely more than seven thousand and fought Sarl and fifty thousand conscripts, plus Nasaug's ten thousand warriors, to a two-year stalemate. Give him what he wants."

Lararl was silent for a moment more. Trumpets blew in the city, and a mounted force of several hundred Canim warriors rode their taurga toward the eastern gates of the city—an advance party for the larger infantry force that had to be preparing to march to the Shuaran interior.

The golden Cane shuddered again. Then he flicked his ears in a sharp gesture of assent, spun to face Tavi fully, and beckoned him with a curt gesture of his hand as he strode toward the door leading back into the tower. "Demon—" He paused and growled deep in his chest, baring his fangs. "Tavar. Come with me."

"Crows," Max breathed under his breath. The big Antillan took his hand from his sword. "How did you know about the Vord?"

"I guessed."

"You *guessed*?" Max hissed. He shook his head. "You take too many chances, Calderon."

"It was necessary," Tavi said. "Besides, I was right."

"One of these days, you're going to be wrong."

"Not today," Tavi said. "Stay here so that Crassus can make contact."

Max frowned at Tavi worriedly. Then he saluted. "Be careful."

Tavi put a hand on his friend's shoulder. Then he turned and strode down into the darkness of the tower, following Lararl.

CHAPTER 25

Tavi wasn't sure how long he'd been working in Lararl's cavernous hall when the door opened and a guard, his eyes narrowed against the relative brightness of the torches Tavi had requested, admitted Kitai.

Tavi looked up from his place among half a dozen Cane-sized sand tables. They were meant to be used by a Cane squatting in a comfortable crouch, but were an awkward height for an Aleran—too tall to sit beside them, too short to be practical while standing. His back hurt. He straightened, wincing, as Kitai shut the door behind her.

"Crassus is here," Kitai said without preamble. "He was attacked by the Vord on his way back to the port. He had to circle wide of them on the way back. He's injured."

Tavi chewed on his lower lip. "How bad is it?"

"Maximus is seeing to him, but he's exhausted." Kitai walked closer and gave Tavi a calm kiss on the cheek. As she did, she whispered, "The rest of the Legion's Knights Aeris are at hand, unseen. Crassus says that the Shuarans have several thousand of Varg's people held prisoner in a camp not far from here."

Tavi smiled and kissed her cheek in return. "Tell them to stand by," he breathed in reply. "And to say nothing to Varg."

Kitai gave a slight nod and turned her eyes to the sand tables, examining each of them. Sheaves of paper lay stacked beside them, held down with simple weights made of polished black stone. "What is this?"

Tavi turned to the tables and raked his fingers back through his hair. "The Canim ranges," he replied. He pointed at one of the stacks of paper with a toe. "And reports taken from each."

Kitai frowned at the tables and pages. "You've read all of these?"

Tavi waggled his hand in a so-so gesture. "I'm not as familiar with their script as I'd like to be."

Kitai sniffed. "It's just as senseless as Aleran writing."

"Yes," Tavi said, "but I've had years to practice Aleran."

She smiled slightly. "What have you learned?"

Tavi shook his head. "Plenty. I'm just not sure what to make of it all." He pointed at the first table, where a number of small black stones and white stones marked Vord and Canim forces, respectively. They were scattered everywhere over the table. "Narash. Varg's range. They were the first to be attacked. The reports from there are the most confused and conflicting."

Kitai glanced up sharply at him. "It was intentional."

Tavi nodded. "I think the Vord established several different nests, keeping as quiet as they could for as long as they could, then attacked simultaneously, causing as much havoc and confusion as possible. From what I can tell, most of the Narashan commanders initially thought they were being attacked by their neighbors. By the time they realized the truth, it was too late."

He gestured at the next tables in succession. "Kadan, Rengal, Irgat . . . They all fell within the next year."

He blew out a breath to keep from shuddering. Each Canim nation had been home to a populace nearly as great as Alera's, though settled into a much smaller geographical region. Despite their armies, the dark power of their ritualists, the savagely protective nature of the Canim with regard to their territories, each of them had fallen as steadily and surely as a field of wheat before a farmer's scythe.

Tavi nodded to the next table. "Maraul. They held out for nearly a year. But by then they were cut off from Shuar, surrounded. Then . . ." Tavi shrugged. "Shuar was the only range left."

"What are you looking for?" Kitai asked.

Tavi shook his head. "I'm not sure yet. I've been looking for patterns. Trying to see how they think, how they operate."

"The Vord?" Kitai asked. "Or the Canim?"

Tavi shot her a quick smile. "Yes," he replied. The smile faded. "Though at the moment, I'd be thrilled at the prospect of having the Canim as a long-term worry."

Kitai regarded him with calm, serious eyes. "Crassus says that there are as many as eighty or ninety thousand Vord already in central Shuar."

Tavi frowned at the news. Eighty or ninety thousand. Fighting that many Vord on open ground would be little more than suicide for the Aleran Legions. Their only chance would be to fight beside Nasaug's troops—and that was hardly a proposition that his men would enjoy. Two years of war had made for plenty of hard feelings on both sides.

For just a moment, staring at the sand tables, at the enormous number of black stones, and the relatively few white ones opposing them, Tavi felt at a complete loss. Only a few years ago, he had been nothing but a shepherd. No, not even that. His uncle had been the shepherd. Tavi had been an *apprentice* shepherd.

Oh, of course, now he had a title: His Royal Highness, Gaius Octavian, Princeps of the Realm, heir apparent to the Crown of Alera.

With that and a sharp knife, he could slice bread.

How was he supposed to deal with this situation? How was he supposed to make the choices before him—choices that would send Alerans and Canim alike to their deaths? Was he merely arrogant, to think that he was the best person to decide? Or was he quietly, calmly insane?

Kitai's slim, warm hand slid over the back of his neck, and he looked up into her eyes.

"I don't know if I can do this," he told her in a near whisper.

Her stare grew intent. "You must," she said, just as quietly. "The Vord will not stop here."

"I know," Tavi said. "But . . . I can't even manifest a fury, Kitai. How am I supposed to stop what we've seen out there?"

"Aleran. When has the lack of a manifest fury stopped you before?"

"This is different," Tavi said quietly. "It's bigger. It's more complex. If the Vord aren't stopped . . ." He shook his head. "It's the end. Of everything. The Canim. My people. Yours. Nothing will be left."

He felt Kitai's hand touch his chin and lift his head, turning him quite firmly toward her. She leaned into him, pulling him down, and kissed his mouth. It was a long, slow, heavy kiss, and when she finally drew her mouth from his, her eyes were huge, their green darkened to mere rings of emerald.

"Aleran," she said quietly. "True power has nothing to do with furies." She pressed her thumb firmly to the center of his forehead. "Strong, stupid enemies are easily defeated. Intelligent foes are always dangerous. You have grown in strength. Do not permit yourself to grow in stupidity." Her hand moved to caress his cheek. "You are one of the most dangerous men I know."

Tavi studied her seriously. "Do you really think that?"

She nodded once. "I am frightened, Aleran. The Vord frighten me. What they might do to my people terrifies me."

He stared into her eyes. "What are you saying?"

"Fear is an enemy. Respect it. But do not let it conquer you before the fight has begun."

Tavi turned his eyes to the sand tables again. "I'm afraid," he said, after a moment. "Afraid that I'll fail to stop them. That people depending on me to protect them will die."

She nodded slowly. "I understand it," Kitai said. "Before, there was always someone else, someone above you, who could intervene. Who could shield you. Your mother and your uncle. Maestro Killian. Gaius Sextus."

"Here," Tavi said, "it's just me. There's no one else to rely on."

"And no one else to blame," Kitai said.

Tavi bowed his head for a moment. "I feel . . . too small for this, somehow."

"You would be a fool to feel any other way," Kitai said. She twined her fingers in his. "There are many things at which I am skilled. I ride well. I climb well. I steal well. I fight and dance and love well. My instincts are second to none." She picked up one of the stacks of paper and glanced over it. "But this . . . no. Making sense of a hundred little pieces of information. It is not for me.

"That is *your* gift, Aleran." She offered him the stack of papers. "Knowledge is your weapon." Her eyes glittered. "Kill them with it."

Tavi took a deep breath and accepted the papers in silence.

"Maraul," he blurted, three hours later.

Kitai looked up from where she had sat down with several handfuls of white and black stones, after carrying word back to the roof. She had been playing some kind of game involving scratches marked on the stone with one of her knives, and where the stones sat upon intersections of the lines. She looked at him levelly for a moment, then rolled her eyes, and said, "Why didn't I think of that?"

"Maraul," Tavi said again. "It was right in front of me. That's the point to focus on. Why did they hold out for a year against the Vord when their neighbors fell in three or four months? What was different?"

Kitai tilted her head. "Their armies were more capable? They seem to have the respect of the Narashans."

Tavi shook his head. "By the time they were attacked, the Vord had spread to three other ranges. Superior-quality troops can make up for a world of difference in numbers, but even the best troops get tired, wounded, disorganized. The Vord would have worn them down."

"Better tactical positioning?" Kitai offered.

Tavi shook his head and gestured at the appropriate sand table. "It's a swamp. There are few natural defensive points, and even those are fairly weak."

"What was it, then?"

"Exactly," Tavi said. "What?" He seized the stack of documents next to the model-Maraul table and began reading.

It took him another two hours to turn up a reasonable theory—and even that had only been possible because of the report, precise in its detail, from one of Lararl's Hunters to the Warmaster. Shuaran Hunters, it seemed, had been tasked to observe the fighting in Maraul, to gather intelligence on both their neighbors and the invaders. Somehow that knowledge made Tavi feel a bit more comfortable than he had been before.

The doors to the room swung open, and Lararl entered, with Anag trailing in his wake. The burly, golden-haired Cane strode directly over to Tavi. "Well?"

"Did you post the extra guards?" Tavi asked.

Lararl narrowed his eyes, but his ears flicked in assent. "Every doorway in the tower. No Vord skulker is going to get within a hundred feet of you."

Tavi nodded. "I think I've got an idea of what we need to do."

There was a moment of silence.

"Perhaps," Lararl growled, "you would share your thoughts."

"It is annoying when he does that," Kitai said, "is it not?"

Anag's ears quivered in amusement, but the young Cane said nothing.

"Before I explain," Tavi said, "perhaps Varg should be here, too."

Lararl grunted, and glanced at Anag.

Anag vanished, heading for the stairs to the tower's roof. He returned with Varg within moments. The big, black-furred Cane exchanged a Canim-style nod with Lararl, then Tavi, and walked over to stand over the sand table representing Maraul.

Tavi began speaking without preamble. "Our experience with the Vord has taught us that their greatest strength is also their greatest weakness—centralized leadership."

"These queens you spoke of," Lararl rumbled.

Tavi nodded. "The queens command the Vord around them absolutely— they'll take actions that will result in death without hesitation if she commands it."

Varg let out a low growl. "But they do not think on their own."

"Not very well, at any rate," Tavi confirmed. "Without a queen to lead them, the Vord are little more than animals.

"They operate in a specific manner. The queen who escaped Alera came here and established a colony, somewhere out of sight. She produced two more queens, who would then have departed in order to establish their own colonies, and so on."

"Tripling the number of Vord and queens each time," Lararl said.

"Maybe not," Tavi said. He began picking up the black and white stones from the map of Maraul. "Here is where concentrations of Vord massed for the attack," he said, laying them out again, in more or less separate lines opposing one another at the edge of the range. "According to your reports, Warmaster, the Vord attacked Maraul here, first." He moved one black stone at the northernmost end of the line forward. "Then here." He moved adjacent stones on either side of the center. "Then here, twenty miles farther on each time." He moved the next two stones in succession. "And so on. Each time they advanced, they rippled forward in this same pattern."

Varg narrowed his eyes and studied the map, his tail lashing. "Orders," he said. "That explains the delay. The queen's orders were being relayed up and down their lines."

Tavi nodded calmly. "It took me a while to realize it. In Alera, orders are relayed by furycraft. Separate Legions can move in concord, almost simultaneously. Not as flawlessly as the Vord move, but much faster than word carried by a mounted rider."

"But the Vord in Maraul did not move in unison," Lararl said.

"Exactly. They're moving by some form of relayed command, not by the guidance of dozens of queens working together over distances." Tavi tapped the centermost stone with his finger. "Word had to be taken to each successive element along the lines. The queen had to trigger the attack."

Varg growled in interest. "Theories are air and wasted effort until proven. What other evidence supports this theory?"

"Maraul's major counterattack targeted the northernmost element of the enemy lines," Lararl replied. He paced over to the table and crouched at Tavi's side, openly interested. "Look at the region. It makes no sense to focus a major attack there. There is nothing of strategic value anywhere nearby, and no way to defend it efficiently had it ever been taken." He glanced up at Tavi. "The queen?"

Tavi nodded. "I think that someone in Maraul deduced the queen's existence. I think they waited for her northernmost element to advance again, and hit her with everything they had." Tavi moved several white stones into the northern edge of the Vord lines. He swept up the black stone and dropped it back out at the edge of the range. "They crushed the elements in the north of the Vord line, taking heavy losses. But after that, they spent almost three weeks pushing the rest of the Vord back—the only time it's been done, as far as your records show, Warmaster."

Tavi took up the other black stones, and a pair of the whites, until they were in their original positions again, the forces of Maraul reduced, but in control of the map.

"Three weeks later, the Vord advanced again, with heavier forces." He gestured at the sand table. "They repeated the same pattern, the same battle, over the next year—periods of fierce fighting at the enemy's origination point, followed by rapid assaults from Maraul's warriors that drove the Vord back."

Lararl growled quietly. "Until the Vord ground them away."

Tavi nodded.

"Warmaster," Tavi said, turning to Lararl, "according to your scouts' reports, the Vord fought in undisciplined wave assaults when they attacked Maraul—and yet the horde at the fortifications moves in an extremely ordered fashion."

"True," Lararl said, tilting his head slightly to one side.

"My theory," Tavi said slowly, "is that, for whatever reason, they were short of queens. I think maybe they only had the original and the two daughter-queens she produced."

"Sterile?" Lararl growled.

Tavi shrugged. "They're operating at a disadvantage for no reason, otherwise."

Varg flicked his ears in assent. "The attack on the fortifications is disciplined. Therefore, a queen must be present."

"There must also be one with the flanking force in our rear," Lararl said. He looked at Tavi. "Could a single queen control the entire horde before my walls?"

Tavi spread his hands. "Evidence suggests that she could—but that her ability to control it does indeed have a limited range—somewhere under twenty miles, perhaps even less."

Lararl nodded. "Then we must kill these queens."

"And do what?" Tavi asked him, in a calm voice. "Kill millions more of the Vord in less than three weeks? Because that's how long it would take the original queen to produce a new daughter, if the battles in Maraul were any indication."

Lararl drummed his claws on the stone edge of the sand table. It was a peculiar sound, an almost insectile series of clicks, and Tavi suppressed a shiver.

"What would you have us do, then?" Lararl asked.

"Run," Tavi said simply. "Get as many of your people away from the Vord as you can."

"And go where? All of Canea is overrun."

"To Alera," Tavi said calmly.

Lararl let out a barking cough, a bitter sound. "You would have my folk abandon their home to become slaves in the demon lands?"

"I've got enough problems relating to slavery already," Tavi replied drily. "No." He took a deep breath. "I would have your people and Varg's stand with us against the Vord."

The room became deadly silent.

"They aren't going to stop with Canea," Tavi said. The quiet words fell like lead weights, simple and heavy. "We must stand together—or die separately."

The silence stretched.

Lararl turned his head to Varg.

The black-furred Cane stared at the sand table for a moment. Then he looked up at Lararl. "It would be an interesting fight, would it not?"

The golden-furred Cane turned his gaze to Tavi, his eyes narrowed. "He is truly *gadara* to you?"

Varg flicked his ears in assent. "We have shed blood together and exchanged blades."

Lararl's ears quivered upright in startled surprise.

"His word is good," Varg said.

"And you must understand that we're going to have to trust one another," Tavi said. "Information has to be limited. If I'm wrong about the queens, or if there are other Vord who can see into minds, they could counter us easily. We've got to have the initiative, or none of us are going to live out the week."

Varg and Lararl digested that for a quiet moment. Then Varg twitched his ears in consent.

"You have many ships," Lararl said slowly. "But not enough for all of Shuar."

"Let me worry about that."

Lararl glanced at Varg, who flattened his ears in a gesture that was roughly the equivalent of an Aleran shrug. "Aleran sorcery is far more useful than that of the ritualists, in my experience. They do more than kill with it."

Lararl grunted, then gestured at the sand map of Shuar. "If I divert enough warriors to crush the queen in our interior and safeguard my people, the Vord at the fortifications will surely overwhelm the defenses."

"We aren't going to send your warriors against the queen," Tavi said.

Varg growled. "Your Legions and my forces do not have sufficient supplies to carry out such a campaign, Tavar."

"We aren't going to send them out to kill the queen, either," Tavi said. "We're going to do it ourselves."

"Oh," Kitai said abruptly, her eyes glittering with sudden understanding. "Interesting."

"Ourselves?" Varg asked.

Tavi nodded. "My people here, and yours, together with any Hunters you can find, are going to hunt and kill the queen. Once that is done, and the Vord lose cohesion, all the civilians in Shuar"—Tavi turned to stare hard at Lararl—"every one of them," he said with emphasis, "should have a fighting chance to reach the coast."

Lararl returned Tavi's stare. Then he tilted his head fractionally to one side. "Yes. All of them."

Varg looked back and forth between the other two, and growled thoughtfully. "The queen is in the midst of her horde, Tavar. She will be difficult to reach."

"Let me worry about that, too," Tavi said.

Lararl let out a brief, exasperated growl. "If only you know the details of the operation, how can we cooperate effectively?"

Varg gestured with one paw-hand. "Agreed. Your plan would limit us just as it does the Vord."

Tavi bared his teeth in a smile. "Ah. But we have something the Vord do not have."

Varg tilted his head to one side. "What is that?"

"Ink."

CHAPTER 26

The First Spear strode into the command tent and found Magnus glaring silently at Sir Carleus, the youngest, gangliest, largest-eared of the Knights Aeris in service to the First Aleran. Marcus nodded to the elderly Cursor and returned the young Knight's immediate salute.

"Magnus," the First Spear said, "what's going on?"

"Wait a moment," Magnus said, his clenched jaws making the word tight with tension. "I don't want to have to explain it twice."

"Ah."

Magnus grimaced. "Bloody crows, I don't want to have to explain it at *all*, but . . ."

Just then the tent flap opened and admitted a tall, gangly man; Perennius, the senior Tribune and acting captain of the Free Legion. He saluted the room generally. "Marcus, sir Knight, Maestro. I came as quickly as I could." He paused, then added, mildly, "Why?"

"Please, Captain," Magnus said. "If you will be patient for a moment more, I will explain."

Perennius glanced at the First Spear, who shrugged.

A moment later, there was something of an anticommotion outside; the sudden absence of the camp's usual background noises. Marcus went to the tent flap and peered out, only to see a dozen heavily armored warrior Canim striding through the First Aleran's camp, their paw-hands resting upon their weapons. *Legionares* stood out of the path of the group of Canim, but every one of them kept a hand on his own weapon, as well.

From the markings on their armor—though Marcus was hardly an expert on the intricate customs that infused the Canim practice—it would appear that the soldiers were among the best in the horde that had returned from Alera, their black armor heavily decorated in bands and whorls of scarlet.

Leading them was Nasaug, his own armor nearly solid red across its entire surface. Beside him walked Gradash, the grizzled Cane that Marcus had come to think of as his opposite number among the Canim.

With no discernible signal whatsoever, the escort of Canim warriors came to a halt on the same stride, perhaps thirty feet from the command tent. Nasaug and Gradash continued on, Nasaug tipping an Aleran-style nod to Marcus.

Marcus returned it with the Canim motion, dipping his head slightly to one side, and said, "Good afternoon. Please come in."

"First Spear," Nasaug said. "Word has come from my sire?"

Marcus made a growling sound in his chest. "That isn't entirely clear yet."

Gradash's muzzle wrinkled in distaste. "Secrets. Pah. Hunter-games, is it?"

"Smells like it," Marcus confirmed, and went back inside with the two Canim.

Perennius threw Nasaug a smart salute as he entered, and Nasaug returned the gesture with a slight tilt of his head. "Ah!" the Free Legion's captain said. "Now I see. Word from the expedition inland."

"Gentlemen, please," the old Maestro said. "Wait for the Knight to secure the conversation, if you would."

Sir Carleus sighed, frowned in concentration, then lifted his hand. Marcus recognized the signs of a man strained almost beyond his crafting limits. The young Knight was exhausted—but the windcrafting that snapped up around them and put a brief pressure on his ears was solid enough, and should serve to completely silence the conversation to the world outside the tent.

"Thank you," Magnus told the Knight. He turned to the others and held up a letter, written on the overlarge pages of Canim vellum. "This letter bears the signature and seal of both the Princeps and of Warmaster Varg. According to its text, I was to summon the current company to the tent, ward it from observation, and turn the briefing over to Sir Carleus. Tribune Foss has already worked a truthfinding on Sir Carleus, and found no reason to doubt his claim. Can we agree that the signatures and seals are genuine?"

He passed the letter over, and Marcus scanned over them, finding what he knew the Cursor had already learned. The letter was in Octavian's handwriting, and both seal and signature looked genuine. Granted, the average soldier wouldn't have known the signs of a forgery, so Marcus—perhaps he hadn't completely forgotten intrigue craft, after all—replied, "It seems to be the Princeps' hand to me."

Nasaug took the letter. His ears quivered as he read the Canim script aloud to Gradash. "The tavar is clever. Heed him. Varg."

Magnus winced at the words and muttered something less than gracious beneath his breath. ". . . begotten jackass, thinks that, of course, anyone who disagrees with him must be a drooling old moron—"

The First Spear cleared his throat pointedly.

Magnus flipped his hand at him in an irritated wave, and said, "Sir Knight, your report, please."

Carleus bobbed his head toward the group in general in a brief bow. "My lo . . . uh, sirs. The Princeps wishes you to know that the province of Shuar is the last Canim range that has not been overrun by the Vord. He further advises you that it cannot remain standing for much longer. He and the Shuaran command estimate that the Vord will have engulfed the range entirely within the next three weeks."

The tent was deathly silent. Marcus glanced at the two Canim but could read nothing in their body language.

"His Highness warns you that Vord queens are operating in the area. Their operating patterns and their success thus far suggest that they may be gathering intelligence directly from the minds of their opponents."

Perennius let out a low whistle. "They can do that?"

"Yes, yes," Magnus said, waving a hand at the Free Legion's acting captain in a suppressing gesture. "It was in the documents sent to you at the beginning of the trip."

"Ah," Perennius said, smiling at Magnus rather wolfishly. "Must have missed that detail. I did find something useful to do with the paper, though."

"Perennius," Nasaug rumbled, the faintest hint of a rebuke in his tone.

Carleus coughed quietly. "In an effort to conceal his intentions from the enemy, the Princeps has issued written orders for each of you. The orders are sealed closed, and it is his command that you open them one at a time, in sequence. Instructions for opening the second order will be found within the first, and so on."

Marcus pursed his lips and mused on that. Clever. A spy that can lift information directly from the enemy's thoughts was a dream or a nightmare come true, depending upon whom the spy was working for: But a man could not give away information he did not possess in the first place, no matter how talented the spy might be. It was a simple, clever counter to the Vord's abilities.

In theory, at any rate. Conditions in the field were never static. Whoever was following Octavian's orders would effectively be blindfolded, bound to the chain of orders, and unable to operate upon his own initiative. That was a recipe for disaster. Octavian had a natural talent for that kind of thing, but not even a scion of the House of Gaius could see the future with the necessary accuracy. Every passing hour would make it more likely that his planning and his orders would become hopelessly irrelevant.

"As the Princeps is well aware," Magnus said, "the environment of a military theater is neither static nor entirely foreseeable."

"Yes, sir," Carleus said, nodding. He unslung a heavy courier's pouch from the strap over his shoulder and dropped it on a table with a weighty-sounding thud. "He has done his best to outline the most probable courses of events." Carleus flushed slightly. "It means he's built a number of options into each set of orders, and into each of those options and so on, including the possibility that you might need to act outside his outline. It was quite a bit of writing."

Marcus grunted. "That's something, at any rate," he said. He glanced over at Nasaug. "And you? Are you willing to follow these orders?"

"For now," Nasaug said. "I trust my sire's judgment."

The old Cursor shook his head. "He's going to clever us all into a bloody grave." He extended his hand to Carleus. "If it's going to happen, I'd rather not wait around for it. My orders, please."

The young Knight passed a packet of folded, sealed orders to each of them. Marcus examined his own stack of papers. Each individual order was clearly, simply numbered, and written on an individual, overlarge page of Canim parchment. He found one labeled "Order Number One," and opened it.

Hello, Marcus.

I need you to take every legionare along with Nasaug's troops and the Free Legion, and march directly west at the earliest possible moment. Do not attempt to conceal your movements. Coordinate with Nasaug and Perennius.

Leave your engineers and the entire contingent of Knights behind, along with those of the Free Legion. Maestro Magnus will set them to their tasks.

Take whatever supplies you can. Open the next set of orders when you have marched at least twenty miles.

Octavian

Marcus read it again, just to be sure, then shook his head. "Well. That's cryptic." He glanced up at the old Cursor. "Yours?"

Maestro Magnus glowered at his orders, his face twisted up as if he'd been sipping vinegar. "They are brief and irrational," he said.

Nasaug snorted and refolded his own orders. "The Princeps has flaws that can be exploited," the Cane said. "Predictability is not one of them. Nor is stupidity."

Perennius said nothing, but his eyes were narrowed, the set of his jaw stubborn. For a long moment, no one spoke.

"The question," Marcus said, "is now before us. What will we do?"

He could all but feel the weight of their intent gazes upon his face. He looked slowly around the tent. Nasaug nodded once at him. Perennius followed the Cane's lead. Magnus sighed, and nodded to the First Spear as well.

"Well, then," Marcus said, nodding. "The Princeps has made his will known to us. Let's get to work."

CHAPTER 27

Amara and Bernard took their next major risk about an hour before sundown.

They had been drawn to what had been a small but obviously prosperous steadholt by the presence of several of the lizard-shaped Vord who loitered outside the place, instead of rushing about on the hunt, as had all the creatures they had seen thus far. Amara and Bernard had slipped past the guards and into the steadholt, to find that the Vord had overrun the place and set it up as some kind of base of operations.

A vordknight crouched at the peak of the steadholt's main hall, as motionless as any statue. The *croach* had spread over most of the ground and was growing up the walls of every building. The steadholt's well was completely blocked off by the waxy substance. One of the doors to the barn had been torn from its hinges and lay on the ground, already buried in the wax.

Pale wax spiders glided busily back and forth, tending the *croach* as bees might their honeycomb. All of them that Amara could see emerged from the shadowy interior of the barn and returned to it once their tasks were complete.

Bernard drew close enough to her side to touch her and pressed his fingers lightly against one of her ankles. She tapped his forearm with her fingertips twice, lightly, to acknowledge his signal. Then, one at a time, they slipped on the broadened shoes that they had made specifically for walking on the *croach*. The waxy substance served the Vord as sustenance and as a kind of sentinel. The weight of an adult human would break the resinous surface, spilling out the faintly luminous liquid within like blood and immediately drawing the attention of the wax spiders who stood watch over it.

Bernard and Octavian, in one of their regular written planning sessions, had between them come up with an idea for broad-bottomed shoes that would spread out the weight of an adult onto a larger surface, reducing the stress upon the *croach*. With them, the two should be able to walk, carefully, on the *croach* without breaking its surface or summoning a swarm of its guardians.

In theory.

In practice, the shoes were bloody difficult to use, and Amara suddenly felt very glad that she had insisted that Bernard have a swift-release mechanism built into the pads of leather and still-flexible wood. If they didn't work the way that they had hoped, Amara wanted to be able to get the ungainly things off her feet as rapidly as possible.

With their stealth-craftings still wrapped securely about them, they walked—waddled, really, Amara thought—along the inner wall of the overrun steadholt toward the cavernous barn, until they finally stepped onto the *croach* itself. Amara moved as carefully as she ever had in her life, stepping forward with the awkward motion the shoes demanded, an unusually high lift of the knee, then the first foot forward onto the glowing surface, then the whole of her weight brought slowly to bear upon the forward foot, so that the broad pads of the shoes spread her weight. She supposed that were she a character in a dramatic tale, she'd have one hand on her sword and one eye upon the nearest of the spiders—but that was perfect nonsense. She was a great deal more interested in making sure that she kept her balance and that the edges of the shoes didn't come down at too sharp an angle, tearing the *croach* and revealing their presence to foes who were, in all likelihood, too numerous to fight successfully in any case.

Amara took one step, then another. No whistling, warbling outcry went up around her. She paused to look back as Bernard stepped onto the *croach*. Her husband was a great deal larger than she was, and heavier, and his shoes proportionately wider—and therefore more clumsy. Even from barely more than an arm's length away, Amara could hardly see more than his outline, but she saw him move with the same steady patience with which her husband did everything else as he stepped onto the *croach* behind her.

No cry went up. The shoes were working. So far.

Amara turned her focus back to her own movements, leading the way, and tried to tell herself that she was walking like a graceful, long-legged heron, and not like a waddling duck, in the broad shoes. It wasn't far to the door of the barn—twenty feet, or a little more. Even so, it seemed to take at least an hour to walk the distance. That was ridiculous, of course, and Amara told herself so quite firmly. But her throat was so tight and her heart pounding so loudly that she wasn't sure she could have been expected to hear herself very clearly.

It could only have been a few moments later that she pressed her back against the stone wall of the barn and leaned cautiously forward to peer inside to see what it was that the Vord were standing watch over so diligently.

It was a larder. Amara could think of no other way to describe it.

The *croach* was deeper there, rising in murky swirls to a foot off the stone floor of the barn and more.

People—bodies—were sealed within it. Amara could make out few details. The *croach* was translucent, but shapes beneath it remained murky and mercifully indistinct. The bodies were not twisted in the shapes of death. They simply lay peacefully, as though the folk who had met their deaths there had fallen asleep and been sealed into waxy tombs. Some of the more indistinct shapes, deepest in the *croach*, were too thin to be bodies—but they might, Amara realized, be bones, the flesh eaten from around them by the *croach*.

Except for three who had been standing, sealed into the *croach* where it lined the wall behind them. They had been two men and a woman, their limbs restrained by the waxy resin—and their bodies had been damaged badly before they died.

They had, Amara realized, been tortured.

She took swift stock of the three bodies. They were not clad as holders, but in the greens and browns, in the cloaks and leathers of woodsmen, even as she and her husband were. In fact, taking into account that their faces had been distorted by pain as they died . . .

She felt a chill run through her.

She recognized them all. She'd been at the Academy with the young woman, Anna, who had been from a steadholt near Forcia. She'd gone through her basic training as a Cursor with Anna, before graduating the Academy and being apprenticed to Fidelias.

The Vord had captured, tortured, and murdered three of her fellow Cursors, men and women chosen specifically for this mission for their ability to remain unheard and unseen. For all the good it had done them.

Her belly twisted nauseatingly, and she turned her face away. For a second, she fought to control her stomach. Then she forced herself to look again, to think.

Two more spiders, she realized, were busy repairing a trail of damage in the *croach* inside the building—footprints. Human footprints. They led from the doors to the dead scouts.

The Vord were without pity but also without rancor. None of the other bodies showed signs of torment. They were simply . . . devoured.

Alerans had done this, she realized.

Alerans had done this.

Amara saw in her mind's eye the Alerans surrounding the Vord queen at the battle of Ceres and shivered again—this time with raw rage.

She felt her husband's presence next to her, the brush of his body against hers as he looked at the inside of the barn as well. She felt it when the same realization reached him, when his body tensed suddenly and one of his knuckles made the softest of creaks beneath his gloves as his hand tightened into a furious fist.

She touched his wrist, willing her rage into frozen stillness, and the two turned to begin making their torturously slow way across the *croach* again, and out of the steadholt. They took off the *croach* shoes and ghosted back into the countryside. Without a word, Amara stepped back and let her husband take the lead.

Whoever had tortured the scouts had done so within hours of when Amara had found the bodies. Whoever the culprits had been, they were obviously tied in some fashion to the Vord, to the Alerans who had been helping them—the source of the Vord's furycraft. They were therefore a lead to the heart of Bernard and Amara's mission, and in all probability, they had left a trail.

Bernard took the lead. He would find them.

It took the best part of two days of almost unceasing, agonizingly cautious movement to catch up to the traitors who had tortured the scouts. Their trail led back to Ceres.

The Vord had taken the city.

Croach was growing within the walls. As the sun set, it threw up a sullen green light upon the grey-white stones of the city, making them look eerily translucent, like jade illuminated from within. From outside the walls, the city was eerily still and silent. No watchmen called. No bells tolled. No clip-clop of horses' hooves rattled from the stones. There were no voices, no singing from the wine houses, no mothers calling their children in as the sky settled from twilight to night.

One could hear, very faintly, the murmuring of the city's fountains, still flowing despite the Vord presence. And, every so often, the eerie, warbling call of one of the Vord echoed up from one of the streets or rooftops within.

Amara shivered.

She got close enough to Bernard to be seen clearly and signed to him. *Quarry. Where?*

Bernard pointed at what had been the High Lord's citadel in the middle of the city and added the sign *Maybe*.

Amara grimaced. She'd been thinking the same thing herself. The citadel would be the most secure place in Ceres. If she were an Aleran among a horde of Vord, she would want the thickest walls and strongest defenses around her when she slept. *Agreed. Proceed?*

Bernard signaled agreement. *Begin where?*

A good point. They could do without walking in through the front gates, relying purely upon their furycrafted veils to protect them from detection. Amara, like most Cursors, knew about a dozen different ways to enter all of the High Lords' cities unobtrusively. It was a far easier matter in a large city than in smaller towns, really.

She signaled Bernard to follow her and started for the slavers' tunnels that ran under the west wall of the city.

The tunnels had been sealed prior to the Vord attack, of course, but as she had fully expected, they had been opened by panicked inhabitants of the city as they fled. The tunnel entries all showed the rough, outward-flung ripples of stone moved aside in haste by earthcrafters of mediocre talent, and were wide enough, just barely, for an adult carrying a heavy pack to slip through. Best of all, none of the three entrances within easy reach showed any sign of the Vord, either upon the ground outside or within the tunnels themselves. The only marks were the tracks of booted feet.

It was a good sign. The bulk of the Vord forces had pursued the First Lord and the Legions as they fled to the north. It meant that the city was probably only lightly occupied, rather than being a seething hive. They might be able to move with more speed once they were within.

Amara slipped into the dark mouth of the nearest tunnel. Furylamps were still burning inside, though they were of poor quality and spaced widely.

She drew close to her husband, once within, and crafted a globe of still air about their heads and shoulders that would not allow their words to escape into the close confines of the tunnels. "Lucky," she breathed, her voice a whisper, harsh from disuse. "We still have light enough to move by."

Her husband drew her a little closer to his chest and made a low rumble in his throat. "I'd think it was too convenient if I hadn't lived the past week."

"They can't be strong everywhere," Amara replied. "If there were that many of them, they wouldn't have needed to pursue the First Lord so closely."

Bernard frowned at that and nodded slowly. "He's still a threat to them." He glanced around at the tunnel, his eyes wary but more confident. "What is this place?"

"The slavers in Ceres had a problem," Amara said. "A ready market, opposed by organizations of fanatic abolitionists, who would attempt to disrupt shipments of slaves and murder slavers as creatively as possible. The slavers created these tunnels as secure means in and out of the city."

"Somehow," Bernard said, a hint of a smile on his lips, "I think that whatever happens, that problem has been permanently solved."

Amara found herself tittering on the edge of a half-hysterical giggle. "Yes, I suppose so."

Bernard nodded down the tunnel. "Smells foul, though. Where does it lead?"

"The auction house, in the western city square. It's less than five hundred yards from the citadel."

"Excellent," Bernard said. His eyes went back to hers. "How are you?"

Amara thought it was the simple humanity of the question, in the face of the horror they had seen, that made her chest pang so sharply. She was tired. She ached in every limb and every joint. She was hungry, shaky, and terrified on such a steadily ongoing basis that it had begun to lose its bite and fade into numb indifference. The reminder of a kinder, gentler world, of the times they had shared speaking quietly, or sleeping beside one another, or making love, flared up in a hideously bright, dangerous fire inside her.

She looked away from him and spoke with a shaking voice. "I . . . I can't. Not yet. We still have work to do."

His hands rose to her upper arms and squeezed gently. His voice came out warm, quiet, steady. "It's all right, love. Let's be about it. We need to consider— get down!"

She froze in surprise for an instant, even as her husband's arms drove her to her knees. She lost her balance and would have toppled to one side had he not caught her.

At his curt gesture, she dropped the interdicting windcrafting and they were immediately assaulted by the sounds they would have heard had she not been holding it in place.

Voices echoed in the tunnel. Feet thudded in a careless clatter. Someone— perhaps even their quarry—was in the tunnels with them, and they were crouching in a narrow corridor like perfect fools. No amount of concealing furycraft would do them any good if one of the Vord sympathizers physically blundered into them.

The volume of the voices rose. The tunnels rendered them completely unintelligible, but their tone was clear: an argument. Then a pair of shadowy forms backlit by a dingy furylamp emerged from a cross tunnel ahead of them and turned to proceed farther into the stinking depths of the tunnel that led toward the auction house, away from Amara and Bernard.

She traded a look with her husband. Then the pair of them rose to their feet and began stalking after the retreating figures.

The tunnel widened and became much higher after only a few more yards, its shape far more regular, sloping gently upward as it moved farther into the city. Their footing was good. It was not difficult to move more swiftly than they had in days, their feet, long used to silence, making no more sound on the stones than they had over the soft earth. Amara felt a fierce surge of exaltation spread through her limbs, making weariness vanish, and found her hand upon her sword. She wanted to punish these men, whoever they were, who had turned against their own kind, to butcher them as ruthlessly and efficiently as possible. She wanted to strike *back* at the horrors who had overrun the Vale and visited so much pain and destruction upon its holders.

But vengeance wouldn't bring anyone back. Indulging her own need for action would not assist the First Lord in stopping the Vord. No matter that it *felt* right. She had to be cold, rational, just as Fidelias had always taught her. Or tried to teach her, at any rate. *Crows take his treasonous eyes.*

She took her hand slowly from her sword. There was still a job to do.

". . . and you know what she's going to say when we get back," snarled the voice of a man in the group in front of them. They had drawn close enough to the sympathizers for their discussion to be understood. "That you should have brought them all back here to be processed."

"Crows take the highborn bitch," snarled another man's voice. "She said to find out what the Cursors were up to. She never said anything about recruiting them."

The first man's voice became plaintive, blending frustration and anxiety in equal amounts. "Can't you explain it to him? Before we're all killed for incompetence?"

A woman's voice—a familiar one, though Amara couldn't place it immediately in the echoing tunnel—answered him. "It doesn't matter to me either way. He'll kill the two of you. I have something else to offer him."

"Whore," spat the second man.

"One can retire from whoredom," the woman replied, her tone cool. "Idiocy is for life—which, in your case, is probably about thirty minutes."

"Maybe I should just enjoy myself in the time left to me, then," the man said in an ugly tone. There was the sharp sound of an open-handed blow on skin, followed by scuffling feet and tearing cloth.

"Ranius!" barked the first man, his voice high and panicked.

"She's just a whore," Ranius growled. "One who needs to be put in her place. You can have a turn after I'm d—"

There was the sharp, sudden sound of snapping bone.

It was followed instantly by a heavy thud.

"Oh, *crows*," the first man screamed, his voice rising to a falsetto shriek.

"Apparently he's done, Falco," said the woman, her voice perfectly calm and polite. "Do you want your turn?"

"No. No, no, no, look," Falco babbled, his voice quick and shaking. "I never had a problem with you. Okay? I never tried to lay a hand on you. I never said a thing to you while you were . . . questioning the prisoners."

The woman's voice took on a hard, contemptuous edge. "Those people died for Alera. The least you can do is say the words. Ranius and I weren't questioning them, Falco. We were torturing them to death. And you did nothing. Bloody crows, you're gutless."

"I just want to live!"

"Everyone dies, Falco. Scramble all you want, but in the end you wind up like Ranius, there, no matter what you do."

"You shouldn't have killed them," Falco said. "You shouldn't have killed them. He's going to be furious."

"They died hard," the woman said. "But it was a cleaner death than they would have had if we'd brought them back. Cleaner than we're going to get."

"Why didn't you stop Ranius?!" Falco whined. "You could have stopped him. You know what's going to happen to us when we tell him what happened to the Cursors. You're smart. You knew . . ."

Falco's voice trailed off into tense silence.

"You've still got half an hour," the woman said in a level tone. "You want to be quiet now."

"You did it on purpose," Falco blurted. "You wanted the Cursors dead. So they couldn't talk. You're betraying him." He drew in a breath and his voice turned horrified. "You're betraying *them*."

There was a low sigh from up the tunnel. "Crows take it, Falco . . ."

"You lied to him," Falco continued in a dazed voice. "How the bloody crows did you lie to him?"

"Lying is easy," the woman replied quietly. "Getting people to believe what you want them to believe is considerably more difficult. It helps to be able to distract them with something."

"Oh, *crows*," Falco moaned. "Do you know what's going to happen to us when he finds out?"

The woman's voice was calm—almost compassionate—and Amara finally placed it. "He isn't going to find out."

"The crows he won't!" Falco retorted. "They'll know. They *always* know. I'm not going to have my guts ripped out for those things to crawl in!"

"No," she said. "You aren't."

Falco's voice turned panicked again. "Get away from me!"

There were running footsteps. Then a hissing sound—a knife's blade cutting the air as it was thrown, Amara judged. Falco let out a scream of agony and, from the sound of it, stumbled and fell. There was the sound of quick, light footsteps, then a gurgling sigh.

Amara moved forward until she could see the woman clearly.

She wasn't pretty, precisely, but she was fit, her features strong and appealing. She wasn't particularly tall, but her stance was confident, her motions brisk and sure, blending into a sense of competence that permeated her entire presence. She wore leather flying trousers and a dark blouse. The latter was silk, and it was torn, revealing a swath of smooth skin. Her eyes were the color of rich earth after a rain. Blood speckled her face.

A large man's body lay on the tunnel floor, his head twisted at a grotesque angle, his tongue protruding from between motionless lips: Ranius. A second man lay prone at her feet. He wasn't dead yet, technically, though the blood pumping from his slit throat into a pool on the stone floor was beginning to slow. A small throwing knife protruded from the hollow of one of his knees, precisely centered, sunk to the hilt.

The woman crouched down over him and smoothed the man's hair with her hand. "I'm sorry, Falco," she said quietly. "I can't let you give me away. I'm sorry you had to be afraid for so long. But your life ended weeks ago."

The man on the floor let out a small moan that ended in a little rattle. There was a terrible finality to the sound.

The woman bowed her head for a moment, then took her hand from the man's hair and spoke, her tone a quiet eulogy. "There are worse things to be than a coward. It was cleaner than anything they'd have given you."

She then began cleaning the bloody knife in her hand on his clothing. Once that was done, she jerked the throwing knife from the corpse's leg and cleaned it as well. She rose, her motions still brisk—then froze.

Amara hadn't made a sound or moved, but the woman shifted her grip on her knife and turned to face back down the tunnel, toward her, her body moving into a ready crouch, one hand held out in front of her, the little weapon lifted and ready to be thrown. Her eyes were narrowed, questing up and down the hall, her head tilted slightly, one ear a little forward, and her nostrils were wide as if questing for a scent.

Amara felt a second of sharp amusement. In any tunnels other than those leading to slave pens, she supposed her odor, anything but charming after weeks in the field, might well have given her away.

She put a hand on her husband's chest to warn him back, and took two steps forward, letting her feet strike the stone, slowly lowering the veil around her as she did.

The woman froze for a moment, then her eyes widened in recognition. "Countess Amara?"

"Hello, Rook," Amara said quietly. She stepped forward, lifting her empty hands, and faced the former head of the late High Lord Kalarus's Bloodcrows, the mistress of his personal assassins. Rook's defection and subsequent cooperation with the Crown had been responsible, as much as anything else, for Kalarus's downfall.

But what is she doing here?

After a moment, Amara asked, "Are you going to throw that knife?"

Rook lowered the weapon at once, rising out of her crouch a bit more slowly, letting out a long, steady exhalation. Then she slipped the weapon away and averted her eyes. "Don't talk to me."

"It's all right," Amara said slowly. "I'm a Cursor. I understand what you did. I know you aren't the enemy."

Rook let out a low, bitter croaking sound that might have been intended as a laugh. Then she lifted her chin, still without looking at Amara, and tugged the collar of her torn blouse back from her throat.

A simple steel band gleamed there, a familiar slaver's device.

A discipline collar.

"That's where you're wrong, Countess," Rook said quietly. "I am."

·□·□·□·□·CHAPTER 28

Isana met the tribal chiefs of the Icemen two days later, at the same place she had spoken with Big Shoulders.

"This is ridiculous," Lady Placida said, pacing back and forth in the new snow. She was huddled beneath layered cloaks and shivering. "Honestly, Isana. Over the centuries, don't you think someone would have noticed if the Icemen were watercrafters?"

"Don't let the cold make you cross," Isana said, struggling to ignore it herself. There was a certain amount watercrafting could do to mitigate the cold, by keeping blood flowing steadily throughout her own limbs, and by convincing the snow and ice not to be quite as chilling to her flesh as it might be otherwise. Combined with a good cloak, it was enough to make her comfortable, but just barely. She doubted Aria had ever had need to practice the combination of techniques before, and despite the fact that her skills were almost certainly greater than Isana's own, the High Lady was the one being forced to pace back and forth.

"It's a simple bit of f-f-fieldcraft," Aria replied, shivering. Several tendrils of red hair slipped from beneath the green of her hood and danced back and forth over her face in the chill northern wind. "So simple that every single *legionare* in the northern Legions can learn it. And it takes someone of your skill at watercraft to even notice it's being used from five feet away. Surely you aren't saying that not only are the Icemen capable of furycraft, but that they're as skilled as Aleran Citizens, to boot?"

"I don't believe anyone using that firecrafting to stay warm is capable of thinking very clearly when the Icemen are nearby," Isana said calmly. "I believe there is some sort of unanticipated side effect occurring—one that caused you to be provoked quite easily at the first meeting."

Aria shook her head. "I think you're exaggerating the fact that—"

"That you nearly assaulted Doroga, an ally who was there to help us and who had offered us no harm?" Isana interrupted gently. "I was there, Aria. I felt it with you. It was not at all in character for you."

The High Lady pressed her lips together, frowning. "The Icemen hadn't yet arrived."

"Yes, they had," Araris put in gently. "We just didn't know it yet."

Aria lifted one hand in a gesture of concession. "Then why doesn't it happen constantly? Why only when the Icemen are near?"

Isana shook her head. "I don't know. Perhaps there's some kind of resonance with their own emotions. They seem to be able to project them to one another in some fashion. Perhaps we're experiencing some of their reaction to us."

"So now you're saying that they're firecrafters as well?" Aria asked—but her eyes were thoughtful.

"All I'm saying is that I think we'd be wise not to assume that we know everything," Isana said evenly.

Aria shook her head and glanced at Araris. "What do you think?"

Araris shrugged. "From a strictly logical standpoint, it's possible. The Icemen follow the heaviest storms down from the north, so it's always coldest when they meet *legionares*. It stands to reason that nearly everyone would be using the warmth crafting."

"And no one was looking for that kind of influence," Isana said. "Why would they think intense anger at one of Alera's enemies was strange?"

Aria shook her head. "Centuries of conflict over some sort of hypothetical furycrafting side effect?"

"Only needs to happen for a few minutes at the wrong time," Doroga interjected from several yards away.

Everyone turned to regard the barbarian, who stood beside his huge gargant, leaning his shoulders against Walker's tree trunk of a leg.

"First impressions are important," Doroga continued. "Icemen don't look like you. That makes you people nervous."

Araris grunted. "A bad first meeting. Tempers flare. There's a fight. Then more encounters and more fights."

"Happens long enough, you call that a war," Doroga said, nodding.

Lady Placida was silent for a moment. Then she said, "It can't possibly be that simple."

"Of course not," Isana said. "But a single pebble can start a rockslide."

"Three hundred years," Doroga said, idly kicking at the snow. "Not over territory. Not over hunting grounds. No one gains anything. You're just killing each other."

Aria considered that for a moment and shrugged. "It does seem a bit irrational, I suppose. But after so much killing, so much death . . . it takes on a momentum of its own."

The Marat grunted. "Thought I heard someone say something about a rockslide less than a minute ago. But maybe I imagined that."

Aria arched an imperiously exasperated eyebrow at the barbarian.

Doroga smiled.

Aria sighed and shook her head, folding her arms a little closer to her chest. "You don't think much of us, do you, Doroga?"

The barbarian shrugged his heavy shoulders. "I like the ones I talk to. But taken as a whole, you can be pretty stupid."

Aria smiled faintly at the barbarian. "For example?"

The chieftain considered for a moment with pursed lips. "Be my guess that your folk never even considered that you might have it backward."

"Backward?" Lady Placida asked.

Doroga nodded. "Backward. Icemen don't follow the storms when they attack, Your Grace." He gave Aria a shrewd look as a particularly cold gust of wind threw up a brief, blinding curtain of snow. "The storms," he called, "follow *them!*"

The snow kept Isana from seeing Aria's face, but she clearly felt the startled little flicker of surprise—and concern—that suddenly permeated the woman's emotions.

The wind died away, and as suddenly as that, nine Icemen stood in a loose circle around them.

Isana felt Araris and Aria immediately touch shoulders with her and with each other, forming an outward-facing triangle. Araris exuded nothing—no tension, no discomfort, no fear: She sensed nothing but the steady confidence and detachment of a master metalcrafter withdrawn into communion with his furies, ignoring all emotion and discomfort to stand ready against a threat. That presence bolstered Isana, granted her confidence she badly needed, and she studied the newly appeared Icemen closely.

There were differences in them, Isana saw at once. Instead of bearing similar styles of weaponry and adornment, as the group with Big Shoulders had, each of the nine was perfectly distinctive.

Big Shoulders was there again, fur and leathers and a handmade but obviously functional spear in his hands. But the Iceman beside him was at least a foot taller and far thinner, with a barely perceptible orange tint to his white fur. He carried a large club made out of what looked like the leg bone of some enormous animal, though Isana had no idea what could possibly grow femurs six and a half feet long. The fur around his head was threaded with seashells, a hole bored through each of them to make them into beads.

The Iceman on the other side of Big Shoulders was shorter than Isana, and probably weighed three or four of her. He was clad in a mantle and breastplate of what looked like sharkskin, and carried in one hand a broad-headed, barbed harpoon carved from some kind of bone, and wore over his shoulder a quiver of what looked like smaller versions of the weapon.

Walker let out a low, trumpeting huff that was equally a greeting and a warning, and Doroga nodded to Big Shoulders. "Morning."

"Friend Doroga," Big Shoulders said. He gestured to the orange-tinted Iceman beside him, and said, "Sunset." He made a similar gesture to the harpoon-bearing Iceman on his other side, and said, "Red Water."

Doroga nodded to each of them, then said, to Isana, "Sunset is the eldest of the peace-chiefs. Red Water is the eldest war-chief."

Isana frowned. "They have different leaders, then?"

"Divide areas of authority between tasks of peace and tasks of war," Doroga corrected her.

The presence of both the head peace leader and senior war leader was a statement, then, Isana realized. The Icemen were equally disposed toward either outcome. It might mean that they did not want her to sense that they would be reluctant to fight—or they might genuinely *want* to sabotage any possible talk of truce in favor of ongoing hostilities. Then again, perhaps they were simply being sincere.

Isana let out a slow breath, and lowered the defenses with which she habitually shielded herself from the overwhelming emotions of others. She wanted every scrap of insight she could get about the Icemen.

Lady Aria's faint, tightly controlled anxiety became a painful rasp against Amara's senses, as did Doroga's low-key, abiding worry for his daughter. Behind her, very faintly, she could literally sense the presence of Alerans on the Shield-wall, cloaked in their gentle firecraftings against the cold. The wall hummed with a sensation of constant, quiet, long-term emotion that might or might not have stopped short of the line between anger and hatred.

"The young one tells us you are here to seek peace," said Sunset quietly, in accented but intelligible Aleran.

Isana arched an eyebrow and nodded to him. "We are."

Though none of them moved or reacted, Isana felt a ripple of suspicion and uneasiness flicker around the circle of Icemen.

Isana drew in a quick breath, touched Araris's wrist to tell him to stay where he was, and stepped forward, focusing on making her emotions as plain and obvious as they could be. She stepped forward toward Sunset and offered her hand.

There was a flash of suspicious fury, and Red Waters was abruptly between them, the wickedly sharp tip of his harpoon dimpling the skin of Isana's cheek.

Steel hissed as two swords leapt clear of their sheaths, and there was an abrupt surge of light and hot air at Isana's back.

"Aria, no!" Isana snapped in a tone of sudden, iron authority. "You will *not* do this." She turned—a calm, deliberate motion that nonetheless dragged the tip of Red Waters's harpoon against her cheek in a tingling line.

Aria and Araris stood side by side, weapons in their hands. Aria's left wrist was uplifted, and a small hunting falcon made of pure, white-hot fire perched there, wings already spread, ready to be launched skyward at a flick of her hand.

"High. Lady. Placida." Isana spoke into the silence, putting a ringing emphasis onto each word, her voice rolling across the frozen landscape and rebounding from the distant Shieldwall. "You will put your weapon on the ground and dismiss your fury at once."

Aria tilted her head at a dangerous angle, her eyes focused on one of the largest of the chieftains assembled there. "Isana—"

Isana took two strides to Aria and slapped her smartly across one cheek.

Lady Placida all but convulsed in surprise, overbalanced, and fell on her rump in the snow.

"Look at me," Isana said in a hard, calm voice.

Aria was already staring at her with rather wide eyes. It occurred to Isana that it was entirely possible that no one had spoken in such a tone to the High Lady since before her adolescence.

"We are here on a mission of peace, High Lady. You will immediately desist from your efforts to turn my introduction to the principals of a foreign nation into a bloodbath." She lifted her chin, and said, "Dismiss. Your. Fury."

The little fire falcon vanished in a hiccup of smoke.

"Thank you," Isana said. "Now put your sword on the ground."

Aria gave the assembled chiefs a quick glance, then flushed and did so. "Of course, my Lady."

"Thank you. Araris?"

Isana turned to find that Araris, his sword already thrust point first into the snow, was standing with a folded handkerchief at the ready. He calmly pressed it to her cheek as he said, "You're bleeding."

The tingling on Isana's cheek turned to pain as the cloth touched it. She winced. She'd had no idea that the weapon had been *that* sharp. "Ah," she said, taking the cloth and holding it against the cut. "Thank you."

Araris nodded once and turned to offer his hand to Lady Placida, helping her up from the snow.

Isana turned back to the Icemen and walked over to face Sunset again. She calmly lowered the bloodied cloth, and felt a slow warmth spread down her cheek. She very deliberately allowed her discomfort and annoyance to show on her face and in her bearing and stared at Sunset.

The older chieftain turned his gaze on Red Waters, and Isana felt a sudden, uncomfortably sharp spike of disapproval. Red Waters evidently felt it even more intensely than Isana had. He swayed slightly under the force of it and took a step back to stand beside Big Shoulders again, radiating a mild sense of chagrin. Amusement flowed around the circle of Icemen.

The Icemen, Isana realized, had just had their own version of the scene that had played out between her and Aria. Sunset had slapped Red Waters down— and the entire time, they *never spoke*. They hardly *moved*.

On an impulse, Isana opened her cloak and spread her hands, demonstrating that she was obviously carrying no weapons.

Sunset studied her for a moment, then nodded and passed his bone club over to Big Shoulders. Then he offered her his enormous, shaggy, claw-tipped hand.

Isana laid her own into it without hesitation, exactly as she would to convey her sincerity to another watercrafter. Whatever empathic sense the Icemen used, however it was done, it was obviously just as formidable as her own abilities, even though different. She wasn't afraid that Sunset would harm her. The level of emotional control he had exhibited in conveying his displeasure to Red Waters was humbling.

His enormous hand enfolded hers gently, the claws never touching her skin. The Iceman watched her, expressionlessly.

"I have come here to seek peace between our peoples," Isana said, allowing her feelings to flow down her hand and into Sunset's grasp. She felt a brief urge to giggle. It was entirely possible that the Aleran arrogance that Doroga had warned her about was in play again. What made her suppose that she would be *able* to hide her emotions from the Iceman?

Sunset took a deep breath and bowed his head. A brief tide of emotion washed over Isana, every bit of it as real to her as if it was her own; grief, mainly, a sense of loss and regret that had grown to maturity over slow years. But mixed with it was fierce exaltation, weary relief—and tiny, painfully intense sparkles of hope.

"At last," Sunset said aloud. "Your people send a peace-chief."

Isana felt tears washing down her face, stinging painfully as they entered the cut on her cheek. She nodded mutely.

"This will not be easy," Sunset told her. "Too much . . ." A surge of anger hit her, Sunset's own, though it was under his control. The gentle grasp of his hand never wavered. "Too much . . ." He flashed another emotion at her: suspicion, and more than that—the expectation of betrayal.

"Yes," Isana said quietly. "But it is necessary."

"Because of the enemy attacking you," Sunset said calmly. "We know."

Isana stared at him for a moment. "You . . . you do?"

He nodded. "For three years, we have pressed you here, hoping that the enemy would weaken your people in the south. Force you to send your Wall-guardians there to defend your food lands and that your folk would follow and leave us in peace."

And suddenly, Isana understood the attacks of the Icemen of recent years—why the winter storms and howling hordes had always arrived at precisely the correct time to pin the Legions of the north in place. Many folk, she knew, had feared collusion between the Icemen and the Canim—but it had been neither a mindless assault nor a sinister plot. It had been part of a considered campaign.

"That enemy has changed," Isana said. "You do not know this."

"One enemy or another." Sunset shrugged. "It is of little matter to us."

Doroga spoke for the first time. "It should be. Listen to her."

"The foe that comes against us now is not a nation. It does not seek land or control. It is here only to destroy utterly anything that is not itself. It has attacked us without warning, hesitation, or mercy. It will not speak with us of peace. It slaughters innocents and warriors alike—and it will do so to any other than itself whom it meets."

Sunset regarded her for a moment. Then he said, "Until today, I would have said that your people are little different. Many still would."

"This enemy is called the Vord. And when it finishes us, it will come here for you and your people."

Sunset looked at Doroga.

The Marat nodded. "And for mine. The Alerans caused your tribes to set aside your differences. They were a greater enemy. Now comes another enemy—one who will destroy us all if we do not lay our differences aside." Doroga leaned on his cudgel and spoke intently. "You must permit them to withdraw in peace. To let the Wall-guardians travel south and battle our mutual foe. And to leave their people here in peace."

Sunset stared at Doroga for a time. "What have your folk decided?"

"To let the Alerans fight," Doroga said. "My people cannot defeat the

Vord—not now. They are too many, too strong. You know that my people have no love for the Alerans. But we will not attack them while the Vord are abroad."

Red Waters spat, "So we should let their warriors leave, but not drive their peoples from these lands? So that when the battle is done, their warriors return and take up their arms again?"

Sunset sighed. He looked from Red Waters to Isana. "He has a point."

Isana frowned and looked at Red Waters, searching for the right words.

Araris stepped up beside her and bowed slightly to Sunset, then to Red Waters. "My people have a saying," he said. "Better the enemy you know than the enemy you don't."

Red Waters stared hard at Araris for a moment. Then Big Shoulders let out a bark of laughter that was startling in how human it sounded. It spread around the circle of Icemen until even Red Waters shook his head, his rigid demeanor relaxing somewhat.

"Our warriors have that saying as well," Red Waters admitted. He nodded at the blood, now freezing into scarlet crystals, on the tip of his harpoon. "But what peace-chiefs say is not always what war-chiefs do. Let us see your warriors depart. Then we will speak again of peace."

"Antillus and Phrygia will never agree to that," Lady Placida murmured. "Never."

"You come to us asking us for peace," Red Waters said. "But you offer us nothing."

Isana met Red Waters's eyes. "It seems to me that peace is not a gift one can give away. It can only be exchanged in kind."

A sharp pulse of approval came from Sunset.

Red Waters answered him with a surge of sadness and caution.

Sunset sighed and nodded. He turned back to Isana, and murmured, "As I said. It will not be easy."

"Too much anger," Isana said. "Too much blood."

"On both sides," Sunset agreed.

He was right, Isana thought. Certainly, Lord Antillus had been less than willing to accept the possibility of peace. The most he'd been willing to believe possible was that he could shake the Icemen up, disrupt them enough to send a single Legion south—

The steady, buzzing hostility of the Shieldwall hummed against Isana's senses.

She had a sudden, horrible suspicion and every Iceman in the circle around her suddenly became more alert.

"Lady Placida," she said quietly. "Can you tell me if there are any Knights Aeris aloft?"

Aria arched a pale copper eyebrow. Then she nodded, closed her eyes, and lifted her face to the snowy skies. A moment later, she drew in a sharp breath. "Furies. More than a hundred. Every Knight Aeris under Antillus's command. But why . . ." She opened her eyes wide, suddenly, staring around at the assembled chieftains of the Icemen.

"Sunset," Isana said, "you must leave. You and your people are in danger."

"Why?"

"Because what peace-chiefs say is not always what war-chiefs do."

Thunder rumbled suddenly overhead.

Red Waters snarled and made a swift, sharp gesture. The chieftains gathered around him and Sunset. Big Shoulders wordlessly handed Sunset's bone club back to him. Sunset glanced at Isana and sent out a surge of regret. Then he grasped the weapon in his hands and turned to begin shambling away through the snow, the other chieftains gathering around him as the wind began to rise again.

"Too late," Aria hissed.

Thunder rolled louder and the clouds whirled in a wide circle and parted, revealing a wheel of Knights Aeris aloft, tiny black shapes against the grey clouds with a circle of blue sky far above. Lightning danced from cloud to cloud and gathered into a wide circle, dancing between the Knights like the spokes of an enormous wagon wheel. Isana could feel the power gathering as the lightning prepared to fall on the retreating chieftains.

Aria cursed under her breath and threw herself aloft, wind rising in a roar to lift her into the skies—but even as she did, lightning burned a searing streak across Isana's vision and struck the ground several yards behind the Iceman chieftains. The wheel of Knights above shifted, and the lightning burned its way toward the Icemen, digging an enormous furrow in the earth as it went.

Isana watched in horror, helpless and furious, searching desperately in her thoughts for some solution. But there was nothing there for the Icemen. Words and good intentions meant less than nothing in this harsh land of stone walls and steel men, covered in ice and . . .

Snow.

Isana tore off her glove and thrust her hand into the snow, calling upon Rill as she did. The snow was, after all, water. And she had learned, during the desperate battle at sea the previous year, that she was capable of far more than she had ever believed. There had never been, upon her steadholt, a cause to push her abilities to their limits, except in healing—and she had never failed. When she had needed a flood to save Tavi's life, she had managed one, though at the time she had believed it merely the result of her familiarity with the local furies.

But in the ocean, she had learned differently. The limits she had known before had never been imposed upon her by Alera. They had been assumptions within her own mind. Everyone knew that holders were never truly powerful, even in the wilds of a place like Calderon, and she had let that unconscious assumption shape her self-perception. There, immersed in the limitless immensity of the sea, she had found that she was capable of far more than she'd ever believed.

Snow was water. Why *not* command it as she would any other wave?

She was the First Lady of Alera, by the Great Furies, and she would *not* allow this to happen.

Isana cried out, and the vast snowfield around the Icemen surged like a living sea, responding to her determination and will. She lifted her arm, feeling a phantom strain around her shoulders as the snow surged around the Icemen and piled up into a vast mound behind them. The lightning surged into that sea of snow, throwing out enormous billows of steam, its heat drowning before it could do harm.

Isana felt it when the sky above them suddenly changed, lightning flowing in from everywhere, surging from over the horizon in every direction to center itself in the whirling eye of the vortex above, its color shifting, changing from blue-white to bright gold-green. The burning shaft thickened and intensified, and Isana felt the surge in power behind it as some other enormous will added its power to the strike.

"Antillus," she heard herself gasp.

The weight settling on her pressed on her chest and drove her to one knee—but she did not yield. She cried out again, lifting her hand, and the snow and steam and ice that continued to shield the retreating Icemen washed and flowed into shape to mirror her fingers, her hand lifted in a gesture of defiant denial. The endless cold of the north clashed with the fire of the southern skies, and steam began to spread from the clash, blanketing the countryside.

"Isana!" she heard Araris call. "Isana!"

He shook her shoulders, and she looked around dazedly at him. She wasn't sure how long she had upheld the defense against Antillus Raucus's strike, but she couldn't see the Knights Aeris. Araris's voice sounded oddly distant.

"Isana!" Araris called. "It's all right. The Icemen are gone! They're safe!"

She lowered her hand, and heard an enormous whuffing rumble behind her. She turned to see fine powdery snow rising in a huge cloud, through the steam, as though settling after a sudden avalanche.

Doroga regarded the steam and settling snow for a long and silent moment. Then he looked at Isana appraisingly.

"I ever invade Calderon again," he said, "it will be in the summer."

Isana stared wearily at him, and said, "I'd see to it that you never got those sweetbread cakes you like. Ever again."

Doroga gave her a wounded look, sniffed, and said to Walker, "Alerans don't ever fight fair."

"Help me up," Isana said to Araris. "He'll be coming."

Araris did so at once. "Who?"

"Just stay by me," she said. She caught his eyes. "And trust me."

Araris lifted his eyebrows as he helped her up. Then instead of answering, he leaned forward and kissed her. After a moment, he drew back from her, and said, "With my life. Always."

She found his hand with hers and squeezed it very hard.

Seconds later, wind roared, and two forms plummeted through the mist and powder. Antillus Raucus landed hard, sending up a cloud of powdery snow. Lady Placida came down beside him, and immediately put one hand on his arm in a gesture of restraint.

"Raucus," Aria said. "Crows take it, Raucus, wait!"

The heavily armored High Lord shook off her arm and stalked straight toward Isana. "You little idiot!" he snarled. "That was our chance to throw them back, force them to reorganize enough to send some relief to the south! What do you think you were doing, you high-handed—"

When he reached her, Isana drew back and smacked him coldly across the face. Hard.

Raucus's head rocked to one side, and when he looked back at her, his lower lip had been cut against one of his teeth and was bleeding slightly. The surprise in his eyes began to be replaced by more anger.

"Antillus Raucus," Isana said, in the instant of unbalance. "I accuse you of cowardice and treachery against the authority of the First Lord and the honor of the Realm. And here, in front of these witnesses, I formally challenge you to the *juris macto*." She drew in a deep breath. "And may the crows feast on the unjust."

Chapter 29

Ehren didn't have the full military experience of a true Legion officer, but he knew enough to know that the retreat from Ceres had not gone well. The battered Legions had barely been able to stay ahead of the pursuing Vord, despite the advantage of the furycrafted causeways. The Vord simply outnumbered them too badly. A man could march for hours or for days when he had to, but sooner or later, he had to sleep—while the Vord simply kept coming.

Though the Legions did everything they could to keep the civilians moving out ahead of them, they couldn't help everyone. The Vord had spread through the countryside, and Ehren did not like to think of what would happen to the poor folk who were left behind each time the road was cut, ending any possibility of escape for the poor holders who had been fleeing toward the hope of safety the road had offered.

Ehren paced in the hall outside the First Lord's room, a suite in an inn in the town of . . . Ehren wasn't sure. Uvarton had fallen after the Legions had taken barely a night's rest. The vordknights had caught up to them and begun dropping takers behind the town's walls. Ehren was still having nightmares about the fourteen-year-old girl, taken by the Vord, whom he'd seen rip the heavy wooden tongue from a wagon and beat half a dozen *legionares* to death with it before being cut down herself. That was only after she'd set half a dozen buildings on fire with a simple candle. Others had seen much worse, and the chaos wreaked by the takers had been severe enough to force the Legions to abandon the city before the Vord reached them.

After Uvarton had come . . . Marsford, he thought, where the Vord had poisoned the wells, then Beros, where the Vord had brought up enough wind that, combined with the cold, the Legions had lost one in thirty men to frostbite, then Vadronus, where . . .

Where the Vord had driven them back again. And again. He'd slept in spare moments, half an hour, here and there, for the past . . . some number of days. He wasn't sure. The First Lord had taken even less than that—which was why he had collapsed.

The door to Gaius's room opened, and Sireos the healer emerged. As the personal physician to the First Lord, the thin, silver-templed Sireos was a familiar sight near the capital—which was less than a day's hard ride on the causeway from there. Sireos exchanged nods with the guardsmen at the door and turned toward Ehren.

"Sir Ehren," Sireos said. He had a long, mournful face and a very deep, very resonant voice. "Could I speak to you privately, please?"

He accompanied the physician to the end of the hallway and spoke in a quiet voice. "How is he?"

"Dying," Sireos said in a level tone. "I was able to stabilize him, but he's got to get regular food and regular rest, or he won't last the week."

"And if he does?" Ehren said.

"Weeks," Sireos said. "Months, if he's lucky. He's using furycraft to ignore the pain and strengthen himself, or he would know exactly how bad his condition is."

"Isn't there anything you can do?" Ehren asked.

Sireos gave him a steady look, then sighed. "I've been working on him for years—and never mind what he's been able to do for himself. He's every bit as skilled as I am at watercraft, even though his education as a physician is incomplete. His organs are simply breaking down. His lungs are the most obvious among the symptoms—he had pneumonia several years ago, and they've never been right since then. His spleen, his liver, his pancreas, one of his kidneys— they're all breaking down as well."

Ehren bowed his head.

"I'm sorry," Sireos said. "He's a remarkable man."

Ehren nodded. "You've told him all of this?"

"Of course. He insists that he has a duty. Even if it kills him."

"Have you seen what's out there, sir?" Ehren asked.

Sireos's face turned even more mournful. "I'm under the impression that I will."

Ehren nodded. "It would seem so."

"The world can be a hard place. We all have to face it as best we can, son." He put a hand on Ehren's shoulder. "Good luck, Sir Ehren. I'll be nearby."

"Thank you," Ehren said quietly.

He turned away to look out the inn's window as the physician retreated.

Retreat seemed to be in fashion.

A muffled voice came from the First Lord's room, and the guard opened the door. Gaius strode out, clean from his time in the healing tub, dressed in fresh clothing. He moved with brisk purpose, but Ehren fancied that he could see the frailty underneath the calm surface.

"Sire," Ehren said, as Gaius walked over to him. "You should be in bed."

Gaius regarded him steadily for a moment. "I would be better off. Alera would not."

Ehren bowed his head again. "Yes, sire. At least you should eat something."

"There's no time for that, Cursor. I want you to collect the latest intelligence reports and—"

"No," Ehren said in a firm voice. "Sire."

The two guardsmen glanced at each other.

Gaius arched his eyebrows. "Excuse me?"

"No, sire," Ehren repeated. He planted his feet and looked up at the First Lord. "Not until you've eaten something."

Boots treaded on the stairs, and Captain Miles of the Crown Legion appeared. He was a stocky man of medium height and build, his plain steel lorica dented and nicked with use, and he wore a similarly unadorned, functional, and well-used sword at his side. He sized up the situation in the hallway as he came to a halt, and saluted sharply to Gaius.

"Sire," Miles said, "the defenses are prepared, and the Crown Legion stands ready to serve you."

"Good to see you, Captain," Gaius said, his eyes never leaving Ehren's. He smiled, very slightly, to the young Cursor and inclined his head to such a slight degree that Ehren thought he might have imagined it.

Gaius turned to Miles. "I was just about to take some . . . breakfast?" He glanced at Ehren.

"It's more like lunchtime, sire," Ehren supplied.

"Lunch," Gaius said firmly, nodding. "Join me, and we'll discuss the defenses."

"Yes, sire," Miles said firmly.

Ehren bowed slightly to Gaius as the First Lord returned to his quarters with Captain Miles. Then he went to see to it that food was brought up to the room before Gaius changed his mind.

It was only after he was several steps down the stairs that he realized the import of Gaius's words, and realized what was happening. Ever since Ceres, Gaius had been retreating from the Vord—and for the last several days, Aleran forces had barely put up any resistance at all. But the Crown Legion was Gaius's single most trusted and capable force, and would certainly be present in any decisive confrontation with the enemy. If the First Lord had sent the Crown Legion ahead to prepare Alera Imperia, it meant that Gaius never intended to prevent the Vord from reaching the Realm's capital.

Gaius wasn't being driven back by the Vord.

He was luring them forward.

If the retreat had been such a terrible strain on Alera and her Legions, it had to be pushing the Vord's resources, too. Savage and deadly as they might be, the Vord still had to eat, and they apparently needed their *croach* as food. By forcing them to stay on the move and in pursuit of the Aleran forces, Gaius was also keeping them ahead of their supply lines, advancing far faster than the *croach* could grow.

Meanwhile, the Crown Legion was preparing Alera Imperia herself for battle.

Gaius was drawing the Vord into the most vulnerable position he could arrange for them, tiring them with the campaign—only to prepare to turn upon them at the high point of his power, the heart of the Realm, Alera Imperia.

It was the gamble of a desperate man, Ehren thought. If Gaius won, he would crush the Vord strength in the Realm. If he lost, the center of Aleran commerce, travel, and government would fall with him.

Ehren hurried forward, to get the First Lord a solid meal.

CHAPTER 30

The taurga rolled east at their lumbering trot, crushing the miles beneath their cloven hooves.

"I still don't understand," Kitai murmured, close to Tavi's ear. She rode behind him on his taurg, her arms around his waist. Even carrying the two of them, their taurg was less burdened than any of those bearing one of the Canim, and led the group in fine spirits—which was to say, it tried to toss them off every mile or so. "Why do we keep traveling east when we know the queen we must destroy is to the south?"

Tavi grinned and called back to her, "The best part about this plan is that I don't have to explain anything to anybody."

She slipped a hand under his armor and pinched him hard on the flank. "Don't make me hurt you, Aleran."

Tavi laughed. "All right, all right." He glanced back down the line of taurga. "The Shuaran warriors are engaging the Vord to the south of us. We're going to ride around the main area of engagement, come in from the side."

"And encounter less resistance from the Vord," Kitai said.

"Or interference from the Shuarans," Tavi said. "It isn't as though we can expect every officer in the field to know that a group of Narashan Canim and Alerans—"

"And a Marat," Kitai said.

"And a Marat," Tavi conceded, "are traveling on a special, secret mission with Lararl's approval, even with Anag here to explain things. Simpler and faster if we avoid them."

She frowned. "Tell me something."

"Hmm?"

"Has it ever struck you as strange that the Vord never seem to notice you and me when we are near them? How they simply accept our presence unless we directly oppose them?"

"When we fought them in the tunnels beneath the capital, you mean," Tavi said. "I thought it very strange, yes."

"Did you ever wonder why they did so?"

"Oftener and oftener, the past few days," he said.

"I think it is because we were responsible for waking them," Kitai said. There was gravity in her voice.

"When we went down after the Blessing of Night, you mean," Tavi said, his own tone growing more sober. "We had no way of knowing what was going to happen."

"No," Kitai said. "But it does not change the fact that the first queen stirred after *we* stole the Blessing from the center of the Wax Forest. That it emerged and tried to kill us that very night."

"Until your father threw a big rock at it."

Kitai let out a low laugh. "I remember."

"In any case, it isn't as though they *all* ignore us. The queen I fought under the Citadel certainly saw me, and was more than willing to fight." Tavi chewed on his lip. "Though the lower-intelligence Vord, the wax spiders and takers and so on, haven't ever attacked me unless I attacked them first. It's almost as though they think we're other Vord, somehow, until we start getting rowdy."

"An advantage we could use."

"Possibly," Tavi said, nodding.

She rode in silence for a time, then said, the words rushed together, "I'm frightened, *chala*."

Tavi blinked and stared over his shoulder.

She shrugged. "What fool would not be? What if I lose you? What if you lose me?" She swallowed. "Death is real. It could take either of us, or both. I cannot think of living without you. Or of you without me."

Tavi sighed and leaned back slightly against her. He felt her arms tighten around his waist.

"That isn't going to happen," he told her. "It's going to be all right"

"Fool," Kitai scoffed gently. "You do not know that."

"Sometimes you don't know the most important things," Tavi said. "You believe them."

"That is completely irrational."

"Yes," Tavi agreed. "And true."

She shifted her position, and he felt her lay her head against his back. Her hair tickled the back of his neck. "My mad Aleran. Making promises he cannot keep."

Tavi sighed. "Whatever happens," he told her, "we'll be together. *That* much I can promise."

Her arms tightened again, enough to make him strain a little to draw in his next breath. "I will hold you to that, Aleran."

Tavi turned to her, awkward on the broad saddle, but enough to kiss her. She returned the kiss fiercely.

Until the taurg bellowed, bucked, and threw them both twenty feet through the air and into an enormous puddle of shockingly cold sludge almost two feet deep. Then the enormous riding beast bellowed in victory and went charging off the road, tossing its horns and bucking all the way.

The shock of the water was so cold that Tavi had trouble catching his breath as he struggled up out of it and onto his feet. He turned to find Kitai still in the muck, her green eyes narrowed as she regarded him.

"I am stuck," she informed him. "I blame you."

The other riders caught up to them, their taurga thundering to a halt, bellowing protests along the way. Max and Durias, each on his own beast, stopped closest to them. Durias's expression was dutifully neutral, but his eyes shone. Max was grinning.

"My lord," he said, sweeping a particularly florid bow from his saddle, flourishing one hand as he did. "Are we to take our leisure here for a time, then?"

Tavi gave Maximus a steady glare. Then he turned, slogged through the mud to Kitai, put his hands under her arms, and hauled strongly to pull her free of the mud. She popped out abruptly, his feet slipped out from under him, and they both fell back into the freezing mud, Kitai atop him.

"We could put up curtains for privacy if you like, my lord," Durias said soberly.

The Canim, atop their own mounts, remained a few yards off and none of them were looking in Tavi's direction—but they all sat with their mouths open, teeth showing, their grins requiring no translation.

Tavi sighed. "Just throw us a line, Max. And catch that bloody taurg before he runs into the ocean."

"You hear that, Steaks?" Max said to his own taurg. "It wasn't the Princeps' fault. Your bloody friend way over there was rebellious. Just you watch and see what happens when royal displeasure falls on uppity insurrectionists."

"Maximus," Kitai said. "I am cold. Speak another word, and I will strangle you with your own tongue."

Max laughed, and produced a coil of rope from his saddlebags.

The country that the Vord had emerged into from the tunnel they'd used to by-pass the Shuaran defenses was composed of rolling, rocky hills sparsely covered in pine trees. Varg's three Hunters had determined what Tavi was doing before half the day was gone, and had proceeded ahead of them, fanning out widely as outriders for their group. Though they wore their shapeless grey cloaks, they fairly bristled with weaponry, and each of the silent Canim wore a large, lumpy pack on his back filled with who knew what other instruments of mayhem.

Once they had taken the lead, Tavi simply followed the Hunters, who were sure to know the country better than he did. They turned off the main road and began traveling cross-country by midafternoon, leaving the plain and entering the first of the lightly forested hills Lararl's maps had shown at the interior of the Shuaran plateau.

By sundown they found the Vord.

The Hunters had led them to the vague Canim equivalent of a steadholt. Like the buildings of the Narash fortifications, it looked like a solid block of stone, a rectangle perhaps three stories high—or perhaps two, given the greater height of Canim ceilings. They rode the taurga into it through a relatively nar-row doorway, and found that the lower floor of the Canim steadholt was one enormous, cavernous hall, evidently used in the same way Alerans would a barn, if the scattered droppings were any indicator. No livestock were in sight, though their scent was still strong on the air.

One of the Hunters leapt down after tying his mount to a ring on the wall, and picked up an oddly lumpy pole nearly eight feet long. He began working with it, and Tavi realized that he was unrolling a net or mesh made of wire, which was wrapped around the pole. The Hunter unrolled the pole completely, and sank one end of it into a socket on the floor, and Tavi noticed that there were many such poles and wire fences around the hall.

"Clever," he said.

Beside him, Max grunted. "What's that?"

Tavi gestured at the Hunter, who was erecting a second wall around the tired taurg. "It lets them use this space to pen livestock when they need to, but when they don't, they can clear it out for other uses. They can change the size of the pens, or set it up so that you can cut some animals out and leave the rest penned up. That's handy."

Durias just blinked at Tavi.

Max snorted. "Don't tell anyone," he told the centurion, "but our Princeps was brought up on a steadholt. Herding sheep, if you can believe that."

Durias looked skeptical, but his tone was polite when he asked, "What breed?"

"Rivan Mountain Whites," Tavi replied.

Durias's eyebrows shot up. "Those monsters? Hard work."

Tavi grinned at the former slave. "There were days."

"Tavar," Varg growled. He and Anag stood by a steep stone staircase at the far end of the building. "Best see what can be seen."

Tavi nodded and kicked the taurg lightly in the back of the head. The beast tossed its head and bellowed, and while it was distracted, Tavi passed the reins back to Kitai, who quickly took up the slack again before the animal could realize that it was no longer being held under tight control. Tavi slid off the taurg's back and to the ground, then went up the stairs with Varg and Anag.

They passed the second floor, evidently quarters for whoever had lived there. They were as silent and as empty as the lower floor had been. The stairs continued on up to the building's roof.

Even that space was practical. Long stone troughs were filled with rich, dark earth. A great many vegetables could be planted there during what was sure to be a short summer, to take maximum advantage of the sunshine. A winch-and-pulley rig beside a large bucket at the roof's edge indicated that irrigating the rooftop gardens would be taxing, but not impossible.

It wasn't the same as an Aleran steadholt, but the practical, conservative thought behind its design was no different. Tavi felt oddly comfortable there.

Anag and Varg walked to the western edge of the roof and stood staring out for a time. Tavi followed, hopping up onto one of the stone planting troughs to put his head on a level with theirs.

Perhaps two miles to the west, as the ground rose gently, the green glow of growing *croach* was visible through the sparse trees.

Anag snarled in pure, quiet hate.

Varg glanced aside at Tavi. "How fast does it grow?"

"From what I read in Lararl's study, it depends on several things— temperature, weather, how much plant cover is on the ground, as well as how large it already is." Tavi shook his head. "Maybe other things we don't know about. And the bloody wax spiders spread it when they want to cover a new area, too."

"Not far," Anag growled quietly. "It was not growing until the Vord emerged."

"He's right," Tavi said. "A mile, two at the most. We're near their hole.

Though I'll wager that we probably passed dozens of smaller patches today in the daylight, without seeing them. They set them up like outposts."

"More like spreading seeds," Varg rumbled.

Tavi gave the big Cane a sharp glance and nodded.

"Then it is possible that we have been observed," Anag said.

"Probable," Varg corrected him.

"If so, then why have they not attacked us?"

"Because they don't care," Tavi said, smiling slightly. "We're fewer than a dozen, after all. What threat could we be? We're not in a position to hurt them from here—and if we approach closely enough to do something that might inconvenience them, we'll have to cross the *croach* to do it. That will warn them in plenty of time to act."

Anag's tail thrashed left and right. "Then how shall we find and kill this queen creature? We can't even be sure where she is."

Varg tapped his skull.

"Warmaster?"

The older Cane growled, the sound amused. "Explain it to him, please, Tavar."

"Unlike Lararl," Tavi said, "the Vord queen doesn't have a trusted subordinate she can leave to secure vital rear areas—like the mouth of that tunnel. Without her to control them, the Vord aren't nearly as effective—but as long as the tunnel back to the area they already control stays open, she can throw away as many unguided troops as your warriors can kill. She'll always have more to draw upon. If the tunnel is shut, the Vord are cut off from reinforcements and supplies."

"She must protect it at all costs," Varg rumbled, ears flicking in agreement. "We will find her there."

"She will be strongly guarded," Anag said. "And she will seek to avoid us."

"Without question," Varg said.

"And more Vord will be pouring in through the hole in a constant stream."

"Undoubtedly."

Anag nodded. "Then we must fight through her guard, and all those nearby Vord, *and* any others she can call to her once we reach the edge of the *croach* and alert them of our presence. We are few. Can it be done?"

"If it's all the same to you," Tavi said, "let's not find out."

They waited for three hours, until night was fully on the land. While the Hunters kept watch, the others took what rest they could, until the evening was mature, and the half-frozen rain that had fallen every other evening had begun to speckle the night. Then the group set out on foot through the sleet and darkness toward the glowing beacon of the *croach*.

"I'm going to catch a cold," Max muttered. "These cloaks soak up water like towels."

"That's because they *are* towels, Max," Tavi answered in a low voice. "The Vord sense the heat of our bodies at night. These cloaks are going to hold cold water, help hide us from them."

Max gave Tavi a sour look. "I'm going to have rusty armor. Are you sure this works?"

"I've done it," Tavi said with perfect confidence.

"But does it work?"

One of the Hunters turned to them and bared his teeth in pure threat.

Max muttered something under his breath, about someone smelling like wet dog, but subsided into silence.

They reached the edge of the *croach*, and Tavi shivered. The tall, dark forms of the Canim were just as threatening as the eerie landscape. The *croach* looked just as it had before, a coating like the drippings from an unimaginable number of candles, covering ground and stones and trees with a faintly luminous green sheathing. It spread out before them, nightmarishly beautiful, unsettling, and alien.

Nothing moved within—but that meant little. The Vord could hide dozens of their number virtually in plain sight upon the *croach*, and have them go as undetected as anything hidden by a windcrafter's veil.

Tavi signaled Kitai with a motion of his hand, and the two of them moved up to the edge of the *croach*. Tavi crouched close to the ground to examine it, frowning. He beckoned Kitai, who ghosted over to his side, her green eyes shadowed inside her damp cloak, watching the spectral-lit forest steadily.

"Look," Tavi whispered. "The *croach*. It's thicker here than it was in the Wax Forest."

She bent down and examined it quickly before returning to watching the forest before them. "You're right. But why?"

Tavi pursed his lips, and frowned. "The Vord here have modeled themselves after the Canim. Each one is larger, and much heavier, but not quite as big as a Cane. The *croach* is growing thicker, maybe so that it won't break under the weight of the Vord—just under that of a Cane." He looked up at Kitai. "That's one of the things the *croach* is designed for. It's a kind of watchman. The Vord can alter their forms. They must alter the *croach* to be able to better serve their needs."

Kitai regarded him steadily. Then she nodded, and said, "Then let us test it."

Before Tavi could protest, she had prowled out onto the surface of the *croach*.

Tavi held his breath.

Kitai's feet did not break the surface, though it sank slightly beneath her weight, and slowly restored itself to its original shape after she had passed. She took a dozen steps, body crouched, her bright eyes watching the forest, and returned to Tavi's side.

"Your turn," she whispered.

Tavi eyed her. But then he rose and tested the surface of the *croach* beneath his shoes, glad that he had opted for the lighter pair rather than his heavy, hob-nailed infantry boots. The surface of the *croach* had a bit of give to it, and almost seemed to push up against his feet as he stepped away from it, something like a furycrafted causeway did, if far more weakly. Tavi signaled Max and Durias to come forward, and the two men did. Max, like Tavi, had worn lighter riding boots, but Durias had nothing but his infantry footwear. He grimaced and began taking them off, and stepped out onto the *croach* in his bare feet a moment later.

"Well," Durias murmured, looking around warily. "At least it's warm."

"So far so good," Tavi murmured. "Time to test the Canim's new shoes."

Varg was the first to approach. As the largest of the Canim, he would be the most likely to break the surface of the *croach* and attract the presence of the wax spiders who maintained and repaired it. The big Cane approached with exaggerated steps, a peculiar tilt to his ears that Tavi had never quite seen before on one of the wolf-warriors. Broad discs, almost like dishes, really, of green-black Vord chitin were secured to each of his feet.

"These . . ." he switched to Aleran for the word, "shoes." He shook his head. "I cannot move well in them."

"They'll distribute your weight," Tavi told him. "I hope enough that you can walk the *croach* without breaking it."

"Who taught you the use of these things, Tavar?"

"Some of my people use something like them to move more easily over deep snow," Tavi replied. "Though the original design was made of wood and leather. I thought the chitin was more logical."

"Perhaps if it does break the *croach*, it will not sense the presence of Vord hide as an outside attacker," Varg growled.

"Worth a try," Tavi said. He waited a beat, then added. "Anytime now."

Varg eyed him without amusement. Then he swept his red-eyed gaze around the nearby forest and took a slow, cautious step onto the *croach*.

The shoes worked. They held him up.

Varg growled, a satisfied sound, and gestured once at the other Canim.

Anag and the three Hunters prowled forward onto the glowing *croach*, almost comically cautious about where they placed their chitin-shod feet.

Tavi nodded at them once. Then he turned to Kitai, who flashed him a feral grin and started through the forest in deliberate silence, as scout and pathfinder.

The rest of them followed her, into the glowing green night, and toward the architect and epicenter of that eerie new world.

CHAPTER 31

"The less you say, the better," Rook said. "The less I know about why you're here, the less harm I can do you should the information be taken from me."

Which is precisely why I did not inform you of Bernard's presence, Amara thought.

They had stepped from the slavers' tunnel into one of its adjoining chambers. There was a heady odor coming from a number of tightly fitted barrels against the far wall. Amara recognized the smell of preprocessed hollybells, the flowers from which the drug aphrodin was made. The slavers, it seemed, had used the tunnels as an entry point for smugglers as well as for moving their own merchandise in and out of the city. Doubtless, they had demanded their own extortionate piece of the lucrative enterprise.

"That's a risk I need to take," Amara told her calmly in reply. "You can tell almost as much about my intentions from the questions I ask as from anything I say. If I can't ask you questions, whatever you tell me is going to be of limited use."

Rook smiled grimly. "Believe me, Countess. I think I can make a fair guess at all of your questions."

"Then you must already know what I'm doing here."

"I suspect," Rook said, raising a finger to the collar and shuddering. "I do not *know*. There is a difference."

Amara studied the other woman for a long moment before she shook her head. "How do I know that you aren't feeding me misinformation?"

Rook considered the question seriously for a moment before answering. "Countess, the First Lord himself came to me on the steadholt where my daughter and I were living. It was seventy-four miles south of here."

Amara had to suppress a shiver. The past tense was certainly appropriate if the steadholt they had seen earlier that very day was any indication. The region that far south of Ceres had certainly been overrun by the Vord.

"He told me what was happening. He told me that if I served him on this mission, he would see to it that my daughter was taken to safety—to anywhere in Alera that I chose. And that if I returned from it, I could join her."

Amara could not suppress the curse that slipped from between her lips. Gaius had given Rook no choice at all: Do what he wished, or perish with her daughter before the oncoming menace. "Rook, I don't know why you—"

Rook held up her hand for silence. Then said, simply, "I sent her to Calderon."

For a moment, Amara couldn't find a response. "Why Calderon?" she finally asked.

Rook shrugged a shoulder and gave her a weary smile. "I wanted her as far from the Vord as possible. With the most capable, forewarned, and best-prepared people I knew. I know that Count Bernard has been trying to warn folk of the Vord for years. I assumed that he would begin preparing his own home to resist them. If I betray you, Countess, my daughter has no one to protect her. I would rather die screaming with blood running from my nose and ears than that."

Amara bowed her head. It was an accurate description of the kind of death that awaited anyone who defied a discipline collar too severely or for too long, or should anyone try to remove the collar save whoever had put it there. The locking mechanism on the collars was fiendishly complex, but Amara had no doubt that Rook could bypass it whenever she chose, given the proper tools.

It would, of course, kill her to remove it.

Rook had defied High Lords and Ladies—and the First Lord himself, in her effort to secure her child when she had been held prisoner against Rook's loyalty by the late High Lord Kalarus. Amara had no doubt whatsoever that the woman would sacrifice her life without hesitation if she thought that by doing so she could protect Masha.

"Very well," Amara said. "What can you tell me?"

"Little," Rook said. She made a frustrated gesture at the collar. "Orders. But I can show you."

Amara nodded once.

Rook turned back to the tunnel and beckoned her. "Follow me."

Veiled to the utmost of her ability, Amara crouched on a blackened rooftop beside Rook, overlooking the city's former Slave Market, the Vord's "recruitment" area.

She'd seen merrier slaughterhouses.

There were several dozen Vord, the low-slung garimlike versions, assembled in the courtyard, waiting in patient coils of gleaming black exoskeleton next to every entrance to and from the place, and Amara suspected that she would see similar sentries at every crossroads and gateway within the city.

Besides the Vord, several hundred Alerans filled the Slave Market. The majority of them were imprisoned in the various different cages required to hold strongly gifted furycrafters. Firecrafters were those imprisoned beneath the steady rain-shower trickle of water that poured down from pipes overhead. Earthcrafters were being held in cages suspended several feet from the ground. The windcrafters, as Amara well knew, would be inside the low brick cubes of solid stone, with no access to air but for what could come in through a few holes no larger across than Amara's thumb. A metal cage sufficed for woodcrafters, though they were placed far opposite the courtyard from the heavy wooden beams that restrained the metalcrafters inside.

Most interesting were the cages that had to take multiple layers of precautions to contain their prisoners—doubtless the captured Citizenry. One metal cage that swung high off the ground and was simultaneously drizzled with water and fine black dirt caught Amara's eye, particularly. The cage held a number of damp, mud-spattered figures, only two of them armored men captured during the battle. The other four were women, probably taken when the Vord overran their homes to the south. All of them—and most of the prisoners Amara could see, for that matter—lay in the loose-limbed stupor of the aphrodin addict.

Amara watched as a pair of silver-collared guards dragged a drug-disoriented prisoner from one of the stone windcrafter pens, a young man in shattered armor. They dragged him across the courtyard to the stage where the auctions were held, and up onto it. They slammed him down hard onto the surface of the stage, though the young man—a boy, really—hardly seemed to be in any condition to stand upright, let alone offer resistance.

A pair of extremely attractive young women on the stage, wearing little more than scraps of cloth and gleaming silver collars, approached him. One of them silently began unknotting the thong of a necklace or amulet the young man wore on his neck and took it away, drawing the first feeble stir of protest from him that Amara had seen.

The second girl knelt and caressed his hair and face for a moment, before sliding a slender-necked bottle to his lips. Amara saw the girl's lips urging him to drink. The young man did, his eyes still dazed, and a moment later slumped even more wearily to the floor of the stage—more drugs.

And then Kalarus Brencis Minoris mounted the steps and walked over to him, his movements brisk.

Amara shivered, staring at the son of High Lord Kalarus, the young man whom she had last seen weeping and running for his life on the slopes of some fury-forsaken mountain near his former home, stumbling over the corpses of hundreds of recently deceased elite soldiers. Brencis was dressed in fine silks of pure white, unsoiled by any mud or blood. His long dark hair curled gorgeously, as if freshly touched by hot curlers and a brush. His fingers were crusted with rings, and chains lay in looping ranks upon his chest.

They didn't conceal the silver collar around his throat.

Fascinated and repelled, Amara gestured, willing Cirrus to carry the words on the stage, dozens of yards distant, to her ears.

"My lord," said one of the scantily clad girls. Her words were slurred with wine or aphrodin or both. "He is ready, my lord."

"I can see that," Brencis said testily. He reached into an open chest that lay on the stage and drew out a handful of slavers' collars, shaking them in careless irritation until only one remained in his grasp. He settled in front of the dazed soldier, slipped the collar around his neck, drew a knife, and cut his thumb with it. He shoved his bloodied thumb viciously against the catch of the collar, drawing a choking gasp from the young man.

Amara shivered.

She watched as the collar went to work on him. She was familiar with the basic theory behind the device. It used multiple furycrafted disciplines to flood the targets' senses with ecstatic euphoria at first, pacifying them completely. Not that the collar needed much help in the case of the young soldier, dazed and drugged as he was. Even so, there was a visible arching of his body, and his eyes rolled, then fluttered closed.

That would go on for a while, Amara knew. Long enough that when the sensation ceased, it would almost seem like pain, all on its own. When the brutal agony the collars were capable of inflicting at their owner's will set in, it would seem that much worse by comparison.

"This is the truth, soldier," Brencis said, wiping his bloodied thumb on the man's tunic. "You serve the Vord queen now, or her highest representative. Which means that for the moment, you serve me, and anyone I choose to place over you. Take any action you know is against your new loyalty's interests, and you'll hurt. Serve and obey, and you will be rewarded."

By way of demonstration, Brencis idly shoved one of the half-naked girls across the soldier. She made a purring sound and nuzzled her mouth against his throat, sliding one of her thighs over his.

"Listen to her," Brencis spat, contempt in his voice. "Everything she says is true."

The girl pressed her mouth against the young man's ear and began whispering. Amara couldn't make out much of what she was saying, beyond the words "serve" and "obey." But it seemed simple enough to work out—the girl was emphasizing what Brencis had already told the soldier, reinforcing the commands while his mind was being bent out of shape by the collar and the drugs.

"Bloody crows," Amara whispered, feeling sick. She'd known that the collars had been developed for the control of even the most violent criminals—and she'd heard it argued many times that the potential for abuse in the collars was far greater than most of the Realm realized, but she'd never seen it before. Whatever was going on down there, it must have its roots in the techniques High Lord Kalare had used to create his psychotic Immortals.

And, Amara thought, it gave them control of previously free Alerans. It worked. Or at least it worked often enough to give the Vord queen an Aleran honor guard. Those who had never really been motivated by anything higher than self-interest, it seemed, were easily turned, if the men accompanying Rook were any kind of measure.

"Brencis!" came a croaking cry from one of the cages. "Brencis, please!"

Amara focused on the source of the voice—a young woman in the Citizens' cage, probably attractive, though it was difficult to tell through the mud.

Brencis sorted through various collars in the chest.

"Brencis! Can't you hear me?"

"I hear you, Flora," Brencis said. "I just don't *care*."

The young woman sobbed. "Please. Please, just let me go. We were *betrothed*, Brencis."

"It's funny, life's little twists and turns," Brencis said conversationally. He glanced up at the cage. "You always did like to play with aphrodin, Flora. You and your sister." His mouth twisted into a bitter sneer. "A pity there are no Antillans around to complete the evening for you."

The young woman started sobbing, a broken little sound. "But we were . . . we were . . ."

"That was in a different world, Flora," Brencis said. "That's done now. In a few more weeks, there won't be anything but Vord. You should be glad. You get to be a part of the winning side." He paused to run an idly admiring hand over the flank of the whispering young woman lying atop the dazed soldier behind him. "Even if you wind up with too little mind to do anything but help soothe the new recruits. The process does that to some of them, which is just as well. So we clean them up into little aphrodin dream boys and girls and let them whisper."

Flora wept harder.

"Don't worry, Flora." He directed a venomous gaze at the cage. "I'll make sure you have a pretty boy to keep you company when it's your turn. You'll enjoy the process. Most of them do. Volunteer to go through it again, usually." He looked at a pair of the collared guards nearby, and said, "What are you two standing around for? Get the next one."

Amara crept slowly back from the edge of the building and settled down next to Rook. Then she turned and descended to the relative safety of the building, which had been a prosperous tailor's residence, before the Vord came. Rook followed her.

Amara sat for a moment, simply absorbing the horrific, machinelike pace of the way the captured Alerans' very humanity was being destroyed.

"I know you aren't supposed to speak of it," Amara said quietly. "But I need you to try."

Rook swallowed. She lifted her fingers to the collar at her throat, her face pale, and nodded.

"How many have been taken?" Amara asked.

"Several h—" Rook began. She sucked in a breath, squeezing her eyes shut, and her face beaded with sweat. "Seven or eight hundred at least. Maybe a hundred who didn't need to be . . ." Her face twisted into a grimace. ". . . coerced. Of the rest, only a little more than half of them come out of it . . . functional. The rest get used to help recruit more or are given to the Vord."

"As slaves?" Amara asked.

"As food, Countess."

Amara shivered. "There were hundreds of people up there."

Rook nodded, her breath coming in steady, consciously regulated timing. "Yes. Any strongly gifted crafter captured by the Vord is brought here now."

"Where are the collars coming from?"

Rook let out a bitter, pained laugh, and withdrew what must have been half a dozen slender silver collars from a pouch on her belt, tossing them aside like refuse. "Dead slaves, Countess. They litter the ground in this place."

Amara bent over and picked up one of the collars and stared at it. It didn't feel like anything other than metal, slightly cool, and smooth underneath her fingertips. "How is it done?" she asked Rook. "The collars, the drug. It isn't enough to do *that*."

"You'd be surprised, Countess," Rook said, shuddering. "But there's more to it, as well. Brencis does something to each collar as he attaches—" She jerked in pain, and blood suddenly ran from one of her nostrils. "As he at-taches it," she gasped. "His father knew how and taught him. He won't t-tell anyone how. It p-protects his life, as long as the V-Vord want more crafters to s-serve them."

She clenched her teeth over a scream and pressed one hand to her mouth to muffle the sound, the other to the center of her forehead, as she crumpled slowly to the floor.

Amara had to look away from the woman. "Enough," she said gently. "Enough, Rook."

Rook rocked back and forth on her knees, falling silent, her breath coming in gasps. She nodded once to Amara, and slurred, "Be 'llright. Minute."

Amara touched her shoulder gently, then rose to stare out the window at the courtyard without through a window that had been broken, its jagged edges stained with drying blood. The cages were packed. Amara began to count the number of prisoners, and shook her head. Hundreds of Alerans waited there to be taken into the service of the Vord.

Brencis had just put the collar around the throat of a woman in a fine, soaking-wet silk gown. She writhed on the platform while he stood over her, an expression of revulsion and hunger and something Amara could not put a name to on his beautiful face.

"You'd better report in," she said quietly. "Do your best not to give anything away."

Rook had recovered somewhat. She held a cloth to her face, cleaning the blood from her mouth and chin. "I'll die first, Countess," she whispered.

"Go."

Rook departed without a further word. Amara watched as she entered the courtyard a few moments later, walking briskly toward Brencis. Again, she beckoned, and Cirrus brought the sound to her.

Brencis looked up at Rook as she approached.

Rook's stance and bearing had changed completely. There was a liquid, sensual grace to her movements, her hips shifting with a noticeable, swaying rhythm as she walked.

"Rook," Brencis spat, his voice irritated. "What took you so long?"

"Incompetence," Rook replied in a throaty purr. She pressed her body full-length against Brencis's and kissed him.

The young slaver returned the kiss with ardor, and Amara's stomach twisted in revulsion.

"Where are the two I sent with you?" he growled.

"When they realized I was going to tell you what they'd done, they thought they'd leave my body somewhere dark and quiet. After they'd raped me." She kissed his throat. "I objected. I'm afraid they're the worse for wear. Should I go recover their collars, my lord?"

"Tell me?" Brencis said. The anger had faded from his voice, a different kind of heat replacing it. "Tell me what?"

"The fools questioned the Cursors too hard," Rook said. "I told you we should have recruited them."

"Couldn't take the chance that they'd . . . mmmm. That their minds would break down." He shook his head. "You're earthcrafting me, you little bitch. Mmmm. Stop it."

Rook let out a wicked little laugh. Her ripped shirt chose that moment to slip, exposing naked skin. "You love it, my lord. And I can't help it. I took them with my bare hands. It was close. That always leaves me in a mood." She pressed against him in a slow undulation of her body. "You could take me here if you wished it. Who could stop you, my lord? Right here, before everyone. There are no rules any longer, no laws. Shall I fight you? Would that please you, to force me?"

Brencis turned to Rook with a growl, seizing a handful of her hair in a painful grasp, jerking her head back as he kissed her with near-bruising violence.

Amara turned away, sickened. She would return to the tunnels until nightfall.

She had killed men before.

But this was the first time she'd ever *wanted* to.

CHAPTER 32

Isana had been back in her chambers in the wall for perhaps two minutes before there was a diffident knock at the door, followed by the decidedly nondiffident entry of High Lady Aria Placida.

"That will be all, Araris," she said over her shoulder, her tone neutral. She shut the door firmly and folded her arms as she stared at Isana.

Isana arched an eyebrow at the other woman, then moved her hand in a rolling gesture, beckoning her to speak.

Lady Placida's face quivered through several half-formed expressions that never quite congealed into any single emotion before she finally blurted, "Have you lost your mind?"

To her own complete surprise, Isana burst into laughter. She couldn't help it. She laughed and laughed until she had to sit down on the edge of the small chamber's bed, her eyes watering, her sides aching.

It took a few moments to get herself under control again, and when she did, Aria was staring at her with a distinctly uncomfortable expression on her face. "Isana . . . ?"

"I was just thinking," Isana said, her words still quivering with the edges of the laughter. "Finally. I know how it must feel to be Tavi."

Aria opened her mouth, closed it again, and let out an exasperated sigh. "From a watercrafter of your skill, that's a remarkably ironic statement."

Isana waved her hand. "Oh, you know how teenagers are. There's so much emotion piled up in them that you can hardly sort out one from the next." She felt the smile fade a little wistfully. "That was the last time I spent more than a few weeks around him, you know. He was fifteen."

Some of the rigidity went out of Aria's stance. "Yes. My own sons were off to the Academy at sixteen, then the Legions after that. It hardly seems fair, does it?"

Isana met Aria's gaze. "My son doesn't live under my protection anymore. But that doesn't mean that he doesn't need it. That's why I challenged Raucus today."

Aria tilted her head. "I'm not sure what you mean."

"Without the northern Legions, the Vord could destroy us all," Isana said, her voice quiet and firm. "When my son comes home, Alera is still going to be here."

"Isana, dear. I understand *why* you did it. What I don't see is how the bloody crows you think killing yourself is going to accomplish your goal."

"Reasoning with him is useless," Isana said. "He's too wrapped up in the conflict here, in the loss. You saw him at the funeral."

Aria folded her arms against her stomach. "He's not the only one who feels that way."

"But he is the only one who commands the loyalty of Antillus's Legions." Isana frowned. "Well. I suppose Crassus or Maximus might be able to do so. Crassus has the legal right and Maximus has served multiple terms as an infantryman. I suspect that would give him a strong popularity with—"

"Isana," Aria interrupted quietly, "you're babbling. My nieces do this to my sister when they're trying to avoid discussing something."

"I am *not* babbling," Isana said.

"Then at the risk of making you feel somewhat foolish, I should point out that neither Maximus nor Crassus is in Alera. Even if you succeed in your duel—which I regard as something as close to impossible as anything can be— then what will you have gained? Raucus will be dead, in which case the Legions will almost certainly not abandon their posts on the walls. Anyone that is appointed to stand as regent until Crassus returns will certainly not pursue a radical change in policy.

"And," she added, "if you lose, you will be dead. Raucus will almost certainly do exactly as he has been doing."

"I'm not going to lose," Isana said, "and he's not going to die."

"In a duel to the death—one which *you* instigated." Aria shook her head. "I know you didn't go to the Academy, but . . . there is something called 'diplomacy,' Isana."

"There isn't time," Isana said quietly. "Just as there wasn't time earlier today, Aria." She felt her cheeks heat slightly. "When I hit you. For which I must now apologize."

Aria opened her mouth, then pressed her lips into a line and shook her head. "No. In retrospect . . . it may have been for the best."

"Necessary or not, I wronged you. I'm sorry."

Some of the rigid tension eased slowly from Aria's stance, and the sense of angry restraint around her faded slightly. "I wasn't thinking very clearly," she said. "Afterward, I . . . I felt the way they were communicating with one another. I've never sensed anything like that before. And you felt it yesterday." She shrugged. "You were right about them. I didn't—" Aria's eyes widened, and she looked up at Isana with her mouth open. "Great furies, Isana. That's what this is. You're slapping Raucus across the face to get his attention."

"If I'd thought a slap across the face would do the job," Isana said wryly, "I would have stopped *before* I dropped the challenge onto him." She shook her head. "I have to reach him. I have to get through his anger and his pride. And there's no *time*, Aria."

Lady Placida stood silently for several long seconds. Then she said, "I've known Raucus since I was fourteen years old. We were . . . close, back then, at the Academy. And this is dangerous, Isana. Very dangerous." She glanced at the door and then back to her. "I'll go talk to him."

"It isn't going to change his mind about the duel," Isana said.

"No," Aria said calmly. She gave Isana a slight smile. "But perhaps there will be a miracle and his stiff neck will bend half an inch." She nodded. "At least I can lay a foundation you might be able to build upon."

"Thank you," Isana said quietly.

"Thank me if you survive," Aria replied, and slipped quietly out of the room.

Several hours later, Isana had taken a private meal and sat reading dispatches from the south, sent by water fury and transcribed for her and for Lord Antillus.

Matters had grown worse. Ceres was overrun, and the Vord were harrying the Aleran forces, who had been forced to fight a series of desperate actions to slow the advancing horde enough to allow desperate civilians to flee. Teams of engineers were dismantling causeways as they went, destruction that would take decades of effort to repair—if it ever was.

Losses in the Legions were hideous—worse than anything seen in Kalarus's rebellion or in the battle with the Canim. Militias were mobilizing all throughout Alera, with priority given to those younger men who had most recently left the Legions—but virtually every male in the Realm had served at least a single two-year term in the Legions, and everyone was being called upon to take up arms again.

The problem, of course, was in supplying those arms. *Legionares* were not allowed to keep their weaponry and armor upon leaving the Legion—they were left to be used by the recruits arriving to take their places. Most *legionares* retired to their steadholts, where the only weapons readily available, affordable, and necessary were bows and the occasional hunting spear.

In the cities, of course, there were the civic legions—but they were peace-keepers and investigators, not soldiers. Lightly armored, generally more familiar with truncheons than swords, and used to operating in an entirely different manner than armies in the field, they were of more use organizing refugees and preventing crimes among the displaced population than in actual combat with the enemy. In both cities and in the smaller towns, each lord and Count would generally maintain a small body of personal armsmen, but those rarely consisted of more than twenty or thirty men. There were similarly a limited number of professional soldiers, generally roving from job to job, plying the trade of violence out from under the rigid structure of the Legions. But all in all, there were fewer weapons available than hands to wield them, and peaceful steadholt smithies across the Realm were desperately forging steel for use in Alera's defense.

The thought of that chilled Isana. Back at her own steadholt—her former steadholt, she supposed wistfully—there would be a flurry of activity. Harvest would have been well over a few weeks ago. Elder Frederic would be at Araris's old forge, laboring on weapons instead of horseshoes. Children would be gathering slender branches, smoothing and straightening them into arrow shafts, while their older siblings were taught how to fletch feathers, fix nocks, and secure arrowheads onto them.

Isana bowed her head and set the dispatches aside. She had seen what war could do to the steadholts of the Calderon Valley. She had seen the slaughtered livestock, the burned-out buildings, the broken, discarded bodies. Isanaholt had been spared the scythe, so far. But it could easily, *so* easily, be her own stock that was hacked apart, her own outbuildings fired, her own people piled in pathetic windrows of empty flesh on the bloodied earth.

She set the dispatches aside and bowed her head. Was it selfish of her to worry so for the people on her own steadholt when so many other steadholts were in danger? When so many other steadholts had already been overwhelmed by the enemy? She was claiming the title of First Lady. She had a responsibility to far more people than the folk of a single tiny steadholt—yet they were Alerans, too.

Besides, was there really any choice? Could she *not* fear for them?

There was a brisk knock at the door and Isana looked up as the door opened to reveal Antillus Raucus. She could hear the movement of feet on stone in the hallway outside. Evidently, the High Lord had been accompanied by *singulares* when he came calling. Isana wasn't sure if she was amused by the fact that he might have felt threatened enough to need them. More likely, he had brought them as witnesses to verify that he had not attempted any wrongdoing in coming to speak to her.

Or to restrain Araris while he *did* carry out said wrongdoing.

The big Antillan High Lord filled up the doorway, a broad-shouldered, ruggedly handsome man who looked, Isana realized, a great deal more like Maximus than his legitimate son, Crassus. That explained a great deal about Maximus's upbringing.

She rose and inclined her head with as much poise and restraint as she could convincingly pretend to. "Your Grace."

Raucus ground his teeth as he returned the gesture with a bow, then said, voice tight and hard, "Your Highness."

"Have you come to concede and accompany me south with your Legions, sir?" Isana inquired.

"I have not."

She arched an eyebrow at him. "Then what brings you here? Strictly speaking, you should have sent your second to speak to mine."

"I already spoke to your second," Raucus replied. "And I don't send others to do things for me when it's clearly my obligation to act."

"Ah," Isana said. "I did not send Aria to you, sir. If she has spoken to you, she took it upon herself to do so." She reflected for a second, then added, "As out of character for her as that seems."

Raucus's mouth twitched at one corner, more bitter than amused, and he shook his head. "She couldn't talk you out of it either, eh?"

"Something like that," Isana said.

"I came here to offer you a chance to leave," Antillus said, his tone steady, his words carefully neutral. "Take Rari and Lady Aria and get off my land. We won't mention your challenge again. To anyone."

Isana considered that for a moment. It was a significant gesture. Many folk in the southern portions of the Realm often sneered at the tendency of the more conservative to defend vigorously such notions as their sense of personal valor, but the fact was that in the war-torn north, such a thing was a survival trait. Without the personal courage to face his foes—and more importantly, his *legionares'* belief in that courage—Antillus Raucus would face a horde of problems that could otherwise be avoided. When men had to stand on the battlefield, their courage itself a weapon that was every bit as deadly to the enemy as swords and arrows, one could not afford to appear as a coward to one's men.

By offering Isana a chance to simply depart, Raucus was running the very real risk of appearing, to his men, to have been skittish about taking her on—particularly after the clash of their furycraft before the walls earlier that day. Granted, if Isana left quietly, and no one said anything further about it, that damage would be minimized, but there were bound to be rumors, regardless.

She supposed it made sense, from Raucus's perspective. The man simply could not accept that the threat facing the Realm was greater than that which he'd spent his entire life—and the lives of who knew how many of his *legionares*—fighting.

"I'm sorry," she said quietly. "I can't do that."

"You're strong," he said in that same distant, uninflected tone. "I'll give you that. But you aren't stronger than I am." His gaze was steady. "If you see this through, I'll kill you. Don't think I won't."

Isana gestured at the table. "You've seen the dispatches. You know the danger."

His features shifted subtly, hardening. "I've spent my life fighting a war no one in the south can be bothered about. Burying men no one down there mourns. Seeing steadholts devastated. I know what they're going through, Your Highness. I've seen it more than once, visited on my own people."

"Then it should make you more eager to stop it—not less."

His eyes flashed in sudden anger. "If I take my Legions from the Wall, the Icemen will slaughter thousands of holders who can't protect themselves. It's as simple as that. Never mind what will happen to the rest of Alera if the Icemen decide to press south and grind us to pieces between two enemies."

"What if they're willing not to do that?"

"They aren't," Raucus growled. "Whatever you talked about in half of an hour today, take it from someone who has spent a lifetime dealing with them. They'll fight. That's all there is to it."

"You use that phrase a great deal," Isana said. She rose and lifted her chin, meeting Raucus's eyes. "What if you're wrong, my lord?"

"I'm not."

"What if you *are*?" Isana demanded, her voice still gentle. "What if you could achieve a truce with the Icemen and take your forces south to the relief of the First Lord? What if you could be saving thousands of lives, right now—but you aren't?"

His gaze never wavered. A long, silent moment passed.

"I'll make sure your coach is standing by," he said quietly. "Be gone by morning, First Lady."

He bowed to her again, his back and shoulders stiff, then turned and swept from the room.

Isana felt herself begin to shake a moment later, in simple reaction to the tension and stress. She grimaced and folded her hands in her lap, closing her eyes and willing Rill into her own body, to exert some measure of control over her nerves. She urged blood to flow more smoothly, calmly through her limbs, and felt her hands warm up a little. She crossed the room to sit by the little fireplace, her hands extended, and took deep breaths until her quivering fingers stilled.

Araris entered silently and shut the door. He stood there, a silent presence against her senses, his concern a small thing beside the steady warmth of his love.

"He called you Rari," Isana said, without turning.

She didn't need to see him to know that a small smile had quirked up the unmarred side of his face. "I was in my first term at the Academy when he and Septimus were in their second. I followed them around a lot. Raucus bought me my first . . ." He coughed and she felt a flush of mild embarrassment from him. ". . . drink."

Isana shook her head, and enjoyed the feel of the smile that came to her mouth. "Thirty years ago. It doesn't seem like it should have been such a long time."

"Time goes by," Araris replied. "But yes. It doesn't feel like it was all that long ago to me, either." His mouth quirked into a small smile. "Then my knees ache and I see grey hairs in the mirror."

She turned to face him. He was leaning back against the door, legs crossed, arms folded over his chest. Isana walked over to him and ran the fingers of one hand lightly over his hair, caressing the silver that peppered the dark brown. "I think you're beautiful."

He captured her fingers in his, and kissed them delicately before murmuring, "You *have* gone mad."

She shook her head, smiling, and pressed herself against Araris, laying her head on his armored chest. His arms slid around her a moment later.

"You're taking an awful risk," he told her.

"I have little choice," she replied. "The only way to take the Shield Legions south is with Raucus's cooperation. You know the man. Do you think he would murder an essentially unarmed woman in cold blood?"

"Not back when I knew him. But he isn't the man he was when we were young," Araris said. "He's harder. More bitter. I know you want to try to reach out to him, Isana, but bloody crows."

Isana said nothing. She just held on to him.

"Maybe you should think about his offer," Araris said. "Maybe there's another way."

"Such as?"

"Take him south. Let him see the Vord for himself. Reading dispatches is one thing. Seeing it with your own eyes is another."

Isana inhaled and exhaled deeply and closed her eyes. "Open eyes are of little use when the mind behind them is closed."

Araris stroked her hair with one hand. "True enough."

"And . . . and there's no *time*." How could it go so quickly when you needed it most?

"If he . . . hurts you," Araris said calmly, "I'm going to kill him."

She lifted her head sharply and met his eyes. "You mustn't."

His scarred face was completely immobile. "Mustn't I?"

She framed his face with her hands. "The point of this is to reach his heart, Araris. He's built up layers and layers of defenses around his emotions—and being up here, it's easy to see why. He's channeled his passion into protecting his people, fighting the threat that's right here in front of him. Even if I die, trying to reach him, I might get through. I think he's a decent man, beneath the calluses and scars. If my blood is what it takes to wash them away, so be it."

Araris stared down at her for a long moment.

"Bloody crows," he whispered, finally. "I've never known such a woman as you, Isana."

She found her face warming, but she couldn't look away from his steady gaze.

"I love you," he said, simply. "I'll not try to carry you off before you can go out and get hurt tomorrow. I won't try to change what you are."

She didn't trust herself to speak. So she kissed him. Their arms slid around one another, and time went by on the wings of a falcon.

When he finally broke the kiss, though, there was something cold and hard in his voice.

"But I'm not changing who I am, either," he said in that same calm, steady voice. His eyes flashed and hardened. "And if he hurts you, my love, I'll leave his corpse out there on the snow at the foot of his precious Wall."

CHAPTER 33

Tavi walked slowly forward, shivering beneath the damp coldness of his body-heat-concealing cloak. The weather had cooperated with them remarkably well. Cold rain, mixed with soft-frozen sleet, continued to fall, and the wind had died down to almost nothing as night closed in and slowly drew talons of ice across the face of the land.

As surprise assaults went, it was the most miserable one he could remember actually participating in. His nose was running freely, and he had already, he thought, caught the cold Max had glumly predicted. He didn't want to keep sniffling, and yet wiping at his face with a cloth wasn't something he could spare attention for, either. As a result, his face looked like a small child's—all in all a great deal less dignified than befitted a Princeps of the Realm, he was certain.

Kitai walked on his left, and slightly ahead of him. Her senses were sharper than his, and though he didn't like the idea of letting the young woman be the first to step closer to oncoming danger, he knew better than to ignore the advantage to be gained by doing so. To his right, and slightly behind him, Maximus walked with his hand on his sword. His rough-hewn friend's expression was placid, distant, his eyes focused on nothing, though Tavi had no doubt that Max was perfectly aware of everything around him. He doubtless had a number of furycraftings held ready to use, and doing so was an effort of will and concentration that demanded the most out of the young Antillan.

On the opposite side of Kitai from Tavi, Durias kept pace with a distinctly unhappy expression on his face. Granted, that might be because the blocky former slave was just as cold and wet and uncomfortable as Tavi. It might also be because Tavi was leading him into the stronghold of a horde of nightmare creatures in an alien land two thousand miles from his home.

Max and Kitai had both faced gratuitous amounts of danger with him before—and not always for reasons as desperate and concrete as those before them now. Durias, though, was a new companion. He'd gotten where he had in life by being a man of both competence and conviction, and Tavi had never seen him comport himself with less than complete integrity and sound reasoning.

Durias had to be wondering what he had done to deserve *this*.

As if sensing Tavi's gaze, Durias turned to him, an inquiring look upon his face. Tavi gave him what he hoped was a reassuring nod, and sternly kept himself from smiling. It just wasn't the proper time for it.

Behind them, the Canim walked upon their broad shoes, leaving dish-shaped impressions in the thick surface of the *croach*. Thus far, none of their steps had actually broken that surface. The steady, cold rain barely had time to begin to fill each dent before it vanished, the surface of the strange substance rebuilding itself.

Kitai abruptly lifted a hand, and every member of their hunting party froze in place.

The woods ahead of them shivered, then a trio of the enormous, froglike Vord came into sight, not twenty yards away. They padded by on broad, flapping feet, their movements sinuous and awkward at the same time.

Tavi tensed, and found his own hand moving toward his sword. They weren't yet halfway into the *croach*-covered area around the Vord's tunnel. If they were seen now, they might never have a chance to strike down the queen—or of escaping the Vord's domain alive. Should one of the frog-Vord notice them, it could mean their lives.

But none of the three even glanced toward Tavi and his companions.

Tavi let out a shuddering breath and closed his eyes in relief—just for a second. He could sense the same reaction from the others.

Kitai waited until the Vord had passed from sight, then glanced back at Tavi, nodded, and started forward again. They all followed her, their pace deliberate and steady, avoiding thin patches of the *croach* that might be more easily broken than other places.

It was during one such detour that Tavi came across a broken section of *croach*. Three parallel claw marks, perhaps an inch apart, had been raked through the thin sections of *croach* at the base of a fallen tree. The marks were oozing fresh, brightly glowing green liquid, and Tavi stared at it in horror.

The wax spiders would already be on the way. His group would shortly be discovered, and they hadn't even been responsible for the alarm that would surely be raised. It wasn't so much the thought of being killed that bothered Tavi—though it certainly did. He just hated the idea of dying because some *other* fool had made a mistake. He stared at the damaged *croach*, thinking furiously, and motioned the others back.

Everyone obeyed, except for Varg. The scarred old Cane came forward, his strides exaggerated but confident upon the broad shoes, and froze when he saw what Tavi was staring at. The Cane's eyes narrowed instantly, and began flickering at the trees all around them, his lips peeling back from his fangs.

Tavi began to back up, only to realize that it was too late.

One of the wax spiders had come, gliding across the ground toward them. It had too many legs to be a real spider, of course, but that was the closest thing Tavi could think of in form and movement. Its body was covered in a translucent white chitin, and it was about as big as a medium-sized dog, perhaps thirty-five or forty pounds in weight, though its long limbs made it look larger. A number of glossy eyes glittered greenly on its head, just above the bases of a pair of thick, thorn-shaped mandibles, fangs that Tavi knew bore a swift-acting, dangerous poison.

Tavi dropped his hand to his sword without thinking.

Varg's huge paw-hand closed over his. "Wait," the Cane rumbled. "And do not move."

Tavi blinked at the Cane, then back to the spider. The creature was barely a dozen feet away. It would be sure to notice them around the damaged *croach* and raise the alarm. As Tavi watched, the spider abruptly oriented on them, turning its entire body on its many legs, and began bobbing up and down in agitation, a precursor to the whistling shrieks with which it would warn the rest of the Vord.

Before it could make a sound, something exploded out of the darkness beneath the thick branches of the fallen pine, a dark-furred blur that moved in perfect silence and hit the wax spider like a stone from an old Romanic war engine. The spider was driven across six feet of *croach*, its legs flailing helplessly as its attacker ripped savagely at the joint of its head and body.

Before Tavi could fully register that the attack was happening, the creature ripped the spider's head from its body, and the rest of it collapsed to the surface of the *croach*, its legs twitching and flailing.

Tavi blinked. The animal that had dispatched the wax spider crouched atop its corpse. Its fur was dark, and it had a long, sinuous body. Its limbs were powerful, solid, spreading into clawed paws like those of a mountain lion. Its head, though, was more like that of a wolf, or a bear, with a broad muzzle full of sharp and—obviously—wickedly effective teeth upon what looked like incredibly powerful jaws.

Tavi recognized a deadly predator when he saw it—and even if that one weighed no more than the wax spider, it had dispatched the Vord as easily as it might have a rabbit.

The beast turned its glittering yellow eyes toward Tavi and Varg, and silently bared its impressive, green-spattered fangs.

"Do not make eye contact," Varg rumbled quietly. "Back away slowly. Do not lift your hands."

Tavi glanced at the Cane, then they both began backing away. Tavi glanced back, and saw the other Canim looking on, weapons actually drawn and in their hands. The Hunters hadn't drawn when the Vord had come close to them—but this creature, it seemed, merited more of their respect.

Once Tavi and Varg had reached the Hunters, they all continued backing away, until the site of the kill was a good fifty or sixty yards off, before the Hunters seemed to relax, putting their weapons away.

"Close," Anag said.

"What was that thing?" Max muttered to Tavi. "I couldn't see."

Tavi described it briefly to Max, and turned to Varg. "Is that animal native to this land?"

"To all of Canea," Varg said. "One of the finest hunters in it. Strong, swift, intelligent."

"Smart enough to set a trap for the Vord," Tavi mused. "It had clawed open the *croach* specifically to attract a wax spider."

Varg flicked his ears in assent. "It does not surprise me. They are wise enough to use such ruses."

"They are mad," Anag said. The golden-furred Cane crouched, watching in the direction of the small hunter, his body language tense, wary.

"Mad?" Tavi asked.

"Brave to the point of insanity," said the eldest of the Hunters. Tavi turned to blink at the Cane, who had been silent since he had spoken to Varg on the roof of Lararl's headquarters. "It will fight anything to protect its territory, or its kill. It fights without hesitation, without fear, without reservation."

Tavi lifted his eyebrows. "But it is so small."

The Canim looked at each other, amusement in their body language. "Aleran," Varg said, "do not be deceived by its size. I've seen one kill a full-grown, armed warrior. It gutted the fool while it tore his throat out, and was gone before the body hit the ground. Even if you fought and killed one, it would do everything in its power to take you with it. I've never heard of one being slain without leaving scars."

"Look," Kitai said quietly.

Tavi looked up, and saw three more wax spiders approaching the area. The hunting beast was nowhere to be seen, nor was the body of the dead spider. Instead of raising an outcry, though, the worker Vord simply went about repairing the damaged *croach*, then beat a hasty retreat.

"Not even the Vord want more trouble from him tonight," Varg rumbled.

The Hunter nodded, and said, in the tone of someone quoting a proverb, "Only a fool seeks a quarrel with a tavar."

Tavi blinked again, first at the Hunter, then at Varg.

"Come, Tavar," Varg growled. "Let us go around, and leave your little brother to his meal."

Twice more, Kitai signaled them to halt, and twice more, enemy Vord passed by. Once, they were more of the frog-things they had already seen. The second group was farther away, larger, and more indistinct. Neither encounter resulted in an outcry.

Tavi was sure they were getting close when they encountered the first active wax spiders, gliding silently through the glowing green pines in a row that stretched out into the distance to the north, like a line of ants trundling back and forth from their nest to a fallen fruit tree, each bearing a swollen bellyful of glowing green *croach* with it, partially visible through their translucent bodies.

It wasn't hard to imagine where they were going—to spread the gelatinous substance over the bodies of the dead. It wouldn't matter to the spiders whether the corpses were of their own kind or of the Shuaran warriors who had already engaged them. To the Vord, any dead flesh was simply food to be covered and consumed by the *croach*.

At a nod from Tavi, Kitai adjusted their course, and they began following the wax spiders' back trail, searching for their point of origin. As they did, they saw other Vord, traveling in a solid file on the far side of the spiders, also heading to the north. These creatures, though, were far larger. Many were the tall, lean, Cane-shaped forms they had seen at the fortifications. Most were the thin-limbed frog-things. Others were larger than either of the first—much larger, nearly the size of a gargant, but scuttling along like crabs or lobsters. They must be the warrior forms his uncle had described from the Vord incursion into the Calderon Valley, but they were too far away to be seen any more distinctly. He proceeded with caution.

A shape rose through the trees in front of them, something that looked like an enormous tumor on the smooth surface of the *croach*. It was the size of a small building, and Tavi recognized it at once. Whirls and loops of the eerie wax substance had been piled up to form the building. He had seen two others like it—once in the Wax Forest, back near Calderon, and once in the labyrinth of caverns beneath Alera Imperia.

In the *croach* all around it were hundreds of smaller shapes, almost identical to the structure in form, but on a much-reduced scale, perhaps the size of a large pitcher of beer. The nearest of the lumpy shapes was no more than thirty feet away, and Tavi stared intently at it.

Something inside the lump of *croach* stirred fitfully, a movement of shadows against the green luminescence, and went still again. A small portion of green-black chitin pressed wetly against a surface as translucent as murky green glass.

Tavi inhaled slowly, understanding.

It was a nursery.

That would be the time to enact the plan, then.

He signaled the others to hold their position and, to his considerable surprise, they complied—even Kitai. That had been the part he was most concerned about, the most unpredictable part of the plan. He'd had a number of different contingencies thought out, if they'd been necessary, but it looked like the basic shape of the past couple of days had carried some momentum. They'd listened to him without question.

One worry down, he supposed.

He moved slowly forward, studying the nearest alien blister, or egg, or whatever it was, fascinated, comparing it to the far larger hive structure in the near distance. Each of the smaller shapes contained a Vord of some kind, perhaps taking sustenance from the *croach* that surrounded the blister. He thought he could see the vague shape of one of the frog-form Vord, in miniature, in the nearest hive. A few feet away, a second blister of *croach* contained a half-sized version of a wax spider. The queen, it seemed, was already working on creating more of her kind.

Tavi continued slowly forward. Each hive occupied a circle of *croach* perhaps five feet across, and he could see the glowing substance inside the waxy covering flowing up into the hive—nourishment for the infant Vord within. Tavi counted the hives nearby, and did some math in his head. Presuming this queen had only been busy creating more of her kind here since the Vord had broken out a few days ago, it meant that she could create hundreds of Vord every day—perhaps more. What's more, they could come forth with a great deal less fuss and bother than their Aleran counterparts—and fully armed and ready for battle, to boot.

Bloody crows. No wonder the Vord had wiped out the Canim. His imagination painted him landscapes of conquered territories, glowing with *croach* and covered in hives that spawned fresh nightmares by the thousands. Once these . . . hatcheries were planted and maturing, fresh Vord would emerge by the company, ready to replace those that had been slain by the Canim. Once they were given a chance to establish themselves, it would be all but impossible to be rid of them.

He suddenly found the silence of the *croach*-covered pine forest oppressive and heavy—far too much so.

What mother, Tavi thought, ever left her children unguarded if there was any choice in the matter?

No sooner had the thought crossed his mind than the *croach* itself stirred, and half a dozen of the Cane-form Vord rose silently around him, huge and menacing. Eight feet tall, and lean like the Canim, the Vord's arms were tipped with long, vicious talons, and their beaklike muzzles were serrated and terrifying.

"You are right, of course," said a quiet, alien voice from somewhere nearby— the Vord queen, Tavi was certain. "I would not leave my children unprotected." A dark shape, eyes glowing with a green-white light of their own, appeared behind the hulking shapes of the Cane-form Vord. Tavi thought he saw a faint glitter of light on sharp white teeth. "Kill him."

CHAPTER 34

At one time, Tavi would have been terrified by his situation. He was completely surrounded, outnumbered by implacable foes, and cut off from any of his support. Oh, certainly, Max and Kitai and the Canim were only a hundred yards away—but that was far enough to prevent them from intervening over the next several seconds, which were quite possibly all he had. He would have been helpless to prevent his fate from being decided by someone else.

Tavi still found the situation terrifying; but he wasn't nearly so helpless anymore.

He called upon the furies of the wind, borrowing of their speed, and time slowed as the nearest Cane-form Vord lunged for him. He drew his sword from his side and turned to meet it, focusing on the steel as he went, upon the furies in the blade, and its edge cut through the Vord's armored forearm as smoothly as if passing through water.

He ducked the Vord's second set of talons, took that arm as well, then drew up power from the earth to deliver a hard kick in one of the creature's heavy thighs. The blow flung it back from Tavi to land several feet away, thrashing at the *croach* and ripping through its surface to the glowing green "blood" that ran through it.

By then, a second Vord had closed in on him, and its talons slammed into the armor over his spine. The Aleran steel resisted the creature's claws, though the blow drove Tavi several steps forward, into a third Vord. His sword cut through the creature's thighs, and he drove his shoulder into its belly, knocking it to the ground as well. Then Tavi dropped straight down to his heels, spinning as he went, and his blade lashed out in an arc less than six inches from the ground, literally cutting the Vord behind him off at the ankles. It fell, shrieking and gushing green-brown blood like the others.

He'd killed three Vord in the time it would have taken to count them out loud, something he'd never have been able to do even a couple of years before— but that wasn't what made him dangerous in that situation.

"Wait!" Tavi shouted toward the Vord queen, still lurking behind the rank of Cane-form Vord. "You have a more profitable and efficient alternative!"

Another of the warrior Vord came at him, and Tavi struck away its hand with his sword in a shower of blue-and-scarlet sparks. The clawed hand whirled through the air and landed on the ground near the Vord queen's feet.

"How many more warriors do you want to lose?" Tavi called, slipping aside from the next blow. "It costs you nothing to hear me out!"

The attacking Cane-form Vord suddenly slowed, then halted in place.

The Vord queen spoke again. Her voice was eerie, multilayered, as if coming from several throats simultaneously. The creature herself was—rather obviously—feminine in shape, though Tavi could see nothing of her but an outline against the glowing green of the large hive behind her—and glowing green eyes that matched it. "It is unlikely that you are here to assist us. It is more likely that you are engaged in deception."

"Against a being who can read minds?" Tavi asked. He kept his eyes on the Vord that had suddenly ceased its attack. It was well within range to strike again. "That would seem to be an irrational act."

A figure covered in a dark, hooded cloak appeared from behind one of the nearby warriors. She walked a few steps toward Tavi, the cloak swaying, revealing rigid-looking, green-white flesh each time she took a step forward. The queen was considerably shorter than Tavi. Within the darkness of the hood, twin candles of green light burned with faintly luminescent fire. "Indeed," the queen murmured. "Though desperation can sometimes drive non-Vord intelligences to acts beyond reason."

Tavi felt himself baring his teeth in a smile. "It would be simple for you to determine if such desperation drove me. You just have to come closer."

The Vord queen was silent for a moment, her eyes narrowed to slits of green fire, but she did not move. "How did you approach so closely without being detected, creature?"

Tavi smiled at her and said nothing.

The Vord queen looked past him and made sniffing sounds. "More of the local apex predators are nearby. Though I was told the Narashan strain had been eliminated."

Tavi, stretching his watercrafting senses to the utmost, felt it then—a quiver of . . . not fear, precisely, but something akin to it, if infinitely more ordered—apprehension, perhaps. "Told? By whom? Who would withhold that kind of information from you? And why would such information be withheld?"

The queen stared at him, eerily motionless.

"It is possible that an opportunity for mutual gain through cooperation exists," Tavi said. "If you are willing to listen to me, perhaps we can work together to accomplish a shared goal."

The queen's voice dropped to a buzzing whisper, her voice like locust wings. "What goal?"

"The removal of a mutual enemy."

The queen stared at him for a moment more. Then she turned and began walking toward the hive. The warriors on either side of her took a step back, making way for Tavi.

The queen looked over her shoulder, and said, "Come this way."

The Vord queen entered the hive through a wide, unsettlingly organic-looking doorway. It reminded Tavi, somehow, of the nostril of some great beast. Vord in various forms crouched upon the hive, silent shadows against the glowing green wax. Wax spiders sat everywhere, blending into the background, and Tavi was certain that there were more in evidence than he could see.

Tavi found his feet dragging as he approached the entrance to the hive.

Well, of course they dragged. The interior of the hive was certain to be a death trap. He still remembered the Cane in the caverns beneath the Citadel, and how the Vord, possessing the bodies of the warrior's former comrades, had forced him into the hive—and how he had emerged, taken, moments later, without expression or mind or will. Only a fool would go in there after the Vord queen unless the situation absolutely necessitated it.

His did. Besides, he told himself, going into the hive wasn't an entirely hideous decision, tactically speaking. On open ground, the Vord could come at him from every direction. Inside the building, he could at least put his back to a wall.

Granted, he would probably find himself sinking into it to be slowly devoured by the *croach* if he did, but there would be a wall there nonetheless.

Tavi entered the hive, sword still in hand, dripping the watery, foul blood of the Vord. The interior was a simple dome, and though the glowing *croach* around them was translucent, the light flowing from it rendered the night beyond in complete blackness. Inside, though, Tavi could see as clearly as by any furylamp.

The Vord queen turned to face him, and Tavi sucked in his breath.

The creature looked like Kitai.

There were differences in this Vord queen and the last one he had seen. Her skin was nearly human instead of dark chitin, though it had an odd greenish sheen to it. She had hair, as pale as Kitai's, but worn full and long, hanging down to her hips. Her green eyes, burning with light from within, were multifaceted like an insect's, and her hands and feet sported dark, gleaming, deadly-looking nails as long as a predator bird's talons.

Beneath her cloak, she was also naked. Intensely so.

"Aleran," the queen said, and Tavi shuddered at the familiar phrase from a familiar face delivered in such an utterly alien voice. "You are far from your home."

"A coincidence," Tavi said. "I had business in the area."

"Speak of what you can do to help the Vord."

Tavi paused for a fraction of a second before he spoke, to order his thoughts. His next words could get him killed if he didn't choose them carefully.

"I know," he said, "that the Vord do not usually operate in the pattern you have been following on this continent. I know that your queens normally produce other queens, frequently, the better to perpetuate your kind."

The Vord stared.

"Yet that has not been the case, here," Tavi continued. "The queen that created you has, evidently, taken away your ability to create subordinate queens of your own."

"What makes you think that I am not the senior queen?" the creature asked him, her voice flat and expressionless.

"Logic," Tavi replied. "The operational patterns of your attack on Maraul suggested that the senior queen regarded the subordinate queens as expendable assets. Why would she place herself in such an exposed position here when she could send one of her juniors in her place? If any of you can produce more queens, why are there only three of you instead of the dozens there should be by now?"

The Vord queen was silent for several aching seconds. Then she nodded once.

"And further," Tavi said quietly, "I presume that she is not here. That she has left you and another junior queen to finish off the Canim."

"This is information I already possess," the queen hissed quietly. "It is worth nothing to me."

The walls of the hive stirred, and a dozen wax spiders appeared from where Tavi would have sworn no creature could have been hidden.

"Why?" Tavi asked. "Why has your queen changed you in this way? Does it not hamper the growth of the Vord?"

The queen's eyes narrowed. "Of course. But . . . she acts improperly. Irrationally. She has sampled too much of the blood of your breed."

The Vord's words were uninflected, calm, but the surge of emotion that screamed across Tavi's senses as the queen spoke was painfully intense. The young queen was filled with raw, unadulterated rage, with jealousy, and with intense, ambition-driven hate, the emotions as pure and intense as those produced by infants, unrestrained by any sense of self-control.

Tavi had to fight to keep his jaw from dropping. The Vord queens had, somehow, become more human. Distrust, the need to rule, the emotions *themselves* could all be used against them.

"I think she's returned to Alera by now—or at least she's on the way. What if I told you I would be willing to remove her?"

The Vord tilted its head to one side. "Why would you do such a thing?"

"Survival," Tavi replied. "If we are to survive, we must eliminate her—and you must let us escape unharmed in order for us neutralize her."

"Let you escape . . ." The queen leaned forward slightly. "Who?"

"All of my people and the Canim of this land," Tavi replied promptly. "All of them. They will return to Alera with me. They are necessary to deal with the threat."

She looked slowly around the interior of the hive. Then her green eyes focused on Tavi.

"It costs you nothing," Tavi urged her gently. "Slow the offensive long enough for the Canim to escape the continent. They will no longer be a threat to anything you've built here. You won't have to fight them anymore."

The queen's eyes flared with a brighter light, and she took a step closer. Tavi felt a sudden rush of thoughts flicker through his head—irrational fear sputtered through his body for no apparent reason. (He considered *entirely* rational the fear that he was surrounded by nightmarish creatures which might kill him, or worse, at any moment.) A rush of memories went by, bringing with them a dozen scents so distinct that he was half-certain that they were real, and not mere memories.

"There are others nearby," the queen said, slowly. "They came with you. But you have not told them your true purpose here."

A chill went down Tavi's spine as he realized that the creature was actually examining his thoughts. "No," he answered. "They never would have accepted what I planned to do." He smiled faintly. "They aren't the negotiating sort."

"You are sincere," the queen murmured.

"What is the point of attempting to deceive a being who can read your

mind?" Tavi asked. "I've accomplished a lot of things by finding common interests between myself and my enemies."

"An enemy who becomes an asset is defeated as surely as one who is
killed," the Vord queen said.

"More so," said Tavi.

The Vord queen gave him an odd little smile.

The dark-armored shapes of Vord warriors began to fill the entrance to the
hive behind him. The Cane-form Vord came forward slowly and silently, moving
awkwardly in the confined space.

Tavi's stomach seemed to drop into his boots.

"Your logic was sound but for a single, flawed assumption," the Vord queen
said. "You assumed that because the junior queens had been created without
the ability to create their own subordinate queens, that they would still have the
desire to rule. It is a shortcoming of individuality."

Wax spiders emerged from the walls and flowed over the floor between Tavi
and the queen in a miniature flood, crawling over one another until they were
chest high, walling her away from him as surely any pile of stone.

"Your breed seek authority, leadership, as an extension of your personal
identity. You know nothing of devoting yourself to something larger. You know
nothing of truly subordinating the self for the greater good of all."

Tavi glanced around the interior of the hive again, but there was no escape.
Warrior Vord filled the doorway. Spiders continued to crawl from the walls—
and ceiling, it seemed. He would never be able to get out. He'd known it was
a risk, that his proposal to the Vord could be rejected—but he truly hadn't believed that it would happen. The cold intellect of the Vord, from everything he
knew about them, should have compelled them to protect their nearest hive
and kin.

But what drove this queen was . . . entirely too human. It was a devotion to
her senior queen—to her *mother*, Tavi realized, his senses flushed with an intensity of emotion coming from the junior queen. That was mixed with a horrible and abiding need that was closer to physical *hunger* than anything else—a
need to expand, to overcome, to grow. And mixed with all of that was contempt—
contempt for humanity, for the creatures that fell before the united might of the
Vord.

Tavi realized that he was never going to leave the hive, and suddenly felt
very, very tired.

Well.

Well, then.

He had been held in contempt before. If there was one thing Tavi knew, it
was how to take advantage of being underestimated.

Tavi took a deep breath and tightened his hand on his sword. Then he reached to the short blade on his right hip, and drew it slowly into his left hand. Enough earthcrafting should give him the strength to bull through the wall of wax spiders. He'd be bitten as he did it, many times. The poison would kill him, but not for a minute or two at least.

He had another advantage: The cramped quarters inside the hive, combined with the reinforcements blocking the only exit, would prevent the queen from escaping every bit as much as it trapped Tavi. She wouldn't be able to simply cut and run.

He'd have to kill the queen quickly, with all the windcrafting he could muster. He remembered well the blinding speed a Vord queen possessed—but he would have another advantage she probably did not expect. He could accept a lethal stroke if it allowed him to deliver one in return. Metalcrafting would let him ignore the pain of a death blow long enough to deliver a killing strike of his own.

Provided he was fast enough, this hive would become her tomb. With the queen dead and the Vord undirected, Kitai, Max, and the others should have a real chance to escape. And as long as Crassus and the First Aleran had done their jobs, Varg and the Canim should escape as well, to assist Alera against the common foe.

Really, he thought, planning became a great deal simpler and easier when one didn't have the additional bother of working out how to *survive* said plan.

"It looks like I'm not the only one to make a flawed assumption," Tavi told the queen quietly.

Her eyes narrowed, and he felt the quivering pressure of her mind on his thoughts again.

Her eyes widened.

Princeps Gaius Octavian called upon rock and wind and steel and shifted his body forward into the rush that would—if he was lucky—kill them both.

CHAPTER 35

The windcrafting infused Tavi's senses with the slowed-time alertness of fury-born speed, or he might not have seen what was about to happen.

The Vord turned on one another.

The nearest Cane-form Vord, the one Tavi had wounded, suddenly jerked and was flung viciously forward as the Vord behind it tore into its back with its talons. Its blood splattered the walls of the entry tunnel as it fell into the open space at the center of the hive, and stained Tavi's boots as the newly dead Vord slid to a halt at his heels. In an instant, three more of the Cane-form Vord bounded into the room, and Tavi realized what had happened.

Varg's Hunters had arrived.

The meaning of the odd, lumpy packs each of the Hunters had carried finally became clear to Tavi. The silent Canim had clad themselves in Vord chitin, somehow fastening enough of the green-black material to themselves to pass for true Vord, at least momentarily—and now they were inside the queen's hive beside him.

"Tavar," growled the eldest of the three Hunters.

"Take her!" Tavi cried.

He surged forward with the Hunters at his side, and the Vord queen let out a piercing shriek.

The wall of wax spiders shivered and collapsed toward them, breaking in a wave of flailing legs and dripping fangs. The spiders bounded through the air, raced across the ground, and skittered across the walls and ceiling to attack. Tavi had an instant to be terrified by the sheer number of spiders, then they were upon him.

He struck one spider out of the air as it leapt at his face, his sword moving with the speed and power and deadly sharpness of all the furycraft at his command. He felled the second and third and fourth in less than a second—there were so many of the creatures that even in the dreamlike slow motion of wind-crafted alacrity, there was no time to think, ponder, or plan. He could only react, and strive to make his every movement work against the enemy.

The air was full of slashed corpses of the wax spiders, with spraying blood and severed insect limbs, but despite the web of steel Tavi wove with his swords as he strode forward, the Vord began to break through. He felt one slam into his side, and a sharp, loud pinging sound told him that his armor had held against the spider's fangs. Another seized onto his boot, simply clinging, and threw him off his balance.

Then three more dropped onto his helmet and shoulders, and he twisted wildly as venom-dripping fangs flashed by not an inch from his eyes.

Something slammed against his shoulder, a heavy blow that rang with steel on steel, and one of the Hunter's battle chains crushed the spider beneath it. Tavi managed to turn so that his unwanted passengers were more exposed to the Cane, and several more whiplashing flicks of the heavy chain cleaned the spiders from him.

The other two Hunters took up positions on his left and right, oddly curved swords in hand, flinging the heavy spikes that had wreaked such havoc in Aleran encounters with them during the war in the Vale. Tavi regained his momentum, his own blades whirling, killing—and suddenly found himself face-to-face with the Vord queen.

She moved with a horrible, arachnid grace, and at such speed that even from within his windcrafting, Tavi felt his body responding sluggishly by comparison. Her cloak flew one way as she darted to one side, but the move proved to be a feint, and the hem of the garment cracked like a whip as she reversed her move and raked her talons at Tavi's thigh.

Tavi couldn't respond in time to avoid the blow, so he simply drove his blade hard at the queen's throat.

Her speed astounded him, even as white-hot fire enveloped his leg. She managed to get a hand into the way of the blow, pushing the sword's tip down, but not entirely away from herself—the Aleran steel bit into the pale, rigid-looking flesh in a shower of scarlet-and-cerulean sparks. Her skin, then, was still Vord chitin—it merely looked like human flesh. His sword did not plunge deeply through the armor, despite the earthcraft and metalcraft behind it. An inch or two of blade sank into her abdomen and drew a howl of surprise and rage from the queen.

She bounded directly up to the ceiling, the movement so abrupt that it ripped the blade from Tavi's left hand, and began scuttling like a spider toward the entry tunnel.

Before she could get there, a pair of bloodred steel chains, their ends weighted, whipped up from the ground like lariats. One settled around her wrist, the other around a thigh, and with a snarl, the two Hunters hauled the queen from her ceiling and back to the floor of the hive.

Tavi slashed another pair of spiders from the air as he charged the downed queen. The two Hunters had kept the chains tight, taking the queen's balance from her each time she tried to regain her feet. Spiders were swarming over them, but the two Hunters, in their Vord-hide armor, ignored them and hauled with all their enormous strength on the chains.

Tavi slammed a leaping spider from the air with his left fist, killing it, whirled his longer blade over his head, reaching up to take it in a two-handed grip, and began the downward stroke that would kill the Vord queen.

She shrieked again and twisted in desperation, and her hood fell back revealing—

Kitai's terrified face.

Tavi held back his strike for a startled instant, and in that hesitation, the Vord queen twisted her shoulders and ripped her own trapped arm from its socket.

The Hunter who had been holding the other end of the chain stumbled backward at the sudden lack of resistance and fell.

The spiders swarmed over him, burying him completely.

The queen rolled, scuttling sideways like a crab, and seized the other chain in her remaining hand. With a twist of her hips and shoulders, she ripped the chain from the grip of the other Hunter, lashing it at Tavi as she did.

Tavi had to fling himself back to avoid the chain, and the queen turned to fling herself at the hive's exit.

There was a flash of light and a roar of superheated air, somewhere beyond the hive, lighting the walls to near transparency for an instant as a sphere of white-hot light appeared at ground level outside. Bits and pieces of heat-shriveled Vord armor and anatomy flew in through the hallway, and close behind them came another enormous form—Varg, his sword in hand, his black-and-crimson armor liberally smeared with the ichor. The Canim Warmaster slammed one foot down on the ground, then the other, settling his weight with the immovable mass of a mountain, and raised his sword to a high guard over his head.

"Come, creature," he snarled. "Come through me if you can."

The Vord queen let out a shriek and blurred toward Varg.

Tavi cried out and charged—realizing, as he did, that his wounded leg was no longer responding to the commands of his mind.

The Vord whirled the chain at Varg, who caught it with the blade of his sword. The queen screamed her frustration and tried to rip the sword from the Cane's grasp, but Varg set his body against the pull and, with a sudden surge of motion, dragged the queen across ten feet of floor and into range of his blade. He struck with a brutally swift economy of motion, and Tavi knew that it would have cut through a tree as thick as his own thigh in a single stroke.

The Vord queen dropped the chain and swept her arm into the path of the blow. Varg's sword pierced her armored skin, hacking almost to the bone, just as another firecrafted explosion illuminated and shook the walls of the hive. She reeled back from Varg, just in time for the Hunter whose chain she had taken to send a throwing spike into the back of one of her knees. The armored hide must have been less strong there, because the spike sank into it, while the raw power behind the heavy bar of steel sent one of her legs flying upward, taking her hips with it, so that her shoulder blades crashed to the floor.

She used the rebound of the impact to roll backward and to her feet, and as she did she drew the spike from her leg and sent it flying back to the Hunter who had thrown it. He dodged, but she'd either anticipated him or gotten lucky. The spike hit him in the throat, and a fountain of dark Canim blood clouded the air as he fell and was buried under more spiders.

Varg bellowed in rage and threw his weapon at the queen. It spun and tumbled through the air, and she leapt back and away from it—

—and into Tavi's two-handed swing. His sword struck her across the nape of the neck, and a fountain of blue-and-red sparks exploded from her flesh. The blade cut swift and true, never slowing, and the queen's head—Tavi's mind screamed silent horror at him, horror he couldn't allow himself to feel, as he saw Kitai's face, her mouth open in silent shock—tumbled away and went rolling across the floor.

The Vord's behavior changed in an instant. Wax spiders let out chirping squeals of alarm and raced aimlessly around the hive. Outside, Tavi could hear an entire chorus of alien shrieks that went up at the same time, the sound deafening.

The third Hunter appeared from behind Tavi, recovered Varg's sword, and tossed it to him.

Varg turned to the downed queen, and with four swift, heavy blows, dismembered the body. He glanced at Tavi and found the Aleran staring at him.

"Best to be sure," Varg rumbled.

Tavi whipped his sword through another spider that had leapt at him, dispatching it. Though they no longer came at them in an enormous wave with a single purpose, the spiders were naturally aggressive, and it was probably a bad idea to stay in the hive any longer than was absolutely necessary.

"Come on!" Tavi called, heading for the exit, and the two Canim came behind him.

Outside the hive, Tavi found a low set of earthworks around the entrance, doubtless earthcrafted by Max and Durias to serve as a fortification. The two Alerans were behind it, bloodied weapons in hand. Max's sword was wreathed in flame, and dead Vord were piled over the top of the little rampart. Kitai stood between them, her own sword stained as well, while Anag, his axe in hand, his blue-and-black armor covered with ichor, stood behind them, where he must have used his greater height and longer reach to good advantage.

The eerie, green-lighted world of the Vord was in chaos. All manner of nightmarish creatures filled the fey twilight, racing about in what seemed like sheer, unreasoning madness. One Cane-form Vord was clawing and biting a nearby pine tree, while one of the toad-shaped Vord repeatedly bounded forward into the side of the hive, righted itself, and tried again. Wax spiders glided calmly, bounded in tremendous agitation, or fought madly with one another, a seemingly endless number of legs flailing.

"Come on!" Tavi cried. "We're leaving!"

"Aleran!" Kitai said sharply. "Your leg."

Tavi looked at her blankly for an instant before he understood what she was talking about and looked down. His leg, where the Vord queen had torn at him with her claws, was bleeding—not fatally, but if it wasn't stopped, that could change. He'd been drawing upon enough metalcrafting that he hadn't even noticed the pain of the injury, which seemed as much a part of the background as the howls and shrieks of the disoriented Vord.

"Got it," Maximus said. He slammed the tip of his sword into the earth, jerked a flask from his belt, and passed it to Kitai. "Pour this over my hands as I close it," he told her.

While the others warded off any Vord who approached, Tavi felt Max's hands clamp down on his leg. As Kitai slowly emptied the flask over the wound, the big Antillan's grip burned like fire for an instant, then two, then for a hideous little collection of seconds. Tavi ground his teeth and concentrated on keeping his sword in his hand, until Max released him.

"There," the Antillan said. "Good enough."

Kitai glanced to Tavi, a feral smile stretching her mouth, and gave him a hot, swift kiss. "Lead on."

Tavi oriented himself and set out at the mile-devouring trot of the Legions toward the ruined steadholt where they had left their taurga. The others followed in his wake.

"What was that?" Tavi demanded. "What the bloody crows did you think you were doing?"

He could hear Kitai's grin again. "Why, whatever do you mean, Aleran?"

"The attack!" Tavi snapped. "The disguises! That wasn't something you threw together at the last minute."

"Naturally not," Kitai agreed. "The Hunters in Canea have been using suits of Vord chitin since six months into the invasion. There were several available. We just had to fit them."

He turned to give her an exasperated look. "That's not what I mean and you know it! Why didn't you tell me?"

Behind Kitai, Max's mouth spread into a wide grin. "Couldn't be helped, Your Highness."

"And what is *that* supposed to mean?"

"Operational security," Kitai said smugly.

Tavi blinked. "What?"

"There is no lying to a being who can read your thoughts, Aleran," Kitai said. "The only way we could be sure that she wouldn't expect the attack was to make sure that *you* could not expect an attack."

"You . . . You, it . . . How did . . . You can't just—"

"Why else would we have let you approach the hive by yourself without so much as a comment about what a foolish idea it was?"

Tavi stared at her helplessly, and nearly killed himself tripping over an out-thrust root.

"Do not look so astonished, Aleran," Kitai said. "It was not difficult to anticipate what kind of strategy you would favor. You have something of a history of successfully negotiating with your enemies. Even making friends of them." Her green eyes sparkled. "In some cases, very close friends."

Tavi shook his head. "You used me."

"Yes."

"You *used* me," Tavi said.

Her smile widened. "And it worked. You are a marvelous stalking cow."

"Horse," Tavi corrected wearily. "Stalking horse."

Kitai tilted her head. "What idiot would so endanger a perfectly good horse?"

Max and Durias both burst out in laughter.

A Cane-form Vord exploded from a copse of small pines ten feet away, bounding forward to the attack. Varg met the attacker in midleap, the speed and power behind the blow astonishing, and the attacking Vord fell to the *croach* in two pieces.

"Tavar," Varg growled, still on guard, his eyes scanning the trees around them. "Now is not the time."

Tavi stared at the still-twitching Vord for a second, his heart racing with surprise at the sheer speed of the attack. He nodded at Varg and grunted his agreement. "But we're going to talk about this," he said, glowering at Kitai.

She smiled, unperturbed, and said nothing as they continued making their way out of the confusion and anarchy that covered the landscape every bit as thoroughly as the *croach*.

CHAPTER 36

Amara returned to the Slaver Market that night, once dark had settled on the occupied city. Furylamps burned in the streets, but infrequently: The only Aleran lights remaining had been burning since they had last been put in place by Ceres' former residents. They wouldn't last more than a day or two more, at most. For the moment, though, they created broad swaths of shadow, which made it simple for Amara to move unseen.

The greenish light of the glowing *croach* within the city was bright enough, cast up on nearby buildings, that Amara had no trouble avoiding the various bits of wreckage on the ground in the alleyways leading up to the Slave Market. Twice, a Vord keeper prowled by, long legs scything in a rippling motion, the translucent shell of the spiderlike being glowing from within with the dim light of the glob of *croach* it carried inside whatever passed for its belly. Once she saw one of the creatures begin to vomit up blobs of *croach*, smoothing it over the sill of a window, where the waxy substance evidently began to take root and grow.

Ceres was still habitable by human beings, technically speaking. But the Vord clearly intended to change that.

Amara hurried her pace.

She came in from a different direction than Rook had shown her. The former chief of Kalarus's Bloodcrows had obviously worked out a way to strongly influence Brencis's focus—a young man, alone in an alien world, suddenly granted both physical gratification and emotional reassurance, in the form of someone he was familiar with, hardly had a chance against a manipulator of Rook's skills. All the same, Amara knew that Rook's hold on Brencis was made of whispers and cobwebs. If he ever realized they were there, it would be a simple matter to brush them away—and if he had done so in the intervening hours, Rook might already have been forced to betray Amara.

And if not . . . well, it never hurt to be cautious.

The Slave Market was lit by furylamps and a glowing mound of *croach*, bulging up like a cyst from the paving stones and covered with spiderlike keepers. A few more Vord were in evidence than had been there during the day. Were the creatures predominantly nocturnal? Or was there some other explanation for their increased presence.

The "recruiting" operation maintained the same pace she had seen before. Half a dozen dazed Alerans, newly collared, lay on the auction platform. A number of sleepy-eyed slaves were draped over them, whispering and . . . and other things, in the light of the dancing furylamps. Amara shivered and looked away.

Brencis sat at a small table beside the platform, drinking from a dark bottle. He set it carelessly aside and began wolfing down food. Rook sat on the bench beside him, her hair mussed, her clothes in attractive disarray. A fresh bruise decorated one cheek—a testament to Brencis's attentions, Amara wondered, or evidence of Rook's discovery and coerced treachery?

Amara saw the glittering eyes of a vordknight, crouched upon the roof she had used earlier that day to spy upon the courtyard. A coincidence? Or had the collared Rook been forced to inform them of what she knew of Amara's presence and movements.

Amara grimaced. There was no help for it. She'd simply have to press on and hope for the best.

Veiled behind layers of windcrafting, blending with the weirdly lit night in her furycrafted cloak, Amara stalked silently forward.

Murdering a powerful furycrafter like Kalarus Brencis—and surviving the experience—was a dubious proposition at best. His innate gifts at watercrafting meant that only a sudden and massively traumatic injury had a real chance of killing him; a slash that opened anything less than a major artery would be rapidly repaired. She had to be swift. His skills at windcrafting would grant him deadly swift reaction speed to any attack, and the raw strength granted by his earthcrafting meant that if there was any sort of struggle, he would literally tear Amara limb from limb. Worse, if she struck, missed, and, sensibly, tried to flee, he would probably kill her before she had covered more than a few yards. His firecrafting would make that simple.

Most dangerous of all, his metalcrafting would warn him of any steel weapon as it approached him. It would not give him anything but an instant's warning, true, but that would be more than sufficient. In order to kill Kalarus Brencis Minoris and survive the exchange herself, Amara would have to open up his throat wide with the stone-bladed dagger she held in her hand. Or else sink it to the hilt in one of his eyes or ears. There was absolutely no room for error.

Brencis, on the other hand, could snap her neck with a thrust of his arm, burn her to bones with a flick of his fingers, or sweep her head clean of her neck with a single motion of his excellent-quality sword.

It seemed a trifle unfair.

But then, she'd never really expected a series of equitable situations when she'd joined the Cursors.

Crows take you, Gaius. Even when I walked away from your service, you managed to draw me back into it.

Moving silent and unseen had become second nature to her over the past days. She drifted past the guards standing about the courtyard, walking slowly, calmly, and carefully. She paused several times, to let one of the collared Alerans pass nearby, before she continued. Stealth had a great deal more to do with patience and the ability to remain calm when there was very little reason to do so than with any amount of personal agility.

It took her perhaps ten minutes to move from the shelter of the alley to the side of the platform opposite Brencis's table. It took another five to slide around the platform and stop beside the stairs leading from the floor of the courtyard up to the auction stage. When Brencis finished eating, he would go back up the stairs to collar the next victim, and Amara would drive her dagger into his brain. He would fall. She would take to the skies immediately, and be gone from the meager light of the furylamps before anyone could react. It couldn't be simpler.

In matters such as that, simplicity was a deadly weapon in its own right.

It took Brencis several more moments to finish dinner, before he pushed his plate away and rose.

Amara settled her grip on the handle of the stone knife and relaxed her muscles, preparing for the single, blindingly swift strike that was her only chance at success.

Brencis glanced at Rook, then down and said, "I hate this."

"Just remember," Rook told him. "You have what they want. You can't be replaced. They don't have the power. You do."

Amara felt herself freezing into place.

Brencis touched the collar at his own throat. "Maybe," he said.

"Don't show weakness," Rook cautioned. "You know what will happen."

Amara took a moment to admire Rook's delivery, as her words went home in as deadly a fashion as any sword thrust, planting discord and division among the enemy while remaining concealed as simple self-interest. Amara could think of any number of women and men who had urged their mates in a similar fashion, attaining position and prestige by proxy. Crows, but the woman had guts. Amara could not say if she would act with as much courage in the same circumstances.

Suddenly, half a dozen vordknights simultaneously leapt into the air from rooftops around the courtyard, their wings making a heavy, thrumming burr of the evening's silence.

"She's here," Brencis murmured in a numb tone.

The oppressive buzz of Vord wings faded—and then grew louder again, and louder, multiplying in volume, until it filled the stone-enclosed courtyard with thunder. An instant later, a veritable legion of vordknights descended from the night sky. They came down like locusts, all at once, landing upon buildings, cages, and cobblestones alike, covering everything in sight in a living carpet of gleaming black chitin. It was sheer luck, Amara knew, that one of them landed a bare couple of inches beyond where the tip of her outstretched fingers would reach, rather than upon her head, and it was only the practice and discipline of the endless days of stillness and silence that prevented her from flinching into a spasm of motion that would have concluded with her fleeing for safety and finding only disaster.

Instead, she held her place and waited.

From somewhere near the center of the courtyard, a Vord screamed, a high-pitched, chittering shriek that ripped at Amara's ears.

A second after it had faded, the cry was repeated from above them.

This time, the courtyard filled with the thunder of windstreams, as Knights Aeris in gleaming silver collars descended from above, in an armored-guard formation around a pair of figures Amara recognized at once:

The Vord queen.

And Lady Aquitaine.

Of course, the Knights Aeris can't fly among the vordknights, Amara thought, with clinical detachment. *Their windstreams would make it too difficult for the Vord to use their wings.*

It was the training she'd had as a Cursor. One never allowed emotions to control one's reactions. Whether those emotions were abject terror or bitter hatred so vile that it made her mouth twist at the taste, they couldn't be allowed to take the upper hand. When you felt it happening, you focused on details, the practical, connecting one fact to another, until the surge of fear and hate washed by and receded somewhat.

Only after she had done that did Amara look back at the would-be authors of Alera's destruction.

The Vord queen was shorter than Amara had expected her to be—not even as tall as Amara herself. She didn't know why she had thought it would be otherwise. Thinking back on it, the queen she'd fought and helped to kill in Calderon had not been particularly tall or imposing, physically. It had been a human-shaped creature, but there had been nothing human about it.

This queen was different.

Her cloak was finer, for one thing. The other queen had been dressed in cloth that could have come from a not-too-recent grave. This one wore a great cloak of black velvet so deep that it rippled with illusory colors in its folds. She stood in the courtyard with something else in her posture and bearing, too— something alert, almost electric. The other queen had never projected anything but cold and alien patience.

The Vord queen reached up with slender, *pale* hands, and drew back her hood, revealing a face that was youthful, beautiful, and shockingly familiar.

She looked almost precisely like the Princeps' lover, Kitai.

Amara stared in such shock that she almost forgot to maintain the veils around her. The queen in Calderon had looked human in form, but had been covered in gleaming, green-black chitin, much like the vordknights. This one, though, looked almost entirely human . . .

Except for the eyes.

The eyes were a swirl of black and gold and green, in hundreds of glittering facets. Without those eyes, the Vord queen could have walked down any street in Alera without raising eyebrows—beyond the fact that she was, except for the cloak, apparently naked.

The queen turned those alien eyes in a slow circuit of the courtyard, and with a collective sigh that approached a moan of adoration, or terror, the collared Alerans as one sank to prostrate themselves upon the ground before her.

The queen's mouth curved into a small, satisfied smile. Then she moved her right hand in a liquid, precise gesture, and Lady Aquitaine stepped up to stand beside her.

The former High Lady stood well over a head taller than the queen. With her hair drawn back into a tight bun, and clad in the formfitting black chitin of the Vord, Lady Aquitaine looked more slender than the richly cloaked, smaller figure before her. From that close, Amara could see the creature crouched upon her breast. It looked almost like a wax spider, but smaller, and clad in a dark shell. Its many legs circled Lady Aquitaine's torso and, Amara realized with a start, had actually sunk their clawed tips into Lady Aquitaine's flesh. Worse, the creature's head, sporting what must have been mandibles as long as Amara's fingers, was sunk into the flesh of her torso, just over her heart. The thing shivered and pulsed oddly—and in the rhythm of a heartbeat.

"My lady," Lady Aquitaine said smoothly.

"Judge the male taker's progress," the Vord queen murmured. Her voice was a buzzing thing, as inhuman as her eyes, and sounded like many young women speaking in almost-perfect unison.

Lady Aquitaine inclined her head again and turned to Brencis. She walked over to him, her chitin-coated feet clicking sharply into the silence with each step. Then she knelt over the prostrate young man and ran her fingers lightly through his hair.

Brencis shuddered in reaction to her touch, and looked up with eyes as heavy and hopelessly adoring as any of the other slaves in the courtyard.

"Tell me what you have accomplished, dear boy," Lady Aquitaine murmured.

Brencis nodded. "I've been working without stop, lady. Recruiting more Citizens and Knights, with a focus on earthcrafters, as you commanded. Another hundred and twenty are now ready to accept orders when you wish it."

"Very well done," Lady Aquitaine said, her tone warm with approval.

Brencis jerked in place, shivering in forced pleasure, and his eyes rolled back into his head for a moment. A moment later, he stammered, "Th-thank you, lady."

"Sixscore?" asked the Vord queen. "Too slow."

Lady Aquitaine nodded. "Brencis," she said, "it's time for you to tell me how the collaring is accomplished."

Brencis closed his eyes. His body tensed and twisted again, though this time it was obviously not in pleasure. His face twisted into a grimace, and he said, through gritted teeth, "I. Will. Not."

"Brencis," Lady Aquitaine chided, "you're going to hurt yourself. Tell me."

The young man ground his teeth and said nothing. A trickle of blood suddenly coursed down from one nostril.

Lady Aquitaine did not move for a long second. Then she rose, and said, calmly, "Very well. Another time. You may remain silent."

Brencis gasped and almost seemed to melt into the earth. For several seconds, the only sounds were his panting sobs of release from agony.

"I'm sorry," Lady Aquitaine said, turning to speak to the Vord queen. "The standard collar I fitted him with can't match whatever it is he does to alter the bonding process. I can't compel the secret from him."

The Vord queen tilted her head slowly to one side. Dark, glossy black hair fell in gentle waves from beneath her hood. "Can you not cause him to fit himself with this same collar?"

Lady Aquitaine shook her head. "He is collared already, my lady. A second such crafting wouldn't take."

The queen tilted her head the other way.

"It would have no effect on him," Lady Aquitaine clarified.

The queen blinked slowly, once. Then turned her gaze past the sobbing Brencis.

To Rook.

"Why was this one pleased when he resisted?" the queen asked. "She restrained a smile. The facial indication of pleasure, is it not?"

"It is. Though there are nuances of meaning to smiles that can become complex," Lady Aquitaine said. She looked past the subjugated Brencis to Rook, who also lay prostrate, her face downward. "A young woman. Perhaps she has attached herself to his future. Encouraged him to remain silent, so that he could preserve all the power he could."

The Vord queen considered that for a moment, and paced silently toward Rook, standing over her. "So that she could benefit herself."

"Correct."

"Individuality is counterproductive," the queen said, her voice calm. Then her form blurred, and Amara saw a gleam of dark, green-black chitin at the tips of the pale queen's fingers as they ripped half of Rook's throat away.

Amara's heart all but stopped at the sheer, sudden viciousness and speed of the attack. She had to fight down a scream, and with it the impulse to fling herself to the wounded woman's defense.

Rook made a sound that was more of a wet, wheezing gasp than any word. She rolled partly onto one side in reaction, her arms and legs thrashing weakly. Blood rushed from the gaping wound in her neck.

The Vord queen stood over the dying woman with a mildly interested expression on her face, staring down at her with unblinking eyes.

"What," the queen asked, "is Masha?"

Lady Aquitaine looked on impassively, her expression remote. Even so, she averted her eyes from the dying woman and said, "It is a female proper name. Perhaps her sister or her child."

"Ah," the Vord queen said. "What is Countess Amara?" Her head tilted slightly, and her unsettling, faceted eyes glittered in the light of torches and furylamps. "A woman. Ungroomed."

Lady Aquitaine's head snapped around toward the queen abruptly. "What?"

The queen looked up at her without expression. "Her mind. There is an increase in activity preceding death."

Lady Aquitaine hurried to Rook's side, reaching down to turn her face slightly to one side, and her eyes widened in recognition. "Bloody *crows*." She looked up at Brencis, and snapped, "Healing tub, *now*."

She clamped her hands over the gaping wound in Rook's neck, her eyes narrowing. "You've . . . Crows, the wound is . . ." She looked up and snarled, "Brencis!"

"What are you doing?" the queen asked. Her tone was politely interested.

"This woman is an agent of Gaius Sextus," Lady Aquitaine said, her voice tight. "She might have information that—" She broke off suddenly, shuddering.

"Dead," the Vord queen said, her voice clinically detached. To punctuate the word, she lifted the scoop of bloody flesh she still held in the taloned fingers of her hand and nipped off a small bite. A spot of Rook's blood, still hot, sent out a wisp of steam into the cool night air as it smeared the Vord queen's chin.

"What did you see about Amara?" Lady Aquitaine asked.

"Why?"

"Because it could be important," Lady Aquitaine said, frustrated exasperation hidden in her words.

"Why?"

"Because she, too, is an agent of Gaius," Lady Aquitaine said, rising a bit unsteadily from the body. "She and Rook have worked together before and—" Her eyes narrowed abruptly. "Amara must be *here*."

Amara felt a surge of terror join the helpless rage and sickened pity in her breast, and pushed them both aside to call upon Cirrus. Borrowing swiftness from the wind fury, she drew back her arm and flung the stone knife at Lady Aquitaine, the weapon letting out a sharp crack like a whip as it tumbled toward her with an almost lazy grace to Amara's fury-heightened senses.

Amara's aim was true. The heavy stone knife hit Lady Aquitaine just right and center of her chest, upon the form of the quivering Vord . . . *thing* that crouched there. The knife, furycrafted from heavy granite, would have made a poor tool, its blade too dull to be of everyday use, but for its intended task of parting the flesh of a single victim, it more than sufficed. The sheer mass of the thing made its tip as deadly as any arrow or blade of steel, especially at the speed with which Amara had thrown it. The knife plunged through the Vord creature as easily as through a rotten apple, and continued on to the flesh beneath, cracking bone with moist snapping sounds, hurling its target from her feet and to the ground.

Amara gritted her teeth at how badly wrong the plan had gone, but there was no help for that now. Brencis had gone running off to fetch a tub, and had been nowhere in sight, and Lady Aquitaine—no, *Invidia*, Amara thought viciously, for she was no Aleran Citizen anymore—would have circumvented

Amara's veil in seconds. So before Invidia's feet had hit the ground following the impact of her shoulders, Amara had turned and leapt skyward, calling Cirrus to bear her aloft.

Amara's feet were perhaps seven feet from the ground when she felt hands like stone wrap around the ankles of her soft boots. Desperately, she called upon Cirrus to bear her up with even more force, even as she drew her steel dagger from her belt and twisted to thrust it down at her attacker with the instant, blindingly swift violence of trained instinct.

Yet as fast as she was, the Vord queen was faster.

She released one of Amara's legs to spread the fingers of one pale hand wide. Amara had time to realize that the queen's hand was still wet with Rook's lifeblood, as the tip of her dagger pierced the queen at the center of her palm.

There was no more reaction than if Amara had thrust her knife into the ground. Without any expression beyond one of steady concentration, the Vord queen twisted her wrist, the knife still trapped in her flesh, and tore it from Amara's grasp. Amara kicked one leg, trying to get loose of the queen's remaining grip as they continued to rise from the courtyard, albeit slowly, but the Vord's grasp was inhumanly strong. Her alien eyes glittering more brightly, the Vord queen swarmed up the length of Amara's body, hand over hand, and Amara felt the tip of her own dagger thrust twice into her flesh in hot bursts of tingling pain.

Then an iron bar pressed against her throat, and her vision darkened.

Amara struggled wildly, but it was useless, everything spinning down to a tunnel. She saw the walls of Ceres rushing at her, and in a last burst of defiance called Cirrus with every remaining ounce of her strength to rush them both toward the obdurate stone.

Then nothing.

▢▢▢▢ Chapter 37

Amara awoke with a gasp as water trickled into her nose. She coughed and tried to lift her arms to her face, but couldn't move them. Her body ached in every joint and muscle, and she was ravenously hungry. She flung her head back and forth, and realized that she was almost entirely submerged in something liquid and warm.

Her eyes flew open in a panic, images of sleeping bodies wrapped in glowing green *croach* filling her thoughts, her body contracting and convulsing to pull her free. Her arms flexed but refused to move from her sides, and her legs stayed firmly clasped together. Pain burned through her biceps, her thighs, and the warm liquid covered her face entirely as she slipped lower into it.

"—her head out of the water befo—" shouted a woman's voice.

It was cut off completely. Then a fist seized her by the hair and hauled her up, out of the warm liquid.

"—ld have warned me she was about to wake!" said a petulant male voice. The hand grasping her hair kept hauling, and she suddenly fell over a slippery barrier of some kind and onto hard, cold stone.

Amara coughed the water—for it *was* water—clear of her nose and lungs and lay panting for a moment, dizzy and drained with the aftereffects of a watercrafted healing. She looked down at herself and found her arms bound to her sides, her legs trussed together at thigh and ankle. She was still clothed, though her outfit was soaked entirely through.

"Welcome back, Countess," came Invidia's voice. "We feared for you for a time."

The voice of the Vord queen buzzed weirdly against Amara's senses. "I did not."

Amara shook her head, blinked the water from her eyes, and looked up at them. If she didn't show them defiance quickly, the cold air of the deep night would suck the warmth from the water soaking her clothes and leave her shuddering and freezing. She thought the defiance might be less convincing if she waited for that.

Invidia sat in a chair that had been brought out from one of the nearby buildings. She looked hideous. There were dark circles under her eyes, and her skin was a deep, sallow shade of saffron. The Vord creature upon her chest was gone. Holes like little gaping mouths in the pale flesh beneath where it had been leaked dark fluid that only faintly resembled blood.

"Invidia," Amara said. "Finally, the outside matches the inside. Treacherous, cowardly, petty."

Invidia sat in her chair and slowly withdrew a hand from the waters of the healing tub. She tilted her head at an angle that made Amara acutely aware of the fact that she currently lay bound at Invidia's feet. Other than that one motion, she did not move, until she turned her head to the Vord queen. "Well? She lives."

"Yes," the Vord queen said. She walked past Amara's view, pale ankles and delicate feet tipped with green-black toenails walking with deliberate grace across the stones and stepping over Amara's bound form. She stopped behind Invidia's chair.

Invidia shifted her body, settling her back upright against the chair's straight back and gripping the arms with weak fingers. "Countess," she said. "As ever, swift to judge."

"Perhaps you're right," Amara said. "You must have an excellent reason to explain why you are toadying for the enemies of the Realm and murdering and enslaving her citizens. Any reasonable person should be able to forgive and forget. Surely."

Invidia narrowed her eyes. "Does it look like I would be here if I had a choice, Countess?"

"I don't see a collar on you, *Invidia*," Amara said.

For the first time, the other woman seemed to notice the way Amara had entirely omitted her title. Her expression flickered with surprise, then offended anger, then—for just an instant—with what might have been a flutter of regret.

"The people here, the ones you've had broken and enslaved, *they* didn't have a choice. You took that from them."

The Vord queen settled her fingers lightly upon Invidia's neck. The tips of her green-black talons dimpled the delicate skin of the former High Lady's throat. She shivered and *rippled* hideously, as if some other creature entirely had writhed in its sleep beneath her skin. Her fingers tightened, and tiny trickles of blood coursed over Invidia's pale white skin.

"After your mentor betrayed me," Invidia said, her mouth spreading into a rictus, "and left me bleeding on the ground with garic oil poisoning my wounds, I fled and was found by my new liege." She tilted her head slightly back toward the Vord queen. "She made me an offer. My life for my loyalty."

"You make it sound like barter," the queen murmured, her faceted eyes half-lidded. "It is not so much an exchange as an ongoing arrangement." Then she closed her eyes, and shivered again, something undeniably alien in the motion, and Invidia fell silent.

Amara shuddered and stared, revulsion and fascination competing for her thoughts.

The Vord queen smiled slightly, let out a little sigh, and parted her dark, soft lips. Impossibly long, spidery legs slowly began to emerge from between them. As they appeared, they grew like the branches of a tree, but with horrible rapidity. Once they reached better than a foot in length, they began to stir, slowly, waving about like weeds growing in the sea near the shore.

The queen opened her mouth wider, and a bulbous body emerged from it, shaping itself as it came, until it settled into the form of the creature Amara had seen on Invidia before, albeit a bit smaller.

The Vord queen lifted her hand to her mouth and took up the creature in it, as gently as any mother handling her newborn. She reached slowly around Invidia's body and held the creature against the Aleran woman's chest. The creature spread its legs, fluttering them lightly over Invidia's torso, and, in an abrupt motion, struck with every leg at once, nearly a dozen limbs lashing out in separate serpentine motions. The creature clutched hard to Invidia, then slammed its head forward, long mandibles burying themselves in the Aleran woman's flesh.

Invidia closed her eyes for a moment, shuddering, but not moving or struggling against the creature. It seemed to adjust itself for a moment, then settled, its legs each sinking a talon into her flesh, drawing more dark fluid from her.

Within seconds, her color had begun to improve, and Invidia let out a shuddering sigh. She blinked her eyes open a moment later. "Ah. My thanks."

The Vord queen simply stared at Invidia for a moment. Then she shifted her attention to Amara.

"Now," Invidia said. "Where were we, Countess?"

"Fidelias," Amara said. She struggled to keep her voice calm, but she couldn't do it. The cold had settled into her soaked clothes, and she began shivering. Her voice shook with her.

"Yes," Invidia said, her voice growing steadier by the word. "Dear Fidelias. I don't suppose you know where he is?"

"To the best of my knowledge he was in your company," Amara said. "Or dead."

"Really?" Invidia asked. "That hardly seems likely. You were close to him, after all. He was your *patriserus*."

Amara clenched her teeth to keep them from chattering. "He was a traitor."

"Doubly," Invidia mused. "I had thought your type had a name for that sort of thing, but perhaps I was mistaken." She glanced down at the creature on her chest and shifted her shoulders gently. Its legs flexed slightly, and she winced. "Mmmfh. He could hardly have struck at a better moment. I was incognito. Had he succeeded, I would have been buried as a nameless camp follower, an unfortunate casualty of war—and one of Gaius's most capable foes would simply have vanished. A High Lady of the Realm, gone without a trace."

"I can't see where he failed," Amara replied. "I see no High Lady here."

Invidia stared at her in deadly silence for a long moment.

Amara bared her teeth at her in a humorless smile. "You may have lived through the attack, but High Lady Aquitaine didn't survive it."

"Enough of her survived to settle accounts, Countess," Invidia said in a quiet voice. "More than enough to deal with you. And your husband."

Amara felt a little chill of fear go through her.

Invidia smiled. "Ah. I thought as much. Where is dear Count Calderon? I can't imagine him to be the sort to let you accept a mission such as this alone."

"He's dead," Amara said, keeping her tone as flat as she could.

"Liar," replied Invidia, without an instant's hesitation. "Oh, you could deceive me about many things, child. But not about him. He's too close to your heart." She rose slowly, eyes again on the creature upon her breast. This time, it didn't stir as she moved. "This needn't be any more unpleasant than it already has been, Countess."

"Meaning it will go easier for me, if I cooperate with you, I presume," Amara said.

"Precisely."

"Go to the crows. And take your friends with you."

Invidia's smile widened. "Where is your husband, Countess?"

Amara faced her in silence, except for the rattling of her belt buckle against the stones of the courtyard as she shivered in the cold.

"I told you," Invidia said, her smile widening.

"Some of your people adequately understand the situation," the Vord queen said, stepping forward to stare down at Amara. "But so many of the others refuse us. Even given the chance to survive, they ignore their own best interests in favor of . . . intangibles. There is no gain in it, no sense, no reason."

Amara had felt the touch of a Vord queen's mind before, though she had not known it at the time. It was a subtle thing, a fluttering of thought and emotion as tenuous and delicate as a strand of spiderweb stretched across a wooded path.

"Where is Bernard?" Invidia prompted in a gentle voice.

Amara ground her teeth and focused upon her surroundings, upon how cold she was, separating herself from her thoughts and emotions—just as she would when attempting to deceive a skilled watercrafter. And then she drew up every memory of Bernard that she could summon—his steady silence in the field, his gentle humor telling a story of his day over dinner, the granite strength of his body as it pressed against hers in their bed, his laughter, his eyes, the scratch of his short beard against her throat when he kissed her neck—and a hundred memories more, running through every one of them, everything he was.

The Vord queen exhaled slowly, and said, "Her mind is disciplined. She hides him from me." The pale, strange-eyed being turned away, and Amara felt the touch of its thoughts vanish. "Interesting."

"Give me an hour," Invidia said. "She'll be less able to concentrate once we've spent some time with her."

"We have work to do, and no time to waste on such pursuits," the queen replied. She looked over her shoulder and stared at Amara, dark eyes glittering. "Come."

Invidia rose, but looked at Amara with narrowed eyes. "That could cost us her mind, along with its contents."

The Vord queen hadn't slowed down. "The order of probability that she will know anything more useful than that we have already gained is very low. The risk is acceptable."

"I understand," Invidia said. She stared at Amara for another moment, then shook her head. "Farewell, Countess. When next we meet, I suppose it will be on friendlier terms."

Amara's heart pounded harder as the fear grew. "What do you mean?"

The shriek of the Vord queen echoed across the courtyard, and seconds later the air was filled with the thunder of Vord taking to the night sky on green-black wings.

"Brencis did an excellent job on my ribs, my lung, and my stomach," Invidia said. "So don't fear, Countess. I leave you in capable hands."

Brencis stood over Rook's motionless corpse, his face empty of anything but an odd, fey heat. He looked from the corpse to Amara, very slowly, his eyes unfocused.

"Brencis," Invidia said, as the collared Alerans began to gather around her before she took to the sky. "Collar her."

Amara's scream of protest and horror was lost in the howl of a dozen wind-streams lifting Invidia and her escort away from fallen Ceres.

CHAPTER 38

Isana could count on her fingers the number of times she had worn trousers. It wasn't because it would have been terribly outrageous. Plenty of women could and did wear them on steadholts, especially those involved in gathering herbs in the forest, working around animals, or laboring in the fields. She'd simply preferred her gowns and dresses.

The flying leathers felt decidedly odd, especially the trousers, but they were quite warm. That was a necessity, Araris had cautioned her, when wearing metal armor in such cold weather. The metal itself would be cold enough to freeze to her skin if it had the help of a droplet of sweat or spittle. Or tears.

Or blood.

She shivered and adjusted the sword belt that held her long, armored coat closed. She checked the weapon again, sliding the *gladius* a bit out of the sheath and back in. The cold could freeze the weapon into its sheath if one wasn't careful.

Aria, standing beside her, said, "There they are. Finally."

Isana glanced up at the dark grey sky. "He was hoping for the weather to worsen," she said. "A blizzard would make a public duel problematic."

Aria sighed. "Probably."

Isana didn't turn around to face the Shieldwall. Once again, they stood on the meeting ground where they had spoken with the Icemen. The snow all around it was stirred into odd hummocks and bare spots, where the massive watercrafting she had wrought had disrupted the usual pattern of smooth drifts.

"Aria," Isana said. "If I should . . . If today should not end well for me . . ."

"Ahhh," Aria said. "That's why you chose me to be your second instead of Araris."

"I don't think he'd be able to help himself. He'd tear into Antillus immediately."

"And what makes you think I won't?" Lady Placida asked, her tone completely calm.

Isana glanced aside at the High Lady and noted that Aria wore her slender sword at her side.

"Oh, not you, too," Isana sighed.

Lady Placida gave Isana a smile that was startlingly wolflike. "Never fear. I'll leave his hide intact. But I'll flay his conscience from his bones."

Isana nodded. "If nothing else . . . I think it will give you a genuine chance to talk him into doing the right thing." A motion toward the edge of the trees drew her eye. A massive shape loomed there in the shadows of early dawn—Walker, the gargant. Doroga appeared from the shadows and leaned on his long-handled cudgel, a hundred yards away. He gave her a slow, respectful nod, which Isana returned.

Aria sighed. "I can't believe it's come to this. I can't believe the young man I knew would . . . do this. But Raucus changed, after he married Kalarus Dorotea. They could barely stand one another, but their fathers had arranged it all. It was supposed to unite the northern cities with the south, you know." She shook her head, and said, "Here they are."

Isana turned slowly, gravely, to face Lord Antillus.

She honestly wasn't ready for the sight that greeted her.

Every member of the Legion and every single person who was part of the Legion's support structure, or so it seemed, had come to the top of the Wall to watch the duel. A river of humanity stretched for a mile, perhaps more, along the dark, massive structure. When Isana had walked out in the dark before dawn, she hadn't really been paying too much attention to what was going on around her, she supposed, and it hadn't been light enough to see very far.

Her potentially useful death, it seemed, would have an enormous audience.

Something about that irritated her. It was one thing to give one's life for one's Realm—but it was quite another to be forced to do so with every soul for twenty-five miles looking on, evaluating her, and making individual judgments. She was not there to put on a crowbegotten *spectacle*.

Not for them, at any rate.

Antillus Raucus walked to them through the snow, stopping a few yards away. Beside him walked Aria's son, Garius, his face grim, his armor and uniform immaculate. Isana understood Raucus's choice of seconds at once. It was the second's duty to intercede should anyone of the other duelist's party attempt to interfere in the duel. Not only would Garius doubtlessly be a formidable furycrafter himself, but her own second, Aria, would be immediately disinclined to attack Raucus if it would mean that she found herself faced with her own son.

Isana tried to be charitable. The choice might have been as much diplomatic as tactical. Since Garius would be just as unwilling to initiate hostilities against his mother as she was against him, his presence might have been meant as a reassurance—even as an overture, from a certain point of view. Raucus clearly did not want this fight.

She met the gaze of the man who might be killing her in a few moments and lifted her chin slightly. He had not worn his usual heavy Legion lorica, opting instead for a coat that she thought was probably armored like her own. His boots were heavy, lined with fur against the snow and the cold. He wore a *gladius* at his side, rather than the longer sword she'd seen him with before.

He's matched his weapon and armor to mine, Isana thought. *So that at least he'll be able to think to himself that he killed me fairly.*

Doroga strode forward, then, cudgel swinging over his shoulder.

"I am the Master of Arms," the barbarian said. He tapped a round case hanging by a thong from his belt. "I read up on your trial by combat law. It means I come over here and tell you all the rules, even though everyone here knows them better than I do."

Antillus spared an irritated glance for Doroga. Isana had to suppress her smile.

"Lord Antillus, there, is the challenged. He gets to choose how the duel will be fought. He's chosen steel and fury. Which basically means anything goes, which is how fighting ought to be done in any case."

The young man beside Lord Antillus said, "I'm not sure it's the prerogative of the Master of Arms to give editorial comment on the *juris macto.*"

"Garius," Aria chided. The tone was exactly like that Isana had heard in her own voice, time after time, when cautioning Tavi to restrain his words. Garius subsided.

"Isana is the challenger," Doroga continued, as if no one had said anything. "Which means she gets to choose the time and place of the duel. She has chosen here and now. Obviously. Or none of us would be standing out here in the wind."

Antillus Raucus sighed.

"Lord Antillus," Doroga said. "As the challenged, you have the right to let a champion stand in your place. In case you don't want to get hurt, I guess." Doroga's tone was completely neutral and polite, but somehow the barbarian managed to infuse it with contempt, nonetheless. "Do you wish a champion to stand for you?"

Antillus gritted his teeth. "I do not."

Doroga grunted. "There's that much at least." He looked back and forth between them. "Now I am supposed to ask you to tell me why you're fighting. Isana."

"The Realm is in need," Isana said quietly, never taking her eyes from Raucus's. "The First Lord has called the Shield Legions to battle the Vord. Lord Antillus not only refuses to heed his rightful lord's command, but he actively tried to destroy the truce I might have wrought with the Icemen that could potentially have given him no further excuse to do continue defying the First Lord's will. If he would avoid this duel, he must immediately mobilize his Legions and militia and march them south to defend the Realm."

Doroga grunted. He nodded to Antillus. "Your turn."

"My first commitment is to my people, not to Gaius Sextus or the crown he wears," Antillus rumbled. "I have no desire to pursue this duel. But I will not abandon my responsibilities." He gestured with one hand at the wall behind him and the people on it. "You want to know why I'm fighting? I'm fighting for them."

"You're both fighting for them, Raucus," Aria said in a quiet, saddened voice. "You're just too stiff-necked to see it."

Doroga shook his head. "Isana. You willing to back off?"

"I am not," Isana said. She kept her voice from shaking, just barely.

"How about you, Antillus?"

"No," Raucus said.

Doroga opened the case and consulted a rolled piece of paper, before nodding once and saying, "You both sure?"

They both replied in the affirmative.

Doroga read the paper carefully, his lips moving, and nodded. "Right. Both of you turn and take ten paces when I count."

"I'm sorry," Raucus said. He turned his back on Isana.

Isana turned around without replying. Her legs were shaking as she took one step forward, and Doroga counted off the paces out loud. Then she turned to face Raucus again.

The Marat chieftain lifted his club overhead. "When I lower the club," he said, "my part in this ritual is over. Then you two fight."

With a deliberate, practiced motion, graceful and implacable, Antillus Raucus, the most personally dangerous man in Alera, put his hand to his sword.

Isana swallowed and mimicked him, though her own motion was jerky by comparison, and her hand shook and felt weak.

Doroga dropped his club to the ice-bound ground—

—and Antillus Raucus blurred into motion so swift that it barely seemed that his limbs moved at all. There was simply a streak of dark leather and bright steel coming toward Isana before she could draw half the length of her little sword from its sheath.

He wants it over quickly, mercifully, she thought. By then Raucus was barely a long stride away, his sword gleaming in the rising sun, and she had lifted her hand and cried out to Rill.

The snow and ice beneath Raucus's feet shifted and rose into a long rise— an icy ramp, to be more precise. Isana let her trembling legs give out completely, and dropped to the ground, as the slippery incline turned Raucus's own blinding speed against him. The High Lord went sailing over her head, his arms windmilling.

Isana completed drawing her sword and came back to her feet, her eyes tracking Raucus's flight—which turned into literally that before he actually returned to earth, a windstream rising to carry him clear of the ground. He banked in a broad circle, gestured with his left hand, and a sudden sphere of fire blossomed less than a foot in front of her face.

Isana reacted without thought, gathering more snow from the ground to surge up and swamp the white-hot firecrafting. She crouched away and down, keeping the surge of snow flowing up over the fireball like a lumpy white river. Steam billowed out and would have enveloped her, in any case, had she not kept more snow flowing upward, dousing the fire, refreezing the steam, carrying it all up and away from her.

She didn't see Raucus coming until he plunged *through* the column of steam and snow in a howl of wind, shards of frost and ice flying in every direction.

Hours and hours of instruction and practice with Araris had taught her reflexes a great deal more than she had realized. Her sword came up in a parry meant to deflect the tremendous force of the blow rather than opposing it outright, sure that she would not be able to match the power of the charging High Lord. The swords met. A shower of bright blue sparks flew up, and Raucus's sword peeled a long strip of metal from one blade of her *gladius* as easily as a man might slice the skin from an apple. Then he was past her and gone, recovering his own balance in the air.

Isana stared at the mauled sword for a split second, the edge of the sliced area glowing red with shed heat, and knew that she had been more than merely fortunate. Raucus hadn't been able to see *her* as he charged, just as she hadn't been able to see him coming. His blow had been badly aimed—which was to say, slightly less than perfect. Her defense had happened to meet it well, but doing it once was no guarantee that she could do it again.

And it was terrifyingly clear that she could not meet him sword to sword for long. He would slice her weapon apart like a stick of chilled butter. For that matter, she doubted that her armor would stand up to his blade any better. If she allowed Raucus to keep diving upon her, he would carve her to bits one pass at a time. She had to ground him.

With another lifted hand, the snow around her began to whirl in another vortex, rising in a blinding, stinging curtain to veil her from his sight, to make swift charges through the curtain of snow an unattractive option.

Instead, she maintained the watercrafting that kept the snow stirring around her and cooled her still-hot sword in the snow at her feet while she waited.

A moment later, a shadow broke the whirling snow, a dark shape, and Antillus Raucus appeared, frost clinging to his beard, his hair, and to the leather of his armored coat. His sword was in his hand.

On an impulse, Isana maintained the snow curtain, and waited.

"Bloody crows, Isana," Raucus said. His voice was not loud, and was more tired than angry. "An excellent choice of a dueling ground."

"Thank you, Your Grace," Isana said quietly.

He shook his head. "All you're doing is drawing things out. You're determined, and you think quickly. But this is only going to end one way."

"I can't help but wonder," Isana said quietly, "why you are so obstinate about refusing to cooperate with me."

"I think we've just about talked this to death," he said bleakly, and started forward.

Isana lifted her sword. "I'm not so sure, Raucus. Is this because of me? Or because of Gaius. I think you owe me that much of an answer."

"Owe you? *Owe* you?" Raucus said, and with a flick of his hand sent a gout of flame rushing toward her.

She raised a shimmering shield of ice halfway between them, and the flame vanished into a cloud of steam.

"As you point out, I can't really do more than draw this duel out, Your Grace. I'm well aware of that. It seems a small thing to ask of you in exchange for my life."

Raucus gave her a hard, bitter smile, hovering just outside what Araris had taught her would be the striking range of his weapon. "Gaius would be reason enough. That treacherous snake doesn't deserve the loyalty of the worms that will feast on his corpse."

"As much as I would like to," Isana replied, her tone frank, her sword at a low guard position, one that would be easiest on her arms to maintain, "I cannot say that I disagree with you, sir."

Raucus frowned. His stance shifted subtly, as he lifted his sword to a high guard, both hands on the weapon's handle, the blade almost directly in line with his body.

It was something of a ludicrous ready stance for such a short weapon, but all the same, it dictated that Isana had to adjust to the new potential threat. She lifted her blade to a similar stance, overhead, but with her arms slightly to one side, holding the weapon's length across her body.

"Eastern style," Raucus noted in a calm, professional tone. "Araris always loved bringing out that Rhodesian tripe in his high defense."

He took a step forward, closing into range, and swept a blow down at her. Isana managed to divert it, at the cost of another long sliver of steel from her blade, but then Raucus's shoulder and hip slammed into her as he continued forward, his entire mass impacting simultaneously along the center of her balance. Isana was flung violently back to the snow, and desperately wrought a working, flattening it to smooth ice, so that she slid several yards backward.

Raucus had taken quick steps forward to follow up the attack, but as his feet touched the slick ice, he was forced to slow. Another effort of will, and the snow gathered beneath her, lifting her to her feet again. She brought her sword up, her back against the wall of whirling snow that still enfolded them, and faced him, ready.

Raucus lifted his weapon to her in a smooth salute. "The Rhodesian school never allowed enough for brawling techniques, in my opinion." He began to pace around the icy patch, stalking her. "What do you have against Gaius?"

"He murdered my husband," Isana said, with far more heat than she'd intended. "Or stood by and allowed it to happen. It's the same to me."

Raucus froze in place for an instant, before he continued his stalk. "Then why are you here toadying for him?"

"I'm not," Isana replied. "I'm here for my son." She decided to test a theory, and took a quick step forward, lashing out in a conservative slash at the fingers gripping his sword.

Raucus parried her with the automatic ease of ridiculously disparate skill, nearly taking the sword from her hands—but he waited for her to step back out of range, rather than immediately counterattacking.

He wants to talk. Just keep him talking.

"Your son," Raucus said. "You and Septimus."

"Yes," Isana said.

Raucus's eyes flashed in anger, and his arm blurred. Three inches of steel simply vanished from the tip of her sword and went spinning away to land hissing on a patch of ice. Isana hadn't even *felt* the impact, it was so focused and powerful.

"The Princeps now," Antillus spat. "Proper and proud."

And it suddenly struck her, like blinding light on snow.

She knew the source of Antillus's obstinate rage.

She retreated from the next attack. "It isn't about Gaius at all," she breathed aloud. "It's about *me*. And it's about Maximus."

Raucus flung another burst of flame at her, hot but badly aimed. She was able to defend against it with more snow raised about her.

"You don't know what you're talking about," he snarled.

"Yes, I do," she said. "At first I thought you must have hated Tavi—but he's your friend's son, Raucus. You and Septimus knew and trusted one another. And I don't think that even after all those years, you're the kind of man to forget a friend."

"You've got no idea what you're *talking* about!" Raucus snarled. His sword whipped out twice more, biting away another inch of her blade each time.

Isana's voice shook with fear, and she smoothed the ground between them to ice, trying to create more space between them. "I do. Septimus did something you did. He fell in love with a freeman—with me. But he did something else you didn't dare to do. He married her."

"You think it's that *simple*?" Raucus demanded. He gestured once at the ground and—

—and fire blossomed *within the earth itself*. Isana felt the sudden rush of ice and snow melting, sublimating at once to mist as the ground warmed to the heat of a southern summer in the space of an instant.

"Crows take you," Raucus hissed, and came forward, sword raised to kill.

She couldn't fight the heat in the earth, to send ice through it to cool it again—not in time to save her life. But she *could* use that warmth. She reached out to all that mist and vapor and forced it down, into the warm earth—transforming it almost instantly to soupy mud that swallowed Raucus to midthigh.

And leaving her suddenly, viciously weary. She'd performed too many craftings, done swiftly and powerfully rather than with grace and efficiency, and it was taking the inevitable toll.

The High Lord let out a roar of frustration and simply flung his sword at her.

Isana's sword—what was left of it—snapped in an immediate, basic parry, one of the first Araris had taught her, and one of six that that he'd said he had time to drill into her muscle memory.

It simply wasn't fast enough.

She felt her mangled *gladius* brush the oncoming weapon, then a tremendous impact in her belly, and she was lying on her back in the snow.

She turned on her side, dazedly, and felt something horribly *wrong*. It wasn't pain, precisely. It was more like a quivering, trembling, silvery sensation that shot up and down her spine and throughout her limbs.

She looked down and saw that the High Lord's sword had sunk to its hilt in her abdomen.

Her curtain of snow had fallen. Silence had swallowed the land. From the walls, there was not a single sound, not a cry, not a single human voice.

Scarlet was spreading onto the snow around her.

She lifted her head to see Raucus just staring at her. His face had gone pale. His right hand was still lifted from his throw, fingers loosely curled.

"I don't think it was simple," Isana gasped. The words hurt to speak. "I think you were young. I think you fell in love with a freeman, Max's mother. And I think your father, your mother, whoever might have been in your life was horrified. There was a war to be fought along the Shieldwall—always a war. W-w-what would happen if the heir of Antillus didn't have the furycrafting talent he needed to fight it?"

The cold was getting through her coat. Or following her blood back up to her veins. Or she was simply bleeding to death. Regardless, Isana had little time to reach the man.

"Y-you had n-no way of knowing if M-maximus would be strongly talented. I th-think you had to set his mother aside to marry. F-for strong bl-bloodline. For alliances with Kalare and its watergrain fields."

Raucus began slogging his way out of the mud, moving toward her.

"Y-your f-father was k-killed on the Wall that year. Wh-when Crassus was born. You must have been gone most of the time after that. F-fighting." She nodded to herself. Of course he would have had to be gone. Learning how to command, proving himself to his troops. It would have taken enormous effort and dedication to do so.

"You w-were in the field when Septimus died. And when Max's mother died."

"Isana, stop," Raucus said. He pulled himself from the mud.

The cold grew deeper, but somehow less unpleasant. Isana laid her head on one outflung arm and tried to keep her eyes open. "And you knew Max suffered at Dorotea's hands. But there was nothing you could do. You couldn't acknowledge him over Crassus. You couldn't cut yourself off from Dorotea to wed his mother. You must have t-tried and been denied by Gaius." She smiled faintly. "He'd never have let you v-violate the traditional laws of legitimacy. Kalare would have raised a crowstorm over it in the Senate. And you were young. And Septimus's friend. Easier to ignore you."

"Stop talking," Raucus said.

Isana let out a small laugh. "No wonder you challenged him over Valiar Marcus. He'd not *dare* to deny you that acknowledgment, one that was within your rights to grant. And you'd have been too happy for an excuse to fight him if he did."

Raucus grasped the hilt of his sword.

Isana put her hand on his wrist, gripping it as hard as she could. "And then, after denying you, he acknowledges Septimus's son by a freeman. A son without furycraft to his name. And after he's already manipulated Maximus into being friends with him, to boot. You must have been so angry."

She leaned up, seeking his eyes desperately. The grey sky had begun to turn black. "I'm sorry. I'm so sorry that happened to you. That the Realm made your life this way. That you lost the woman you loved and were forced to keep one you hated. It's unjust, Raucus. Septimus would never have allowed it to go on.

"But he's *gone*. And if there's going to be a future, for your friend's son, for your sons, for the Realm, you have to set that a-anger aside."

She couldn't see anything at all by then.

"Please, Raucus," she said. She knew her voice wasn't coming out in more than a whisper. "I'm asking you to take a horrible chance. But without it, there won't be anything for any of us. Please. Help us."

There was a wrenching burst of fire in her belly. She didn't move, though. It was easier not to. She could hear footsteps somewhere.

"Aria!" Raucus screamed, his voice anguished.

Cold. And blackness.

CHAPTER 39

Shuar was dying.

As they rode toward the ships, Tavi realized that the roads of the last free nation of Canea had become charnel houses. Though the majority of the Vord emerging from the tunnels had flowed toward the north and west, to assault the fortifications from their unprotected rear, thousands more had spread out to haunt the roads of the land. There, they had found easy pickings in fleeing Canim families as panic descended upon the countryside. Corpses of the Canim makers—their farmers and artisans—lay exposed to the weather, untended. Their cattle had been slaughtered beside them.

The Canim had not died easily. Corpses of Vord attackers were heavily mingled with the fallen wolf-people, and in places it seemed that larger groups had managed to fend off their attackers. In others, what had probably been mounted patrols from the fortification had attacked the Vord, pursuing them off the roads, leaving trails of crushed chitinous forms into the rolling landscape. All the same, the previous few days had been a nightmare of blood and death for the Shuarans.

Without the steady reinforcements from the Vord's tunnel or the coldly logical will of the Vord queen to guide them to where they were needed, the roads had become less deadly. The Vord still lurked across the countryside, but they were fewer in number, their movements random and unfocused—if no less deadly for anyone caught outnumbered in the open or by surprise. Of course, if the second Vord queen commanding the enemy forces at the Shuaran fortifications changed position, the Vord's lack of coordination could change in an instant. Tavi's group raced along the roads, pressing the taurgs to their best pace.

Twice, they were attacked by small groups of wandering Vord, but Max's firecrafting and Varg's and Anag's balests shattered the armor and wills of the Vord before they could close to combat, and once they had traveled far enough from the site of the Vord emergence, encounters with the enemy and their handiwork declined abruptly.

They rode for the night and the rest of the day, stopping only occasionally to water the taurga. An hour or so before sundown, they came across a small stream where perhaps two hundred Canim had stopped to rest and drink. None of them wore armor, though many carried the sickle-swords that were, for them, simple harvest tools. Several of the makers were wounded, some badly so. Though Canim were never a particularly noisy people, the silence that fell on the group as they came riding up was tangible. Tavi could acutely feel the weight of their stares.

He wondered, for an amused moment, if they found the Alerans as strange and intimidating as he had found Varg and the guards of the Canim embassy in the Citadel, the first time he had encountered them.

"Let me speak to them," Anag said. The golden-furred Cane slipped off his taurg, and it spoke of the weariness of the beast that it didn't make even a desultory effort to bite or gore him as he dismounted. Anag strode over to the refugees, heading for a tall, grey-and-golden furred Cane who seemed to be their leader.

Tavi got his taurg down to the water and led Max's beast as well. The big Antillan, weary from the intensive crafting and fighting he'd done at the hive, simply flung himself down on the ground and slept.

Tavi found himself alone at the side of the stream, except for several taurga too tired and thirsty to cause trouble, and the lone Hunter who had survived the attack on the Vord queen.

"Thank you," Tavi told him quietly. "You and your people saved my life."

The Hunter looked up at him, ears quivering in surprise that he quickly suppressed. He bowed his head, Aleran-style.

"What were their names?" Tavi asked.

"Nef," growled the Hunter. "And Koh."

"And yours?"

"Sha."

"Sha," Tavi said. "I am sorry for their loss."

The Hunter became very still for a long moment, staring down at the stream.

"It is the way of your people to sing over the fallen," Tavi said quietly. "I've heard it before. Is there anyone to sing for Nef and Koh?"

Sha moved one paw-hand in a negative gesture. "Their kin sang their blood song long ago. When they became Hunters."

Tavi frowned and tilted his head.

"We are as the dead," Sha said. "Our purpose is to dedicate our lives to the service of our lord. And, when it is necessary, to surrender those lives. When we become what we are, we lose our lives—our names, our family, our homes, and our honor. All that remains is our lord."

"But their sacrifice may have saved thousands," Tavi said. "Is it the way of your kind to let such courage go unmourned?"

Sha studied him in silence for a long moment.

Tavi thought about the Cane's words, then nodded slowly, understanding. "They served well, and they died well and with meaning," he said. "What is there to mourn?"

Sha bowed his head again, more deeply this time. "You understand." The Cane's eyes gleamed as he looked at Tavi. "You were ready to die in that place as well, Tavar. We Hunters know what it looks like."

"I hadn't intended it to work out that way," Tavi said. "But I knew it was a possibility. Yes."

"Why?"

Tavi blinked at him. "What?"

"Why lay down your life?" Sha said. He gestured at the makers. "Varg is not your lord. These are not your people. They will not serve as soldiers if your plan to use our warriors against the Vord comes to pass."

Tavi thought about his answer for a moment before giving it. "It is my purpose to defend those who cannot defend themselves," he said finally.

"Even if they are your enemy."

Tavi smiled at Sha, showing his teeth. The Hunter had used the Aleran word, not one of the many Canim variants on the term. "Perhaps I wish your people to be *gadara* to mine. Perhaps I wished to tell you so in such a way that would leave no doubts as to my sincerity."

Sha's ears quivered with surprise again, and he stared hard at Tavi, his head tilted to one side. "That is . . . not a thought I have heard given voice before."

"His mind is strange," came Varg's rumbling voice, "but capable." The dark-furred Canim Warmaster had approached in silence. He checked the straps on his mount's saddle. "There is news on the roads. Couriers have passed by."

Tavi straightened. "And?"

"The fortifications have fallen," Varg said. "When Lararl sent a portion of his strength back to attack the Vord in the interior, the heaviest assault he had yet seen fell on the fortress."

Tavi frowned. "Then the pressure that had been put on the fortress for the past weeks—it was a ruse."

Varg nodded. "Convincing Lararl of the strength of his defenses. Causing him to send away more troops than he would have were he not confident that those remaining could hold. They waited for him to weaken himself, then . . ." Varg smacked his paw-hands together.

Tavi shook his head. It had cost the Vord untold numbers of their creatures to maintain the charade—but then, they had had bodies enough to spare. Mathematics had decided the war, probably months before the attack on Shuar began. "How bad?" Tavi asked.

"Lararl sent out couriers to spread the warning and dug in to hold the Vord for as long as possible. But the last couriers to leave saw the Vord entering the city at the top of the cliffs. What warriors escaped are fighting to slow the enemy—but a queen commands them."

Tavi nodded. "She'll drive for our only means of escape—Molvar. And she'll be gathering more and more troops to her as she heads this way."

Varg flicked his ears in assent. "We must return to the ships at once. The Shuarans may already have seized them."

"No," Tavi said. "We head for the hills west of Molvar."

Sha glanced up sharply at Tavi at this blatant contradiction of Varg's words.

"Tavar," Varg said quietly, "there is no winning a battle against the Vord on this ground. And there is not room on the ships for a tenth of those who will wish to flee Shuar. To do other than reach the ships and sail away is death."

Tavi stared at Varg, smiling.

Varg looked up from his saddle. "You meant it when you told Lararl you could get his people away?"

"How many times have I lied to you?" Tavi asked.

"I have never taken you prisoner," Varg replied, his tone pensive. "Lararl had. And some of your folk are truthful only in preparation for the day when they need one critical lie to be believed."

"If that is the case," Tavi said, "then that day has not yet come." He nodded at the camp of miserable-looking makers. Maximus had risen from his near stupor on the ground and was standing with Anag over one of the worst-looking of the wounded, supervising moving the injured Cane into the stream for a water-crafting. "We're getting them away from here."

Varg looked at Tavi, then at the makers. "Tavar, I sometimes think you are insane."

"Are you coming with me?"

Varg glanced at him, and Tavi swore he could see something offended in the big Cane's body language. "Of course."

Tavi showed him his teeth again. "Glad I'm not the only one."

By a few hours after midnight, they had reached the Aleran defenses.

A rising moon, nearly full, and the mercurial nature of Canean weather had swept the sky clean of clouds and bathed the land in silver light. A line of hills west of Molvar had been transformed by several days of furious labor on the part of the Narashan Canim and both Legions, aided by Aleran furycraft. Where there had been only gently rolling land, the combined forces had erected an earthworks twenty feet high, faced by freshly cut stakes of pine, in front of a trench very nearly as deep as the wall was high. Only a few narrow passages had been left through the defenses, which arched in a line nearly five miles long around Molvar. Refugees from the invaded territory had flooded the area inside, and the interior of the hastily erected, enormous fortress was already filling with Canim.

Even with all of Nasaug's troops and both Aleran Legions, the defenses around the town were spread thin, though it was clear that the Shuarans had thrown what forces they had into the same effort. More were arriving at every moment, as well—stragglers, Tavi supposed, who had been separated from their battlepacks, and what looked like the occasional wayward company who had been cut off from the larger portion of their command and had found themselves nearby. The wounded, too, were pouring in, as were the Shuaran taurg cavalry, whose riders came and went in constant activity.

Max brought his mount up beside Tavi's as they approached the earthworks, and whistled. "There's a lot of work. That's what the Legion's been up to?"

Tavi nodded. "We need a defensible position. It's going to take time to move this many Canim and all the supplies onto the transports."

"Transports?" Max asked. "What transports?"

Tavi shook his head.

Max sighed wearily. "Tavi, I'm tired. We know there were only two queens on the whole continent. You and Varg diced one of them, and the other one is busy leading an army toward us. We don't need to worry about anyone's mind being picked over. So talk."

"Max," Kitai said from behind Tavi on their shared taurg. "What we do *not* know is the location of those two queens' mother."

"Oh." Max was quiet for a moment. Then he grunted, and said, "Good point. Shut up, Calderon."

"Durias," Tavi called.

Durias nudged his weary taurg forward. "Highness?"

"Ride ahead and let the Legion know we're coming," Tavi said. "I'll need to speak to Marcus, Nasaug, and Magnus immediately. See if Crassus can be there as well. Oh, and Demos."

Durias saluted and kicked his mount into a lumbering trot.

"Did you see that, Maximus?" Kitai asked. "He just helped, without whining or indulging in foolish questions. Perhaps when you grow up, you will be more like Durias."

Max glowered at Kitai, then saluted Tavi, and said, "I think I'll just go help him now." He nudged Steaks into a trot and caught up with Durias. Tavi heard him muttering darkly under his breath as he went.

"That wasn't very nice," Tavi said quietly, once Max had gone.

Kitai sighed. "You weren't looking at him when you spoke to Durias. He's so tired he was about to fall off his taurg. Now he's grumpy enough to get back to camp while awake—and more quickly."

Tavi let himself lean back against Kitai, feeling the weight of his own fatigue. "Thank you."

"I know how important he is to you," she said quietly. "And I love him, too, *chala*."

Tavi nudged his own mount into a walk. "So you manipulated him into doing what you thought was in his best interests."

"I did what was necessary to protect him. Yes."

Tavi glanced over his shoulder and met her intent green eyes. "You deceived me."

She didn't even blink. "You lied to me, Aleran. When you promised me we would be together. You knew you were about to go out on your own. That you could die."

"This is about more than you and me. You shouldn't have decided to kill the queen without talking to me about it."

"Only speed and surprise could enable us to succeed. If you had known—"

"That isn't the point, and you know it."

Her eyes narrowed. "The Vord are not to be reasoned with. They are to be killed."

"You didn't know that for certain. We couldn't, until we made the attempt."

She sighed and shook her head. "Aleran. You are a good man. But in some ways, you are a fool."

"Swords and fire don't solve every problem."

"And some can be solved no other way," she replied, her voice fierce. "The Vord all but destroyed my people in the past. They are gutting the corpse of what is left of the Canim now. Open your eyes."

"I *did*," Tavi said, and suddenly he felt so weary that it was hardly worth speaking. He turned back to the front, and his head felt too heavy to hold up. "And I feel like I'm the only one who can see the truth."

Kitai was quiet for a moment, and when she spoke again, her voice was more gentle. "What do you mean?"

"*Chala*," he said quietly. "Look at what the Vord have done to the Canim. If the only option we have is to fight . . . I don't think Alera could do any better. How am I supposed to lead people into a fight I know they can't win? Ask them to die in vain? *Watch* them d—"

His vision blurred for a moment, and his throat felt tight.

Kitai's arms tightened around him, and he suddenly became intensely aware of her love for him, her faith, her trust, wrapping around him as tangibly as her embrace. "Oh, *chala*," she said quietly.

Several moments passed before he could speak. "What do I do?"

Her hand touched his face. "I know that you feel as if you need to find some clever alternative. Some way to overcome the Vord, to save lives, to avoid bloodshed. But this is not an enemy who might live with you in peace for a time. The Vord want nothing but to destroy. And they *will* destroy you if they can. They will use your desire for peace against you."

She gently turned his head until he could meet her eyes again. "If you truly want peace, if you truly wish to save lives, you must fight them. Fight them with everything you have. Fight them with everything you are. Fight until there is not a breath left in your body." She lifted her chin. "And I will fight beside you."

She was right, of course. He knew that. When the Vord finished with the Canim, they would come for Alera. The advantage of numbers they had was formidable, but it wasn't impossible. Not if all of Alera worked together.

That was the problem. There were too many divisive elements in play at home. Oh, certainly, once Alerans at large realized the danger, they would respond together—but by the time they did, it might already be too late. His uncle had been trying in vain to warn Alera about the Vord for years. Many Alerans regarded the Canim as little more than animals with weapons. His countrymen would never believe that the Canim civilization had been so large, so developed, and consequently its destruction would lack credibility as a warning of the danger to come.

Worse, he himself represented another enormous element of division. Many Citizens had tacitly refused to recognize his legitimacy as heir to the Crown. He had escorted Varg's people back to Canea precisely because his presence was such a potent disruption. Crows, he'd felt fortunate to avoid any encounters with assassins before he left.

Gaius was wise and powerful, but he was also aging. Fighting a campaign of the scale of this one would be would be taxing even on a young man—and it was the kind of fight the old First Lord was not suited to in the first place. He was a master of politics, of manipulation, of the critical strike delivered at precisely the right instant with precisely the force needed. He was used to being thoroughly in control.

But war wasn't like that. You never thought of all the possibilities. Something always happened to throw off your plans. Supplies could be delayed or lost. Soldiers could encounter sickness, bad terrain, parasites, faulty gear, hostile weather, and a million other factors that would prevent them from performing as expected. Meanwhile, the enemy was doing everything in his power to kill you. No one could control that kind of chaos. All you could hope to do was keep your eyes open, make sure everyone was working together, and stay a couple of steps ahead of disaster.

A united Alera would have a chance. Probably not a good chance, but if led correctly, they could make a fight of it. Oh, certainly Gaius had the training, but the study of books and the stories of old generals and models on a sand table were a far cry from war's horrible reality. Could Tavi's aging grandfather change his thinking as quickly and drastically as this war would demand?

The first step, Tavi supposed, was to believe. Believe that victory was possible. Believe that he could make it happen. Then bring that same belief to others. Because sure as crows on a corpse, anyone who fought believing they would lose had lost already. He had to trust in his grandfather, the single most formidable person Tavi had ever known, to guide the Realm through this storm. And if he was to trust and serve the First Lord, then he had to give the fight everything he had.

There would be no surrender.

"All right," he said quietly. He looked up at the earthworks and nodded. "Let's get inside. There's a lot of work to do, and not much time to do it in."

Kitai's arms tightened hard on him, and he felt her fierce pride and exultation as if it were his own.

Tavi rode toward the last defenses of a dying land to do everything in his power to take a host of deadly allies to the man who was Alera's only hope.

CHAPTER 40

For the first time in history, Alera Imperia braced herself for war beneath a canopy of wheeling crows.

Ehren stood on a southward-facing balcony of the First Lord's citadel, where Gaius was the center of a swarm of activity while the Legions prepared to defend the city. From there, he could overlook all the prepared defensive positions, descending through the city's defensive rings.

Alera Imperia had been built to withstand a siege—originally, at any rate. Her avenues ran in concentric, descending circles around the citadel, with cross streets laid out in straight lines from the city's heart, like the spokes of a wheel. Each avenue was approximately fifteen feet above the next level of the city, and the stone buildings lining each avenue had been reshaped by Legion engineers, so that their outer edges had become defensive walls. The streets had been sealed, except for a single avenue between each level, alternating on opposite sides of the city. Now, the only way to the citadel was a long corridor of streets faced with stone walls, so that even if the enemy took one gate, they would be faced with another and another before they reached the citadel itself.

Against conventional tactics, Alera Imperia could theoretically hold against an attacker almost indefinitely.

Against the Vord . . . Well. They would soon find out.

". . . and Third Rivan will also be on the first tier," Aquitainus Attis was saying, nodding to the city gates behind the actual, massive walls of battlecrafted stone, far below the citadel. "First and Third Aquitaine, Second and Third Placidan, and the Crown Legion are camped on the north side of the city, outside the walls."

"I cannot agree with this measure," muttered a man Ehren recognized as the senior captain of the Rhodesian Legions. "We may not be able to open and close sally ports to get your men back inside when the Vord arrive."

"It's the right move," Captain Miles said. "A mobile force can exploit any opening they leave us as they approach the city. They could inflict more damage than months of fighting from defensive positions."

Lord Aquitaine gave the Rhodesian captain a very level stare.

"Of course," the man said, averting his gaze.

Aquitaine nodded once and continued speaking as if he hadn't been interrupted. "Further reinforcements from Forcia, Parcia, and Rhodes are unlikely at best, though they may be able to strike into the enemy's flanks in the Vale."

Which, while it could prove important in the long run, would *not* help them now, Ehren thought.

The First Lord cleared his throat and spoke in a quiet, clear tone. "What is the status of the civilian evacuation?"

"The last of them are leaving now, sire," Ehren supplied. "All who were willing to leave, at any rate. The Senatorial party offered their personal armsmen as a security force."

"I'm sure," Gaius murmured. "The southern refugees?"

The people who had already fled so far from their homes had been heartbroken when they were told that the capital held no safety for them. Many of them were too sick, weary, hungry, or wounded to keep running. "We made sure those who were worst off were given space on wagons, sire," Ehren said. "We also gave them all the food they could carry."

Gaius nodded. "And the food stores?"

"We've enough to feed the Legions for sixteen weeks at normal rations," Miles responded. "Twenty-four if we immediately begin cutting them."

No one responded to that, and Ehren was fairly sure he knew why: none of the men there felt confident that they had sixteen weeks remaining to them, least of all the First Lord.

The voices of the circling crows were harsh.

Ehren entered the First Lord's private chambers and found Gaius Caria at the liquor cabinet.

"My lady," he said quietly, surprised. He paused to bow his head to her. "Please excuse me."

Caria, Gaius's second wife, was tall and lovely and fifty years younger than the First Lord, though the natural appearance of a skilled watercrafter kept her looking even younger than that. She had long hair of dark chestnut, narrow, clean features, and wore a blue silk dress of impeccable style and cut. "I should say so," she said in a calm, cold voice. "What are you doing here?"

"The First Lord ran out of his tonic. For his cough," Ehren said, all but stammering. Whether or not he'd had legitimate business here, he wasn't comfortable with the concept of being alone with another man's wife in his own bedroom. "He sent me for another bottle."

"Ah," Caria said. "And how is His Majesty?"

"His physician is . . . concerned, my lady," Ehren said. "But of course, he is handling the matter of the defense of the Realm quite well."

Her voice gained the faintest hint of a sharp edge. "Of course he is. Duty before all." She stepped aside from the cabinet, then turned to walk out of the First Lord's chambers.

Ehren hurried over to liquor cabinet and found its door unlatched.

That meant nothing, in itself—but Ehren knew Gaius. He was not the sort of man to leave doors unlatched behind him. He opened the cabinet and found the various bottles inside standing in neat rows—except for one. The full bottle of the First Lord's tonic was askew, and the cork that sealed it was improperly seated.

But who would have tampered with the First Lord's . . .

Ehren turned and was across the room in several long strides, seizing Lady Caria's wrist, and spinning her toward him. He dug his fingers into her wrist, twisting, and a small glass vial fell from her fingers and to the floor. Ehren released her and snatched it up.

"How *dare* you!" Caria snarled, and fetched him a backhanded blow that fell on his chest and flung him back across the room.

Ehren managed to fall correctly, or he might have broken something on the marble floor. Even so, the fury-assisted blow had driven the breath from his lungs.

"How dare you lay a *hand* upon me, you arrogant little slive," Caria snarled. She turned one palm upright, and fire kindled between her fingers. "I should burn you alive."

Ehren knew that his life was in very real danger, but he could barely move his arms and legs. "The First Lord," he wheezed, "is expecting me with his medicine."

Caria's eyes flicked down to his chest and back up to his face. Her expression twisted in something like frustration, and she clenched her fist, snuffing the fire that had sprung there.

Ehren glanced down as well. The silver coin on his necklace, the unofficial sign of a Cursor working personally for the First Lord, had fallen free of his tunic.

"I suppose it hardly matters now," Caria said, her tone positively vicious. She turned with haughty deliberation and began walking away again.

Ehren looked down at the vial in his hand. It was stoppered tightly, with perhaps half a fingertip's width of grey-white powder at the bottom. Poison, almost certainly.

"Why?" he croaked. "Why do this now, of all times?"

Caria paused at the doorway and looked back over her shoulder, a small smile on her lips. "Habit," she murmured in a velvet voice.

Then she left.

"Helatin," Sireos said in a firm tone of voice. The physician sat at a table in an antechamber next to Gaius's command center, a dozen glass vials of colored liquid in wire racks in front of him, along with the now-empty vial Ehren had taken from Caria. "More specifically, refined helatin."

Ehren shook his head. "I don't understand. I thought that was a medication."

"Medicine and poison are separated by quantity and timing," Sireos responded. "Helatin is a stimulant, in small quantities. It's part of his tonic, in fact. The body can process a small amount without harm. Larger amounts, though . . ." He shook his head.

"This would have killed him?" Ehren asked.

"Not at all," Sireos said. "At least, not alone. Helatin taken in larger amounts is deposited in the brain, the spine, and the bones. And it stays there."

Ehren breathed out slowly over a sick sensation in his stomach. "It accumulates over time."

"And degrades the body's ability to restore itself," Sireos said, nodding. "Eventually to the point where—"

"Where organs begin dying," Ehren said bitterly.

Sireos spread his hands and said nothing.

"What can be done?"

"I believe the penalty for poisoning is death by hanging," Sireos responded. "Of course, that's always been after a trial before a committee appointed by the Senate."

Ehren blinked at the physician. "What happened to 'first, do no harm'?"

"I love life," Sireos said, his eyes hard. "I do not revere it. Caria was once my student at the academy. She used that knowledge to hurt another human being, and has earned the retribution of the law. I'd tie the rope."

"But that won't help Gaius," Ehren said.

Sireos shook his head. "The damage helatin does takes years to build up, and it is subtle. I'd have to have been looking for it specifically, and unfortunately the poison's effects look a great deal like the effects of simple age."

"Wouldn't Gaius have noticed it?" Ehren asked.

"Because he's grown old before, and should know what it feels like?" The physician shook his head. "Part of what the helatin did would have reduced Gaius's ability to detect it for himself. Even if he was a young man, the best we could hope for would be to manage it. As things are . . ."

"Habit," Ehren said bitterly. "How long has it been going on?"

"Six years, at the least," Sireos said. "Given the idiocy of that business in Kalare, I'm frankly surprised that he's alive right now, much less on his feet."

"For some reason," Gaius said quietly, "I find it comforting to know that growing old isn't this painful for everyone."

Ehren looked up to see the First Lord standing in the doorway. He coughed, a wheezing sound, and pressed his hand to his chest with a grimace. "In my tonic, you say?"

Sireos nodded. "I'm sorry, Sextus."

Gaius took this news without expression. "How much time did she take from me, do you think?"

"There's no way to be sure."

"There seldom is," Gaius said, his voice slightly harder. "How long, Sireos?"

"Five years. Maybe ten." The physician shrugged.

A small smile quirked the corners of the First Lord's mouth. "Well. I suppose that makes the two of us even, then."

Ehren turned to him. "Sire . . ."

Gaius waved a hand. "I've taken as much from her, and better years, at that. She was a child, caught up in games she had no way to understand or avoid. I'm not willing to waste what time remains to me on the matter."

"Sire. This is *murder*."

"No, Sir Ehren. This is a footnote. There is no time for arrests, investigations, and trials." Gaius reached out to a weapons stand that was set up beside the door and buckled on his sword belt. "I'm afraid the Vord have arrived."

Gaius stood on the broad balcony, looking down as the Vord came for Alera Imperia. At his murmured word, the edges of the balcony had become one enormous windcrafting, focusing the view into a greatly magnified image whenever one stood at the rail and looked down. All Ehren needed to do was stand at the railing and stare at a particular portion of the lower city, and his view of it would suddenly rush forward, showing him the outer walls, more than a mile away, in crystalline clarity.

It was a little disconcerting, and gave him an odd, spinning sense of vertigo.

This must be how the Princeps felt aboard a ship. Ehren reminded himself to be somewhat less cavalier about Tavi's discomfort in the future.

If there was a future.

"Ah, I thought so," Gaius said. "Look."

Ehren came to the First Lord's side and stared in the direction he indicated—south, over the plains surrounding the capital. The Vord had crested the most distant ridge that could be seen from the Citadel in a solid black line, like a living shadow that rolled steadily forward. Most of the ground troops were the four-legged creatures that they had seen before, but for every dozen or so of them, there walked a single creature shaped something like an enormous ape. The behemoths had bandy legs and enormous apelike arms, and they rolled forward using their forelimbs as well as their feet for locomotion. They were huge, better than twelve feet tall, and covered in plates of Vord armor that looked inches thick.

"Siege units," Gaius murmured. "They'll use them for breaching gates and walls, and probably to spearhead assaults."

Ehren stared at the behemoths and shivered. "Look behind them."

Gaius fell silent for a moment as he studied what Ehren had noticed.

Behind the first wave of Vord came an enormous line of Alerans.

They weren't alive, of course. Thanks to the windcrafting, Ehren could see that much. Their skin was mottled with postmortem bruising, and in some cases their bodies bore disfigurements or injuries that would have rendered any human immobile. The taken holders—and the vast majority of them *were* obviously holders, dressed in common clothing—walked without any expression whatever on their faces, their eyes focused on nothing.

"Where are the vordknights?" Ehren murmured.

"Staying out of sight, massing for an attack, most likely," Gaius said. "They can't have much fight left in them."

"They've been harassing us all the way here," Ehren said.

"Exactly," Gaius said. "It takes an enormous amount of power for them to keep themselves aloft. They must eat like gargants to be able to sustain the muscle they'd need for that sort of activity—and even with the patches of *croach* that they planted in secret, ahead of their advance, we've yet to discover one more than an acre in size." The First Lord shook his head. "Badly supplied infantry can fight on to some degree. But I think the vordknights are more like cavalry. Short cavalry of supplies, and they become ineffective far more rapidly. She'll save them for a critical stroke."

"The queen, you mean?" asked Ehren.

Gaius nodded. "She is the key to the entire battle." He fell silent again as they watched the Vord swarm over the plains toward the capital.

"So many of them," Ehren breathed.

For an instant, the First Lord's eyes glittered with a wild, fey light. "Aren't there, though." He nodded and turned to one of the Legion trumpeters at hand. "Signal the first attack."

The courier nodded and raised his trumpet. Its call sounded clear over the quiet city, and in its wake the Legions roared.

Thousands of Citizens stood among their ranks, called forth to fight for their land, to demonstrate the obligation that went with the privileges of their title. Among the Citizenry, earthcrafting was by far the most common talent, and now those Citizens unleashed their furies upon the Vord.

Just ahead of the Vord ranks, the ground erupted, swelling into hillocks and blisters of stone that burst to disgorge furies of the earth. Gargants, wolves, serpents, great dogs, and nameless things—both beautiful and hideous—came bounding and slithering and charging out of the very soil of the land, to fall upon the first wave of the alien horde.

The battle that ensued had a ghastly sort of beauty to it. The Aleran furies, like statuary come to frenzied life, slammed into the Vord. Furies of the earth, though not swift, were viciously strong and difficult to actually harm—and the Vord were packed in close to one another as they came for Alera Imperia. Ehren watched as a bear made of black-and-grey marble slammed its paws down with methodical precision, crushing a Vord at every blow. A gargant of flint and clay thundered into the Vord ranks without being noticeably slowed, leaving destruction in its wake. A great sandstone serpent wound swiftly around one Vord after another, crushing the howling creatures in its coils and slithering on. The earth furies broke Vord quadrupeds like toys, and shrugged off blow after blow in response.

The behemoths, though, proved tougher than the Vord-lizards. Ehren saw one of them accept a pair of hammerblows from the great bear without flinching, and in response it simply bent and heaved the fury's form up off the ground. The granite was riven and shattered, and a few seconds later, the "crack" of protesting stone reached the citadel. The behemoth smashed the bear-form down to the ground, where it crumbled into motionless rubble.

Gaius winced.

"Are you all right, sire?" Ehren asked at once.

"Just feeling sympathy for whoever called out that bear fury," the First Lord replied. "That sort of thing . . . leaves a mark."

Ehren turned his eyes back to the battle and watched for several moments more as the Vord reached the earth furies and simply enfolded them, pouring around them, all but ignoring their presence as dozens of their fellows were crushed. Earth furies could only focus on a task for as long as the one who compelled them, and as the earthcrafters who called them forth began to grow more weary, their furies began to move more slowly and with less purpose. Here and there, a behemoth would meet a fury—those battles ended only one way. The enormous Vord had to be possessed of absolutely awesome strength, to so deal with beings of living stone.

"Enough," Gaius said. "Sound the recover."

Again, the trumpet blast rang over the city, and at once the earth furies began to recede into the stone. Down on the walls, Ehren saw exhausted earthcrafters dropping down to sit with their backs against the battlements, while Legion runners brought them water—and while medics hauled away no few Citizens who had collapsed, presumably of exhaustion or because their furies had been ravaged by the behemoths.

Thousands of the enemy had been slain—but they poured forward, unaffected and unslowed, on the last several hundred yards of their approach to the city walls, through the rough wooden buildings and shanties that surrounded them.

"Fire it," Gaius said calmly.

At another signal, flame bloomed up in a hundred places at once, and a wind sighed down from above and began to blow more and more strongly. Within a minute, fire had leapt up to raging proportions within the wooden outlying buildings, and completely engulfed the leading elements of the Vord advance. Smoke and heat and flame made it impossible to see what was happening within, but Ehren could vividly imagine the damage that the inferno was wreaking among the Vord.

The horde suddenly stopped in its tracks—by the tens of thousands, they simply ceased moving forward at the precise same instant. A moment later, the closer elements of the enemy force withdrew slightly from the flames.

And waited.

"Mmm," Gaius said, nodding. "The queen is nearby, to so control them. Let's see if she'll send her captured crafters to deal with the problem."

Meanwhile, the rest of the horde continued to advance behind the front ranks, spreading out to the sides, slowly filling in along the outer edges of the ring of flame. It took only moments for their easternmost elements to reach the banks of the Gaul, the river that flowed past the capital. Then the Vord focused on expanding their lines to the west. The enormous black force was slowly engulfing the city.

After a quarter of an hour had passed, Gaius murmured, "Apparently not." He turned to a nearby Knight, and murmured, "Inform Lord Aquitaine of the disposition of the enemy."

The man saluted and took to the air at once, flying toward the north side of the city, on the far side of the horde.

Ehren swallowed. "What are we going to do, sire?"

"The same thing they are, Cursor," Gaius said calmly. "We wait."

It took the rest of the day and the first three hours of night for the outbuildings to burn down. Smoke hung in a haze over the city below them, and if that wasn't enough, fog had begun to roll up off the river. The citadel almost seemed to float among clouds—clouds lit hellishly from below by the burning buildings of the capital. The crows wheeled overhead all the while, chuckling and croaking to one another in the darkness.

Gaius had retired to the antechamber, where Sireos did what he could to fortify the dying First Lord. At Ehren's insistence, he'd eaten another meal and was dozing on a couch when horn calls blared up from the unseen city below, ghostly in the mist.

The First Lord snapped awake at once—and from his seat nearby, Ehren saw Gaius's face contort with pain. Then the old man closed his eyes, took in a determined breath, and pushed himself up off the couch to stride toward the balcony. Ehren rose at once to follow him.

Gaius listened to the horn calls for a moment and nodded to himself. "They're coming through. Here is where we force their hand, Cursor." He pointed at the trumpeter without looking back at the man, and said, "Sound the attack."

The clarion call of the charge, universal among the Legions, rang in Ehren's ears, and was answered by hundreds of horns in the city below.

Gaius raised his hand and cried out, and the chilly northern wind rose to an abrupt gale that threatened to throw Ehren from his feet. The wind roared down over the city, and carried away the pall of smoke and fog—while fanning what was left of the fires to vicious life.

Ehren paced the balcony at Gaius's side, and saw that the Vord had surrounded nearly half the circumference of the city—and were surging forward in a unified attack.

Once more, earth furies rose to battle, among the fires and ruined buildings, disdaining the heat. In addition to that, spheres of white-hot fire began to erupt among them, some of them large enough to engulf a behemoth and the Vord-lizards all around it. Knights Aeris erupted into the skies all around the city, and teams of the men streaked along over the outlying buildings, using their windstreams to fan fires and to topple ruined buildings upon the foe.

The Vord advance was slowed—not because they had begun to waver, but simply because the Alerans were killing them faster than they could run forward. Ehren stared at the naked destruction in awe and terror. The ground itself was being rent by the fires unleashed by the Citizens of Alera, gouging out chunks of earth as easily as one might scoop butter from its container. The Vord shrieked and writhed and died, and Ehren could hear their cries even from atop the balcony.

The First Lord was staring hard around the city, though, his eyes searching. "Bloody crows," he muttered beneath his breath. "Bloody crows take that arrogant slive. Where is he?"

"Who, sire?"

"Aquitaine," Gaius growled. "This is the moment to strike them, when they are all focused forward on the walls. He had plenty of time to move into position. Where *is* he?"

No sooner had Gaius said the words than the mighty Gaul suddenly convulsed. The great river, shining silver beneath an almost-full moon, rose from its banks and flowed abruptly toward the rear of the Vord positions, the water cutting smoothly across the plain outside the city, spreading in the midst of the Vord ranks, driving some forward and others back.

Then, impossibly, trumpets sounded from the suddenly empty riverbed, and with a sea-crash roar of furious voices, the full strength of five Legions came charging out of the trench where the river had flowed. They smashed into the flanks and rear of the enemy horde, their flank secured by the new course of the river, and began driving hard into the Vord lines.

"Bloody crows!" Ehren all but screamed.

Even the First Lord arched his eyebrows at the sight. "He must have used his watercrafters to convince the river to flow over and around his troops. Windcrafting to keep the air in the bubble fresh. Earthcrafting to solidify the silt so they could march on it." Gaius shook his head. "Impressive."

The city's defenders roared in defiance. As the endurance of the Citizenry below began to flag, the Vord began to reach the outer wall and *legionares* went to work with sword and shield upon the battlements. The enemy immediately began changing its formation, its westernmost elements turning to come in and support the threatened eastern half against Aquitaine's Legions—but Alera Imperia was a large city, and they would have to travel miles to be of any assistance to their fellows.

The whole while, Aquitainus Attis and the Legions under his command would be cutting the Vord to bloody ribbons.

Ehren focused on the battle, hope surging in his heart, as the scarlet star of fire that marked the blade of the High Lord of Aquitaine flickered and flashed. Through the magnification of Gaius's windcrafting, Ehren could see Aquitaine himself in the front ranks of his Legion, surrounded by heavily armored bodyguards. As Ehren watched, the High Lord braced a pair of behemoths.

With a flick of his hand, a tiny sphere of fire erupted upon the face of one of the huge beasts, and, while it roared in pain, Aquitaine dodged the thunder-

ing downswing of the second. In several dancelike steps, he struck an arm and
a leg from the second behemoth, sending it crashing down, and in the course of
returning to the ranks he slew the burned, screaming beast before it could recover from the pain. His men howled in a frenzy of rage and encouragement,
and the entire force continued on inexorably, like a single, vast scythe cutting
down wheat.

Then the Vord queen struck back.

The taken Alerans turned as one to charge Aquitaine's lines. Even as they
approached, fire and earth and wind erupted toward them, slaughtering the first
several dozen to draw near.

But the hundred who came after them let out eerie screams, raised their
hands, and turned fire and earth and wind back upon the Legion lines. Men
died screaming in blasts of fire, or were hauled into the earth by hideous shapes,
never to be seen again. Wind cast dust and ashes into their faces in thick
clouds, and their formations began to falter. More and more taken Alerans arrived, and the furycrafted pressure against Aquitaine's force doubled and doubled again, as each new taken seemed to feed upon the energies being unleashed,
adding its own to the struggle.

"Knights Aeris to their aid," Gaius said calmly. "Focus on the enemy crafters
and take them with blades alone."

Another courier screamed skyward, and within a moment several cohorts
of Knights Aeris rose from the city and streaked toward the battle. It took them
only seconds to land among the taken and attack, wielding steel alone. Aquitaine's
Legions realized what was happening as the pressure on them began to ease,
and they surged forward in a desperate effort to reach the Knights Aeris before
they were engulfed by the oncoming horde.

It was then that the vordknights pounced.

They suddenly burst up from the ground on the far side of the redirected
river, where they must have slipped into position once the sun was down. They
were barely a half mile from the battle, and they swept down upon the Knights
Aeris of Alera like a swarm of bees. The Knights found themselves suddenly be-
set on all sides, and did what any of them with any sense would do—they called
their furies and prepared to take to the air.

Until the taken began throwing salt at them.

Windcrafters screamed in agony as the salt crystals ripped holes through
their furies, dispersing and weakening them. Several made it off the ground and
managed to escape—but most didn't. Though the Legions tried to push forward
to shelter the exposed Knights Aeris, they had lost too much of their momentum to reach them in time. In seconds, the masters of Alera's skies were all but
drowned in armored bodies and hacking limbs.

And then the true death blow fell.

Crows by the tens of thousands suddenly plummeted into the capital's streets, buildings, and rooftops. Several of the creatures even fell to the stones of the balcony upon which Ehren stood. The crows, upon landing, fluttered in bizarre spasms, then went still.

Ehren and the others stared around the balcony and out at the city, perplexed.

"Great furies," Ehren breathed. "What was that about?"

Gaius's pensive frown suddenly froze in place. His eyes widened slightly, and he said, "No. Cursor, ware!"

The bodies of the crows erupted with Vord takers.

They weren't impressive things to look at. Each was about the size of a scorpion, and vaguely resembled one, except for dozens of flailing tendrils sprouting from all parts of its body. They were swift, though, as quick as startled mice, and half a dozen of the things scuttled toward those upon the balcony in a blur of green-black chitin.

Ehren spun and stomped a foot down upon one of the takers, and slapped a second from the back of his thigh. One of the couriers stomped at another one, missed, and lost his balance. Three takers swarmed up his body, and, as he cried out in surprise and revulsion, one of them plunged into his mouth.

The man screamed once, and then fell backward in convulsions, his eyes rolling back into his head. Another cry died as it was born—and then his eyes went flat, and swiveled toward the First Lord. He came to his feet and lurched at Gaius.

Ehren flung himself in between the First Lord and the taken courier. He seized the man's tunic, and with a panicked effort of his entire body the young Cursor threw the doomed courier over the balcony railing.

There was a bright flash of light, a crackling snap, and the sharp smell of ozone. By the time Ehren was finished blinking the spots from his eyes, he realized that several takers lay curled up and dead on the balcony floor. The First Lord stood over them, his right hand out, flickers of lightning dancing between his spread fingers.

"Crows," Gaius said simply, glancing up at the nearly empty sky. "I didn't spare them a second glance."

Screams began to echo up through the city. Not a minute later, a house or a garden one tier below the citadel level caught fire.

Outside the city, the Vord's collared crafters came onto the field. They drove forward toward Aquitaine's forces, and the redirected river began to waver and writhe like a vast, living serpent.

A scream of agony echoed through the halls of the Citadel, behind them.

"Never a second glance," Gaius said, sighing quietly. Then he raised his voice to a tone of firm command. "Clear the balcony."

Everyone there withdrew, except for Ehren. Gaius went to the balcony's edge and stared down at Aquitaine's desperate Legions. The High Lord had already realized his predicament, and his men were executing a fighting retreat, struggling to get away from the Vord before they were cut off, drowned, or overwhelmed.

Gaius bowed his head for a moment, then looked up again, and calmly took a pair of folded, sealed envelopes from his jacket. He passed them to Ehren.

Ehren blinked and looked down at it. "Sire?"

"The first is for my grandson," Gaius said simply. "The second, for Aquitaine. There's a tunnel concealed behind my desk in my mediation chamber in the deeps. It exits two miles north of the city, on the road to the Redhill Heights. I want you to take the messages and Sireos and go."

"Sire," Ehren said, "no, I couldn't . . . We should all go. We can retreat toward Aquitaine or Riva and prepare a better—"

"No, Ehren," Gaius said quietly.

Another scream echoed through the citadel.

"I'll be dead before we can establish another stronghold—and the seat of my power is here," Gaius said. "This is where I can hurt them the most."

Ehren's eyes stung and he looked down. "We're to sound the retreat then?"

"If we do," Gaius said quietly, "there's no chance of the queen's exposing herself. Their forces will disperse to pursue us, and the roads will become abattoirs." Gaius turned haunted eyes toward the city's defenders below. "I need them. If there's to be any chance at all . . . I need them."

"Sire," Ehren breathed. Though it didn't feel as if he was crying, he felt his tears falling on his hands.

Gaius put a hand on Ehren's shoulder. "It was an honor, young man. If you should see my grandson again, please tell him . . ." The old man frowned slightly for a moment before his lips turned up in a sad, weary smile. "Tell him that he has my blessing."

"I will, sire," Ehren said quietly.

Gaius nodded. Then he untied the thong that bound the scabbard of his signet dagger, the symbol and seal of the First Lord, to his side. He passed the dagger to Ehren, and said, "Good luck, Sir Ehren."

"And you, sire," Ehren said.

Gaius smiled at him. Then he put his hand on the hilt of his sword and closed his eyes.

Gaius's skin changed. At first, it became very pale. Then it began to gleam in the moonlight. Then it gained a silvery sheen, and within seconds it actually shone like freshly polished steel. Gaius drew his sword, and his fingers clinked against it, steel upon steel.

Ehren simply stared. He had never even *heard* of such a feat of crafting before, much less seen it.

Gaius took one look at Ehren's face and smiled again. The motion made his shining steel visage moan like metal under stress, though his teeth looked normal, and his tongue seemed almost unnaturally bright pink. "It doesn't matter," he told Ehren. His voice was rough, oddly monotone. "I hadn't planned on lasting much longer in any case." The smile faded. "Now go."

Ehren bowed to the First Lord. Then he turned, clutching the letters, and ran.

Ehren and Sireos exited the tunnel an hour later and began making their way to the causeway so that they could attempt to catch up with the fleeing civilian refugees. Most of another hour of running with the effortless ease of fury-assisted travel brought them into the hills north of Alera Imperia, the beginning of the Redhill Heights, and they paused there to look back.

The capital was burning.

Vord swarmed all over it, like some kind of gleaming mold. Aquitaine's Legions had apparently made good their escape—though he had only three of them remaining, not the five he'd begun the operation with. They had managed to cross the Gaul, then bring it back into its normal course, and were withdrawing to the north.

White and violet fire like nothing Ehren had ever seen suddenly flashed from the top of the First Lord's tower. Vordknights swarmed through the air toward it. Knights Aeris, presumably the enemy's, rushed toward it upon gales that sounded hollow in the distance. A star of scarlet-and-azure light suddenly blazed upon the tower top—the First Lord's sword, kindled to life.

Ehren held up his hands and brought the air between them into focus. His gifts at windcrafting were, at best, modest. He would not be able to see nearly so well through his visioncrafting as he had through Gaius's. But it would have to do.

He couldn't see much more than a gleam of silver and the blazing sword upon the top of the Citadel, but he knew that it had to be Gaius. Vordknights buzzed around the tower like moths around a lantern, so thickly that they sometimes obscured the light almost completely.

Lightning crackled down from the sky to strike the tower, but immediately flashed back upward again, bouncing off like light against a mirror. Vord began to scale the tower, hundreds of them, clawing their way directly up its sides.

Then the figure atop the tower raised both arms above his head, and the earth itself bucked and shook like a stallion at the bite of a horsefly. Ehren was thrown from his feet to the ground, and he lost his visioncrafting—but he could not look away.

The ground rippled like the surface of the sea, shattering buildings like so many toothpicks. The earth split open, great, yawning cracks spreading out for a mile in every direction from the citadel—and then those cracks began to glow with inner, scarlet light. The tremors stopped, and for an instant everything was perfectly silent, motionless.

And then fire like nothing Ehren had ever seen, rock so hot that it had begun to flow like liquid, erupted upward from the ground in a column that was literally miles across. The magma clawed for the sky like a fountain in a city square, and hundreds, then thousands, then tens of thousands of winged forms erupted from the fiery spray, eagles which spread their great wings and streaked through the air, leaving blazing columns of fire in their wakes. The wind rose violently, the superheated air reacting to the eruption, and the fire-eagles swept and spun in great circles, crying out in shrieks made tiny by distance.

Fire filled the skies over Alera Imperia. Cyclones of flame spun away from the city, deadly funnels that seemed to lift everything they touched from the ground, only to incinerate them to ashes.

The ground beneath the city and for miles around began to buckle. Falling walls and buildings added their own gravelly screams to the night's cacophony. The Vord died by the thousands, the hundreds of thousands, devoured by insatiable flame and ravenous earth.

With a final scream, Alera Imperia collapsed into the earth, lowered like a corpse into its grave and consumed by the fires that raged there.

So died Gaius Sextus, First Lord of Alera, his pyre lighting the Realm for fifty miles in every direction.

Ehren sat numbly, staring at the end of the Realm. The three Legions who had escaped with Aquitaine had nearly reached them. Their outriders came pounding up the causeway on horseback, and one of the weary-looking men drew to a halt as he reached them.

"Gentlemen," the outrider said, "I'm afraid I'm going to have to ask you to get moving or else clear the road. The Legions are coming through."

"Why?" Ehren asked quietly. "Why run now? Nothing could have lived through that."

"Aye," the outrider said in a subdued voice. "But there were some of those things that weren't close enough to get burned up. They're coming."

Ehren felt sick to his stomach again. "So what Gaius did . . . it was for nothing?"

"Crows no, young man," the outrider said. "What's left ain't half a tithe of their numbers—but we've only three exhausted Legions left to us and no strong defensive position. It's more than enough for them to do for us." He nodded to them, then kicked his horse up into a canter, riding on down the road.

"Sir Ehren?" asked Sireos wearily. "What do we do?"

Ehren sighed and bowed his head. Then he pushed himself to his feet. "We retreat. Come on."

▭▭▭▭▸Chapter 41

Placidus Aria looked down from the Redhill Heights at the embattled Legions below.

Smoke blackened the skies, so thickly that not even the omnipresent crows were at hand. Where the smoke would part for seconds at a time, the sky to the south burned a sullen scarlet. What disaster could have done that to the skies? Only the release of one of the Great Furies, surely. But the only place south of here where one of the Great old Furies might rise was . . .

"Merciful furies," she breathed.

Far below, a mass of humanity fled through a nightmare.

The vast majority were freemen, men and women and older children trundling along the road at the steady lope of those propelled by furycraft—dodging the occasional cart or mounted rider. Many of them, though, either did not have the ability to utilize the causeway or else were too young or too old to keep the pace of the panicked flood of refugees. They made their way as best they could at the side of the road, mostly through fields barren for winter. Recent rains had made the ground into little more than mud pits stretching for miles. The unfortunate refugees struggled through them at a snail's pace.

Behind them, spread out in a broad bar of muscle and steel came three Legions, marching side by side, straddling the road in tight formation. Their march was slow but steady, their engineers moving ahead of them, earthcrafting the mud into more tractable footing as they approached and restoring it to mud as they passed.

Behind the Legions came the Vord.

The front edge of the enemy pursuit was a ragged line, the swift-moving Vord as slowed and separated by the horrible footing as the fleeing Alerans. But the farther back from that front edge one looked, the more coherent and organized the Vord became. The lizard-wolf creatures ran together in ranks, centered around the enormous hulking mass of the Vord warriors, or around the still-larger giants that covered the ground in strides yards long. Overhead swarmed the black-winged form of hundreds of vordknights, clashing and skirmishing with Knights Aeris covering the retreating Legions.

The three bars of Legion steel were badly outnumbered by their pursuers, but the black-and-scarlet banners flying from the center Legion flew bravely in the breeze, and the discipline of the troops held them in good order as the foe closed in on them.

"Bloody crows," Antillus Raucus breathed. "Crows and bloody furies."

"Do we attack?" Lady Placida breathed.

Gaius Isana, First Lady of Alera, nudged her horse to stand between Aria's and Raucus's. "Of course we do," she said in a firm voice, ignoring the twinge of discomfort from the still-tender wound in her stomach. "I didn't go through all of this and march these Legions all the way down from the Wall to stand around and watch things happen."

High Lord Antillus's mouth spread into a wolfish smile. "Looks like the boys are going to earn their pay today, then."

"Look at the banners in the center Legion," Lady Placida said. "Do you know who that is?"

"An Aleran," Isana said, her tone steady. She felt Araris's steady presence at her back, and looked over her shoulder to find him, on his horse, hovering a few feet away from her, his eyes focused on nothing and everything at the same time. "An Aleran in trouble." She turned to Raucus, and said, "Attack, Captain."

Raucus nodded sharply. His horse danced a step sideways, evidently picking up on his rider's excitement. "I recommend we wait, Your Highness," he said. "Let them advance another mile down that causeway, and I'll leave those ugly things in pieces."

Isana felt the confidence flowing from him, and arched an eyebrow. "You're sure?"

"They're coming with maybe thirty thousand troops. I've got three standing Legions, three Legions of veteran militia, better than a thousand Knights and every bloody Citizen in Antillus. *Pieces*, Your Highness," Raucus replied, vicious satisfaction in his voice. "Little ones."

"As you think best, High Lord Antillus," Isana said.

He threw back his head and laughed. "Hah! That's a good one." He turned his horse and said, "There are preparations to make. If you will excuse me." He saluted Isana and turned his horse—then hesitated, glancing back at Isana.

"Your Grace?" Isana asked.

"It's a battle. Things can happen." He reached into his coat and withdrew an envelope. It was brown with water stains and brittle with age. He held it out to her and said, "In case I'm not able to give it to you later." He nodded to them. "Ladies."

Isana took the envelope and watched as Raucus rode back to his senior centurion and the captains of his Legions.

"What is that?" Aria asked.

Isana shook her head. "I think it's . . ." She opened the letter hurriedly—and instantly recognized Septimus's liquid, precise handwriting.

Raucus,

My insides are whole again, and I'm getting ready to leave the back end of nowhere. I expect that the holders here in Calderon will be just as happy to see the Crown Legion go. Too many handsome young men for all these pretty young hold-girls to resist—which reminds me that I've been meaning to tell you that I've got a surprise for Father. He's going to choke on it, but Mother will make him see reason. More later, old friend, but I'll need you to find some time to cover my flank during an important engagement.

Murestus and Cestaag just got back from Rhodes. I had them following the money trail of those cutters I told you about. They didn't find anything that could go to a court, but I think I might like to visit Rhodes and Kalare with a few good friends once I wrap up my current obligations. Interested? I wrote Attis already, and he's in.

Invidia got my letter. She was furious that I told Father no, though you had to read between the lines to see it. You know how she is—polite and cold as a fish, even when she's about to beat someone senseless. Father will be in a rage about me turning her down, though what else is new? To tell you the truth, though, I was never really sure about her. Oh, gorgeous, intelligent, strong, elegant, everything Father thinks I would need. But Invidia just doesn't give a crow's feather about people in any sense other than how they can profit her. It means she fits right in with everyone at the capital, but at the same time, I'm not sure she's entirely sane.

Give me passion—and compassion—any day.

I'm glad I can write you. There are fewer and fewer people I can speak

my heart to, these days. Without you and Attis, I think I'd have lost my bloody
mind after Seven Hills.

Here's truth, old man.

The next few months are going to bore future students of history at the
Academy for decades.

The three of us will get together again with the old gang from the fencing
hall—minus Aldrick. Then we'll sort some things out.

Are you in, snowcrow?

Sep

PS—How's the little snowcrow? He set anything on fire yet? When do I get to
meet him? And his mother?

Isana stared at the letter and blinked away tears.

Septimus. She could *hear* his voice as she read the words.

She sniffed before anything could dribble down her nose and looked at the
date on the letter. A second letter was visible in the envelope. She opened it and
read it is as well.

The handwriting was not Septimus's. It was angular, sharply leaning to the
right, and in places the paper had been torn, as if the quill had been pressed too
viciously to the surface of the fine paper upon which it was written.

Raucus,

By the time I got wind of anything and made it to Calderon, it was hours
too late. But I was there when they found him. I know that by now the official
story has reached you, but it's nothing but smoke.

Septimus died with five of the finest blades in the Realm in a circle
around him. And it wasn't the Marat alone who did for him. Firecrafting and
earthcrafting were both involved. I saw it with my own eyes.

Septimus was the only heir, and his father was arrogant or incompetent
enough to allow him to be murdered, despite Septimus's appeals for his aid,
for pressure upon the Senate, for direct action against the ambitious bastards
who eventually killed him. The First Lord did nothing, and our Realm is
doomed to division and self-destruction as a result. He doesn't deserve my loy-
alty, Raucus. Or yours.

I know you won't believe me, you slow-witted northern snowcrow. And
even if you did, you'd never come with me down the road I've chosen.

If the House of Gaius can't defend and protect its own child—and a soul like Septimus's at that—then how can it do so for the people of the Realm?

I don't ask you to help, old friend.

Just stay out of my way.

Good-bye.

Attis

"My Lady Isana?" Araris asked quietly.

Isana blinked and looked up from the letter.

Behind them, the Antillan Legions prepared for battle, men rushing about with the calm hurry of practiced professionals. On the fields below, the Vord had engaged the surviving Legions. Isana watched as the First Aquitaine, banners surrounding High Lord Aquitainus Attis himself, literally threw itself into the teeth of the pursuing Vord and stopped them cold, not a hundred yards from the slowest of the fleeing refugees.

"Attis Aquitaine was never his enemy," Isana breathed, her voice numb. "Rhodes. Kalare."

"Isana?" Aria asked.

Isana wordlessly passed her the letters. "A week. It's dated a week before we wed. He was almost the same age Tavi is now."

Aria read the letters. Isana waited until she looked up again.

"Rhodes and Kalare," Aria said. "Gaius killed Kalarus personally. And he as much as sent Rhodes out to be butchered by the first Vord attack."

"Revenge," Isana said quietly. "It took him more than two decades, but the old man had it all the same." She shook her head. "And Invidia Aquitaine had sought marriage to Septimus. I never knew that. He never said anything." Isana smiled faintly, bitterly. "And he spurned her. For a steadholt girl from the back end of nowhere."

"She was a part of it," Aria whispered. "The cabal that killed him. That's what Septimus's letter means. If one reads between the lines."

"Citizens and lords," Isana sighed. "Wounded pride. Ambition. Vengeance. Their motivations seem so . . . average."

Aria smiled faintly and nodded toward Raucus, who was the center of the swirl of activity. "I think you've been given ample opportunity to observe that Citizens and lords can be idiots as easily as anyone else. Perhaps more so."

Isana gestured at the letters. "Read the letter. It's in every flourish and scratch. Attis hated Gaius. Hated the corruption, the ambition of his peers."

"And became what he hated," Aria said quietly. "It's happened to many men before him, I suppose."

Fire blossomed in the midst of the First Aquitaine, the light of a burning sword that was clearly visible, even from that distance, in broad daylight. The Legion roared in response, the sound distant, like the surge of waves crashing on a shoreline. The Legion drove into the mass of the Vord, killing and crushing, lances of fire lashing into the largest of the Vord, spheres of white-hot flame enveloping the heads of the behemoths and sending them crashing down to crush their fellows.

Cavalry alae, launched from the Legions flanking the First Aquitaine, pressed into the gap, harassing and crushing the disordered Vord—while the Legion reformed and retreated, screened by the shock of the cavalry's charge. The Legion withdrew perhaps three hundred yards from its original stand against the Vord and reset its lines as the cavalry retreated, in turn, behind them.

Again the Legion clashed with the Vord, who were coming thicker and in greater coordination. The First Aquitaine was joined by its brother Legions on either side—Second Placidan, Isana thought, and the Crown Legion, judging by the banners. Again, the Vord were driven back. Again, the cavalry charged and covered the infantry's withdrawal. Another three hundred yards were gained— but more and more armored forms were being left still and silent on the ground, to be overrun by the inhuman foes.

Isana watched as the Legion repeated its maneuver against the enemy, but each time the Vord came more thickly, and each time the Legions gained less ground before they were forced to turn and face them again.

"Why hasn't Antillus attacked yet?" she asked. She looked over her shoulder to Araris, who waited patiently at her back. "If they don't move soon, the Legions down there will be destroyed."

Araris shook his head. "No. Aquitaine's got them right where he wants them." He pointed at the thickening lines of the Vord. "He's tempting them into concentrating, readying for a final push."

"Bloody right he is," Antillus Raucus said, riding his horse closer, and surveying the battlefield below. "His fliers have spotted us up here. He's gathering all those great bloody bugs into one place so that I can—" He smashed one fist into the open palm of his other hand, the sound shockingly loud in the comparative quiet of the hilltop. "Not bad work," he added, in a tone of grudging admiration, "for someone who isn't much more than an amateur."

"How long?" Araris asked him.

Raucus pursed his lips. "Five minutes. Next retreat, they'll push up, and we'll have them." He signaled one of the Legion staff waiting nearby and called, "Five minutes!"

The call went up and down the lines of troops and officers, spreading with rapid and precise discipline. Antillus nodded to himself, a sense of confidence and satisfaction radiating from him, now that he was close enough for Isana to sense his emotions. He cleared his throat, and said, "Your Highness?"

"Yes?"

"May I have a moment to speak to you alone?"

Isana arched an eyebrow, but inclined her head to him. "Lady Placida. Araris. Would you give us a moment, please?"

Aria and Araris both murmured assent and walked their horses several yards away. It wasn't solitude, precisely, but it was as close to a private conversation as they were likely to come by, in the midst of an army preparing to move.

"You never asked me," Raucus said bluntly. "You never asked me why I had given the order to bring my Legions south. Why I had decided to trust my people's safety to your word. You just got out of bed and demanded a horse so you could come along."

"Politely," Isana said. "I demanded politely. I distinctly remember using the word 'please.'"

Raucus showed his teeth when he laughed. "Crows and bloody furies. It looks like Septimus knew what he was talking about after all."

Isana returned his smile. "I assumed you would tell me when you were ready."

"You never asked why I was . . . so set against you, either, when you came to the Wall."

"I assumed the same."

He gestured at the letters she once again held in her hand. "You read them?"

"Of course."

"You could have been with them," he said, simply. "You could have been one of the treacherous slives who killed him. Get a child on him, kill him, and put the child on the throne once he was grown. "

Isana drew in a slow breath. "Do you think that now?"

Raucus shook his head. "I followed you here because of what you showed me on that field at the foot of the Wall."

"What was that?"

The High Lord stared at her for a moment, and then out at the desperate battle unfolding below them. "Any man with a brain in his head looks for three things in anyone he'll follow: will, brains, and a heart." His eyes grew distant. "Gaius has the first two. He's one fearsome old cat." He gestured at himself. "I've the first and last. But those things aren't enough. Gaius never felt much for his people. He had their fear and respect. Never their love. I took care of my men as best I could. But I let my fear for them blind me to what else was happening."

"I still don't understand," Isana said gently.

"Septimus had all three, lady," Raucus replied. "You showed me your will when you stayed my attack on the Icemen, and when you challenged me and wouldn't back down. Even when you bloody well knew you should have.

"You showed me your heart when you fought me as you did—to the death, without flinching. When you lay bleeding with—" He shook his head, as though flinching from the image, but forced himself to continue. "With my sword in your guts. But your concern was for me. I felt it in you. It was no act, lady. You were willing to die to open my fool eyes. There was no scheme in that, no puppet strings. You meant what you said."

"Yes," Isana said simply.

"That's two," Raucus said. "But when I realized that you staged the whole thing to happen where the Icemen could see—and bloody *sense* everything that was going on, you showed me you had the brains as well. Sunset came alone into my personal chambers, after we'd seen to your wounds, and gave me his hand and his word that his folk would abide by the truce until we returned from battling the Vord." Raucus shook his head, and a small note of what might have been wonder entered his voice. "And he meant it. It won't resolve everything overnight. Maybe even not in my lifetime, but . . ."

"But it's a start," Isana said.

"It's a start, Your Highness," Raucus said. "Septimus, my friend, chose you. And chose well." He bowed his head to her, and said, simply, "I am yours to command."

"Your Grace," Isana said.

"Highness?"

"These creatures have destroyed our lands. Murdered our people." Isana lifted her chin. "Pay them for it."

When Antillus Raucus looked up, his eyes were hard, cold, and clear. "Watch me."

CHAPTER 42

Once Lady Aquitaine and the Vord queen were gone with their retinues, the courtyard was strangely silent. Only a handful of Vord remained, along with a similarly reduced contingent of collared guards—and the prisoners, of course.

Of which, Amara was very much aware, she herself was currently the most endangered.

She shivered in the cold, her muscles aching from the effort, hardly able to do more than curl her body up as tightly as possible to keep from succumbing to the chills.

"You and your husband crippled my father," Kalarus Brencis Minoris said in a quiet, deliberate tone. He walked toward her, the silver band of a discipline collar in his hand. "Not that there was a great deal of love lost between Father and me, but my life grew harder after the old slive was trapped in his bed. Do you have any idea how much damage you had to do to his spine to leave him broken like that?"

"H-h-he should have held still," Amara said. "I'd have been glad to kill him."

Brencis smiled. "My father always appreciated defiance from his women. I never really had the same tastes—but I'm beginning to see the appeal." He crouched over Amara, the collar swaying in front of her eyes. "Rook was my first, you know. I think I was about thirteen. She was a couple of years older." He shook his head. "I thought she liked me. But I realized later that she must have been acting under orders." He bared his teeth, a hideous expression, completely disconnected from anything resembling a smile. "Just as she must have been doing tonight."

Amara stared at him for a long, silent moment. Then she said, "It's not really your fault you were raised by a monster, Brencis. M-maybe you never really had a chance. And I can't bl-blame you for wanting to survive." She smiled back at him. "So I'm going to give you one last chance to do the right thing before I k-kill you."

Brencis stared at her for a second, uncertainty flickering in his eyes. Then he let out a short bark of a laugh. "Kill me? Countess," he told her, "in a little while, I'm going to my bed. And you're going to be happy to go with me." He glanced idly around the courtyard. "Perhaps I'll bring one of my girls, so that she can bathe you. We'll see if we can broaden your horizons."

"Use your head, fool," Amara said. "Do you think for one moment that you're going to survive the Vord?"

"Life is short, Countess," he replied, bitterly. "I have to take what I can from it. And right now, I'm taking you."

She hadn't noticed that he'd smeared his bloodied thumb to the collar, but it went around her neck like a band of ice.

And ecstasy turned her world into a single, endless white blur.

She felt her body arch against her bonds, and was helpless to stop it. The pleasure wasn't merely sexual—although it *was* that, too intensely so to believe. But atop that rapture were layers and layers of other sensations. The simple satisfaction of a hot drink on a cold morning. The heart-pounding excitement she felt when seeing Bernard for the first time in days or weeks. The joy of soaring up through dark, heavy clouds into the clear blue sky. The fierce pleasure of victory over intense competition in the Wind Trials, when she had been at the Academy. The bubbling laughter that followed after the third or fourth excellent joke she'd heard in an evening—and a thousand more, every single happiness, every single joy, every wonderful thing that had ever happened to her, every individual gratification of the body, mind, and heart, all blended into a single, sublime whole.

Brencis, the courtyard, the Vord, the Realm, even her husband—none of it mattered.

Nothing mattered but feeling *this*.

She knew she'd be weeping if she'd had thought enough for such inanities.

Someone was whispering to her. She didn't know who. She didn't care. The whispers didn't matter. All that mattered was drowning in the pleasure.

She came back to herself, slowly, inside a warmly lit room. It looked like an inn room, a fairly lavish one. There were soft hangings on the walls, and an enormous bed. It was warm—blessedly warm, after the hideous cold of the courtyard. Her fingers and toes were tingling, so intensely that it would have hurt, if anything she felt could have been interpreted as anything but pure pleasure.

She was standing in a tub, and one of the barely clothed girls was taking off her travel-stained blouse. Amara stood in blissful disinterest. The girl began bathing her face and neck and shoulders, and Amara reveled in the warmth, the feeling of the soft washcloth against her skin, the scent of soap in the air.

She became aware of Brencis walking in a slow circle around the tub, unbuttoning his shirt as he went.

Despite his faults, she thought, he really was quite beautiful. She watched him, though the effort of moving her head simply became too much to sustain. She let her eyes follow him, tracking his movements through her lashes when the simple pleasure of feeling herself being cleaned of weeks of grime became almost too delicious to endure.

"Lovely, Countess," Brencis said. "You are lovely."

She shivered in response to his voice, and her eyes closed completely.

"Don't forget her hair," Brencis said.

"Yes, my lord," murmured the girl. Warm water cascaded over her head, and a gentler, softer-scented soap was applied to her hair. Amara just reveled in it.

"It's too bad, really," Brencis said. "I had hoped that you would put up more of a fight than this. But you were brittle, Countess. The ones who go this far under, this swiftly—they don't come back. Do they, little Lyssa?"

Amara felt the girl standing close beside her shiver. "No, my lord. I don't want to come back."

Brencis stopped in front of her, smiling slightly. "I'll bet she has pretty legs. Very long, very slender, very strong."

"Yes, my lord," Lyssa agreed.

Amara found herself sleepily returning Brencis's smile.

"Take the trousers, off, Amara," he said, his voice holding a quiet, snarling promise in it.

"Yes, my lord," Amara said drowsily. The soaking-wet leather was stubborn against her pleasure-numbed fingers. "I . . . it's too tight, my lord."

"Then be still," Brencis said, his voice amused. "Very still."

A dagger, its tip glittering with fascinating, wicked sharpness, appeared in his hand, and he knelt by her side. "Tell me, Countess," he murmured. "Were you here on Gaius's orders?"

"Yes, my lord," Amara murmured. She watched as the knife's tip, doubtless enhanced by Brencis's furycraft, sliced effortlessly through the hem of the leather flying trousers over her ankle. He began cutting slowly upward, his knife opening the garment as readily as a boy might peel a fruit.

"And your husband," Brencis said. "He isn't dead, is he?"

"No, my lord," Amara said sleepily. The knife slid over her calf. She wondered if she would feel it if such a sharp blade opened her flesh. She wondered if, in her current state, it would feel good.

"Where is he?" Brencis continued.

"Nearby, my lord," Amara replied, as the knife moved past her knee. "I'm not sure where, exactly."

"Very good," Brencis said, in approval, and placed a kiss on the naked flesh at the back of her knee.

Amara shuddered in anticipation.

"What are his intentions?" Brencis asked, returning to cutting his way up Amara's leg.

"He's waiting for my signal," Amara said.

Brencis smiled grimly as the knife opened the leather encasing Amara's thigh, slicing slowly up toward her hip. "To do what?"

"Free the captives, my lord."

Brencis laughed. "Ambitious of you. And what is to be the signal for him to begin? There doesn't seem to be much left of you, but when we take him, I can at least make sure that you are the one to whisper in his ears when he is captured and recruit—"

Metal scraped on metal, and Brencis paused, frowning in puzzlement.

Amara looked down, to see that his knife had parted the leather over the top of her thigh—where the discipline collar her husband had bound to her, hours before, nestled tight against pale flesh.

Brencis's eyes widened in stunned realization.

Amara called upon Cirrus, her hands lashing out. She caught Brencis by the wrist of the hand that held the knife, twisting toward his thumb, the motion taking him by surprise, so swiftly that he had no time to resist with his normal strength, much less with fury-enhanced power. The knife came free of his grasp, and Amara seized it with what seemed like lazy precision to her own accelerated senses before it could even begin to fall.

Brencis had seized upon his own wind furies by then, his hands beginning to rise to defend himself—but he had not been quick enough. Amara slapped his hand aside with one hand—

—and with a flick of her wrist, passed the fury-sharpened dagger through both of the arteries in his throat.

Blood flowed out in a torrent, a cloud. It splashed over Amara's naked leg and torso, hot and hideous, as she stumbled, thrown off-balance by the speed of her own movements, and fell back out of the tub and out of the reach of Brencis's hands.

The young Aleran lord arched his back, his hands thrashing out wildly. One of his clenched fists struck the wooden frame of the tub and shattered it, sending soapy water, the bubbles stained with spraying blood, rushing out over the floor. He twisted, flailing toward Amara, and one of his thrashing shoulders struck a dazed Lyssa in the stomach, flinging her back like a doll.

"The signal?" Amara hissed, her body singing, alight with rage and with the silver-white pleasure flowing from the metal collar bound about her thigh. "The signal is your *corpse*, traitor. You will never *touch* my husband."

He tried to say something, perhaps, but no sound emerged—the dagger had parted his windpipe as well.

It was nearly impossible to strike down a furycrafter of Brencis's power without employing comparable furycraft to accomplish it.

But only *nearly*.

The last scion of Kalarus crumpled to the floor of the inn, shrinking like a bladder being slowly emptied of water. His blood joined the perfumed water on the floor.

There had barely been a sound to betray the murder.

Amara stumbled back against the wall of the room, fighting the euphoria still being forced upon her by the collars. She wanted, very badly, to just sink to the floor and let the pleasure have its way with her once more—

—but the collar on her leg ceased sending its pulses of ecstasy through her at the very thought. She had, at her own insistence, been instructed otherwise. If she ignored those instructions, it would shortly begin inflicting hideous pain instead of bestowing rapture, and Amara felt little bubbles of entirely involuntary panic rippling through her at the very thought.

She forced herself to stagger to the room's wardrobe, conscious of Lyssa's wide eyes upon her as she moved. The collared girl had her mouth open in horror, and tears had flowed down her face, cutting streaks through the flecks of blood spattering her features. Amara opened it, and seized one of Brencis's tunics, quickly donning it, then tossed one of his capes over her shoulders. They fit her like sacks, but they would do. She took Brencis's sword from the belt at his hips a few seconds later, moving quickly, half-terrified that his stillness might be a ruse—but the dead man never stirred. Like the clothing, the sword was too large to fit her comfortably—but like the clothing, it would do.

"I'm sorry," Lyssa sobbed. "I'm sorry. I'm sorry."

Amara turned to look at the girl, and caught her own reflection in a mirror hung upon the wall. She wore a dark green tunic and cloak, and the color contrasted sharply with the almost-solid scarlet staining her face, her hair, her hands, and the bare skin of her leg. She bore a bloodied knife in one hand, a bright sword in the other, and her eyes were wild and dangerous. For an instant, Amara frightened herself.

"Stay here," she told the girl, her voice hard and clear, "until you are instructed otherwise."

"Ye-yes, my lady," Lyssa said, pressing herself abjectly to the floor. "Yes, yes, I will."

She turned to the window, unlocked and opened it. The window overlooked the Slave Market courtyard, which looked much as it had when she had last seen it—full of prisoners, though with rather fewer guards than there had been. Only a few Vord were in sight—but the green glow of the *croach* was brighter, from other parts of Ceres, than it had been the night before.

She couldn't be sure of any of the collared Alerans. Some of them could have been collaborators like the two with Rook when they'd bumped into one another. Some of them could have been more deeply conditioned by the modified collars than others. Some might be able to fight against the collars' control and help them—but Amara had no way to know one from another.

So she had to regard each of them as the enemy.

Amara stood in the window for a moment, fully aware that she could be seen in the candlelight of the room. Dimly outlined, feminine shapes appearing in that window would doubtless be a familiar sight to those below—and she had no way of knowing where Bernard was, to be able to give him a more specific signal. She would simply have to trust that he had been keeping track of where she had been taken and would be in position to watch the building to see her standing there like a practice target. She counted slowly to thirty, then closed the curtains again.

She went out of the room on silent feet, wrapping herself in a windcrafted veil that should keep her unseen to anyone beyond the reach of her sword—a potent advantage if she decided to attack, but not an overwhelming one. A skilled enough metalcrafter would not need his eyes to know where her sword was, and the Vord didn't seem to have kept anyone alive who was not at least wielding the skill of a Legion Knight at his given talents.

There were several collared Alerans in the main room of the inn, apparently off duty. Three were watching one of Brencis's whisper-girls dance to music no one but she could hear. Another trio played listlessly at cards, and a silent pair were deep in their cups, drinking with grim, methodical determination. Amara went through the room with every ounce of stealth she could muster, wary of her own balance under the befuddling aftereffects of both collars' euphoric bonding process. She managed to pass by them without attracting attention, and glided into the Slave Market.

She headed straight for the stone box-cages that held the captured windcrafters.

The cages didn't have locks, thank goodness, and were held closed by simple bolts. In her current condition, she wasn't sure how quickly she would have been able to open a more complex mechanism, even though she still had her tools in a pocket on the trouser leg that had survived. Snoring came from some of the cages.

Brencis had to have been slipping them the drugs in their water. She would just have to hope that some of the Alerans inside had been aware and determined enough to refuse it, hoping for their chance at escape.

Amara and Bernard were about to give it to them.

Or at least, she desperately *hoped* Bernard was.

"Can you hear me?" Amara hissed into one of the slots just under the top lip of the first cage.

It took a moment for someone to answer, "Who is there?"

"I'm a Cursor," Amara whispered. "And keep your crowbegotten voice down."

Confused murmurs came from the cage, sleepy voices speaking in blurred words. They were immediately shushed by other voices, which probably made more noise than all of the confused murmurs together.

"Quiet," Amara hissed, looking around, certain that someone was going to notice the muted commotion any second. "We're going to get you out of here, but we're going to get as many people out as we possibly can. Stay alert. Everyone who can fly in a straight line needs to be ready."

"Open the cage!" someone rasped.

"Be *ready*," Amara responded. "I'll be back." Then she slipped over to the next cage, and repeated the conversation. And the next. And the next.

The Vord discovered her as she reached the fifth.

She had just shushed the final stone cage filled with captives when one of the lizard-form Vord twenty yards away raised its head, whuffling in through its nose, and let out a shriek that vibrated from the stones of the courtyard.

It must have smelled the blood still on me, she thought. Most animals would react strongly to the scent of bleeding prey. She should have taken a moment to clean herself better—but it was too late for that.

Speed was everything now.

Amara dropped the veil to call upon Cirrus for speed, and slammed open the bolts to the cage before hurling herself back down the line to the next cage and repeating the process.

"Alerans!" she cried, the words oddly elongated to her altered perceptions. "Alerans, to arms!"

She slammed open the bolts to the last cage as a chorus of Vord shrieks arose around them. The captive windcrafters began shoving their way out of the cages in their wake, screaming cries of their own.

"Alera!"

"Fight, you miserable bastards!"

Only Amara's heightened senses allowed her to see the flicker in the air above her, where the Citizens were caged under multiple layers of counters to their furycraft. There was a small explosion of sparks, where steel had met steel—and another burst of sparks, where a second arrow had struck another of the hinges on the hanging cage with impossible force and precision, and a dozen Citizens were abruptly dropped fifteen feet to the wet stones of the courtyard floor.

Sparks exploded from the second cage of hanging Citizens, and more cries went up.

"To me!" Amara cried, leaping up onto the nearest cage. "Alerans, to me!"

"Cursor, look out!" screamed someone in the darkness.

Amara whirled, sword in hand, to find the Vord that had first raised the alarm bounding toward her. She waited until it was in the air to lean far to one side, striking with Brencis's sword, and felt the blade crunch through the Vord's chitinous armor. She had misjudged her balance, though, crows take those bloody collars, and she fell to the stones with the Vord, bleeding vile, dark fluid, scrambling to find her.

There was a crack like a miniature thunderbolt and the creature dropped as still and dead as if crushed by an enormous hammer. One of Bernard's arrows protruded from the base of its skull, sunk all the way to the green-and-brown fletching.

Amara looked up to see her husband leap from a low rooftop to the back of a wagon, bow in hand, and from there to the courtyard beside her. He strode to the nearest wooden cage, presumably filled with metalcrafters, and ran his hand along the top. It immediately groaned and warped and fell to pieces, freeing the prisoners inside.

"Are you all right?" Bernard asked, extending his hand to her, his eyes wide with fear. "Are you hurt?"

She took it, and he hauled her to her feet. "I'll . . . yes, all things considered. I mean, I'm fine. The blood isn't mine. It's Brencis's."

"Oh," Bernard breathed, his face sagging in nearly comic relief. "Good."

Pleasure washed through her from the collar bound about her thigh at his approval. "Oh," she breathed. "Love, please. Be careful of your words."

Bernard blinked at her, then seemed to understand. His face clouded and he stepped in close to her, setting his bow aside. He growled in his throat, seized the steel collar about her throat and snapped it clear of her neck with his bare hands. "I never found the key to the first one," he told her, kneeling. The collar about her thigh was rather a tighter fit, and his fingers felt warm and rough, sliding beneath it. "Hold still. It could cut you."

She saw him pause for a heartbeat, and she had a wild thought that he was being tempted. He didn't have to take the collar off her, did he? No one could except for him, after all. What if he simply left it on her? The collar pulsed with pure bliss again at the very thought, and Amara swayed on her feet, struggling to remember why that would be a bad thing—

And then there was another sound of snapping metal, and her thoughts were abruptly clear again.

"Foul thing," Bernard spat, rising with the broken steel circlet in his hand.

"Vord!" screamed one of the prisoners still trapped inside a wooden cage.

One of the lizard-forms had swarmed over a nearby wall and leapt down onto one of the water-drenched cages holding the miserable firecrafters, raking at them with its talons.

Bernard spun, lifted the steel circlet, and threw it with fury-born strength. The metal struck the Vord in midlimb and ripped through it like paper. The Vord fell, shrieking and spraying filthy-looking blood all over the courtyard around it.

Amara tossed her sword to one of the freed metalcrafters as more Vord swarmed over the walls. She pointed at the other cages, and snapped, "Free them!"

"Yes, my lady!" shouted the man. He spun to the nearest suspended cage of earthcrafters and slashed it open with the fine steel blade, the bars parting in a shower of sparks, before he moved on to the one beside it.

Bernard had taken up his bow again, and Amara watched as he calmly shot a pair of oncoming Vord from the walls. "We can't hold them," he said. "Get the windcrafters and get them out of here."

"Don't be ridiculous," Amara retorted. "We're all leaving together."

"There are too many of them. Our people aren't armed. Half of them can barely stand," Bernard said. A vordknight buzzed down from above, and he shot it through the center of its chest. It fell to the ground like a wounded pheasant, and one of the freed earthcrafters smashed it with a heavy iron bar ripped from the walls of the cage that had recently held him.

But more Vord were coming. Many more. They swarmed over the walls from every direction, and the thrum of vordknight wings quivered in the air all around them, before materializing into half a dozen of the winged horrors, diving upon some of the still-dazed, defenseless prisoners.

A sphere of white-hot fire erupted abruptly in the air—not among the Vord, but immediately above and behind them. For an instant, Amara thought that the firecrafter's aim and timing had been badly off, but the wash of heat blackened and curled the Vord's relatively delicate wings, and the eruption of hot wind from the firecrafting sent them spinning and tumbling completely out of control to crash haphazardly to the ground.

"Bloody crowbegotten bugs!" roared a gravelly voice, and a blocky old man, his silver hair still shot with streaks of fiery red limped into sight, being supported by the slender, bedraggled young woman Brencis had called Flora.

"Gram?" Bernard said, surprise and delight on his face.

The old firecrafter squinted about until he spotted Bernard. "Bernard! What the crows are you doing in the south?"

Bernard shot one of the crashed vordknights who had survived the fall and risen to its feet in the courtyard. "Rescuing you, apparently."

"Bah," Gram growled, and Amara finally placed the old man as the previous Count of Calderon. He raised his hand and waved it in a circle, and a sheet of fire arose atop the walls surrounding the courtyard, a red-hot curtain that came from nowhere and drew howls of pain and protest from dozens of as-yet-unseen Vord. "Move to the Vale, Gaius says. Retire in wealth and comfort, he says. My ass, the crowbegotten old confidence man." He squinted at Bernard. "Figure us a way out of this mess, boy. I can't hold this for more than half an hour or so."

"Half an *hour*?" Bernard asked, grinning.

"The wooden cages," Amara said. "We can use them as wind coaches, long enough to get clear of the city at least."

Bernard turned to her and kissed her hard on the mouth. Then he drew his sword and tossed it to another freed metalcrafter. He pointed at that man and the one who had taken Amara's sword. "You, you. You're on guard. Kill anything that gets through." He jabbed a finger at the freed earthcrafters. "Arm yourselves with something and help." He spun to the Citizens, gathering loosely around Lord Gram. "Anyone with any watercrafting, do what you can to help the others shake off the aphrodin, starting with Citizens and windcrafters."

One of the Citizens, a man who would have been pompously impressive if he'd been clean, groomed, and standing in a civilized part of the world, demanded in a dazed voice, "Who do you think you are?"

Bernard took one step forward and rammed his clenched fist into the dissenter's mouth.

The other man dropped bonelessly to the ground.

"I," Bernard said, "am the man who is going to save your lives. You two, toss him into one of the wooden cages. He'll slow us down less when he's unconscious. *Move* it people!"

"Do as he says!" bellowed Lord Gram.

Citizens scrambled to obey.

"Bloody crows," Amara breathed. "Do you know who that was?"

"An idiot," Bernard said, his eyes sparkling. "He can challenge me to the *juris macto* later, if he likes. Shall we get to work?"

"What should I do?"

"The windcrafters and coaches. Get them ready."

Amara nodded. "Bernard, the slaves . . ."

"We'll take whoever disarms himself and wants to go," Bernard said. "If there's room." He leaned down and kissed her swiftly, again, then growled, "When I get you out of here, Countess . . ."

A thrill ran through her that had nothing to do with furycrafted collars. "Not until we've both bathed. Now, don't make me punch you in the mouth, Your Excellency."

He winked at her, then turned, barking orders as the freed Aleran Citizens and Knights prepared to make good their escape.

Half an hour later, dozens of makeshift wind coaches sailed up from the captured city, Vord shrieking useless protest behind him. Perhaps a score of vord-knights attempted to stop the coaches, but were driven away by half a dozen firecrafters, and moments later the coaches were too high and moving too swiftly for any winged pursuit to catch up with them.

Amara vaguely remembered working as hard as she could to help keep one of the coaches aloft, and bringing it in for a brutal but nonlethal landing an endless amount of time later, as the sun began to rise. Then someone put a stale piece of bread into her hand, which she ate ravenously. A moment later, there was a warm fire—a real *fire*, by the great furies, and its heat wrapped her in blessed warmth.

Bernard pressed her head gently down onto a cloak he'd spread on the ground, and said, "Rest, my Countess. We'll have to move again soon. I'll keep watch."

Amara was going to protest that he needed rest, too, she honestly was, but the fire was beautiful and warm and . . .

And for the first time in weeks, Amara felt *safe*.

She slept.

CHAPTER 43

Tavi stood atop the earthworks and stared out across the rolling plain. His armor and helmet had been scoured clean and freshly polished by the First Aleran's valets, and gleamed in the setting sun.

Since they had arrived the night before, thousands more refugees had appeared, and the flow of Canim makers fleeing the Vord was only growing heavier. The crafters of the Legions had made sure that there was freshwater available, but food was in much shorter supply, and shelter was almost nonexistent.

Heavy, purposeful footsteps marched up behind Tavi and stopped.

"What is it, Marcus?" Tavi asked.

"Your Highness," Valiar Marcus replied. He stepped up beside Tavi and stood in a natural-looking parade rest. "Did you sleep?"

"Not nearly enough," Tavi said. "But that's going around." He nodded at the berm that was Molvar's only defense. "You and your people must have worked without stopping."

"It was the Canim, sir," Marcus replied, his voice serious. "The ground around here has got a lot more rock than earth in it. Thousands of them were out here, moving stones. I knew that some of their warriors were strong, but bloody crows." He shook his head. "You should see what some of their makers can do. The ones who lift heavy things for a living, I mean."

"Impressive?"

"Terrifying," Marcus said. "This berm is as much rock as earth. Considering that Your Highness sent all of our engineers on a different mission, our men had to work like mad to keep up with the Canim."

Tavi nodded. "Well, it shouldn't have surprised us. We saw evidence enough of what they could do at Mastings, and even more since we've gotten here."

"Yes, sir."

"Do you have the latest reports?"

"Such as they are," Marcus said. The faintest trace of reproach laced his voice. "We could do a lot better if our Knights Aeris were available, sir."

"They're busy," Tavi said. "How much time do we have?"

"The Canim mounted packs have been encountering the Vord closer and closer to the port, sire. They're steering refugees in this direction."

"What is the count on refugees?"

"Just over sixty thousand, give or take."

Tavi grunted. "Has there been any contact with the main body of Lararl's forces?"

"No," Marcus said quietly. "But on the positive side, no sightings of the Vord main body yet, either."

"I'd almost feel better if we *had* seen them," Tavi said. "They have a way of turning up where they aren't expected."

"Your Highness is becoming paranoid," Marcus said. "I approve."

"Highness!" called another voice, and Magnus came puffing up the terraces to the top of the berm. The old Cursor's hair was in disarray, as if from sleep, and he clutched a sealed letter in his hand. He came and passed it over to Tavi, still huffing. His eyes stayed steadily on Marcus. Marcus stolidly ignored him.

Tavi took the letter, glancing between them. "Something I should know about, gentlemen?"

"Not that I know of, sir," Marcus said. He glanced at the old Maestro. "Magnus?"

Magnus stared at the First Spear for a moment more before he turned to Tavi. "No, Your Highness."

Tavi eyed them both again, then opened the letter and read it. "Hah," he said. "Crassus will be back sometime tonight. Marcus, do you remember those stairs we were talking about crafting into the cliff face when we first got here?"

"Yes, Highness."

"Make it happen, three times, on the farthest outthrust promontories within the fortifications—near where I've had you stockpiling supplies." Tavi frowned, thinking. "We'll need some lamps or furylamps set up on the stairs, too, so that they can be seen from the sea. If we don't have enough of our own, ask the Shuarans. They use a lantern that looks like it's designed to handle mist and spray."

Marcus and Magnus both blinked at Tavi.

"We're going to need a means to load people and supplies onto the trans-ports," Tavi told them. "The wider the stairs, the better. Wake Maximus. He's good with stone."

"Ah, sir?" Marcus asked carefully. "What transports?"

"The ones Crassus is bringing."

The old Cursor frowned. "And the reason these transports cannot avail themselves of the Shuarans' perfectly respectable port is . . . ?"

Tavi found himself grinning at them. "They wouldn't fit."

Both of the men frowned severely at him.

"Meanwhile," Tavi continued, "we should start getting all of our own non-combatants loaded up. Magnus, get that in motion, if you would, and make sure our captains are ready to set sail. After that, I want you to coordinate with the Tribune Logistica and work out the fastest way to get our men from the for-tifications down to the ships and out to sea."

"Tavi," Magnus blurted. "Slow down. Are you sure you wish to ask our men to engage the Vord when we have no watercrafters to tend the wounded and only a score of Knights to support the *legionares*."

"With luck, they won't need to," Tavi said. "And our crafters will be back before the night is out. If we've done it quickly enough, we might be able to slip away without taking on the second queen at all." He turned his eyes to the low-ering sun, frowning. "Time is the critical factor, here, gentlemen."

Marcus and Magnus struck their fists to the hearts and, after one last ex-changed glance, they turned to be about their duties.

"Captain!" Durias called. Tavi glanced down to see the stocky *legionare* waving frantically at him from the back of a puffing taurg at the base of the ter-raced wall. "They made it! They're here!"

Tavi turned and hurried down the berm. He took Durias's offered hand and swung up onto the taurg behind the former slave. "Take me to Varg."

They found Varg walking the earthworks on the opposite side of the city from Tavi. Varg's militia—though they could scarcely be called that anymore after nearly two years of training beside Varg's warriors and conflict against the Aleran Legions—was spread around the fortifications, and the Canim Warmaster had placed blocks of heavily armored warriors at regular intervals around the wall. The militia would hold the line, and the warriors would be used as a reserve, ready to lend their tremendous power to the militia should the Vord breach the defense.

"Varg!" Tavi called. "There is something you should see."

The big Cane looked down from the wall, and his ears twitched in mild amusement. "Is there?"

"I do not know," Nasaug said, the Cane's resonant voice coming from where Nasaug sat upon his own taurg beside Durias's mount, along with a spare beast for Varg. "He would tell me nothing."

Varg grunted. "Only a fool seeks a quarrel with a tavar." He came down the terraces, slammed the open taurg on the snout when it tried to snap at him, and mounted.

They rode to the single opening in the earthworks that bestrode the road leading out of Molvar. "When are the engineers going to close this up?" Durias asked him.

"They aren't," Tavi said.

Durias blinked. "Why build the wall if you're only going to leave an enormous and obvious weakness in it?"

"Because it means we know where the enemy will concentrate his strength," Varg growled. "The defenses are thin. The enemy is many. If every spot was as good as any other, the Vord would simply attack at random, and we would have no way to predict where to concentrate our strength against them."

"Leave them a big, obvious opening to exploit," Tavi said, "and we can be certain where their main thrust will fall. This is where the Legions will fight."

Durias nodded, looking around. "That's why we're putting up the lower berms inside, then, along the road. They can't be seen from the outside. When the Vord come through, they'll be walking into a death trap."

"It'll be worse than that," Tavi said. "You've never seen what firecrafters can do in an enclosed area." He glanced up at Varg, and added, with very mild emphasis, "Neither have you, Warmaster."

Varg paused a moment, meeting Tavi's gaze, before he replied just as mildly, "My ritualists will be there as well, *gadara*. It should be interesting."

Tavi carefully suppressed a quiver of unquiet at the thought of some of the things he'd seen the Canim ritualists do. He showed Varg his teeth, and said, "That's for later. My scouts spotted something I think you'd want to know about." He pointed across the rolling landscape outside the earthworks.

Varg exchanged a look with his son, then the pair of them stood up in their stirrups and peered out across the land. They stared for a long, silent moment.

Nasaug let out an explosive snarl, and lashed his startled taurg into a sudden, ground-shaking gallop that made the other two taurga bawl and rumble in complaint. Half a dozen Shuaran refugees who were just arriving had to throw themselves out of the way before the taurg flattened them. Durias and Varg brought their beasts under control again. Varg growled low in his throat, glanced at Tavi, then dismounted and tossed the reins of his beast to Durias.

Tavi dismounted as well, dodged a sullen kick Durias's taurg aimed at him, and hurried after Varg, who was striding up the terraces to the top of the earthworks beside the gateway. Tavi came to a stop beside him and watched Nasaug's progress.

Out on the plain outside the earthworks, a large group of refugees was moving together. Unlike the majority of the Shuarans, though, these Canim were all dark-furred. Among them moved, often with the aid of canes and crutches, warriors in red-and-black armor, and at the heart of the group, a long spear bearing a simple twin pennant of red-and-black cloth stood above the rest of the group.

"My people," Varg said, his voice very deep and very quiet. "Some of them survived."

"Ten thousand or so, according to my scouts," Tavi agreed quietly. "I know that isn't many."

Varg was silent for a moment before he growled, "It is everything, *gadara*. Some of our warriors live among them." He arched one paw-hand, dark claws spreading fiercely. "We did not fail them entirely." He turned his eyes to Tavi. "Where were they?"

"Lararl had them near the fortress."

Varg turned pensively back toward the plain, then narrowed his eyes, a growl shaking his chest. "His ritualists needed blood."

Tavi said nothing.

Nasaug reached the group a moment later, and all but broke his taurg's neck hauling it to a halt. The mount snapped at his arm as Nasaug dismounted, but the Cane struck it between the eyes with one enormous fist, staggering the three-quarter-ton mount as easily as if it had been a drunk staying too late at a wine house.

The arriving Narashans let out cries and howls as Nasaug reached them and began striding through them, toward the banner at the heart of the group.

"That was what it meant, back in Lararl's chambers," Varg said. "When you told him that everyone was to leave."

Tavi said nothing.

Varg turned to him, and said, "Lararl would not have given up a military resource in such a desperate situation without cause. You demanded it of him, Tavar."

"I couldn't tell you they were near," Tavi said quietly. "You would have gone to get them, and to crows with the circumstances."

Varg narrowed his eyes and growled deep in his considerable chest. It made Tavi acutely aware of exactly how large the Cane really was.

Tavi took a steadying breath and turned to meet Varg's eyes. He cocked an eyebrow at the Cane, daring him to deny the statement, and hoped that Varg's intense passions on the subject weren't about to express themselves at his expense.

Varg looked back out at the plain and let his growl rumble away to nothing. After a long moment, he said, "You protected them."

"And the Shuarans," Tavi said in a very soft, very nonchallenging voice. "And myself. We're all standing in the same fire, Varg."

Varg rumbled out another growl, one containing a tone of agreement. Then he turned from Tavi, strode down the terraces, and out onto the plain, toward the oncoming group of Narashan survivors.

Tavi watched them come. A moment later, Durias climbed the stairs beside him, and asked, "How'd he take it when he realized you didn't tell him?"

"He didn't like it," Tavi said. "He understood it."

"It's a strength of their mind-set," the young centurion said, nodding. "Working through the logic of others dispassionately." Durias smiled. "Though if they'd come to harm because of it, it wouldn't have stopped him from gutting you."

"Don't I know it," Tavi said. "But I didn't have any good choices."

Durias squinted out at the Narashans for a second, then his eyes widened. "Bloody crows."

Tavi glanced at him. "What?"

"That banner," Durias said. "That isn't a common symbol among them."

"What does it mean?"

"Warriors rarely use spears," Durias said. "They gave the Free Aleran a hard time because our standards were mounted on them. They're considered to be a female's weapon."

Tavi lifted his eyebrows. "So?"

"So the spear standard in the colors of the range means a matron of a high warrior bloodline," the young centurion told him. "And I—"

His voice was suddenly drowned out when ten thousand Canim throats erupted into wordless howls, and though the sounds were not human, Tavi could hear the emotions that drove it—raw celebration, sudden and unexpected joy. He traded a glance with Durias, and the two leaned forward, watching.

As Varg approached, the small sea of singing Canim parted, and Nasaug appeared, walking beside a Canim female as tall and as dark-furred as he, their hands joined. Even as they walked, half a dozen young Canim, one of them scarcely larger than an Aleran child, came bounding out of the crowd and rushed Varg, baying in high-pitched tones. The Warmaster planted his feet, and was shortly inundated in delighted, furry children and wagging tails. A gang wrestling match ensued, in which Varg pinned each of the children to the earth with one hand and nipped at their throats and tummies, to squeals of protest and delight.

"Bloody crows," Durias breathed again. The young centurion turned to Tavi, and said, "Your Highness. Unless I'm very much mistaken, you just saved the lives of Varg's family. Nasaug's mate, and their children. Furies, you practically brought them back from the *dead*."

Tavi stared out at the plain for a time, watching as the female caught up and dragged the pups from their grandsire, then exchanged deep bows of the head with Varg, showing him the deference of a confident subordinate to a much-respected superior. Then they embraced, after the Canim fashion, their muzzles touching, heads resting together, their eyes closed.

"Maybe," Tavi said. His throat felt a little tight. "None of us have survived this yet."

The night was clear, and when the scream of the windstreams of the Legions' Knights Aeris drifted across the fortifications, Tavi emerged from the command tent and looked up to see the forms of his Knights speckling the face of the almost-full moon. The sentries were taking note of it at the same time, and horns rang through the camp, alerting officers of the return of the Aleran fliers.

"Yes!" Tavi snarled, as Marcus came out of the tent behind him. "They're here! Magnus!"

The old Cursor was already hurrying toward the tent, from where he'd been resting briefly nearby, still tugging his tunic into place. "Your Highness!"

"Get everyone who isn't fighting into the ships, now! I don't want to lose a minute."

"Very good, Your Highness."

"Gradash!"

The grey-furred old Canim huntmaster came out of the tent on Marcus's heels, squinting up at the sound of the incoming windcrafters. "I am here, Tavar."

"I think you should send word to your people now, and get them moving toward the piers as we discussed."

"Aye." He turned to a pair of whippet-thin young Canim runners who had been waiting nearby, and began growling instructions.

"Marcus," Tavi continued. "I want you at the breach with the men. The minute you see the signal, fall back to Molvar and get to the ships."

"Sir," Marcus said, banging a fist to his breastplate. The First Spear turned, barking orders, and was shortly mounted and riding out to the earthworks.

Kitai and Maximus came out of the command tent, and stood watching with Tavi as the Knights Aeris came in to land in two groups, one dropping into the landing area of the former slave Legion, the other landing in the First Aleran's—except for a single armored figure that came down not twenty yards from the command tent.

"Crassus!" Tavi called, grinning. "You're looking well."

"Sir," Crassus replied with an answering smile. He saluted Tavi, who returned the gesture, then clasped forearms with the young officer. "I'm glad to see you got back in one piece."

"Tell me," Tavi said intently.

"It's working," Crassus hissed, his eyes bright with triumph. "It took us a bloody lot of crafting to pull it off, and the witchmen aren't at all comfortable, but it's working."

Tavi felt his mouth stretch out into a fierce grin. *"Hah!"*

"Bloody crows!" Maximus said, frustration and delight warring in his voice. "In the name of all the great furies, what are you two *talking* about?"

Crassus turned to his half brother, grinning, and embraced him. "Come on," he said. "See for yourself."

Crassus led them all to the cliffs overlooking the sea below Molvar. In the silver light of the moon, the sea was a monochrome portrait of black water and white wave-caps—and riding upon that dark sea were three white ships, ships so enormous that for a moment it seemed that Tavi's eyes had to be lying to him. And he'd known what to expect.

He turned to see the faces of the others, who were simply staring in disbelief at the enormous white vessels. They watched as tiny figures moved about on the decks of the sail-less ships—engineers of the First Aleran, whose tiny forms upon the white decks showed the true size of the ships: Each of them was nearly half a mile in length and more than half as wide.

"Ships," Max said, his tone dull. "Really. Big. Ships."

"Barges, really," Gradash corrected him, though the old Cane's own voice was sober and quiet. "No masts. What's making them move?"

"Furycraft," Tavi replied. "Witchmen are using seawater to push them." He turned to Crassus. "How many levels deep?"

"Twelve," Crassus said, something smug in his voice. "Cramped for a Cane, but they'll fit."

"Ice!" Kitai exclaimed suddenly, her tone enormously pleased. "You crafted ships from ice!"

Tavi turned to her and nodded, smiling. Then said, to Gradash, "I remembered the ice mountains you showed me as we arrived. And if the leviathans truly avoid them, we should have no problems with them on the way back to Alera."

The old Cane stared at the ships, his ears quivering. "But the ice mountains. They roll like taurga with itchy backs."

"The keels go fairly deep, and are weighted with stone," Crassus assured the Cane. "They should be stable, provided they don't take a big wave broadside. They won't roll."

"Roll, crows," Maximus sputtered. "Ice *melts*."

"It also floats," Tavi said, feeling a little smug himself, though he probably didn't deserve it. He hadn't been working himself to exhaustion for days to make them happen, after all.

"The firecrafters have been making coldstones nonstop," Crassus told Max. "There are enough of them there to keep the ships from melting for three weeks, by which time they'll have made more—and the engineers stretched a granite frame throughout. They think they'll hold, if we can avoid the worst of the weather."

Tavi slammed a fist on the pauldrons of Crassus's armor. "Well *done*, Tribune," he said fiercely.

"So," Kitai said, smiling. "We get everyone on the ships, and we leave the Vord screaming their frustration behind us. This is a fine plan, Aleran."

"If the weather holds," Max said darkly.

"That's what Knights Aeris are for," Crassus said calmly. "It will be hard work, but we'll do it. We have to do it."

Canim horns brayed from the earthworks, pulsing out in odd, baying signals. Tavi held up a hand for silence and watched Gradash.

The old Cane took in the horn calls and reported, "The first of the main body of Lararl's regulars have been sighted, Tavar."

Max whistled. "One crowbegotten fine retreat, if they held together all the way from the fortress."

Tavi nodded agreement. "And that means that the Vord won't be far behind. We need to get moving, people. The enemy is close." He began giving rapid orders, rounding up a couple of couriers to get them out to the right portions of the Legion, when a surge of terrified realization from Kitai hit him like a punch in the belly. He stopped in the middle of his sentence and turned to her.

"Aleran!" she said, staring out at the breach in the earthworks where the First Aleran was stationed.

Tavi spun to see the First Aleran under assault. Enormous blue-armored Canim had, in the midst of passing peacefully through their positions, suddenly whirled to attack. In the bright moonlight, Tavi could see the Shuarans hacking into the surprised Alerans, fighting in perfect unison and entirely without regard for their own lives.

He sucked in a breath and realized what had happened. "Taken," he spat. "Those Shuarans have been taken by the Vord." He turned to the others, and said, "The Vord aren't close. They're *here*."

Chapter 44

The Vord surged toward the defenses around Molvar in a great, dark wave, and the last defenders of Canea rose to meet them in a single, enormous roar of defiance and hate. Signal horns, Canim and Aleran alike, bayed and shrilled across the fey, silver-lit landscape, and from the west poured a great wave of the enemy, chitin gleaming and winking beneath the great eye of the winter moon.

Tavi knew that he was speaking, because orders were flying off his lips more rapidly than he could keep track of them, and all around him officers of the Legion were slamming out salutes and sprinting away, but it seemed that he didn't actually understand anything he was saying. His thoughts were racing, trying to cover every possible outcome of the next minutes and hours, anticipating everything, taking every measure he possibly could. Then he was swinging up behind Kitai onto a taurg and racing toward the battle.

The First Aleran had hacked down the taken Shuarans, suffering ruinous casualties in doing so—anything taken by the Vord was enormously strong, oblivious to pain, and fought with mindlessly suicidal ferocity. Though the taken Canim were down, several Alerans had joined each of the fallen enemy upon the earth—and the enemy's ruse had paid a dividend. The Legion's ranks had been badly disrupted, and the Vord's first thrust came hard on the heels of their opening gambit.

The Legion was being driven back from the breach in the earthworks, while more Vord—always more Vord—assaulted the rest of the defensive positions, preventing the Canim from coming to the Alerans' aid. Now the Legion fought to defend a twenty-foot-wide corridor, the opening in the earthworks. Ten-foot walls flanked the opening, and *legionares* with spears crouched in ranks atop those walls, thrusting their weapons into the press of armored Vord bodies below, while the infantry fought with shield and sword to keep the Vord from forcing their way through the engineered bottleneck and past the fortifications.

Tavi drew his sword and flung himself from the plunging taurg as the beast began to ride through the scattered and reeling *legionares* who had been driven out of position and away from their various centuries. *"Legionares!"* he bellowed. "To me!"

"Captain!" called a dazed *legionare*.

"Form up on me!" Tavi called to the scattered soldiers. "You, you, you, you're spear leaders! Line them up! *Legionares*, fall in on this line!"

Once he had the men organized into a fighting century, a block ten files long and eight *legionares* deep, he sent them forward, to the support of the men already fighting. He did it over and over, until the scattered soldiers were accounted for, and realized as he did that the Vord had imitated the enemy yet again. Tavi's group might have hunted down and killed the nearby queen a few days before, but the Vord were returning the compliment—the taken Shuarans, it seemed, had focused their efforts upon killing the centurions within each century. Crested helms lay far more thickly among the fallen Alerans than they should have and in the press of battle, without the leadership of the men wearing them, the organization vital to the Legion's order of battle had frayed.

The additional centuries helped to stiffen the lines, though Tavi knew that it would only be for a few moments—fortunately, those moments were enough.

The air screamed as forty Knights Aeris swept down upon the battle. Tavi lifted his sword, signaling Crassus, who flew at the head of the Knights—each of whom flew paired with another Knight, carrying a third armored form between them.

"Crassus!" Tavi shouted into the din of battle, pointing to the walls overlooking the bottleneck. "On the wall!"

But the young Tribune hadn't needed Tavi's gesticulations to see where his help was needed. Signing instructions to his men, Crassus touched down on the wall overlooking one side of the breech, along with half of his flight. The other half landed on the other side, where each pair of Knights Aeris deposited the men they'd brought to the fight—the Knights Ignus of the First Aleran.

Tavi couldn't see what happened from his vantage point on the ground, behind the Legion's wall of shields, but heartbeats later, there was an enormous roar and hellish blue-white light flared ahead of him, burning the black silhouette of the massed ranks into his vision. The Legion let out a shout of exultation at the return of their Knights, and surged forward, driving the Vord back into the sudden vacuum the Knights Ignus had burned into their ranks.

Tavi sprinted up to the earthworks to join Crassus, but by the time he got there, the situation was in hand—at least for the moment. The Vord had reeled back from the breach, and every time they began to press in more closely, one of the Knights Ignus unleashed a blast of fire in their midst.

"Max is coming," Crassus panted to Tavi. His face was streaked with sweat from the effort of his recent furycrafting. He turned to point back toward the city, where Max and a column of armored figures were marching at the quick step from the Legion camp outside the city walls. "He's bringing the engineers and our Knights Terra. We'll close up the breach and—"

On the outer earthworks, Canim horns blared and brayed, and at that signal, dozens of ritualists appeared among the Canim on the walls. All of the hooded figures threw back their pale mantles, dipped their hands into the pouches of blood they wore slung at their sides, and cast scarlet droplets into the air. Again, Tavi wasn't in position to see the results of the working, but he saw the great, billowing clouds of greenish mist form and fall, and heard the screams of agony among the Vord as it descended upon them, scouring the earthen walls clean of attackers.

"Form up!" bellowed a strident voice from the breach below. "Crows take your idiot eyes, form up! Dress the ranks before they hit us again!"

Tavi looked down to see Valiar Marcus—absent his crested centurion's helmet—striding among the Aleran lines. The First Spear's armor was horribly dented over his left shoulder, and that arm hung limply at his side—but he carried his centurion's baton in his right hand and made liberal use of it, shoving soldiers into line, rapping them sharply on their helmets to get their attention. Marcus had thought quickly, Tavi saw. The scarred veteran must have realized that his crested helm had marked him as a target when the battle had gotten under way and he'd removed it. A quick scan showed Tavi that there was a notable absence of crested helms among the ranks—but the centurions were still visibly doing their jobs, maintaining their presence by virtue of their batons, voices, and sheer force of will.

"It's going to take us several hours to load the supplies and all the refugees," Tavi said. "We have to hold them. Marcus is in charge of the breach. Support him. I'm going to talk to Varg."

"Aye, Your Highness," Crassus said, slamming a fist to his heart. "We'll do our part, never fear."

Tavi rushed up to the walls, taking advantage of the brief respite in the battle as the Vord recoiled from the massive scourge of acidic blood magic the ritualists had released upon them. He had to pace almost half a mile along the walls until he found Varg, who was striding the wall among his own people.

Tavi nodded to him and began speaking without preamble. "Three hours. We have to hold them that long at least."

Varg looked from Tavi out to the field, where the Vord were still pouring in from all over the countryside. The base of the wall was a ruin of melted chitin and half-formed bodies, all that was left after the ritualists' counterattack. "Three hours. That could be a long time."

"It will take that long for the transports to dock and for our people and supplies to load on," Tavi said. "There's no point in rescuing them now only to let them starve to death at sea."

Varg growled out his agreement. "What of our fighters?"

Tavi laid out the withdrawal plan for him. "None of which matters if we can't hold now."

Already, the Vord had recovered from the sting of the first repulsion, and were beginning to mass again, preparing to assault the earthworks once more en masse.

"We will hold," Varg growled. "We will wait for your signal."

For three hours, more and more Vord poured in from all across the countryside, their numbers growing ever larger, their attacks more focused and cohesive: and for three hours, the last defenders of Canea cast them back.

The casualty rate was hideous, the worst fighting any of them had seen—and for the First Aleran, that was saying something indeed. Once the earthcrafters had closed the breach in the earthworks, the Legions fought to defend a relatively tiny section of the defenses—proportional to their numbers.

It was the Canim who carried the lion's share of the battle.

Shuarans and Narashans fought side by side, reserve forces of warriors charging forward more and more frequently to come to the aid of hard-pressed militia fighters in their far lighter armor. Ritualists screamed to the night sky and sent death in multiple, hideous forms down upon their attackers—Varg had, it turned out, been bleeding volunteers from his people a bit at a time, regularly, on their way to Canea, saving up a store of blood for the ritualists to use. They unleashed it on the Vord, holding back nothing, to terrible effect, until they were pouring their clouds of acid down the faces of the earthworks not to kill Vord, but to further dissolve the corpses that were piling up higher and higher, building a ramp for the Vord that followed in their wake.

For the Alerans, the fight was grueling and desperate. Blocks of *legionares*, working together, could fend off the wave-assaults of the enemy, but when a formation was broken, or when any of the men were isolated, death followed close behind. Antillar Maximus, leading a cadre of Knights Terra and Ferrous, launched himself time and again into the fray, where the more deadly weapons of the powerful Knights would crush the Vord like so many toys, driving them back from the more vulnerable *legionares*.

Tavi did everything he could to make sure the men could fight on stable ground, and to facilitate the rotation of the rear ranks with those in the fore, fighting the exhaustion that was certain to do them more harm, in the end, than any Vord form or poison. Those wounded too badly to be able to walk were taken from the field, stabilized, and loaded onto the ships that waited for them at the bottom of the city of Molvar. Other wounds were quickly closed, then the men were sent back to the defenses, until there was barely a spear in the Legion who wasn't at least half-populated by the walking wounded.

When the Vord press became too great, firecrafters would lend their aid to the defenses—but the Knights Ignus quickly tired, and soon only Crassus remained capable of laying out the supporting fire the Legions required to survive. Tavi could only urge the young man on, silently, from his position at the rear of the fighting, and wonder at how the young Tribune could keep rising to his feet, again and again, to destroy more of the Vord.

Meanwhile, behind the battle, the civilians filed down the stairways hurriedly crafted into the stone, down to the water, there to board the vast ice ships. Canim families bore crushing loads with them, everyone lending a hand to the effort to pile supplies on the ships, the knowledge of the certain death that howled at the earthworks driving them to cooperation and orderly conduct more surely than any law or tradition ever could.

Twice, the Vord breached the earthworks and began pouring down the terraces—but both times, Anag and the Shuaran taurg cavalry charged, shattering the momentum of the advance, which was then pushed back by blocks of Varg's elite warriors, led personally by the Warmaster.

And then, after more than four endless, nightmarish hours, the horns Magnus had stationed at the piers began to sound the retreat.

"That's it!" Tavi screamed, turning to the trumpeter he'd kept near him. "Signal the Canim! Sound the retreat!"

As the silver trumpet shrilled, the First Spear turned to Tavi from his place in the ranks, eyes searching. Tavi flashed Marcus several hand signals, and the veteran centurion began barking orders that were repeated instantly through the ranks.

Once more, the Canim horns brayed, and the ritualists came forward for one last, mass summoning of blood magic. The Vord reeled back from the destruction—and in that moment of opportunity, the defenders turned and withdrew from their positions.

"Go!" Tavi shouted, waving men past him, *willing* them to retreat in good order, to escape, to survive. "Through the city gate and down to the ship! The route is marked by our colors! Go, go, go!"

Four hours of hard fighting made a poor prelude to the mile and a half of hard marching the men would have to make before they could board their ships, but none of them seemed anything less than eager to take to his heels. Despite the hours of slaughter and havoc they and the Canim had wreaked upon the Vord, the enemy numbers outside the walls had not visibly diminished—this was a battle they could not possibly win, and they knew it. They could only hope to survive.

The Vord came over the walls and began to pour down them like a black flood finally breaching a strained levy, pursuing the retreating forces—but the taurg cavalry flung itself forward into the foremost elements of the advance. The taurga, bellowing their fury and fear, smashed into the oncoming Vord with a ferocity and power of impact that Tavi had never seen, an unstoppable hammerblow that left acres of Vord crushed into the Canean soil.

Again and again the taurga charged, and here and there, one of the great mounts fell, pulled down by the sheer weight of numbers, spilling a blue-and-black-armored Canim warrior onto the cold earth to a savage death.

But all they could do was slow the oncoming tide.

Tavi pushed along at the rear of the Aleran forces, a shoulder under one of Crassus's arms, hauling the exhausted young Tribune along by main force. He was exhausted, and every nerve felt strained. Everything happened very rapidly, and at the same time in achingly slowed distortion.

The Canim and Alerans alike flowed into Molvar through the city's several gates, and went rushing down to the docks, where the ships stood waiting for them, lined up in specific order. Boarding instructions were designed for speed, not organization. Each ship would take its maximum load from the first to reach it, then clear the piers in the port for the next.

If Tavi had known, when he was younger, how much of war depended upon vast and complex ways of organizing where people were supposed to walk, eat, sleep, and relieve themselves, he thought he would have had a completely different opinion on the subject.

He was among the last Alerans to enter the city, and he could see the Vord, halfway across the open ground, rushing toward the city as the Canim at the gates swung them closed and locked them shut.

"Go!" Tavi urged them silently. "Go, go, go!"

Outside, he heard the Canim cavalry sound their own retreat, then the taurga racing toward the stone piers. Tavi could not imagine the danger and mayhem that was about to ensue when several hundred blood-maddened Canim guided the battle-frenzied taurga down narrow stone staircases so that they could board the ice ships, but it was plain to him that no sane man would want to be anywhere close.

Even as Tavi kept urging his men to hurry on through the city, their way marked by pennants made from strips of red-and-blue cloth, he saw the Canim on the walls of the city begin to rush through the walls and buildings with lit torches, setting them aflame. The fires had been laid hours before, and spread rapidly, smoke coming up in a sudden veil.

Molvar would burn to shield their escape.

"Max!" Tavi gasped, still hauling Crassus along by one arm. "Here, help me!"

Max appeared from the confusion and smoke and got beneath his brother's other arm. "I can handle him. You should move ahead, get to a ship!"

"Once all of our people are ready to go, I will," Tavi responded. "Stop slowing me down, and get moving."

"Captain!" Marcus appeared out of the smoke, coughing. "West wind is rising! The fire's spreading toward us faster than we can move away!"

"Get to the front of the line with some Knights!" Tavi called back. "Knock down some walls if you have to!"

"Yes, sir!" Marcus saluted and vanished again.

As they got closer to the piers, the line came to a halt, the men backed up in the street, pressed chest to shoulder blades with their fellows. Tavi could hear Marcus bellowing orders in a smoke-roughened voice, somewhere ahead of them. Men had begun to shout and mill about in panic, as the roar of the fire grew nearer, along with the light of the spreading flames.

"Stand easy, men!" Tavi called. "We'll get through. We're going to be—"

Tavi didn't know how the Vord had gotten through. Perhaps it had been one of the first to reach the city, and had plunged through the flames before they had risen to deadly intensity. Perhaps its froglike form had been specifically designed to resist heat. Perhaps it had just gotten lucky. Regardless, Tavi didn't realize that it was there at all until something disturbingly like a hand seized a weary, wounded *legionare* beside him, holding the man's entire head in its grasp, and flung him to his back on the ground.

Just as it happened, there was a surge of motion and a roar of triumph from the Legion ahead of Tavi. Men stumbled forward as the restraining pressure of the bodies in front of them was released.

Tavi screamed for help, but his voice was lost amidst the shouts and the roaring fire and wind. The Vord hunched over the fallen *legionare*, moving with a hideously lithe ferocity. Sparks flew from the armor over the *legionare's* belly as the Vord raked at him with shining green-black claws.

Tavi drew his sword, needing no conscious effort to call upon the furies within the Aleran steel. His sword struck through the arm with which the Vord had the *legionare* pinned, then through its slender neck in a pair of rapid strokes, followed by a fury-enhanced kick that prevented the Vord's mass from falling on the downed *legionare* and pinning him there.

Tavi flashed the stunned-looking man a quick grin and hauled him to his feet. "No lying down on the job, soldier. Watch my back until we get to the ship, eh?"

The man answered his smile with one of his own and drew his sword. "Yes, sir. Thank you, sir."

The two of them hurried through the thickening smoke to catch up with the retreating *legionares*, and Tavi found himself beginning to cough and struggle for breath. There were more of the Vord in the haze, moving as swiftly as shadows, glimpsed for only a second before they were gone again. An eerie shriek rose through the smoke, and others answered it from all around, the cries echoing between buildings and becoming strangely distorted as they bounced around stone.

Elsewhere in the streets, they heard the snarls and roars of fighting Canim, mixing with the shrieks of the Vord. They were under attack, as they descended through their own routes to the harbor.

The smell of seawater, tar, and fish, the odor of every harbor Tavi had ever encountered, suddenly reached him through the acrid stench of smoke. The *legionares* were emerging from one of the several streets to the harbor, where their ships waited to receive them. Enough light shone through the smoke from the burning city above them to light their way, even without the lamps set up along the piers, and Tavi could hear Marcus and other centurions bellowing orders, counting off men to each ship.

"Form on me!" Tavi called, sword still in hand, and began organizing the *legionares* at the rear into an outward-facing defense, swords and shields at the ready, with spears in the second rank, their gleaming steel points protruding in a defensive thicket.

He'd acted none too soon. Vord rushed them through the smoke, half a dozen of the froglike beasts bounding out of the shadows and confusion, only to meet the armor and steel of the readied Legion. Once they were in position, Tavi let a trio of baton-wielding centurions take over the defense, which slowly contracted backward onto the wharves as the *legionares* behind the wall of shields boarded their vessels.

The ships began to warp away from the piers as they filled, turning to sail down the channel and out of the harbor. The smaller Aleran ships had few problems, but the passage was a far tighter fit for the larger Canim vessels, and the process of emptying the harbor was agonizingly slow. It had to be. A ship, if mishandled, could sink in the channel and block it for every vessel behind. Even moving at the most frantic pace that could be managed, the ships practically touching one another as they sailed out, it was more than an hour before the rear of the column stepped slowly backward onto the piers. All the while the smoke thickened, and the fires drew nearer.

Tavi checked to see that Marcus was counting off the last thousand men onto half a dozen ships that had hurriedly thrown lines to the piers and tossed down gangplanks. The *Slive* was the last ship, tying on to the end of the pier, and Tavi could see Kitai standing in the prow.

Tavi counted off men from the last line, sending them back to board a ship one by one, until only he, Marcus, and half a dozen *legionares* remained, marching slowly backward down the stone pier while half a dozen of the frog-Vord ghosted through the smoke, wary of rushing forward after an hour of clashing uselessly against Legion shields.

Only forty yards remained as the last of the *legionares* boarded and the ships cast off. Then twenty. Then ten.

Five yards from the gangplank of the *Slive*, something seized Tavi's leg in an iron grip and hauled him off the pier and down into the cold water of the harbor. He plunged into frigid and utter darkness, and the weight of his armor pulled him down like a sinking stone.

The Vord that had seized his leg had not let go. Tavi felt an enormous hand clutch him around the waist. Something clamped onto his arm at the elbow, fangs sinking into the skin above the steel bracer on his forearm, tearing into his biceps and shook him savagely.

Tavi had to fight not to scream. His long sword would have been useless at such close quarters, so he drew his dagger and thrust it awkwardly at the Vord, feeling the badly aimed tip slip and turn aside from the Vord's armored skin. Surrounded completely by water, he tried in vain to summon strength from the earth, the only thing that might allow him to escape the Vord's grip, but it was useless. He distinctly felt the bone in his arm break as the Vord ripped at him with hideous strength in the dark—and continued pulling, beginning to rip his arm from his body, the pain mounting, bubbles of priceless breath escaping his lips and sliding along his face.

And then his feet struck the icy silt at the bottom of the harbor.

Fury-born strength surged through him and he transferred the dagger to his mouth, gripping the blade in his teeth, so that he could twist around with his undamaged arm. The motion tore his shoulder from its socket, but he drew the steel of his dagger into his mind and the pain became a piece of background datum, like the temperature of the water or the fact that he was hungry. He secured a grip on the Vord's armored limb and twisted his hips, scissoring his legs up, feeling his back strike the mud as the Vord struggled. He locked his legs around what he thought was the Vord's body, closed his good hand in the tightest grip he could imagine and arched his body, crushing his legs together with all his strength.

For seconds they strained in stasis—and then something broke with a horrible crack, and the Vord's grip went loose. Tavi kept ripping and straining until the Vord tore, then shoved the still-twitching pieces away from him, into the water.

His fingers flew to the fastenings on his armor. He'd done and undone them thousands of times by now, and it was an operation he could perform when practically asleep—when he was using both hands. And when the leather fastenings weren't soaked and swollen. And when his fingers weren't numb from the freezing water. And when he wasn't more than half-panicked, his lungs burning, with brightly colored stars dancing across his vision.

He kept struggling with the lacings, and finally managed to slide free of his armor. Only his continued focus on his metalcrafting as his broken arm and shoulder came free kept the pain from curling him into a ball of agony and sealing his fate. He ripped at the buckles of his heavy greaves until they came free, kicked off the bottom with whatever feeble strength he had left, and swam in the direction he thought was toward the surface. The pressure on his lungs and ears was awful, and he needed to *breathe*, and his lungs were collapsing, readying to draw in another breath whether he was clear of the water or not, and the dagger had fallen from his mouth and the fire from his shoulder and arm was simply too agonizing to be real—

Something slapped against his head, then seized him by the collar, and he was rising through the water, choking on the first half-breath of water—as his head emerged into the air.

Kitai jerked his head and shoulders out of the water with unexpected strength, and her panic and fury pounded against his senses. "Aleran!" she cried. *"Chala!"*

He retched out water and choked in a wet, heavy breath, hardly able to move his limbs together.

Something cut through the water nearby them, something dark and large and swift. A shark—or another Vord.

"Go!" Tavi gasped. "Go, go!"

Kitai began swimming, hauling him along by his tunic, and Tavi struggled just to keep his head above the water. They were fifty feet from the *Slive*, and just as far from the pier—which was haunted with Vord. Tavi had just begun to make sense of things again, through the pain in his shoulder and chest and arm, when he looked up to see the bulk of the *Slive*, already drifting back from the pier, moving above him.

Men were shouting, and a line fell into the water. Kitai seized it with one hand, wrapped it several times around her forearm and screamed something. Then she was rising and pulling Tavi up out of the water by the tunic—and his weight all seemed to concentrate itself in his ravaged shoulder.

Tavi screamed at the agony and bucked in entirely involuntary reaction, accompanied by the sound of ripping cloth and a short fall into the water.

He fought his way to the air again as *something* rushed by beneath the surface, brushing against his legs. He saw the ship gliding backward from the pier and away from him, Kitai and the line already out of reach. Her hand was tangled in the rope and she fought frantically to free herself, but she was already yards away. Tavi looked up to see Demos looking over the rail at the side of the ship, the captain's eyes wide, and then there was only the old carved figurehead of the *Slive*, the beautiful woman staring sightlessly ahead with a slight smile on her lovely lips.

Tavi's legs began to fail, and the water reached up for him. He began to sink, the figurehead holding his attention, until it almost seemed to swell in size, growing larger, turning toward him.

He realized with a shock that the carven woman on the *Slive*'s prow *was* moving, and that it was not some trick of his frozen, agonized mind. She bent to him with a grace and splendor belied by the peeling paint of her features, smiling, and extended a strong and slender hand.

Tavi summoned the last of his failing strength and took it, feeling her grip his hand with flexible, inexorable strength. She was drawing him from the water, lifting him through the air, as another frog-Vord struck at his heels in vain. He had a brief and dizzying view of the foredeck of the ship, then he was lying on wooden planks, too tired to lift his head.

"Gotcha," said Demos in satisfaction. "My lord."

"*Chala!*" Kitai shouted. She was there beside him, her own wet tunic clinging to her slender form as she ripped a cloak from a passing sailor and tossed it over him. "Maximus! He's bleeding!"

"Healer!" bellowed Marcus's smoke-roughened voice. "Bring out a tub!"

"Captain," Tavi croaked. "Get us the crows away from here."

"Aye," Demos said, as several willing hands lifted him toward a tub that had been hurriedly brought up from the hold of the ship. "Aye, my lord. Let's go home."

Epilogue

All things pass in time.

We are far less significant than we imagine ourselves to be. All that we are, all that we have wrought, is but a shadow, no matter how durable it may seem. One day, when the last man has breathed his last breath, the sun will shine, the mountains will stand, the rain will fall, the streams will whisper—and they will not miss him.

—From the final journal entry of Gaius Sextus,
First Lord of Alera

The air around the former capital was too hot and too laden with fumes to overfly, Amara thought numbly. She would have to lead their party of rescued Knights and Citizens around it.

She turned course to circle the flaming wasteland, following its eastern edge as they proceeded north. Alera Imperia, the shining white city upon a hill, was only a gaping hole in the ground. Smoke and flame seethed in that cauldron, far below them. The river Gaul poured into it, and steam obscured the land below from time to time in its own layer of thick white mist that lay over the ground like a filmy funerary shroud.

Amara glided in close to the lead wind coach, opened the door, and slipped inside. She sat quietly for a moment, her head bowed.

"Bloody crows," Gram breathed, looking down. "Did the Vord do that?"

"No," Bernard said. Amara felt him take her hand in his and squeeze gently. "No. I've seen something like this before. At Kalare."

"Gaius," Gram whispered. He shook his head, then bowed it. "That arrogant old . . ." His voice cracked, and he broke off his sentence.

"Do you think the horde was there?" Amara asked her husband.

"Absolutely. They weren't shy about leaving a trail. You could see it from up here."

"Then Gaius defeated them," Gram said.

Amara shook her head. "No. I don't think so." She lifted her head and looked out the window at the destruction. "He would never do . . . this, unless the city was all but taken in any case."

"The Vord won," Bernard rumbled nodding. "But he made them pay for it."

"Where would survivors of the battle go, Bernard?" she asked.

"Survive? That?" Gram asked.

Amara gave him a steady look and turned back to Bernard.

Her husband took a deep breath, thinking. "They'd take the causeway north, into the Redhill Heights, until they reached the crossroads. From there, they could turn east toward Aquitaine or northeast to Riva."

The crossroads, then, would be the natural rendezvous point for anyone in the region who was fleeing the Vord-ridden south.

She nodded to her husband and stepped out of the coach, once again willing Cirrus to bear up her weight. Then she signaled to the other fliers in their group to follow her, and took the point position again, to lead her own band of survivors north.

Within half an hour, a hundred Knights Aeris plunged down upon them in a swirling mass of cold air, from such an altitude that their armor was coated with frost. The lead Knight—no, Amara corrected herself, the Placidan Lord who was obviously in command of the unit, flashed her an angry signal, to which she knew no countersign. Shouting at one another amidst so many roaring windstreams would have been an exercise in futility, so instead she simply lifted her head to bare her uncollared throat and lifted her hands into the air. The Placidan scowled at her, but flashed a standard signal at her to land, then signaled a hover, and spun his finger to encompass the rest of her group. She nodded, signaling her own folk to remain in place, and descended toward the ground with the Placidan Lord.

They landed on the causeway, and the lord never took his eyes off her the whole way down. He stopped ten feet from her and faced her silently, one hand on his sword.

"No," Amara told him tiredly. "I haven't been taken."

The man seemed to relax, at least by a fraction. "You understand, of course, that security is a priority."

"Of course," Amara said. "I'm sorry, sir. I recognize that you are of the Placidan Citizenry, but I can't remember your name."

The lord, who looked about Amara's age, but who could have been twenty years older, if he had watercrafting enough, gave her a tired smile. He needed a shave. "Crows, lady. I can barely remember it myself. Marius Quintias, at your service."

"Quintias," Amara said, bowing slightly. "I am Countess Calderonus Amara. The people with me are the Knights and Citizens my husband and I rescued from the Vord. They're tired, cold, and hungry. Is there a haven for them nearby?"

"Aye," he said, nodding as he swept his gaze around. There was a faint, but undeniable note of pride in his voice. "For the moment, at least."

For the first time, Amara looked at her surroundings.

A battle had been fought there, on the causeway beneath the Redhill Heights. The earth was torn with furycraft and the tread of thousands of feet. Black patches marked where firecrafting had scorched the ground. Broken weapons lay strewn about the ground, here and there, along with spent arrows, broken shields, and cloven helms.

And there were dead Vord.

There were thousands upon thousands of dead Vord. They carpeted the earth for hundreds of yards behind her.

"I wouldn't go walking this countryside alone for the time being, Countess," Quintias said. "But if you'll come to the camp, you can sleep safe, at least, once your people have cleared inspection."

"Inspection?" Amara asked.

"No one comes into the camp unless we're sure that they aren't taken or working with the Vord, lady," Quintias said without rancor. "We've had taken trying to slip in and cause trouble since about an hour after the battle."

"I see," she said quietly. "It's imperative, sir, that I speak to the First Lord at once. I have information he will need."

Quintias nodded sharply. "Then let's get moving."

They took to the air again, and Quintias and a dozen of his Knights escorted them ahead, flying low and slow, the effort laborious. They would be exhausted when they landed—which was, she suspected, the point. If they had been intent on causing mischief, their fliers, at least would be in no condition to do so.

It took them little time to reach the camp—a camp set up behind the interlocked palisades of no fewer than *nine* Aleran Legions. Half a dozen of them were flying the blue-and-white banners of Antillus, which was, Amara would have sworn, an obvious impossibility.

Beyond the neat white tents of the Legion camps was a small sea of humanity numbering in the tens of thousands if not the hundreds. Armored *legionares* of one of the Placidan Legions were waiting, and Legion healers were coming forward to help (and presumably to verify the humanity of) the most recent arrivals.

Quintias beckoned Amara, and she followed him through the Placidan camp, to a single Legion camp standing behind the front line. The red-and-blue banners of the First Lord flew over it, and she found herself hurrying her steps as she passed through the Crown Legion's camp, toward its commander's tent. It was awash in activity, with couriers and officers alike coming and going.

"I'll tell the First Lord you're here," Quintias said, and entered the tent. He came out only a few moments later, and beckoned Amara. She followed him inside.

A crowd of officers stood around a sand table in the center of the room, their quiet discussion buzzing. "Very well then, gentlemen," said a quiet, cultured baritone. "We know what needs to be done. Let's be about it."

The officers saluted with the kind of precision and discipline Amara knew never would have been seen during peacetime, a rattle of fists striking armor, and then began to disperse.

"He wanted to hear from you first thing," Quintias told her. "Go ahead."

Amara nodded her thanks to the man and walked forward to speak to the First Lord—and stopped in her tracks in shock.

Aquitainus Attis turned to her, his expression calm and confident beneath the shining steel circlet of the First Lord that he wore upon his brow, and nodded. "Countess Amara, welcome. We have much to discuss."

Isana walked into the command tent at the temporary camp and was unsurprised to find it empty except for Lord Aquitaine. The tall, leonine lord stood over the sand table, staring down at it as if reading a poem he could not quite comprehend.

"Your brother's wife is quite resourceful," he said quietly. "Not only did she arrange the escape of more than three hundred Knights and Citizens who would have been enslaved by Vord, and destroy their capability of adding any more to their tally, on the way here she also managed to compile a surprisingly complete estimate of the spread of the *croach* from the reports of the various hostages and her own observations."

"The only part of that which surprises me is hearing that she shared it with you," Isana replied in a level tone.

Aquitaine smiled without looking up from the map sculpted into the sand on the table in front of him. "Honestly, Isana. The time for our petty squabbles is past."

"Petty," Isana said quietly. "My pardon, Lord Aquitaine. I labored under the misconception that the death of hundreds of my friends and neighbors in Calderon was not a petty matter."

Aquitaine looked up at Isana and regarded her thoughtfully for a moment, the steel coronet at his brow gleaming in the light of the tent's furylamps. Then he said, "Let us suppose for a moment that what happened at Calderon had gone differently—that the Marat had wiped out the population of the valley, just as they did in Septimus's day. That I had positioned myself to stop the horde and won the favor of the Senate and various other parties."

"And if it had happened that way?" Isana asked.

"It might have saved *millions* of lives," Aquitaine said, his voice quiet and hard, and it gained in intensity as he spoke. "A stronger First Lord might have prevented Kalare's rebellion, or been able to end it with something other than a cataclysm that left a quarter of the Realm in chaos and anarchy that became an ideal breeding ground for the crowbegotten Vord."

"And you believed that you were the proper person to choose who would live and who would die."

"You saw where Gaius's constant games and manipulations took us. You can see it in the smoking ruin where Alera Imperia used to stand. You can see it in Kalare and the Amaranth Vale. You saw it the night they murdered Septimus." Aquitaine folded his hands behind his back. "Why not someone else? And if it is to be someone else, why not me?"

"Because you are not the heir to the throne," Isana replied. "My son is."

Aquitaine gave her a brittle smile. "The Realm is on its knees, Isana. Your son is not here to lead. I am."

"He will return," Isana said.

"Perhaps," Aquitaine said. "But until he does, he is a theoretical leader—and we are facing days of deathly practicality."

"When he comes back," Isana said, "will you honor his claim? His birthright? He is Septimus's son, Lord Aquitaine."

Aquitaine's expression flickered and he glanced down at the table again for a moment, frowning.

"If he comes back," he said, with quiet emphasis on the first word, "then . . . we will see. Until that day, I will do as I think best for the Realm." His eyes flicked back up to her, and became hard and cold as agates. "And I will expect your support."

Isana lifted her chin and narrowed her eyes.

"Division in the Realm has all but killed us," Aquitaine continued in a deadly quiet voice. "I will not permit it to happen again."

"Why tell me this now?" Isana asked him.

"Because I would rather we were forthright with one another. It will save time later." He spread his hands. "I have a certain amount of respect for you. I would rather have your support over the next few months. But make no mistake, I cannot tolerate your antagonism. I'll kill you first. Even if I must cross Raucus to do it."

Isana wondered if Aquitaine expected her to cringe in fear. "Do you honestly think you could handle him?" she asked.

"In a duel, one of us would die," Aquitaine replied, "and the other would not win. Neither would the Realm."

"Why?" Isana asked. "Why would you say this to me? I have no Legions to offer you, no cities, no wealth. Why do you need my support?"

"Because Raucus has made it clear to me that he came south for your sake. And Phrygia follows him. Lord and Lady Placida have made it clear that if I am wise, I will treat you with all deference. The heir presumptive to Ceres seems to think you can do no wrong. And, of course, the people love you—one of their own, risen up to wed the Princeps and provide the Realm its desperately needed heir. You have far more power than you realize."

He leaned forward slightly. "But a third of the Realm is *dead*, Isana. What's left is going to die, too, unless we stop stabbing one another's backs and work together."

"If you say so," Isana said stiffly. "You are more an authority than I in matters of treachery."

He sighed, and settled down on a camp stool. He spread his hands, and asked, wearily, "What do you think Septimus would have wished you to do?"

Isana regarded him in silence for a long moment. Then she said, "You aren't the same as your wife, Lord Aquitaine."

He gave her a wintry smile. "We shared a goal, an occasional bed, and a name. Little else."

"You shared a conviction that any methods were acceptable, provided their ends were worthy of them," Isana said.

Aquitaine arched an eyebrow. "It's easy to argue against morality by the numbers—as long as the numbers are small. Millions of people—people we Citizens of the Realm were expected to protect—are *dead*, Isana. The time for difficult decisions is here. And making no decision at all may prove just as disastrous."

Isana turned her face away, absorbing that for a moment. A bitter taste filled her mouth.

What would Septimus have wished her to do, indeed.

"The Realm needs its leaders to stand together," she said quietly. "I will work with you—until my son returns. I will promise you nothing more than that."

Aquitaine studied her profile for a moment, then nodded once. "We understand one another. That is a reasonable beginning." He frowned for a moment, then said, "May I ask you something?"

"Of course," Isana said.

"Do you honestly think he will return?"

"I do."

Aquitaine tilted his head for a moment, his eyes distant. "I confess . . . there is a part of me that wishes he would."

"To free you of responsibility?"

Aquitaine waved a hand in a vague gesture of negation. "Because he reminds me of Septimus. And what the Realm needs at the moment is Septimus."

Isana tilted her head. "Why do you say that?"

He gestured at the sand table. Isana came over to it and saw a map of the entire Realm laid out in the sand.

A quarter of it, perhaps more, was colored in *croach* green.

"The Vord have been beaten down," Aquitaine said. "But they reproduce so swiftly that they'll be back again. Entire forests, within the *croach*, have been filled with trees that bear young Vord like fruit. All the queen need do is wait for a fresh crop, then she will come at us again, as strong as before."

"Can we not . . . burn their crops, so to speak?" Isana asked, frowning down at the sand.

"Possibly. If the causeways to the south hadn't been cut behind us as we withdrew." He shook his head. "And we don't have hands enough to cover all the ground we'd need to cover in the time we have before the Vord's counterstroke. I'll send teams down, certainly, but that will only mitigate the enemy's numbers."

He gestured at the northern part of the map, where a handful of markers indicating Legions stood. "Meanwhile, we're becoming more reliant upon militia for our fighting men, we've lost our trade nexus for the moving of supplies and funds, and the Vord are slowly killing off the most powerful of our crafters."

"What are you saying, Lord Aquitaine?" Isana asked.

He gestured to the north. "I can gather our forces. I can marshal what resources remain to us. I can plan the battles, and I can hurt the Vord. I can feed them to the crows in mountains." He shook his head. "But unless we can get into the southlands and strike at them there, where they breed, it won't matter how many of them we kill. They'll send more. Sooner or later, this war ends in only one way.

"I can give the people of Alera a strong leader, Isana. I can give them time." He bowed his head, and spoke very quietly. "But I cannot give them hope."

Gaius Octavian, Princeps of the Realm of Alera, had gotten over his seasickness nearly an entire day sooner than he had the last time he'd been aboard ship, which meant almost nothing in terms of relative suffering. But he would take improvements wherever he could get them.

Tavi stood on the deck of the *Slive* in the dead of night. They were moored to one of the great ice ships, which had been dubbed the *Alecto*, and even the officer of the watch was drowsing. Tavi had lain on the deck for a while as his head cleared, then made his way to the prow of the ship. He stared up at the great vessel for a time, and out over the gentle sea, where hundreds of other ships rode slowly toward Alera, at barely a third the pace they could have managed had they been alone instead of bracketed by the ice ships. Still, late was much better than never—and a return voyage without the ice ships would encompass far too many nevers for Tavi's taste.

He nibbled on ship's biscuit, stared out at the sea, and waited for his stomach to settle so that he could finally get some sleep. He was entirely unprepared when a voice said, from directly behind him, "What do you find so interesting?"

Tavi all but jumped out of his clothes at the words, and he spun to find a young woman standing behind him.

Or at least, that was his first impression of her.

He took a second, longer look and noticed the way that mist and fog seemed to cling to her in the shape of a common gown. He noticed the way her eyes kept shifting from the hue of one metal or gem to the next. And, most of all, he noticed the depths of her eyes; eyes that belonged to no young woman— to no human being at all.

"What do you find so interesting?" the woman repeated, smiling.

"Not interesting, exactly," Tavi replied. "It just . . . seems easier to consider the future when I'm looking out over the sea. What might happen. What I might do in response. How I might shape it."

The woman's smile didn't widen so much as deepen. "You are all the same," she murmured.

"I don't understand," Tavi said quietly. "Who are you?"

She regarded him with steady, bright eyes, and he noticed that neither her hair nor the mist of her dress stirred with the evening wind. "Your grandfather," she said, "called me Alera."